Angel of

TEMPTATION

MIKKI WALKER

ISBN 978-0-692-40199-6

Angel of Temptation

Printed in the U.S.A.

Editor: Kathy Hill

Book Cover: Karl Moeller

Chapter One

To throw oneself at any man was ridiculous, Alex scoffed, beneath what she thought proper and ladylike. Women behaving this way made her shudder, grateful that she wasn't one of them. Alex knew the proper way to court: the man should call on the lady and the lady should be coy and shy, with delicate, feminine mannerisms. Alex played the part of a lady very well, but was far more headstrong and stubborn than most. These ladies were only showing how foolish they could be, and just how much they allowed society to dictate their behavior.

The hostess of tonight's soirée was apparently striving for a new pinnacle of elegance. Overhead, the ballroom's crystal chandeliers painted the room with a golden glow. Fine damasks adorned the long buffet, set off in an alcove, where bountiful bouquets of fresh, exotic blooms were reflected by old china and crystal. Tall silver candelabra illuminated every table. Chairs and loveseats that had been passed down for a dozen generations, upholstered in soft silken brocades in rich colors, provided cozy seating areas all around the dance floor, except at one end, where a chamber orchestra struck up tune after tune. Dancing were gentry from all over London and the countryside, clad in their finest attire, competing for the attention of the most beautiful or powerful members of high society. With bodies warmed by exertion while clad in many layers of formal garments, along with strongly scented perfumes and pomades, so many candles, the profusion of flowers, and platters heaped with steaming, succulent dishes, the air in the ballroom had grown close and stuffy.

The occasion was very formal, but the outrageous scene in front of Alex finally made her laugh out loud. She could stand and watch no longer. She slipped away to enjoy some fresh air on the terrace.

The spring night was lovely, with a light, low mist that presaged rain: the cleansing of the earth, her father would say. She glanced up at the sky, appreciating how brightly the moon and stars were still shining. "What a perfect night. I should be home in the garden enjoying it to the fullest, but no, instead, I am here wasting my time witnessing foolish women fawning over a man," she thought. Captivated by the rapturous night, she let her mind drift, and momentarily escaped her surroundings.

"Andrew, if you don't get me out of this damn place this instant I fear these silly little ninnies will start attacking me, from the hungry look in their eyes," Gavin hissed, most hostile. "I don't know why I let you talk me into these parties anyway."

"Now Gavin, how could you even think of leaving all these beautiful women? Are you daft, man? Besides it is not my fault that you have to hide from that half-crazed witch you were going to marry. Really, could you not see all the lies and deceit that lay at that woman's feet?" Andrew's reply was too soft to be heard by anyone but Gavin.

"I did not ask for commentary, Andrew, just that we leave," Gavin hissed. "Now, if you wish to remain, I shall be out on the terrace. Do keep these fools from following me."

"I assure you that 'tis one task I really do not mind." Andrew replied quietly, with a lascivious look in his eye.

When heads turned to note the arrival of minor royalty, Gavin discreetly slipped around a tall potted palm and escaped unseen to the terrace. Once out the door, he realized he was not the only one with a need for privacy. Accustomed to drawing the attention of young women, Gavin soon began to wonder why the gentlewoman standing barely ten feet away was not at once swooning over him, as so many others had just been doing. Moonlight caught the golden glow of her hair; he saw she was tall but slim, with a tiny waist. Excellently built, he thought, with stature, her head held high, proud as well as lovely. She seemed the picture of elegance, and looked most innocent as she stood alone gazing at the stars. She looked like an angel.

Alex was so lost in her musings she did not realize she was no longer alone. When the handsome stranger suddenly appeared at her side she jumped back in surprise.

"Forgive me, I did not mean to startle you, I was just wondering what it was you saw up there as you gazed into the stars? Of course, you need not answer me, I realize I am nothing more then a stranger to you."

Thoroughly amazed, Alex stared in awe, never before having beheld quite such a good-looking man. It took her a moment to regain her composure. She grasped that he must have been the center of all that feminine attention inside, subject of so many whispers and rumors. He was tall, more than six feet was her guess, muscular, and his great strength was evident. His hair was dark, rich, and brown, with curls only in the back and worn longer then most men sported. He was so manly and attractive, she imagined he could wear rags and still look good. His dark brown eyes were rich with gold flecks that almost took her breath away, and the lips that moved before her were full, sensuously outlined by a mustache slightly lighter then his hair. Never before had anyone made outspoken Alex lose her tongue, or stare so rudely. But then again, Alex had never known such a strong attraction.

When Gavin repeated his question, she stood straight and tall so he would not think that she was looking him over, as she was. She regained her senses quickly.

"No, I do not mind telling you what I was looking at. However, I doubt you will see it the same."

"Well, perhaps I could be the judge of that," Gavin replied. He seemed polite, and she felt so surprisingly comfortable, she shared her thoughts with him without hesitating.

"When I was a child, my father would tell my sisters and me that the stars in the sky are our Guardian Angels, who shine bright to let us know they are there. This made us feel safe and protected." As she spoke, Alex felt that the same held true to this very day, though she was now a mature woman of twenty.

Gavin stood before her listening intently, and thinking— She truly is an angel! She even speaks like an angel, innocent, carefree and cheerful, as though she had never experienced a bad day. He thought her young in years but mature in demeanor, more mature than any of those slightly older women who had been all over him. She possessed a remarkable beauty, and her sky-blue dress brought out her sapphire eyes and complimented every curve of her body. Her light, shining hair was arranged high on her head, with loose curls that cascaded over her shoulders and well down her back. She is just stunning, he mused.

He endured a deep pang of regret for his vow not to get involved with anyone while getting free of Melinda... who was nothing but pure evil. When he had broken off the engagement upon discovering that she only wanted his money and title— and that she was bedding Antonio!— she had bitterly sworn to search out Gavin to make his life a living hell. Antonio! The recollection still burned.

Antonio, always dismissed as merely a childhood friend! Melinda was deceitful, crafty at lying, expert at keeping secrets. It had taken Gavin three years to discover her duplicitous nature. Before he could seek new romance, he must find a way to disentangle himself from Melinda's wiles. For good. And for his own good.

Gavin shook his head to vanquish painful memories, and concentrated on the vision in front of him. "I understand what you are saying, and I admire the fact that you shared it with me. I too feel a sense of peace by gazing at the vastness of the stars. If I may be as so bold to ask one more question?"

"Of course you may. You need not have my permission to ask a question, for if I did not like it I simply would not answer," she replied coyly.

Gavin threw back his head and laughed. "But of course! I was merely wondering what your name is."

"My name is Lady Alexandra Marie Patience Rosenshire, although most people call me Lady Alex. My father called me Alex from the day I was born, and that is the name that stuck. My mother intended *Alexandra* to be used at all times, but that did not happen." She knew she was rambling, aware she was presenting herself in a more casual fashion than was expected of a Lady.

"Alex is a lovely name. My name is Gavin Blake." He was omitting his title. "It was a pleasure meeting you. I believe I had a more pleasant time out here with you then I had all evening inside. However, I must bid you farewell... I see my cousin Andrew is ready to leave. As I said, it was a pleasure meeting you... Angel."

Gavin turned with a slight bow and strode toward the door where his cousin waited, and they were gone. In a moment his words registered with Alex, that he had called her *Angel*, and she called out to correct him. Too late.

"I know he heard me say my name was Alex. How odd," she pondered. She had to admit that this Gavin Blake deserved all the complimentary whispers in the other room. He was both handsome and charming, if slightly more disheveled than most other men, which only added to his earthy appeal. He also looked a bit older then the twenty-eight years she'd been told was his age.

Perplexed and amused, Alex decided to rejoin the party.

Chapter Two

Almost all the denizens of the sleepy town of Bedford, just north of London, loved to talk about their neighbors' shocking scandals, and any skeletons in the gentry's closets, real or imagined. But Rosenshires escaped the gossip and calumny, for they were widely respected as people with high morals, strong values, and plenty of love to go around. The Rosenshire family was regarded as admirable in every way.

On this bright, sunny Sunday morning all six members of the Rosenshire clan were gathered around their breakfast table talking and laughing, enjoying each other's company in the comfortable and familiar embrace of the rambling family estate.

Alex, second child and eldest daughter, adored and admired her father and mother and felt a strong bond with each of her siblings. Her father Daniel, nineteenth Earl of Bedford, was a powerfully-built man of forty-five. Tall and handsome, his rich brown hair was sparsely flecked with gray. He successfully managed the many enterprises handed down to him as the latest heir, and enjoyed the well-earned respect of peers and villagers.

Alex's dear mother Elizabeth was kind-hearted, with a sweet, gentle disposition. She had never been heard to raise her voice, and she took great pride in rearing her own children, echewing the customary and fashionable involvement of nannies and wet-nurses. She exemplified a great talent for nurturing her offspring and lovingly ushering them into adulthood. A petite woman of forty-three, with beige-blonde hair and green sparkling eyes, Elizabeth looked much younger than her years.

Alex's older brother Richard often kept his distance from the family. He was in a state of youthful rebellion, anxious to explore the world. Twenty-five years old, resembling a slightly smaller version of his father, Richard traveled widely, looking for profitable business opportunities and hoping to prove he could manage independently. Nonetheless he was a happy person and his pleasant disposition was most apparent when he was at home.

Next there was Cassandra, seventeen, just blossoming into her adult beauty and leaving childhood behind. Soon she would have her coming-out, to be introduced to society and put on display for potential suitors. Her extra height did not detract from her appearance. Dark, thick auburn locks accentuated a face similar to her mother's, and highlighted eyes that could be compared to emeralds. Cassandra had shown a wild and rebellious streak that gave her parents much to worry about. Most instances, fortunately, were not harmful or dangerous.

Ashley was the baby of the family, only fifteen. Already a bit tall for a woman, she had inherited all the best features of her father, but accented by the blonde tresses she shared with her mother and Alex. Her appearance held promise of great beauty to come.

Although the family's breakfast conversation was lively and interesting, Alex had something else on her mind: Gavin. It was Gavin in her thoughts all last evening, all she saw in her dreams was Gavin, and even now, wide awake— Gavin. She shook her head as though trying to shake him out of it, but to no avail. He was still there. This bothered her fiercely, for no one had ever consumed her thoughts this way, and she was not at all sure she liked it. Alex had always had control of her emotions, so this state of preoccupation gave her a sense of helplessness, something she did not like, could not afford, did not want to tolerate. She had a need, a determination, to appear strong at all times, no matter what. Now she felt weak, pummeled by her own feelings.

At the advanced age of twenty, Alex was fast approaching spinsterhood. She felt constantly reminded that it was high time she got married, not so much by her family as by her friends and the whole realm of Society. Her parents agreed she should only marry for love— nothing else. So until Alex found the man of her dreams, they would let her be. At times, the gentlest of reminders slipped through, but rarely. In this culture, they could not help but reveal awareness of her age.

Alex was not without suitors. She was currently being courted by a certain Lord Harrison. Wealthy and handsome, yes, but he did not seem to hold any special feelings for Alex, nor she for him. He was tall, with light brown hair and a bulky, burly physique. Unfortunately, he had no personality— or at least Alex could never find one. He liked to think that every girl was delighted by him, and that Alex should consider herself lucky to have such a treasure calling on her. Alex had promised him that they would go riding today, and although she was not looking forward to the occasion, she liked to ride, and she never broke a promise.

Harrison arrived promptly at one-thirty and waited in the drawing room. No one in the family seemed to enjoy his company, so there he sat, by himself. Alex came down the stairs soon thereafter in her new and highly fashionable riding habit, fitting her trim form to perfection. Although it appeared to have a full skirt suitable for sidesaddle equitation, it had been cleverly tailored with a split skirt, the split hidden when afoot by cunning button-back flaps. Thus it permitted her to ride astride, as she had as a child, though gaining her father's permission for this breach of modesty had taken some pleading. He had finally given in when asked whether he would like to try riding sidesaddle to see what it felt like, almost impossible to keep one's balance and control one's mount! The habit was a deep tan in color with navy accents, and she knew it nicely set off the radiant golden hair flowing down her back, with the sides neatly pulled away from her face.

"Lord Harrison, it is nice to see you this afternoon," Alex said with little enthusiasm.

"Alex, you look lovely today, absolutely perfect for what I have planned for you," he responded slyly.

Curious, Alex cautiously asked, "What exactly is it that you have planned?"

"Well, to tell you would be to waste a perfectly good surprise, and I spent a great deal of effort putting it together. So please be patient and come along. My horses are waiting, and I have brought a gentle mare for you."

Surprise? Alex did not like the sound of that! She'd always had a peculiar self-protective feeling on rare occasions when they were alone, but she'd never had a good reason not to trust him. She decided to put her nervousness aside. She suspected that Lord Harrison was getting ready to propose marriage, in which case she would decline. She would be pleased to end their relationship, if it could even be called that. Being with him was a waste of her time. But as a lady of society, sometimes you had to entertain people you didn't much like, however boring they might be. She gestured for him to proceed, through the doors and on toward the courtyard where a groom held the reins of two glossy thoroughbreds.

Once they had mounted, Lord Harrison said, "Alex, if you would please follow me, there is a special spot I would like to take you," and with a short incline of his head he trotted away. Hesitantly, Alex followed, wondering what exactly he might have in mind. There was a bundle behind his saddle; she surmised a woodland picnic would be in store. A pleasant day for a picnic, she thought, no matter the company.

She considered that perhaps her father was right, and she should have brought a chaperone with her. The more she thought about it, the more butterflies fluttered in her stomach, making her more and more apprehensive as they rode along. She wished he had let her ride her own horse, instead of trying to show off the choice mounts from his own stable.

By two o'clock an easy trot on wide trails through flat, sparsely wooded lands brought them to the banks of a small stream clear enough to see branches and fluffy clouds reflected in its limpid surface. Tall trees lined both sides of the brook, with a small clearing along one bank, its mossy surface soft and spongy, green and fresh. There were wildflowers blooming here and there, and the scent of spring welcomed them to this private little bower, lit by a beam of bright mid-day sunlight filtering through boughs above.

Harrison pulled his horse roughly to a halt. Hopping off, he untied the checkered blanket and wicker basket fastened behind his saddle and arranged a simple, light repast of sherry and little delicacies with care. All the while, Alex remained on her saddle, for apparently he had forgotten his manners, and had yet to help her down. After being patient a long while, she took it upon herself to dismount. Lord Harrison stood gazing contentedly over the little glade, waiting for Alex to join him.

"Excuse me, my lord, but perhaps it is time you shared this surprise of yours with me. I cannot stay long; we have come far, and I am soon expected back." She hoped by telling him this he would not drag the occasion out. His demeanor was making her edgy. There was something different about him today that scared her a little.

Grasping Alex firmly by the hand, Lord Harrison led her to the blanket and gestured for her to sit. After giving him a sideways glance, she did, arranging her skirts around herself and fastening their buttons modestly.

"Alex, I have been calling on you for quite some time now, and I feel very strongly toward you."

"My lord, please—" Alex attempted.

"Alex dear, do not interrupt me, and I in turn would then not have to cut you off." He stood over her, pacing back and forth. Alex was annoyed. She was not accustomed to being blithely interrupted in mid-sentence and didn't like being admonished.

"Now, as I was saying. I have been calling on you for some while now and feel that we both are not getting any younger. You will make an excellent wife, you're admired by many, and you get along well with everyone. It is a perfect match if I do say so myself."

And suddenly he was down on one knee, grasping her hand, looking deeply into her eyes.

"Lady Alexandra Rosenshire, will you marry me?"

She looked back at him without saying a word. He was waiting for her response. She was trying to judge his mood, and thinking how best to respond, but she could tell by the look on his face that he was quickly becoming impatient.

"My lord, do you love me?" she finally asked, looking him straight in the eye.

"Love you? Where did that come from?" he replied, dropping her hand and sitting back on his haunches, looking confused and surprised. This was not the response he so confidently anticipated.

"Lord Harrison, please try to understand. I will marry for one reason and one reason only: because I am in love. And the person I will marry must love me back!"

"Lady Alex, that is a childish dream. People marry, and later they may grow to love one another over time. Do not get me wrong. I have feelings for

you, but love is not one of them. Not yet, anyhow."
He spoke as though all feelings were trifling, just a
minor, unimportant fact of life.

"Then I truly am sorry, but the answer to
your question must be no. As I said, though we do
not share the same opinion, I shall only marry for
love."

As Alex rose to her feet, Harrison grabbed
her wrists and yanked her close. She tried
unsuccessfully to pull away from his sharp aroma of
sweat, horse, tweeds, and anger.

In a low growl he scolded her. "I hate to
think that I have wasted five long months on you! I
am Lord Harrison, son of an Earl, and there is no
way you can *not* marry me! I don't care if I have to
ruin you. It will happen." His face was now red, and
his grip on her wrists was becoming painful.

Offended, angered, and defiant, but
remaining calm, Alex swiftly brought her knee up to
where it could do the most damage, and ran for her
horse as he doubled over. But Harrison recovered
quickly, caught up and grabbed a big handful of her
hair. He roughly twisted her to the ground on her
back, then clambered on top of her to control her
limbs.

Alex found herself breathless, trapped
beneath his bulk, kicking uselessly and trying to
scream. Finding air once again in her lungs, she
raged at him.

"Harrison, stop! You don't know what you are doing. You will see in time— this was for the best! Harrison— please stop!" Alex struggled to free her fists to hit him as she screamed out her anger and distress, making as much racket as she could.

Harrison raised his voice to be heard over her screams. "What is for the best, Alex? That you remain alone? I can provide for you, and in time you will be happy! Stop struggling so much! You're making it harder on yourself! I will not have people thinking that I could not get you to marry me. No one rejects me! It is expected that you marry me. Do you not see this, you little fool?"

She continued to writhe beneath him. "I will not let you take me like this, this is wrong and I will not let it happen! Marrying you would be the biggest mistake of my life!" She succeeded in freeing one hand as he struggled with a trouser button, and at last could poke him in the eye with stiffened fingers. As he flinched away, she had enough room to kick, using her knee with as much drive as she could muster, connecting with the best possible target. As he fell away from her, helplessly gagging, Alex quickly got to her feet and ran, this time making it to her horse. The neat buttons of her skirts popping off into the underbrush, she sprang into the saddle, and, not looking back, kicked the startled mare to a gallop while finding her stirrups.

It didn't take Harrison long to collect himself. Energized by anger, wincing in pain, he swiftly mounted his horse and took off after Alex with all the speed he could urge with whip and spurs and loud imprecations.

Gavin was out enjoying the day, with the excuse of looking over some land he was thinking of buying. It was such a beautiful, fragrant spring afternoon. Woodland plants were all in bloom, announcing the summer ahead. He always felt strong and proud astride his black stallion. To make his contentment complete, leaping at his side was his most trusted companion, a pup that had followed him home nearly two years ago. Jack was a mixed-breed of some sort, now a good-sized dog of about 50 pounds with a short thick chocolate coat and a narrow, intelligent face. Jack was there for him through times good and bad, Gavin thought. The two really enjoyed each other's company. A perfect day, he mused happily, with a fine horse, a loyal dog, and brilliant spring weather.

Then Gavin thought he heard a faint scream. Not ready to believe his ears at first in this idyllic setting, he halted his mount, shut his eyes, and strained to listen. Yes, there it was again! Jack cocked his head to one side, validating Gavin's concern. Some woman was screaming, no doubt about it. Looking down over a vast swath of sparsely wooded new-growth forest in the general direction of the noise, he eventually spotted a distant female on horseback, galloping at full speed, headed right toward him.

At first, he couldn't tell what was going on. Then he saw a second rider in pursuit, and realized the woman might be in trouble; the gap between the two riders was closing. Could they be racing? He approached them at a trot, not quite sure help was needed. When they drew close enough for him to recognize the woman he had met on the terrace, and view the expression of alarm on her face, he leaned forward and urged his willing stallion to a gallop.

Like a lightning bolt, Gavin closed in on Alex's pursuer. Wheeling his mount to pull tight alongside the startled man, Gavin dropped his reins and sprang from his saddle fearlessly, grappling the other rider off his horse and following him hard to the ground, knocking the man out with a whoosh of escaping breath.

Glancing back to see the chase had ended, Alex slowed her horse to a walk and turned the mare around, not sure what had just happened or just who might have effected this daring and welcome rescue. Trotting closer, she halted to take stock of the scene. Harrison's horse was blowing heavily and standing near his master, reins about around his ears. Harrison himself lay flat on the ground, not moving, with his head next to a big rock. A tall and glossy black stallion was nearby, riderless, calmly munching a mouthful of underbrush, not even breathing hard. Here comes a nice-looking dog, trotting up to join the stallion. And— sitting on the ground a little way off— Could that be Gavin?

Yes, it is Gavin! She again felt butterflies in her stomach, but now they had nothing to do with apprehension. She dropped a rein and placed a hand on her belly, trying to calm her nerves, unaware of the odd look on her face. Feeling as though an eternity had just passed by, she regained her composure and grip on the reins and urged her mare back to the little tableau of men and animals. She soon reached the scene and dismounted.

Running to Gavin, Alex knelt in front of him without thinking, and cupped his face in her hands. She looked him over with care, searching every inch of his face for any sign of damage, but there were none.

Gavin said nothing. He stared into her sapphire eyes as though they were a piece of blue heaven sent to enrapture him. He leaned forward and placed a gentle kiss directly on her lips, to which she responded warmly.

Suddenly Gavin realized what he was doing and pulled back, and a reserved expression swiftly fell across his features. Alex realized what she had just done was more thanks then she needed to give, and felt that her behavior might make her seem a little wanton.

"I would like to thank you for helping me. I turned down Lord Harrison's proposal of marriage, and he did not take it very well," blurted out Alex breathlessly.

"You're welcome, but you owe me no explanation. What you should do is hop back on your horse now, and escape before the man wakes."

"You're correct. Just one question. Is he going to be all right?"

"He will be fine," he said, rather shortly, wondering why she cared. Rising and dusting off his seat, he walked over to his horse and in one swift graceful motion hoisted himself into the saddle. Looking over his shoulder, he whistled for Jack, growling and hovering over the inert figure on the ground.

Alex, in a bit of a daze, mounted her horse and turned the mare for home, then swiveled in her saddle to call out, "Thank you again, Gavin. It was nice of you to help me."

"You're welcome, but please just go home." Turning his back to her, Gavin did not want her somewhat forlorn look to be mirrored by his own. He had made that promise to himself, the one he had to keep. He didn't want to send confusing signals to Alex, and the only way he knew to push her away was to be mean, and cold, and pretend total disinterest. He knew he could not manage a new relationship, especially one with someone so appealing, so lovely.

Shoulders slumping, Alex said nothing, feeling most dejected as she kicked her ride into an easy trot without looking back. So many questions were unanswered. Why had *he* kissed her like that, only to appear as though *she* had done something wrong? He had shown her such strange coldness, after such a delicious kiss. She could not bear to dwell upon that kiss.

A mile or two from home, Alex pulled her horse up short to pause briefly, questioning her own actions and feelings. I liked it when he kissed me, is that wrong? Did I behave improperly? Well, I shall never know, he dismissed me as though I were nothing. With a deep sigh, tapping the compliant mare gently with her heels, Alex finished the journey at a gentle canter. The further she rode, the more furious she felt at Lord Harrison's unforgivable behavior. She would not make an issue out of it; however, she did not want him anywhere near her. If he's smart, he will send a servant to collect this horse, she fumed. Reaching the stable, she dismounted and handed the reins to a waiting groom, entered the house and rang for her maid to say a restorative hot bath was now in order.

Gavin, meanwhile, felt as though he had descended into madness. He had started off in the opposite direction soon after Alex headed homeward, but had only proceeded a few paces before finding himself turning his horse around as if someone else controlled the reins. He couldn't help it; he felt mesmerized. He told himself he merely wanted to make sure she arrived home safely, with no further interference from her spurned suitor—though the fellow shouldn't be up for a while yet. Finally, he followed Alex home as if attached by a long, invisible leash, careful to keep out of her sight if she should glance back.

When he saw her reach her gates, he started to turn his horse in the direction of his cousin's nearby estate and head there at last. Then, for just an instant, a flash of his kissing Alex appeared before his inner eye: he suddenly knew again the softness of her lips, the sweet scent of her hair, the smooth texture of her brow, the depth of her sapphire eyes, as real in this moment as they had been in the actual kiss.

How in just two brief encounters had this woman been able to arouse such strange sensations in him, ones he had never before experienced? Shaking his head and continuing homeward, Gavin resolved once again that he would not let thoughts of Alex get in his way.

He did hope, however, that Harrison had heard Gavin's stern admonition. As soon as she rode off, Gavin had circled back, quickly dismounted, hoisted the limp figure up by his collar, and in a low and threatening growl, told him in the most definite terms to stay very, very far away from Alex. Consequences were mentioned. Though the man did not seem to be conscious, Gavin nevertheless felt as though his message had been received.

Dalton Harrison indeed understood the message. He had struck his head and lost his wind, but he had never lost consciousness. Having never liked face-to-face confrontation, he had feigned an unconscious state until certain the others were well away. Seething, sore, insulted, pride deeply wounded, and highly offended by the day's events, he silently vowed revenge on both parties. He would stop at nothing to get his vengeance.

Nothing.

Chapter Three

Upon entering the hall, feeling soiled, sullied, damp and exhausted, all that Alex could think of was a long, hot bath. Her usual energy had completely left her. She made her way along the hall, and as she neared the foot of the staircase, Cassandra appeared, coming down.

"Alex, what on earth happened to you? You're an absolute mess!" she said with a shocked look on her face, leaning over the balustrade.

"You would not believe me if I told you, so just let me go take my bath," Alex replied, her tone betraying both annoyance and fatigue. She was suddenly aware of the grass in her hair and the dirt on her clothing.

"Alex, why are you being so short? Did you not go riding with Dalton today? Would that explain your foul mood?"

"All right, Cassandra. If you must know what happened, I'll tell you. Lord Harrison asked me to marry him and..."

"Tell me you did not agree!" Cassandra interrupted.

"No, I did not agree. If you will let me finish, I will explain."

"Sorry, go ahead."

"I told him that I would not marry anyone, unless it were for love. He does not love, me nor I him. He became enraged— and attacked me." She stopped to take a deep breath, reliving the brutality and fear, and fighting off tears that suddenly sprang to her eyes. "Were it not for Gavin, I would have been ruined."

"You mean *ruined*, ruined?" Cassandra gasped, shocked and horrified.

"Yes!" She controlled her tears before they rolled down her face but knew her eyes glittered. She hoped the light of the stairwell was too dim for her sister to notice. "That is what I mean... He tried to *take* me because I refused his proposal, and that is how I became all disheveled. I had to fight him off. When I freed myself from under him and managed to get on my horse and away, he gave chase." She paused again, taking a deep breath. It took her a moment to regain her poise, and her sister said nothing, suddenly aware of her distress.

Alex felt calmer and continued. "If Gavin hadn't stopped him, Harrison would have caught me, and he would have tried again. But I was lucky. Gavin must have heard my screams, as he galloped up and forced Harrison off his mount."

"Goodness, was anyone hurt?" Cassandra gasped, her hand rising to her mouth in horror. "And who on earth is Gavin?"

Alex ignored the second question. "Lord Harrison was knocked out, and Gavin was... well, he was odd, actually." Pausing, Alex walked another step toward the stairs, leaned her weight on the railing, and decided to share the rest of the story with her sister.

"He... *kissed* you!" Cassandra said with surprise. She was much more interested in the romance of a kiss than in the unimaginable physical attack. "He just *kissed* you? Out of nowhere?"

"Yes, but do not get the wrong idea, he kissed me, and then took it back all at the same time."

"Alex, how does one give a kiss and take it back?"

"It was in his actions. He kissed me, and then got up as though nothing had happened and *ordered* me to leave for home." Recalling his coldness, she straightened her spine and put a calm, emotionless expression on her own face.

"You still have not told me how you take back a kiss."

"Haven't you been listening? By not acknowledging that he had kissed me, it was as if it had not happened at all."

"Oh. I see what you're saying. So... you're in love with this Gavin, whoever he is, aren't you? I mean, why else would one harmless little kiss bother you so much?" Cassandra raised one eyebrow in curiosity, enjoying an opportunity to tease her big sister.

"Cassandra, I am not in love with Gavin, he just puzzled me, that is all." Alex spun away, rounded the newel post and started to make her way up the stairs, still attempting to shield her feelings with erect posture and a blank face as she brushed past her sister.

"Well, it seems to me that if you did not care about someone, you would not be so concerned with one silly little kiss. And you would not be so secretive about his identity!" Cassandra chided as her sister passed.

"I am not in love with him, and that is the end of it!" Alex said emphatically as she attained the landing and put a hand on her doorknob.

"Alex!" her sister called up the stairwell. "Wait, I have just one more question."

"What is it?" Alex called back, unable now to keep frustration and fatigue from her tone.

"Will you tell me who this Gavin person is? You're being quite mysterious about him, are you not?"

Alex sighed again, annoyed. She leaned over the rail at the top of the stairs. "Remember last night, when we were at the party, how all those silly women were making fools of themselves over a man standing in the corner?"

"Oh, I see now, Gavin was that man in the corner." Cassandra called up, her amusement apparent.

"Yes, and he introduced himself as Gavin Blake."

"Really, and how did you chance to meet him?" Cassandra's curiosity was piqued.

"I stepped out on the terrace, and so did he. Now I am going to take my bath. I will see you at tea in a little while. And no lectures about not having a chaperone with me!"

Cassandra heard the bedroom door shut with a bang, and resolved to catch up with her sister later.

Alex rang for her maid, Sara, who helped to remove her boots and strip off her once-handsome riding habit. Noticing now its missing buttons, ragged tears, and grass stains, she made a note to have it cleaned and mended. Even though it was new, it had become a favorite. She was not sure she wanted ever to put it on again, but its sturdy twill had shielded her skin from sharp branches during her wild gallop.

Sara had prepared her bath and placed towels within reach. Alex slowly took out her hairpins and gingerly lowered herself into steaming water scented with lavender just the way she liked it. A sigh again escaped her, now signalling her relief as she closed her eyes to try to vanquish the events of the afternoon. Hard to believe so much had transpired in only two hours or so.

However, the scene with Gavin kept replaying before her. Without willing to, she again recalled the moment she had cupped his face to look for injuries, how he kissed her... And how, abruptly, in the next second, he arose and acted as though nothing had happened.

These thoughts were not pleasant. Why do I keep going over this? Why does the kiss bother me more than Harrison's threats, violence and disrespect? One kiss should not be bothering me like this, unless... ? Could what Cassandra said to me be true? Do I love Gavin? This cannot be! I don't even know what love is. Besides, Mother always told me that when you love someone you never question it, you just know. So I could not love this man I barely know, for I am questioning it... and I am making far too much of this!

Around and around went the same thoughts. The heat and scent of her bath slowly helped calm and soothe her. There was a fire cheerfully burning in a nearby grate to keep the room pleasantly warm. Gradually she relaxed and let herself rest.

A knock on the door interrupted Alex's repose.

"Yes, what is it?" Alex asked.

"Lady Alexandra, it is time for tea," Sara answered.

"Thank you, Sara. Please tell my family that I will be down shortly and they should go ahead and start without me." The Rosenshire parents treated servants with respect and courtesy, and they had brought up their children to do the same.

"Yes Lady Alexandra, I will tell them."

Noticing the bath water cooling, Alex felt much restored, rose from the tub, quickly pinned up her damp locks, and soon was dressed in a fresh frock with Sara's assistance. She was feeling almost cheerful now, with her usual strength and energy returning.

When she entered the drawing room, everyone had begun the light repast without her. Richard was absent as he so often was, and Ashley had not yet returned from visiting a neighborhood friend.

"Alexandra, darling, please sit and join us, your tea is getting cold," her mother said.

"Yes mother, I am very hungry," Alex answered, as she surveyed a big, scented pot of tea and an array of delicate little cakes and cream biscuits, fresh fruit and tiny sandwiches neatly set out on the sideboard. She helped herself to generous servings. Teatime was nearly over when Cassandra struck up a new conversation.

"So Alex, have you told Father and Mother about your eventful afternoon?" Suppressing her giggles as she spoke, Cassandra hoped to make her sister uncomfortable.

"Why, no, I had not. But thank you for reminding me," she said, unable to keep annoyance out of her sharp tone. She wanted to keep her thoughts to herself and knew when her sister was baiting her.

"Alex, whatever is Cassandra talking about?" her mother asked with concern, wondering why her eldest daughter had lost her usual polite manners.

Alex stifled a sigh and gave in, knowing she would have to describe her experience, but hoping to minimize the violence so her parents would have less cause to worry. "It's nothing, really. I rode out with Lord Harrison this afternoon, he asked me to marry him, and, before any one gets excited, I refused, and then he grew rather upset."

"He was angry with you?" her father questioned sharply, one eyebrow crooked.

Cassandra impatiently took it upon herself to finish the romantic tale that was taking her sister so long to tell. "Lord Harrison tried to *ruin* her, and a man named Gavin came to her rescue! He even went as far as to kiss her. Is that not right, Alex?"

"Yes that is right, and thank you for telling my story. We did not want to leave any parts out, did we?" she said, flashing her sister a dark look. This sort of interplay had always existed between the sisters, though they were very close.

"Alex dear, now that your sister has given us the bare bones, please feel free to fill in the details." Her father's commanding tone did not leave her any choice in the matter.

Alex proceeded to recount the whole of it, starting with where and when she had met Gavin, and truthfully describing what she thought about a kiss followed by coldness, though the topic made her uncomfortable. Her family listened with full attention and did not interrupt.

Her mother could tell the kiss meant more to Alex than she was admitting. Elizabeth dearly hoped her eldest daughter would find a man to love and to be happy with; she wished this for all her children. She deeply desired for each one to find a love such as she carried for her husband, and he for her, a great blessing not bestowed often, a true and everlasting love. But to come so close to *ruin*... that would be a major disaster!

"Alex, why did you not tell me this at once?" her father asked when she finally came to the end. "And where was your chaperone! How many times do I have to tell you girls that some rules of society exist for a reason. I indulge the lot of you with your independent, strong-willed ways, but when it comes to safety, *your* safety, some rules *shall* be followed.

"I will soon be having a chat with Dalton Harrison, and I will make sure he does not come around again!" Now he was thundering. To his credit, he cared more about her feelings than her reputation.

"Father. I do not want to make a fuss about this," Alex responded, trying to calm him with her most soothing voice. "I just want to forget all about it, and besides, I am not worried that Lord Harrison will try anything so stupid in the future."

"And why would that be?" her father asked, with a little less heat.

"He would have to deal with you, Father, and who would ever cross *you*?" Alex implored, with a childish, pleading look on her face.

"I see! Now wipe that expression off your face, it's not going to work." He thought for a moment in silence, brow creased, then continued more calmly. "For now, I will respect your wishes. However, if anything else should happen relating to this matter, then I will take it upon myself to address it, is this understood? And don't think for one minute that I won't be confronting Harrison at some point. I may speak to his father, he's rather a pompous old fellow, so the thought of scandal may be enough to make him listen. This unforgivable behavior cannot go unremarked."

"Yes, Father," replied Alex meekly.

Teatime ended with an uneasy silence in the room. The afternoon had grown a bit cloudy and chilly, spring weather patterns being variable, and a thunderstorm suddenly struck the windows with a gust of wind and rain. The women settled into comfortable chairs with their needlework, near a crackling fire, and Alex's father adjourned to his library to read over some papers. Richard came in from a long ride to announce he was going out for the evening to dine with friends as soon as he had bathed and changed into proper attire. In spite of Alex's dreadful experience, this was turning into just another day for the Rosenshire family. Alex hoped nothing further would be spoken about her ordeal.

The women of the house sat in silence, each deep in her own thoughts. Elizabeth gazed at her eldest. Was she thinking of that young man? she asked herself. Her musings getting the best of her, she was moved to inquire.

"Alexandra, dear, tell me more of this man who rescued you," Elizabeth coaxed gently. She was leaning toward Alex with her hands folded in her lap, her needlework abandoned.

"Mother, I would like to tell you more, but I do not know very much about him." Alex was staring out the western window at the fading light as if there were something to see beyond the gardens. The storm had already moved on.

"Well then, answer me this. Do you carry strong feelings for this man?"

"No. I do not!" she said rather shortly. Turning to face her mother, Alex continued, "This man helped me out of a difficult situation, which does not mean I care for him as you and Cassandra have suggested. I mean, really, I do not know him!"

"All right, dear, if you say so. But I must tell you... I disagree."

Alex opened her mouth to respond. Her mother raised a hand to gently silence her, and continued. "I see the way your eyes light up, and how perplexed you seem to be over him. I know well the signs of love, my dear. I know, for this is how I felt about your father when I first met him, and it is how I feel about him to this very day." She spoke with a warm, affectionate smile that revealed the youthful beauty of her face.

"Mother, I know you love Father, but I do not believe I am in love with Gavin! I do not know him, and I strongly believe that you must *know* a man before you can *love* him."

"My sweet, innocent child, your *heart* knows Gavin, and it is your heart that you must obey. You are not wrong in your thoughts, but your thoughts are logical, and love is anything but logical. If your heart is telling you that you care for this man, then you should believe it, and you should not fight it. If you do, you could lose him, and I think you know as well as I, had I lost your father I would not be the woman I am today. He makes me whole. Without the man for whom you are meant, you will only amount to a partial person, never really knowing true happiness. So if you do have feelings for this man, as I think you do, do not lose him, Alexandra."

"Thank you for the advice, Mother... I do not think I am ready."

"You may not think so, but I believe the future will prove you wrong. I think you should get to know him now... with a chaperone, of course." She rose and gathered her grown daughter into her arms and held her close as if she were still a child.

To Elizabeth her children would never be too big for motherly hugs.

The rest of the day proceeded the way it normally did, with Richard off playing the rogue with his companions, Ashley returning from her friend's house, and the rest of the family enjoying their usual activities. Daniel rode out to meet a nearby tenant farmer to discuss the spring planting. As the thunderstorm had refreshed the air, and the day had recovered its earlier warmth, Alex escaped outdoors and made her way along a winding path through the manicured lawns and gardens, appreciating how branches sparkled wherever a bright beam of sunshine caught lingering raindrops. Meanwhile Cassandra read and studied in the library, then went to play the pianoforte in the music room. Ashley sat with her tutor for her daily French lessons. Elizabeth met with the housekeeper to discuss the next day's menus and the spring produce starting to appear in the markets.

There seemed to be a tacit agreement not to further discuss Alex's unfortunate experience, for which she was grateful. After gathering for a light sherry before dinner and enjoying a simple but rich repast featuring a roast of beef and buttery new potatoes at eight in the evening, they moved near the drawing room's fireplace for a little more conversation. Upon saying fond goodnights, the women of the Rosenshire family made their way upstairs and closed their doors one by one, as Father settled down in the library.

Alex's bed had been neatly turned down, with her nightdress prettily arranged across the coverlet, and a fire burned low in the grate. As she began to prepare for the night, her earlier fatigue returned like a curtain coming down. Sara placed her garments over a chair one by one, and would take them in the morning to be laundered. As Alex took up her nightdress, nearly naked, she noticed several blue bruises had appeared on her sore arms where she had been so roughly restrained. She was relieved when long beribboned sleeves hid the marks from sight.

As Alex seated herself at the dressing table, the window at the foot of her bed caught her eye; the light shining in was too enticing to ignore. She dismissed Sara and walked over. The stars and moon appeared as always, but one thing was unexpected. A star was shining so brightly it was almost blinding in comparison. She gazed at it for a while, and decided it might be a sign. Perhaps she was to love Gavin just as her mother had told her she would. Squeezing her eyes shut tightly to help her concentrate, she made a wish on the brilliant star.

"I wish for love, and if it is to be with Gavin, then make it so." Opening her eyes, she added in a whisper, *"I will be waiting for a sign if my wish is to be granted."* Turning away from the window feeling rather childish and silly, Alex ran the brush through her tresses in a perfunctory way, and climbed between the sheets with a final sigh of

comfort and relief, and sank at once into a welcome, dreamless oblivion.

Chapter Four

Gavin arrived at his cousin's door in such an agitated state that Andrew at once asked him what had happened. Gavin's tone made it obvious he was in no mood for discussion. With an exasperated sigh he replied, "I helped a young woman in distress, who was being chased by a witless young man, who knows no better then to think with his rod and not with his head! Now I would rather drop the subject, get out of these filthy clothes, take a hot bath, and relax."

"For God's sake, Gavin, what are you so touchy about? I merely asked why you look so beastly. Perhaps there is more to this than you care to discuss." Observing the look of disgust on Gavin's face, Andrew saw he had hit the mark.

"Andrew, why must you question me? I told you what happened and that is that. Perhaps I am a mite touchy because instead of soaking in a hot, glorious bath to soothe my tired body, I am standing here explaining myself to you." Gavin summoned his valet, Stephen, explained his desire for a bath and a snifter of brandy, and stalked off toward his rooms.

Andrew raised one eyebrow as many a question raced through his head. As he wondered about the situation, he moved toward the liquor cabinet to pour his own tot of brandy. Thinking how much fun it usually was to spend time with Gavin,

Andrew was curious as to what had taken hold of the old boy to spoil his spirits like this. Gavin had been distracted this morning. Now he was prickly and abrupt, not himself at all. Finding out the cause might be most amusing. This should make for good banter at dinner.

Andrew was not being cruel. Cousins Gavin and Andrew, almost the same age, loved each other more than brothers. No one knew them better than they knew each other. Gavin and Andrew's fathers had been brothers who had shared the same sort of closeness. As boys, Andrew and Gavin had spent every summer together, most holidays, and any other opportunities that arose, together in everything. And since earliest childhood, they had loved to antagonize each other. A casual observer might conclude they were being mean and hurtful, but to them it was all in good fun, and an unquestioned feature of their deep and abiding friendship.

Gavin bathed at leisure, then remained behind the closed door of his rooms all afternoon to sleep and read, and took his afternoon tea there alone. At times, a passing servant heard the sound of his boots as he paced restlessly back and forth on the carpet before the fire. The other members of the household had gone out visiting, so his reclusive behavior passed unnoticed. At the eight o'clock gong, Gavin emerged to join the family for dinner.

Gavin was the holder of an ancient title, his father having passed on. He could call himself the Most High, Noble and Potent Prince His Grace Gavin, Twenty-First Duke of Arlington, but seldom did. He seated himself at the foot of the table, with his aunt, still the lady of the house, joining him to his right. Lady Amelia Blake still wore mourning garb and had become thinner and older-looking after the death of her husband. Her raven hair had faded to iron-gray as she approached the age of fifty, but she retained her height and her classic beauty. The young Lady Catherine, Andrew's twelve-year-old sister, seated herself opposite her mother. Andrew Blake, Marquess of Arlington, was seated at the head of the table.

As soon as the butler, Gregor, signalled for the footman to serve the first course, Andrew started on his little plan to needle his cousin. "Gavin, you look completely refreshed. Surely your rest had the effect you were hoping for."

"Why yes, Andrew, it did, and thank you for being so concerned," Gavin said with a mocking smile. He could tell the games were about to begin.

"Good, then you won't mind talking a bit. Mother and Catherine did not get to hear of your heroic adventure today," Andrew taunted gently, as a footman spread his napkin across his lap.

"Tell us Gavin, what happened to make you a hero?" Catherine asked with wide-eyed interest, as she spooned a creamy seafood bisque into her mouth. Still a small girl, looking younger than her age, she had bright sparkling green eyes, and wore her long, straight, dark brown hair unpinned. It cascaded down her back to her waist, held back from her elfin features by a broad green ribbon. Very much the baby of the family, coming along so long after Andrew, she had not left behind her childish ways. Both her sisters were much closer to Andrew in age, and had been married and in their own homes for as long as she could remember, more like aunties than siblings.

Gavin answered her with a serious but warm expression. "Nothing really happened today, Catherine. Your brother is just exaggerating."

In a voice so sweet Gavin could not resist, Amelia wheedled, "Gavin, you are so modest! But if my Andrew said you're a hero, then it must be so. Pray go on with the details, and do not omit any parts. I should like to hear it all."

Gavin had no choice but to respond. "I am telling you it was nothing. After luncheon, while riding out to look over that property we spoke of, I happened to hear a young woman calling out in distress. So I went to investigate, and found she needed a little assistance to escape from some brute who had no manners. That is really the whole of it."

"Really, Gavin! Is the young woman all right?" asked his aunt.

"Yes, she is just fine. A little shaken, up but fine indeed."

"And her name, dear?"

"Aunt Amelia, of what importance is her name? I am certain you do not know her."

"You're looking a bit hot under the collar, old chap," interrupted Andrew. "It is so unlike you to dance around the subject. So come now, what is her name?" A satisfied grin on his face betrayed his delight in making his cousin uncomfortable.

Gavin was short. "Her name is Lady Alexandra Rosenshire; she is a young woman I spoke to at the party last night. Is everyone's curiosity quenched now?"

Gavin could not hide his irritation at the interrogation, but he was not angry at Andrew. Perhaps now his cousin would let up. Gavin resolved to have a little fun at Andrew's expense in return for all this needless discomfort, as soon as an opportunity arose.

Andrew pressed on. "Gavin, you must forgive me, but I do not remember your spending time with any particular woman at the party. By God man, that lot was all over you! Help me out here coz, which one was she?"

Smiling thinly back, Gavin continued to play Andrew's game. "Alex was the young lady with whom I was in conversation on the terrace, just before you and I departed. She went out for air while the others were all a-swooning indoors. We introduced ourselves when I happened upon her, making my own escape from the crowd."

"Now that you mention it, I do remember her. A succulent little dish if I do say so myself." Andrew hoped this would antagonize Gavin, and was about to continue in the same vein, but his mother interrupted as he took a sip of wine.

"Andrew, please do not say such things around your sister," scolded Amelia. "She is too young to be listening to such talk. It is improper to speak like that in the presence of any young lady."

"But Mother, you should have seen her! Long, curling golden hair piled high on her head, the bluest eyes you have ever seen, and the face of an seraph... not to mention her figure! Perfect. No other way to describe her. I think I shall call on her. She might make a wonderful wife. I believe the Rosenshire estate is not far from here, next county over... but we do not move in the same circles. Do you not agree she is prime wife material, Gavin?"

Gavin did not think about his response before speaking. "Actually, Andrew, she is not your type. She is quite innocent, something you're not accustomed to. She probably has dozens of suitors. You would be just one more. It would be best for you to steer clear of her, would you not agree?"

Gavin did not take Andrew's purported matrimonial intentions seriously for an instant. He knew his cousin too well. All Andrew was likely to do with Alex was put her great beauty on display in high society, the way he would show off a fine horse or a new carriage, to reflect well upon himself. Andrew was a rogue, if a harmless one, and immature for twenty-eight. He had yet to manifest a sincere desire to settle down and start a family.

This was an unfamiliar impulse for Gavin, to keep the truth from his dear cousin. Though he did not understand his strong feelings for this woman, still very much a stranger, he was determined to keep Andrew well away from her, and to keep these feelings from being known to anyone. He kept imagining Alex as an angel. He would not like Andrew to *use* Alex in any way. For some reason, she felt important to him... and he admittedly felt protective of her, especially after this day's tumult.

Seeing the tension in his cousin's expressive features made Andrew smile. He knew now that Gavin held feelings for Alex, and regardless of what Gavin might say, it was evident those feelings ran deep.

Andrew spoke without revealing his deceit, enjoying the game. "Yes, that is what I am going to do."

Amelia and Catherine sat gazing at Andrew, confused by his words and not quite grasping what was going on between the two men. Gavin's face now began to show a certain ferocity as he read the thoughts and intentions behind Andrew's façade of innocence. They could keep no secrets from each other.

"What is it that you plan to do, Andrew? Why not share it with us?"

"Gavin, Mother, Catherine, I am going to do something I should have done a long time ago." He rose to his feet to make his announcement, lifting his wineglass as if for a toast. "I am going to choose a wife, and I believe I shall start this endeavor by calling upon the very lovely Lady Alexandra Rosenshire. A rather charming name, isn't it? I know just the person to provide the introduction."

Andrew drank down his wine and sat, well pleased with himself. This would certainly cause Gavin enough upset that he would let his true feelings emerge! But... he was wrong.

Gavin was still for a brief moment, then put down his spoon, took his napkin from his lap and slowly rose from the table, though the second course had not yet been served. From the doorway, he turned to Andrew and said quietly, "I wish you luck, Andrew, if that is what you really want." He turned to address his mother courteously. "If you'll kindly excuse me, I am not hungry. I would like to feed Jack his scraps, as he surely is. Pray, enjoy your meal without me."

Gavin hoped a cold attitude might discourage Andrew from his ridiculous charade. With a polite bow to his aunt, he withdrew and headed outside to commune with Jack. Though he wished that calling Andrew's silly little bluff might soon bring this nonsense to an end, he wasn't certain that would be the case.

As the meal progressed, the conversation dwindled as Catherine and Amelia found themselves having difficulty holding Andrew's attention. They spoke with each other politely and left him out, but he did not notice. As soon as they could, they adjourned to enjoy their pudding in the drawing room, leaving Andrew with his thoughts.

Andrew was both surprised and puzzled. Why *does* his cousin deny his perfectly normal feelings so stubbornly? Melinda's escapades had taken a major toll on Gavin, he knew. The reason Gavin was visiting was his desire to distance himself from Melinda's wily clutches. But Andrew felt sure his romance-prone cousin could never shy from seeking a true and appropriate mate. Would he really go through his life without opening his heart again, because of this one unfortunate experience of thwarted love? Surely not. Were not love and marriage just more of proper society's accepted customs, a way to join family to family to the benefit of both– whether or not deep affection was present, as it was for the luckiest ones? For Gavin's sake, Andrew hoped the truth of his cousin's feelings would soon be out in the open. Gavin had had dalliances with several other women, before Melinda, but only in the most superficial way. He had only given his heart to Melinda, to be cruelly disappointed in the outcome. Perhaps he was just mourning the disastrous end of his big romance.

Deep in these musings and mystified by Gavin's reserve, Andrew resolved to take his game a little farther, to force a more forthright response from his cousin. Starting tomorrow, he would put his plan into motion. Realizing his food had grown cold and his mother and sister had quietly excused themselves, Andrew decided to retire as well.

Gavin climbed into his bed early that night after walking through the gardens with Jack, and ensuring that his stallion was well cared for. His body was beginning to ache in spite of his restful afternoon. He asked Stephen to supply a hot water bottle for the worst of his bruises. He had hit the ground hard when tackling Harrison.

As soon as Gavin closed his eyes, he saw once again a vision of his beautiful Angel. He tried to distract himself, to resist, and lay with his eyes open to try to sort out his feelings. He was forced to admit, he was very strongly attracted... such deep emotion rushed through him at the mere mention of her name! And this was odd, as no one had ever made him feel this way, not even Melinda, when such a short time ago he'd been sure he'd love her forever. Hadn't he truly loved her? Apparently, he hadn't reaized what love was... could it be that he had never known true love? He was beginning to appreciate that Melinda was incapable of generating love for anyone but her grasping, deceitful, avaricious self. He remembered his vow— no entanglements! But he felt helpless to go to war with his own heart.

He finally closed his eyes again and Alex's apparition at once materialized before him. Now he found the experience restful and pleasant. He permitted his inner eye to dwell on her angelic image, and in no time was slumbering soundly and dreamlessly.

The next morning Gavin awoke feeling very well, his bruises barely noticeable. He rose early and enjoyed his first cup of tea alone while gazing out the window at the new spring day. Once shaven and dressed, he headed down to the morning room to join the family for breakfast.

It was a surprise to see only Aunt Amelia and Catherine at table. "Good morning, ladies," he greeted them cheerfully. I find it hard to believe that Andrew would miss a repast as divine as this. Where is he?"

Catherine, who was generally quite bubbly in the morning, was all too happy to answer, "Andrew went to call on Lady Alexandra, just like he said he would. Don't you remember, Cousin Gavin?"

"What I remember is that he was thinking about it, not that it was the first thing on his agenda. It's a bit early for a social call." With that, Gavin murmured a few polite excuses and headed out to see to Jack. Breakfast was no longer on his mind.

"Well, Catherine, perhaps he woke up on the wrong side of the bed," Amelia said, enjoying her tea, unconcerned by the apparent tension between the two men who loved each other so well, and the mysterious changes in her normally gregarious nephew's demeanor.

Chapter Five

"Alexandra, don't wolf down your breakfast. It's not ladylike and you will only make yourself sick. What is your hurry?"

Alex answered her mother cheerfully. "Sorry, Mother, but I'm running late. Cassandra and I are riding out this morning and I do not want to waste the day. She must have left already. The morning light is best, don't you agree?"

Riding was Alex and Cassandra's favorite pastime, and they preferred woodland trails to the formal hunt. Their adventuresome spirits led them to take chances they knew would be completely unacceptable if anyone caught them at it. Their father tried to keep them safe by insisting they stay within the bounds of the estate, but it offered plenty of fields, woods and paths, so they were content to obey.

"Indeed, Alexandra, but I would not devour my food so fast that it might ruin my day."

"You're right, Mother, but sometimes I feel like a child and my enthusiasm gets the better of me. Is it strange for a woman my age to act so proper at times and other times, feel like a child inside?" Alex was filling her mouth with a buttery pastry while trying to answer.

"Not so strange, my dear. We all have a little girl locked within us and now and then she likes to show her colors. Just remember that being young at heart keeps you healthy far longer than taking life too seriously does. Do not forget, there is a time and place to be proper. Now, go. Your sister will be impatient."

"Thank you, and do enjoy your morning, Mother. Goodbye!" Alex called over her shoulder, patting her mouth with a damask napkin and pocketing an apple on her way out.

"Do not be too long, and have fun— but be safe."

Elizabeth remained at table. Daniel had gone out early, Richard was not up yet, and her youngest was breakfasting in the schoolroom with her tutor. Elizabeth truly enjoyed this life God had given her, and felt blessed to have a husband she loved with all her heart, who returned her deep affection. Elizabeth was proud of all her beautiful children and thought the world of them. Life had been good to her. Her heart filled with gratitude at moments like this. She contentedly poured another cup of tea and basked in her solitude, and in the sunshine pouring through the windows of the morning room.

Alex was halfway to the stables and buttoning back the skirts of her second-best habit when she spied a gentleman approaching on a very attractive horse, so she paused to take a look.

"Alex, come on! I have been waiting forever and I would like to go!" Cassandra called impatiently.

"Hold on, Cass, I just want to see who this is. Aren't you a little curious yourself?"

"Not particularly! I would just like to get started!" Cassandra replied. She was already mounted and held the reins of her sister's favorite mare.

Andrew saw Alex watching him, and slowed his horse under her direct gaze. She was remarkably beautiful and held a look of complete confidence and poise. The sight was rather intimidating. Andrew preferred a passive woman as opposed to one with a mind of her own. He rode up and innocently asked, "Do you know where I might find the Lady Alexandra?"

Alex, wondering what he could want with her, played her own game. "I might know where to find her. May I ask is who calling?"

"I am Andrew Blake, Marquess of Arlington. I was hoping the lady would enjoy an early-morning ride, if I may be as so bold as to ask. I know we have not met, but I have a letter of introduction from my vicar." He patted his breast pocket. The elderly cleric was always up before dawn, had little to do but comply with requests of the gentry, and his chapel was conveniently located on the route between these two estates.

"She already *has* a riding partner, thank you very much," Cassandra complained, as she led Alex's mare over to her. Cassandra eagerly looked forward to these rides and did not like intruders.

"And she does not go places with people to whom she has not been *properly* introduced." She thought little of letters from country vicars.

"So you are the Lady Alexandra, as I suspected," Andrew said, doffing his hat.

Taking the reins from her sister, Alex mounted Gracie, her beloved and spirited equine friend, and as she found her stirrups she said, "As if you did not know me, my lord. As I recall, you would be Gavin's cousin, and you accompanied him to the soirée the other night. This is my sister Cassandra."

Settling herself and adjusting her reins, she continued, "All this talk is wasting a beautiful morning. If you would like to join us, you may. I will not mind unless you get in our way." She started down the gravelled drive rising to an easy trot, with Andrew and Cassandra quick to follow. In a half-mile, when they turned onto a wide and gently sloping bridle path, finally out of view from the windows of the big house, Alex leaned forward, signaled her mare with her heels, and took off at a fast canter.

Cassandra was right behind her, but Andrew, taken by surprise, fell behind, not believing these two well-bred young women would unexpectedly start a race. Most would keep to a gentle, ladylike trot. It was enlightening to Andrew to see that women could have the same fun as men so often enjoyed. Andrew used his spurs and caught up with the young beauties, and after a mile the three slowed their horses, encountering a rough stretch of path with dangerous footing. They dismounted to walk alongside as the horses picked their way through rocks and frost-heaves thrown up by winter freezes. Alexandra gave Gracie the apple.

"Lady Alexandra, that was quite a show you two put on! Where did you learn to ride like that?" Andrew asked.

"Thank you, my lord. You may call me Alex. My sister and I have enjoyed riding since we were very small. To ride like this is a rare treat, for we seldom have the opportunity these days."

"Yes, our father would have a fit if he knew we rode like that. He would say it was wild and reckless, and young ladies should not behave so. Is that not right, Alex?" Cassandra asked.

"That is true, Cassandra." Turning, she added, "You will not say anything, will you, Lord Andrew?"

"Now that would depend... ," Andrew responded with a smile on his face.

"Depend on what?" Alex asked.

"First, you must call me Andrew. Second, my silence hinges on whether you will dine with me this evening."

"You are most amusing. You see, if you said anything to my father I would just deny it, and, as he does not know you, it would be *my* word he trusted. I might accept an invitation from a friend, but hardly from someone who believes he has to hold something over me." Alex gave him a radiant smile, knowing she had won this match.

"Of course, my lady, whatever was I thinking?" Andrew responded with a laugh.

"Enough of this, did we come to ride or to talk!" Cassandra interrupted, using a convenient stump to help her back into her saddle. Here the path was smooth again, so she urged her willing mount into a gentle canter.

"Well, Andrew, let us not fall behind." Alex gracefully sprang back up on her saddle and Andrew remounted as well.

"Never keep a lady waiting! After you, Lady Alexandra."

They caught up to Cassandra, and the women took turns showing Andrew their special places in the forests and fields of the vast estate. Occasionally they jumped the horses over low stone walls or narrow brooks as they explored. Andrew was enjoying the ride. However, it was not Alex who riveted his attention. Alexandra was beautiful, that was obvious. But to Andrew, Cassandra was exquisite! There was something about her dewy, innocent youth that captured his thoughts and didn't let them go. He found her... what was the word he needed? ...Bewitching.

They arrived back at the stable around one in the afternoon, tired and hungry. The sisters knew a cold luncheon would be waiting, but Andrew declined their polite invitation to share it. Before riding off, Andrew reminded Alex about plans for dinner, telling her he would send his carriage, and she replied that she would be ready around seven o'clock, adding that of course, she would be accompanied by Mrs. Ravenstock, her chaperone. Andrew offered to have the carriage stop there first.

Cassandra stood near the doorway observing their colloquy, having handed her reins to a groom. At first she had been annoyed that he had tagged along. Her sister was so often in London since her coming-out, she treasured any free time with Alex to share their exploits, as they always had in childhood. But during the ride, she had found herself aware of Andrew's every move, and the tall, blue-eyed man on the fine horse had become more than a strange interloper. An unfamiliar twinge of jealousy passed through Cassandra as she went to talk to her mother. Deep inside, she wanted to be the one to dine with Andrew.

Finding Elizabeth at her needlework by the sitting room fire, Cassandra proceeded to share what was on her mind.

"I wish I were Alex."

"Why would you wish that, my dear?"

"Because, if I were Alex, then I would be the one having dinner with Andrew tonight." Cassandra flopped into a chair.

"Sweetheart, who is Andrew... and when did Alexandra make these plans?" Elizabeth set aside her embroidery hoop to pay closer attention.

"Lord Andrew Blake came looking for Alex to ask if she would join him for dinner. He is the cousin of Gavin Blake, and resides at Arlington House, in the next county westward. Apparently he noticed her at that party she attended in London. He said he has an introduction from some vicar. Well, he ended up joining us for our ride... and Mother, he really made an impression on me."

"Oh, my dear, some things in life are not fair, and unfortunately you are taken with someone who is not available to you at this time." Elizabeth's tone was kind and understanding.

"I am well aware of that, Mother." She paused. "How long did it take you to find Father?"

"It took a little while, dear, but just remember one thing: Love always finds you when you least expect it."

"You were young when you married Father. You were only about my age."

"Yes, dear. Debutantes were often younger in those days. And yes, you are indeed very young now."

"Cassandra, Cassandra, where did you go?" Alex called from the hallway.

"I am in the sitting room with Mother."

Alex strolled in and noticed all conversation had apparently ended with her arrival.

"Is something wrong?" she asked, looking at both of them.

"No, dear. Your sister was just telling me that you have a dinner engagement with a man named Andrew Blake. I know of the family. They have a fine reputation."

"Yes, that is true, mother, I was just coming in to tell you myself. This is all right with you, I hope?"

"Yes, but do heed your father about bringing a chaperone." She was pleased that Alexandra had attracted a new suitor from a respected family, but she did not show her enthusiasm, considering the way Cassandra felt.

"Yes, of course. Mother, please will you send a footman to tell Mrs. Ravenstock I need her this evening? The carriage will stop for her on the way here, and it is due at seven. I am hoping that Cassandra will help me get ready later. First, luncheon. I am ravenous! Mother, would you ask Sara to bring a tray to my room before she draws my bath? Would you mind helping me dress for dinner, Cassie?" Alex was thinking of all the tasks ahead.

"No, I do not mind. We'll see what we can do with you." Cassandra's tone was tinged with sarcasm. "Mother, I'll take my luncheon upstairs as well, please." She was feeling a little left out. With that, the sisters courteously took their leave.

At the door, Alex turned and exchanged a questioning glance with her mother. She could tell her sister was bothered, and was not sure why.

After baths and luncheon and an hour or so for resting, the sisters searched through Alex's wardrobes looking for just the right dress. It had to be elegant but not snobbish, fashionable but not too revealing, and, most of all, it had to show off Alex's golden hair. They finally agreed upon an ensemble and sat down at tea to discuss the appropriate ornaments to go with it.

Andrew trotted up to his stable, dismounted and gave the stableboy his reins. As he strolled to the back door of the big brick house, he ruminated over the day's events, wondering what Gavin would say on hearing that the very object of his secret affection would appear in just a few hours! Andrew rang for a servant and strode along to his study, thirsty for a glass of ale before his late luncheon. He had started to open the door when he heard noises inside. Peering in, he was so surprised at the sight before him, he let out a boisterous laugh.

Startled by Andrew, Gavin jumped a foot from his position by the liquor decanters and sprung into a fighting stance, arms raised with fists clenched. Andrew could only laugh again as he looked at his disheveled cousin. Gavin had managed to drink himself into a sorry state.

Andrew wanted some sort of reaction from the man, but this was unexpected. He was not sure how he was going to sober Gavin up enough to behave appropriately. To ensure that Gavin would appear for dinner, Andrew decided not to mention that Alex would be joining them.

"What in the world d'you think you're doing, sneakin' up on me like that," Gavin growled, having a little trouble getting the words out.

"Sorry chap! It's my house, and I didn't realize how drunk you could get in the daytime. What in the blazes is wrong with you anyway?"

"Me? You're the one sneakin' around here like you're some sort of spy," Gavin slurred at his cousin.

"Right! Now, I believe it is impossible to speak civilly with you. Perhaps you might go to your rooms and have a rest before teatime?"

"Why thank you, Andrew. I had not realized that I needed your permission to do so." Now he was enunciating with care, but on leaving the study, Gavin stumbled in the hall and again on the stairs. Andrew assumed he had safely reached his room when he heard a door slam. He went to find his mother to discuss arrangements for the evening repast. He also spoke with the butler to make sure no more liquor would reach Gavin this afternoon. He was not surprised when Gavin failed to appear for tea; there were loud snores emanating from his cousin's chambers. Andrew instructed Stephen to take some hearty sandwiches up with a pot of strong tea when the man showed signs of waking.

As the hour for dinner neared, he felt certain that Alex's presence would ignite Gavin's feelings, and this charade would not have to go any further. Then he saw his cousin descending the stairs, dressed entirely in black, his hair unruly and his shoes unpolished. He must have slept in them. Andrew's famously good-looking cousin looked dreadful!

"Gavin, why not add some color to that outfit? You look like death itself. Maybe you might want to, oh, I don't know...comb your hair perhaps? Have your footwear shined? How could Stephen let you out like that?"

"Andrew, I don't know when you became so fashion-conscious, but why not worry about yourself instead of me?" Gavin replied gruffly. "I gave my man the evening off when he barged in with a tray."

"What? Not feeling well?" Andrew was more than a little concerned.

"No, not really, so do try not to annoy me," Gavin responded in an irritated tone. At least now he was speaking clearly, if not nicely.

"Fine, if that is your wish. But could you please try to fix yourself up a little?"

"I don't know what this obsession is of yours about how I look, but please stop. Besides, it is not as though we were having a dinner party."

Gavin waved Andrew off in annoyance and headed for the study.

Andrew wondered, what am I going to do now? Gavin is going to ruin this entire evening if his mood does not improve. Seeing off a carriage to collect Mrs. Ravenstock and the Lady Alexandra, Andrew hoped his plans would not be ruined by Gavin's unfortunate state. He followed his cousin into the study, where all decanters had been removed.

"Alexandra dear, the carriage is here!" When Alexandra elegantly swept down the stairs a few minutes later, Elizabeth patted her rosy cheek and said, "You look absolutely radiant." Daniel, passing through the hallway, glanced at his child with pride. No longer a child at all, he thought, nodding his blessing.

"Thank you, Mother, Father. Are you sure this gown is appropriate? Cassandra and I took forever picking it out."

"Of course it is. Blue is definitely your color!"

Alex had on a fashionable dress in a rich oceanic hue, cut to show a hint of cleavage, nothing too revealing. Clinging to her slim figure in the right places, it draped softly over her shoulders, plunged almost to the waist in back, and accentuated her curves, trailing to the floor with darker blue lace at the hem. She remembered first wearing it for a dinner dance during her debutante season. She liked its generously cut lace-trimmed shawl and the dyed-to-match elbow-length kid gloves, and she wore just the right shoes for the ensemble.

Cassandra had helped to wash and dry and artfully arrange her sister's hair, and now it was piled high on her head with a few long flaxen ringlets flowing over her shoulders with several more down her back. A light scent of lavender and lily of-the-valley followed Alex faintly.

She was breathtaking, her fine complexion aglow in the lamplight. With her mother and sister looking on from the doorway, she glided down the broad front steps into the courtyard, where a footman stood at attention. He helped her up into a glossy black carriage with a gilded coat of arms on the door. Her black-clad chaperone was seated primly within, a highly respectable clergyman's widow who would rarely get out into the world, or get a good meal, if she did not insist on performing this favor for the nearby gentry. She nodded a greeting as Alexandra settled into the well-sprung seat, and the footman signalled the driver to move along.

Chapter Six

Alex peered out a window as the carriage slowed and pulled up to a grand house, beautiful in every detail and impeccably maintained. Its tall brick frontage was aglow with candles lighting every window, glimmering a welcoming and majestic ambiance. In the early darkness under a rising full moon, rolling green hills could just be made out, embracing the home with its large gardens and neatly clipped shrubbery. The horses arrived at the front steps, and a footman climbed down and helped Alex and Mrs. Ravenstock out. A servant within, hearing the carriage's arrival, was already opening the tall front doors. A moment later, an elderly butler appeared in the doorway to usher Alex and her chaperone inside. Taking their wraps with a welcoming smile, he led them to a parlor to await Lord Andrew's arrival.

The parlor was exquisite. Appointed in emerald green and gold, it was much more elegant than Alex's own. However, she thought hers to be more homelike for family life, whereas this one seemed designed for entertaining. Moving next to a cheery fire as Mrs. Ravenstock seated herself in a dim corner, she admired a painting of a wide, rolling pasture edged by shapely trees and rampant with wildflowers. A servant offered a tray of sherry in tiny crystal goblets.

Andrew soon entered. "My dear, you look absolutely lovely," he said quietly, hoping to make Alex feel comfortable, and bowed to the silent Mrs. Ravenstock with a smile. Andrew was not lying. This vision of beauty really should catch Gavin's eye, he thought to himself.

"Andrew," she said, stepping over to greet her host. "You startled me. I have a habit of getting carried away in my thoughts. I didn't hear you come in. Forgive me. This fine painting caught my eye."

"Don't be silly, Alex. There is no need to apologize. I assure you my feelings have not been affected, except to admire how ravishing you look this evening." Suppressing a grin, Andrew now knew his plan was foolproof.

"Thank you Andrew, it is kind of you to say so. You are looking rather dashing yourself."

"I quite agree with you there," Andrew said, and both succumbed to laughter.

Gavin overheard the laughter from the parlor and recognized his cousin's deep tones. He could swear he recognized the other speaker as well, but could not put a name to her, still feeling a bit befogged. Lady Amelia was hurrying along the hallway and Gavin politely summoned her into the library, where he was slumped into a deep chair, not quite sober and trying to overcome a headache by sipping an icy tonic.

"Aunt Amelia, please, who is the young woman in the parlor with Andrew?"

"Honestly Gavin, I do not know. He told me we were entertaining a dinner guest and her chaperone, but he neglected to tell me the lady's name."

"Why the big secret?"

"I really do not know, Gavin. If you will excuse me, I must go and check on the cook, she had some problem with a scullery maid falling ill." Turning quickly, as if on a mission, Amelia was gone.

Gavin called out to his aunt, "Thank you anyway!" but she was too far down the hall to hear him.

Amelia strode down the hall with a most graceful posture that far younger women might envy. She carried herself well for an older woman. Her skin remained youthful, with hardly a wrinkle. She lived for her children now, as she had been doing in the five years since her husband's sudden death alongside her in bed one night. Despite her loss, Amelia was a happy woman. She often remarked that Andrew was the cause of every gray hair that appeared on her head.

Andrew kept Alex in the parlor until they heard the gong for dinner. He wanted everything to be perfect, and was afraid that by showing her around the rooms, they might run into Gavin, and his surprise would be ruined.

Gavin, Amelia and Catherine stepped up to be introduced as Andrew entered the dining room with Lady Alexandra on his arm, trailed by the quiet Mrs. Ravenstock, who was of a retiring nature and becoming rather deaf. Catherine and Amelia greeted Alex with warm smiles, recognizing her family name as one with high standing in the next county, and a footman soon made sure the bent and arthritic Mrs. Ravenstock was comfortably seated at the foot of the table. No one suspected this was all a ruse on Andrew's part.

Gavin, on the other hand, stood wide-eyed in a doorway, his mouth gaping a little in disbelief. Shocked at the length that Andrew would go to embarrass him... how mortifying! And Alex was lovelier than ever!

Alex, too, was taken aback momentarily on sighting Gavin. She'd had no idea that Gavin would be present and felt a little offended that Andrew had not mentioned it. Nevertheless, she kept her composure and her demeanor did not betray her surprise. As all took their places around the table, a footman pulled her chair out for her, seating her across from Gavin. Andrew moved to the head of the table, his mother on his right, his sister on his left.

Gavin was having a difficult time taking his eyes off Alex. She looked stunning! The sight of her made his blood boil in a way he could not control, and her presence in the room made his digestive discomfort intensify. Something similar was happening in Alex. She had to admit that Gavin looked a little rough tonight. However, he was still highly attractive, and a little twinge of guilt washed over her. She shouldn't think anything at all about Gavin; she was here as the gallant Andrew's guest.

Observing with satisfaction that Alex and Gavin were consumed in each other, Andrew was nevertheless moved to interrupt. "Gavin, don't be so rude, do say hello to our lovely guest for the evening. I know you have met her."

Shaking his head to bring himself back to his surroundings, Gavin said, "Forgive my manners this evening. How do you do, Lady Alexandra?"

"Fine, thank you, and you?" she responded, feeling awkward.

"Fine, thank you," was all he said back to her.

The first course was brought out, wine was poured, and the repast began. Gavin noted the delicate way Alex picked up her wine to sip, how her pinky finger would lift ever so slightly each time she brought her goblet to her sensuous lips.

Alex also studied Gavin. He seemed different from their first encounter, not just disheveled, but lacking in conversation, more reserved. She also noted the way he was stirring his soup around, hardly eating at all. Andrew sat back, noticing how his cousin and guest kept discreetly glancing at each other. Silence around the dining table would never do. Choosing a topic all could join in on, he asked, "Alex, how is your soup?"

"Wonderful, Andrew, thank you for asking, so rich and creamy. My portion is so generous, I don't believe I will finish nearly half!"

"It looks as though Gavin is having the same problem. Gavin, is something wrong with your soup?" Andrew asked.

"Not at all, Andrew. My appetite is just a bit off, nothing to be worried about."

"I hope you're not ill?" Alex said, not realizing how deeply concerned her voice sounded.

"No, I am not ill. I'm just having an... unpredictable day."

"Gavin, were you not drunk earlier today? Perhaps that is the cause of your bothersome stomach," Catherine remarked innocently between spoonfuls of her soup. This caused Andrew to choke a little on his own.

Gavin gave his young cousin a glare that warned, "You better be quiet!" with no uncertainty. Alexandra observed this exchange with a little discomfort.

To change the subject, she inquired, "If I might ask you a question, Lord Gavin?"

"My dear, you need not have my permission to ask a question, for if I did not like it I simply would not answer," he shot back in a sarcastic tone, harsher than he had intended.

Alex felt indignant upon hearing her own words parroted back to her, as she had said them in a much friendlier fashion! "Very well, then... is it very like you, to get drunk in the middle of the day?"

"My dear Lady Alexandra, just because a man drinks in the middle of the day, he is not required to explain his reasons."

Recognizing that he was avoiding her question, Alex decided to give him a taste of his own medicine. "Of course, you need not explain yourself to me. However, I did not at first take you for a drunk, as it would appear."

"A drunk? Ha! I rarely tip a glass in the middle of the day! You caught me on a most unusual occasion, and now you chastise me for it? I think not!" Gavin felt hurt, and was insulted enough to raise his voice, but his bluster did not reveal his pain.

She believed him when he said he wasn't a drunk. He struck her as an honest man, and she had come to this certainty the first time she encountered him. There was a look in his eyes that Alex could not explain to others, but she knew he was telling the truth, and that this was in his deepest nature.

Catherine continued to enjoy her meal as soup plates were whisked away and the second course arrived, despite the twinge of guilt she felt for having started the whole contretemps. When Gavin and Alex stopped talking, unable to control herself, Catherine blurted out: "Maybe I was wrong." Without a second thought, she smiled as the footmen scooped generous portions on her plate from silver trays.

At her remark, Andrew let out a boisterous laugh, but quickly shut his mouth when he saw the look on the face of his cousin. Alex found it difficult to refrain from laughing at the child's remark herself, but on regarding Gavin's expression, she realized he had not found any humor in it.

The cousins sat through rest of the meal hardly saying a word. Amelia tried to make polite conversation with Mrs. Ravenstock, who answered with the shortest and vaguest of replies as footmen served her generous amounts of many delicious dishes. She was too busy enjoying the delights of the table to look up into her interlocutor's face to read her lips, and had little interest in talk anyway. Amelia finally stopped trying. Catherine thought to admire Alex's fancy dress, and was warmly but briefly acknowledged. Alex could not think of a topic that would interest Catherine or Amelia, preoccupied with thoughts of Gavin, with him sitting so near. Amelia and Catherine at last took up the conversation they had been sharing earlier in the day, planning a visit to relatives.

Andrew found he had little desire to develop a friendship with Alex, thinking with some regret that he could have invited Cassandra. Gavin did not speak at all, and dined politely, but without relish, keeping his eyes on his food. Silence around the table was growing more and more awkward. Andrew wondered if his plot was failing.

At last, a tall, rich chocolate cake masterfully decorated with creamy white filling and early wild strawberries was presented with a flourish. Alex had eaten her fill, but she had a sweet tooth, and the cake looked decadent. Gavin did not look impressed with anything, and still had not spoken. Andrew was relieved that the awkward repast was drawing to a close at last.

He was about to take a bite of cake when he detected a distant noise from the front hall. It was quite late for a social call, and the knocking sounded peremptory. Shortly the butler arrived, and spoke softly into Andrew's ear. Andrew excused himself with an apologetic word to the ladies, and followed Gregor down the hall. The others waited for Andrew's return in silence, with Amelia and Catherine exchanging an expression of curiosity. Mrs. Ravenstock was too busy having the footman bring a second slice of cake to notice the disturbance, but she tended to pay little attention to her surroundings. Alex and Gavin sipped from their goblets politely, waiting for a chance to rise from the table, each so aware of the other that their surroundings had faded from their minds.

The footmen cleared away the last crumbs of cake and offered a fine amontillado, which was declined by all. As their host did not reappear, the silence in the room grew uncomfortable. Gavin rose, and begged them to excuse him to determine what urgent business had deprived them Andrew's company. Amelia voiced concern, but Gavin assured her it was probably nothing.

Recognizing a too-familiar voice upon stepping out of the dining room, Gavin quietly ordered the attentive butler to keep the staff well away from the front hall, knowing the havoc that Melinda could wreak. He sighed in disgust that he would need to deal with her.

A moment after Gavin left, Alex heard a loud disturbance from the direction of the front door. Alarmed, Amelia and Catherine exchanged glances and courteously excused themselves. Together they retired through a passage to the back of the house, certain one of the men would soon return to entertain the guests. Feeling deserted, Alex found herself alone with the widow Ravenstock, who appeared to be nodding off, oblivious to these goings-on.

Alex stood and walked to the door, opening it a crack to peer down a dimly lit hallway. *Please,* she thought to herself with a sudden pang of fear, *let everyone be safe.* She caught sight of the butler escorting two frightened housemaids in the direction of the kitchens, then the hallway was empty. She had concern for Andrew, but Gavin was foremost in her thoughts. Not five minutes ago, she and Gavin had silently exchanged a look across the table. In spite of his annoying reticence, there was something special that connected them, and she could still feel it.

Now something must be terribly wrong. She felt this in her stomach as she paused, impatiently expecting the men's return. She could not remain still. Inching her way toward the big front doors, she was soon aware of a woman's loud, shrill threats. Alex heard Gavin's cultured voice answering as she drew closer, finally hiding behind a pillar but peering around it to view the entrance hall. From here she could make out what people were saying and remain unseen.

Gavin was stooped over his cousin's limp body, stretched out on the parquet before the open doors. "By God, Melinda! What have you done to Andrew?" He was trying to interrupt the tiny woman's screeching tirade.

"Oh, stop fretting. He is merely a little stunned." She nudged the form with a dainty toe, and Andrew moaned. Her black, tightly fitted gown matched her raven hair and the jet ornaments on her neck and ears added to the grim effect. Slight in stature, however vicious her nature, Melinda had not arrived alone. The two overbearing giants looming behind her put a menacing power into her threats and insults.

"What on earth do you think you are doing here? I know that you were not invited, so explain yourself quickly before I do to you what you have done to Andrew!" Gavin, now standing, was not joking, regardless of the oversized men at her flank. He was losing patience quickly.

Alex was taken aback by this bizarre scene, and concerned for the groaning heap on the floor. What in the world could Gavin have to do with this... Melinda? As the argument continued, the question went round her head over and over.

"No, I was *not* invited, as you say!" the woman answered with heat. "I'm sure you have not forgotten the promise that I made to you when we had our little... disagreement. I said I would find you, and make your life as miserable as you have made mine!" Her tone implied she had only just begun in this effort and was most enthusiastic to proceed. "You can't hide from me," she sneered.

"Miserable? How dare you blame *me*, you cunning little witch! *You* were the one who was unfaithful. *You* were the one who wanted me only for my fortune and my good name, yet *you* blame *me*. That is both humorous, and indefensible." Gavin kept his tone low, but it betrayed his seething outrage and growing fury.

"I have heard enough from you!" retorted Melinda. "I don't have to stand here and listen to insults!" On her commanding gesture, the two enormous brutes stepped forward. Alex assumed they were somehow responsible for Andrew's lamentable condition.

"And exactly what is it that you think you are going to accomplish with your goons?"

"I don't *think* anything, Gavin. However, I do *know* that these two goons, as you have so rudely called my friends Edgar and Olaf, are going to get you into my carriage. We will journey up to Gretna Green and there be wed, as we should have been months ago. It's a lovely place really, just over the border of Scotland. Only three hundred miles, we'll be there in a week. I hear many scandalous weddings have taken place there. Scotland's marriage laws are much more lenient then our own."

"Over my dead body shall I marry you!"

"As you wish, Gavin, but it would be so much easier if you would just come along."

Again the mean-spirited woman waved her hand, signalling one of her henchmen, and Olaf stepped forward and punched Gavin hard in the midsection without warning, then stepped back.

Bent over and striving to recover his wind, Gavin gasped, "You will not get the words 'I do' out of my mouth." Quickly straightening to his full height, he took a quick breath and continued, "How is it you will deal with that problem? I know, you're going to beat me again, are you not?"

"Don't be so silly, Gavin. By that time, I will not have to force *anything* upon you." Melinda was confident of her charms and now used her most seductive tone.

Alex could take no more. She rushed the last few yards down the hall, and placing herself between Gavin and Melinda, demanded to know what was going on.

"Now, young woman, whoever you are, who *do* you think you are, demanding *anything* from me?" Melinda's voice was low and cold, and she stepped closer to Alex to add to her venomous menace.

Alex did not back away from her diminutive adversary. Standing her ground firmly, she drew herself to her full height and replied heatedly, "You will tell me what is going on, especially why you are yelling at... my husband!"

Horror and astonishment washed over Melinda's face and Gavin also revealed a startled expression, and hid it quickly.

"Husband! Gavin, you are married? This causes a change in my plans."

"You, lady, are no Lady! You have no plans that concern my husband, I assure you of that!" Alex's voice was commanding, still confident, but she began to feel a little desperate.

Gavin, shocked at this turn of events, realized that Alex did not fully understand the dangerous position she was in. He was speechless.

"Look here, you stupid child. I will not be spoken to that way!" Melinda raised her right hand and swung it forcefully to strike Alex's cheek. Alex had not expected that, but maintained her poise. She was not going to let Melinda get away with it. Her cheek was burning. "What is it? Melinda? I believe that is your name, right? Do not think you can hit *me* and get nothing in return!"

Quickly shifting her weight to put it behind her closed fist, Alex punched Melinda straight in the nose, knocking her to the ground. There are times when it is good to have had an older brother to teach you fighting, Alex thought with satisfaction, massaging one hand with the other, but she was becoming more and more frightened as these impossible events unfolded.

"You have made a terrible mistake, princess!" Melinda shouted as she regained her composure and her feet, dabbing her nose with a lacy black handkerchief. "Edgar, subdue this woman. She will be joining us on our little excursion. Use a blindfold. ...Olaf! You know what to do." Her tone betrayed her resolve as changes in her plans took shape in her mind.

Edgar reached into his voluminous coat pockets for lengths of cord, and in no time, Alex found herself bruised, trussed hand and foot, and blindfolded.

As Gavin started to lunge in Alex's direction, he was overcome by Olaf's murderous assault, which knocked him to the floor. The hulking man went over him thoroughly with well-aimed blows, oblivious to Gavin's efforts at defense. Gavin was unmanned by the sight of Alex so helpless and afraid. Furious, outraged, he struggled against his assailant, but was more concerned about Alex than about his own situation. Olaf was twice his own weight, and Gavin's jabs and kicks had no apparent effect.

Melinda found tremendous satisfaction in watching the way Gavin was reacting. The fury and pain she saw in his eyes for Alex pleased her most.

"The woman won't be able to come all the way, of course. That would be silly. How could I marry Gavin if he already had a wife? We will dispose of this *princess* along the way."

"Melinda, you are a cruel, heartless woman, and someday you will get what you have coming to you. Perhaps I will be the one who gives it!" Gavin burst out, just before Olaf knocked him out with a last powerful blow.

Melinda gave orders to put her captives in her second carriage, which had been prepared to hold a captive. Olaf and Edgar roughly threw two well-trussed forms onto floor of the small, nondescript conveyance, piling one on top of the other. Alex fainted when she landed on the hard surface with a whoosh of escaping breath, and did not feel another body land atop her.

By now Andrew lay insensate in front of the open doorway. Catherine and Amelia were sipping bedtime tea together in a back parlor. Mrs. Ravenstock, so often invisible, was snoring in her comfortable chair, forgotten. The servants were gossiping in their own hall by the pantry, under the watchful eye of the obedient, elderly Gregor, who had gotten in his head that of course the dinner guests must have departed before Amelia and Catherine moved to the rear of the house. The household staff seemed pleased to have the evening off from their regular duties, if curious as to the reason and dimly aware of some tumult in the hall. Perhaps their young masters were playing at boxing, or dealing with some intruder.

Chapter Seven

Alex regained her senses soon after the carriages started moving. Dizzy, gasping for breath, lying awkwardly on her back with hands pinned behind her, and aware of something heavy on her chest, Alex opened her eyes. At first everything remained dark, until she remembered her blindfold. Rubbing the knot against the floor, she managed to slide it away from her eyes, and could glimpse that it was Gavin's limp form on top of her in the dim light. Not only did her constricted breathing bother her, but her back and arms ached, her cheek burned, and every bump in the road made her position more excruciating. In a hushed whisper she tried to speak Gavin's name. Wriggling and writhing, she attempted to shift Gavin's weight, but her efforts were futile in such close quarters. She remained pinned, and made herself take slow, shallow breaths. It seemed an eternity before Gavin showed signs of awakening.

"Oh, thank God you're awake! Please, move to the side! I cannot breathe with you on top of me," Alex said in a strained voice.

"Thanks for being concerned with my well-being," Gavin answered with irritation, barely conscious. With some maneuvering, he found a way to roll off Alex and hunch into a semi-sitting position at her feet, bound legs awkwardly crumpled beneath him in the confined space. He leaned against a seat, wanting to rub his lip where he had been bashed and was now bleeding, but his wrists were tightly tied behind his waist. He hurt everywhere. Looking at Alex when a stray moonbeam glanced in the window, he noticed how swollen the side of her face was from the abuse she had received at the hands of that huge, intimidating Edgar, or perhaps this was the result of the slap from Melinda.

His poor Angel beside him looked terrible! And she was obviously in pain. He forgot his own discomforts upon observing hers. He could not stand to see her suffer. He never wanted her to experience anything like this! With a hollow, empty feeling in the pit of his stomach, Gavin shouldered responsibility for their situation. God help those goons. I will get my revenge, he resolved.

Once released from Gavin's weight, Alex soon wrestled her arms and legs free of their bindings, and threw off her blindfold. At once she untied Gavin, straining to make out the knots in the darkness inside the carriage, and helped him onto a seat, all his limbs stiff and sore from the beating and the awkward position Edgar and Olaf had trussed him in. Seating herself on one of the benches, Alex straightened her bedraggled dress and combed her fingers through her tangled hair, rubbing sore wrists and ankles to restore circulation. The pain in her cheek was sharp and hot. She was beginning to wonder just what kind of mess she had gotten herself into. Peering across at Gavin, she noticed his ragged appearance and his split lip as he massaged his limbs. At least he was no longer bleeding. Gavin tried the doors and windows, but all were tightly secured. There was no way they could cast objects out to leave a trail, or get out of the carriage without assistance.

Alex was suddenly overcome with an impulse to hold Gavin and salve his wounds. She also wanted him to take her in those manly arms and tell her everything would soon be fine. Fighting back her feelings, she made herself look out her window and take in the passing scene, hoping she might recognize something familiar or find an opportunity to escape, but they were trotting along some deserted country road in moonlit darkness. Mentally thanking her father passing along his thoughtful habits, she tried to devise some escape. Her determination was overshadowed by an overwhelming mixture of fear, distress and hopelessness.

Soon the route took them well away from the precincts around Arlington House. The moon went behind a cloud and they soon had no clue as to their direction or location.

Gavin could see the forlorn expression on his Angel's face. It made him feel he was dying inside. Hoping she might appreciate some comfort, he painfully shifted his limbs to sit next to her. "Alex, I need to know why you said what you did back there?" he asked in a soft, gentle voice.

Turning toward him, she answered, "I thought if Melinda believed you had gone and gotten married, she would leave you alone. Pretty naive, yes?" She turned back to the window, trying hard now not to cry. Having him so close made her feelings all the more overwhelming.

"It was a kind and generous gesture. Thank you. However, it was really none of your business." He was regretting her pain and involvement, and lamenting their situation, wishing none of it had ever transpired. To Alex, Gavin sounded ungrateful for her brave attempt to help him.

"None of my business! Fine! I was only trying to help, but I have learned a valuable lesson. You, my lord, I shall never help again!" Feeling unbearably hurt and abandoned, Alex crossed her arms over her chest and stared out into the starry night.

"Fine, that is fine by me. I did not ask for your help in the first place, if you recall." Gavin was totally out of sorts now, and his head was aching fiercely. Countless bruises were making themselves known. Moving gingerly back to the opposite bench, Gavin could not understand why Alex had turned so cold and angry, while Alex wondered why Gavin was acting so offensively. It reminded her of the chilly aftermath of his kiss just a short time ago. This man must be insane! She pondered how her escape could be effected.

Gavin shut his eyes in frustration. She drove him crazy! In his mind's eye, Gavin still saw Alex's long, curly golden locks flowing down her shoulders, rising and falling with every breath she took. She was such a beauty, even now, in her distress, disorder and captivity. There was no way he would let Melinda hurt her again! He would save Alex somehow. He just needed to put a plan together in his mind. As looking at her was such a distraction, he would need to remain distant and cool. If Alex were angry at him, he reasoned, it would be easier to remain aloof, and he'd be able to think more clearly.

They jounced along in chilly silence. Alex did not look at Gavin and he tried not to look at her, each gazing out a window on opposite sides of the carriage as it rattled down another narrow unfamiliar lane. Alex finally slipped into a doze, head against the window, he saw from the corner of his eye, glad she could escape into her dreams.

The night was long.

We have been at a steady trot for a full four hours, Gavin was figuring, still in possession of his pocket watch, but with no idea where they might be. He knew the horses could not be pushed much longer without rest and water. He could not come up with a way of escaping while they remained in motion. With either Olaf or Edgar driving this team, any opportunity to get out of the carriage was unlikely. The blackguards were too strong and vigilant. All depended on stopping somewhere.

At last the carriage slowed and the rhythm of the jolting changed, waking Alex. Peering into the moonlight as the horses halted, Alex could make out an insignificant little hostelry close by the side of the narrow, untraveled little road. In a few minutes its doorway was dimly illumined by a bulky shape that must be Edgar or Olaf, hanging a lantern at the lintel. Two front windows started to glow as oil lamps were lit within. The old inn had a shabby look of deep abandonment, as if a new coaching route had passed it by and made it unprofitable some time well in the past. A falling-down stable and paddock were on one end, what must be a burnt-out kitchen on the other. Parts of the roof had lost their thatch. Craning ahead at the other carriage, Alex saw Olaf holding its door open and offering a hand to petite Lady Melinda, helping her down and accompanying her into the building.

"That is quite funny," Alex said, breaking the silence.

"What? What is so funny?" Gavin asked, seeing nothing funny.

"That brute escorted that witch out of her carriage and into this pathetic little roadhouse as if she were a queen. She has no idea what it is to be a lady!" Alex shook her head as if trying to cast aside a painful nightmare. Turning to Gavin she asked, "What is the plan?"

"A plan, my dear? I could hardly devise a plan, considering I do not know where we are or what we are in for. But do not worry, I know how to deal with Melinda. I will not let her harm you." Gavin looked away from Alex, his heart breaking at her look of crushed disappointment, but not wanting to appear too caring.

Alex wasn't reassured. It was only *her* life that was in danger, as his was valuable to their tormentor. She would have to look out for her own safety. First chance, she was going attempt an escape, with him or without him, she made up her mind.

"Edgar, bring me the woman. I have a few questions I need answered. Now go get her!" Melinda barked her orders. "Olaf, see to the horses. Get them fed and watered and bedded down for the night. Make sure all is ready for an early start tomorrow. And be quick about it." Melinda's nose was a little swollen, her voice a little nasal, but she still could make her commands imperious.

With a slight nod, the brute with sandy brown hair lumbered out to retrieve Lady Alexandra. The captives were looking at each other tensely when their carriage door banged open with such force they were taken aback. Before Gavin could react and leap on the thug, Edgar had snatched Alex by her hair, pulled her from the carriage, and flung her violently over his shoulder, roughly slamming the door closed with a strong kick. Screaming imprecations and battering him with fists and knees, Alex was more than annoyed at this unaccustomed treatment.

Gavin sat locked in the carriage. He stared after them glumly imagining what was in store for Alex inside. His helplessness increased his misery.

In the shabby little roadhouse, Melinda ordered Edgar to drop Alex and stand by to control her.

Edgar dumped Alex in a heap on the floor, and took a position in front of the only outer door. "Sit!" ordered Melinda, who was pacing in front of Alex as she started to rise. Melinda wanted to give Alex's fears a chance to build.

Alex took the opportunity to discreetly survey her surroundings. The dusty, cobwebbed space, once the public room of a cozy little inn where travelers could break their journey and obtain fresh horses, was now unfurnished save a scatter of broken-down tables and chairs. Olaf brought in some baskets and parcels and set them down on the innkeep's dirty bar with a thump: a bundle of what might be bread, bottles of wine, candles, articles wrapped in newspaper that must be goblets from their shape, more things Alex could not identify. Opposite the bar was a big fireplace with feathers in its cold ashes. An alcove in the back, opposite the door, led to sleeping rooms and bathing chambers, she surmised. That barred and padlocked door behind the pub counter must lead to the kitchens and pantries with innkeeper's quarters above, now mostly destroyed by fire. The only route to the stables was out the front door, with Edgar barring the way. A damp and musty aroma pervaded the place as if it had sat long empty, unaired, unused and dank. Alex remembered the hole in the thatch and surmised the roof must leak. She wondered if that might be an escape route.

Melinda paused in her pacing and addressed Alex imperiously. "I have a few questions to ask of you, and for your benefit as well as your so-called husband's, I recommend you answer them." Walking back and forth again, Melinda rubbed her hands together with some vigor. "I want to know exactly how you and Gavin met."

Alex smoothed her soiled dress around her and sat up as erect as she could. Holding her head high, she gazed silently up at her captor with grim defiance.

"You will only make it more difficult for yourself if you keep silent," Melinda taunted, spoiling for a fight.

"I don't see how our courtship has anything to do with you," Alex replied civilly.

"I shall not warn you again. Perhaps there *was* no courtship and perhaps you are *not* his wife." Melinda had noticed that Alex wore no rings. "It has only been a scant six months since Gavin and I... went our separate ways."

"We are indeed married! Perhaps that fact is bothering you, Melinda? That he so soon got over you, realized he *never* loved you? That must have hurt! I can see where you would be upset... but to kidnap us? Is that not taking one little rejection a bit too far?" Alex's sarcastic tone brought Melinda to her boiling point.

Walking over to Alex, Melinda leaned down and slapped her again with all her might, aiming well for the red, swollen side of Alex's face. Alex's head whipped around from the blow and she bit back tears. When she slowly turned back to confront Melinda, her hot, bruised visage betrayed only an icy calm.

"Not very ladylike, *princess*. That look on your face is not becoming. I think you had better answer my questions!" Placing a chair directly in front of Alex, seating herself, arranging her skirts and leaning in close, Melinda went on softly, "Again I ask you, where did you and Gavin meet?"

"We met at a party in London." Alex hoped that by telling the truth, Gavin would be smart enough to do the same so their stories would coincide. She stared at the floor, trying to think of a way to end this interview.

"I could not help but notice that you are not wearing a wedding band. Would you explain that to me, please?" Melinda was wheedling.

Color drained from Alex's face for a moment. She had not thought of that detail.

Recovering quickly and recalling young Catherine's remarks at dinner, she looked Melinda in the eye and replied, "My wedding band is a family heirloom, so when we are home or with family, I prefer to keep it locked up. It is just too precious. It was his grandmother's, and when we announced our engagement, she saw it delivered to Gavin, because she thought I was just so *darling,*" She enjoyed the chance to aggravate Melinda. She wanted that evil woman to steep in jealousy.

"A family heirloom? Well *you* must be something. Gavin and I were engaged for many months, and it was never offered to me. I guess they just did not like me." Melinda stood up and sneered down at Alex, this time giving her a glittering stare that would make most women shy away. Alex was not intimidated, and glared up at Melinda with poise and determination.

"I have had enough of this woman!" Melinda exclaimed, more than irritated, almost enraged. She was not getting the snivelling and tears she had expected. She gave a sharp order for Edgar to fetch Gavin. Olaf, just returned from stable duty, stood watch over Alex.

Gavin, firmly gripped by the bearlike Edgar, felt pain and disbelief as he looked down at poor Alex seated so awkwardly on the floor in her nice dress, her face even more swollen and red now, but showing simmering defiance. Noticeable stripes left by Melinda's fingers marred Alex's porcelain cheek.

Melinda nodded to Olaf to give Gavin a spindly chair.

"Melinda! What have you done to my wife?" he demanded with enough fury to scare most people, as he was roughly thrust into his seat.

Melinda was oblivious. "It's her own fault, Gavin. All she had to do was answer my questions, but she refused. Feisty one you have there. However, do refrain from calling her your *wife*. It makes me feel rather ill to hear that. Besides, she won't be your *wife* much longer!

"...Now, my dear Gavin, you are a sight for sore eyes." Her tone had changed in an instant to become coy and inviting. She was done with interrogation. "How about a nice warm bath?"

"A bath! That is really something, Melinda. You want to know if I would like a bath, while the woman I am married to sits on your filthy floor looking worse then myself. You would offer *me* a bath? No! Not unless my *wife* gets to bathe as well." Gavin stood his ground.

"I do not believe you're in a position to bargain with me. Do not make me remind you not to refer to her as your wife!" Infuriated that Gavin would not cooperate, Melinda turned away and balled her hands into fists at her sides. She did not care if she sounded like a shrew.

Gavin almost roared at her. "Melinda! No bath unless my *wife* gets one, and a bargaining position is exactly what I have! If you would like me to stop referring to her as my *wife*, then simply allow my *wife* a bath as well!"

Looking down at his Angel, Gavin desperately wanted to pick her up and carry her far, far away. He noticed his look was mirrored in Alex's expressive eyes, and felt a faint ray of hope.

"So be it then! Olaf and Edgar, prepare *two* baths. Gavin will take his in my room. The *princess* will be in a room all to herself... but Olaf, you will stay to watch over her. Edgar, you will secure the prisoners, and the premises!" She was peremptory. She wheeled to face Gavin.

"Gavin, do not think this is because you are so smart! It is only because I am tired of fighting with you for today." Her voice was shrill again. Heading outside to escape the damp fug and think over her plans for Lady Alexandra's swift demise, Melinda paused to unwrap a goblet, uncork a bottle, and pour a large glass of wine. She turned back toward the room from the doorway and announced with satisfaction, "The sleeping arrangements will be the same."

It took some time for a fire to be lit and buckets of water to be fetched from a pump near the stable and heated, Olaf and Edgar's labors taking place out of sight. There was a noise of hammering from the rear of the building. Gavin and Alex found themselves alone again, bound hand and foot. They spoke in whispers.

"Alex, I am so sorry this is happening. I will get us out of here soon, I promise you that. You must trust me, please." His genuine care was apparent in his voice.

By this time Alex was growing bitter, for it was she who was taking the brunt of Melinda's fury. She was mad to get herself into this situation! She was sitting in dirt and dust in the middle of the night far from home, prey to brute strength and vituperation, and fast losing all the self-control she so treasured.

Alex looked up at him and replied faintly, "Fine, do what you have to do," and glanced away.

They sat in silence, in their bondage, and in bondage to one another. Somehow no escape plan made itself apparent to either. Time ticked by with excruciating slowness.

Olaf and Edgar returned to rummage in the bundles a few times, hauled in clanking pails of water, then returned to yank the captives to their feet. Edgar warily untied Gavin's ankles and marched him to Melinda's room. Releasing his wrist bindings, he kept a steady eye on him, never letting him move out of reach as Gavin quickly undressed and stepped into a small galvanized tub.

Olaf marched Alex into another little bedroom where another tub was set in one dusty corner. Much to her surprise, after releasing her restraints, he turned his head and closed his eyes as she removed her garments with difficulty. The tiny hooks and buttons on her dress, and the fastenings of her corset, demanded the attentions of a maid. The tub was not clean and the water was not deep or especially hot, but she did not feel she had it in her to argue or complain. There was a small chunk of coarse lye soap, looking like it had been broken off a larger bar, and a possibly-clean towel hung from a nail nearby.

"Why did you do that?" she asked, stepping in the tub with her back to Olaf.

"Do what?" Olaf said in a deep voice.

"Turn your head instead of looking."

"Would you rather I looked?" he asked.

"No! But you did not seem to be much of a gentleman, from what I have seen so far."

"This is merely my job, ma'am, not who I am."

"A job? You call this a job?"

"Yes. It is merely a way for my brother and me to make money."

"Are there not more respectable jobs you can do, other than using your superior strength to get people to do as you want?"

"Not as I want. It is what the Lady Melinda wants, for her we use our size and strength. This is not personal, just work. As I said, we are only here to make money, not to make friends. She is our employer, only that."

"I see," was all Alex said. She could not comprehend why anyone would do what Olaf and Edgar chose to do, for money or for any other reason. She soon prepared to rise from her bath, eyeing the lamentable condition of her garments, but feeling less bruised.

Melinda entered the inn again, and refilled her large glass. She headed for her room, hoping to catch Gavin in a state of undress as Edgar continued to stand guard.

"Gavin, you are a fine-looking man," Melinda cooed as she circled the tub, looking him over coyly with her dark, heavily lashed eyes.

"Melinda, save your flattery, it will get you nowhere." Gavin sighed, reaching for his towel and maneuvering it to hide his nakedness from Melinda's shameless stare as he stood.

"That was a clever trick, but a wasted one. My plans for you later will require both of us to be unclothed! Besides, I have seen all you have to offer. I will say that the intention of the bath was to wash off anything your *wife* may have….touched." Laughing, Melinda left the room, enjoying the drama.

Alex managed to don her clothing, and then Olaf tied her limbs. Lying uncomfortably on the small bed, Alex studied the tiny room trying to focus on a way to escape. She had heard him secure a heavy latch as he closed her door.

In a little while Gavin was escorted out to a dirty table in the front room, as was Alex. Both were surprised they were permitted to sit together. Their tormentor stood over them, and the hulks were menacing and watchful.

"Bread and water, Melinda? Tell me, could you not think of anything more creative? We are not that hungry at this hour." Gavin asked sarcastically.

"Gavin, darling, do not complain. Think of it this way: you could be eating nothing at all!" She trilled like a girl, smiling shyly as if she were in the delicate flower of youth. Then she barked out more orders and poured more wine. Her mood shifts were volcanic.

"Edgar, Olaf, remove the hand restraints so they may eat. After all, we did interrupt their dinner! First tie their feet to the chairs so they will not get any bright ideas." The men did as they were told and Alex and Gavin began to pick at the coarse brown bread. Alex had no interest in eating; it was the wee hours of the morning, and she had indulged in that chocolate cake at Andrew's. A meal of any kind at this hour was just another manifestation of Melinda's madness. She took a few bites for the sake of keeping her strength up, and hoped that perhaps, if she were compliant, they would put her back in her room right away. Thinking of escape, she sipped a drop of water to moisten her mouth, nibbled around the edges of her crust, and kept her eyes cast down.

Gavin was not hungry either. He was too worried about his Angel to be interested in eating, especially at this strange hour, after all they had gone through. He did, however, note that Melinda had managed to drink several glasses of wine and was now filling another. She was working on the second bottle, and he doubted Olaf and Edgar had been permitted to take any.

One thing he did know about Melinda... wine made her sleepy. They must attempt their escape at the earliest possible moment, before Melinda was sober enough to act on her intention to murder Alex. He knew what their destination was, but not which route Melinda was taking. For a long stretch before reaching this inn, there had been few crossroads, or signs of towns or villages, just an occasional lonely farmhouse as they rattled down narrow rural lanes. He had been mulling over his knowledge of the countryside north of Arlington relentlessly, but to no avail.

Alex was thinking the same: Tonight, she must try to get away. Wanting to signal Gavin, she raised her eyes to his just as he did the same. They were thinking the same thing. Gavin waited for a moment when no one was looking, then mouthed the words *meet outside.*

Melinda smugly gazed into her claret, enjoying their growing discomfort the longer she made them linger over these insulting crumbs. At last, growing bored with the game, she directed her men to take them to their rooms. First their hands were bound in front of them, then their feet were freed.

As they moved toward their beds in the painful grip of their escorts, Melinda taunted Gavin with a cackle, "I hope you enjoyed that measly little bite you shared with your *wife*, for it shall be her last." She walked toward the outer door, stumbling slightly. Melinda made the word *wife* sound like a curse, and was starting to slur her speech. Alex thought she must be headed for the outhouse, after all that wine, and wondered when she might get a chance to use it herself, but her need was not urgent.

Gavin was alarmed by Melinda's threat and felt it was imperative to get Alex out of her clutches rapidly. Alex understood, with or without Gavin, an early escape was her only hope of survival.

Alex lay feigning sleep after Olaf locked her in, wakeful and determined to find her opportunity. She played out different scenarios in her head, trying not to think about Gavin and Melinda sharing a bed, hoping the big brutes had fallen asleep somewhere. She twisted around on her knees and reached easily to a small window just above her. It had been nailed shut. The nails were not embedded deeply in the frame, and many were bent; obviously, it was a hasty job. She used their protrusions to saw at the cords that joined her wrists. It seemed to take forever as her anxiety built from fear of discovery.

Once freed, she started carefully feeling her way around the little room with her hands and feet. Her eyes had adjusted to the dim light of the moon shining through the window. Some floorboards near the door were worn and splintering. There was a gap where she could just push her fingers through. She grasped this floorboard, pulled on it over and over with as much strength as she could muster, and when it began to loosen, she slowly, quietly freed it from its bed, as nails creaked in resistance. Alex then used the bevelled edge of the hard wood to carefully pry out each nail securing the window to its frame. Finally, she eased the window upward. A quarter of the way up, it caught fast and would not budge.

Discouraged but determined, Alex put her ear to the keyhole to make sure no one was around. She heard Olaf and Edgar in a heated discussion in their room next door. They were not far, but they were so loudly complaining about Melinda, she had no worry they would hear the noise she was about to make. Creeping over to the tub, Alex snatched up the soap and climbed again onto her bed, and rubbed it up and down the window frame. After a considerable effort, the casement finally slid open. Forcing her body through the little window, she heard and felt her dress and stockings rip, then rolled shoulder-first onto the ground, the way she had been taught to take a fall from a horse.

Freedom! She paused to peer around for Gavin. There was moonlight, though the full moon would soon set, but she could not see far. It was still full night. Perhaps soon a first glimmer of pink would start showing in the east.

Alex waited for some time, and when she could wait no more, she crept to the candlelit window and peeked in. Gavin was lying still, clothing in disarray, eyes closed, beneath naked Melinda's limp embrace. Rubbing her wrist where she had been too tightly tied, Alex discovered a bloody scrape from the nailhead she had used to free herself. Backing away into the shadows of encroaching shrubbery, she waited for Gavin to appear. Finally, growing more and more fearful of discovery, she set off.

When Melinda arrived back in her room, she made Gavin soft, coy promises of a night to remember. Setting a lit candlestick on the chair, she lasciviously undid Gavin's buttons, stroked his hair, and whispered about tying his hands to the bedposts, the better to ravish him. Oblivious to his expression of distaste and the coiled tension of his frame, certain in her drunken confidence that he would be a willing and avid partner in a debauch, she blithely stripped off her clothing, and finally loosened the bonds that secured him. Then she flung herself on top of Gavin, naked.

And passed out.

Wine, indeed, Gavin thought, always put Melinda to sleep.

He waited a bit to make sure Melinda would not wake. Soon she began to snore. Sliding gently out from under her passive form, he sat up, then gasped as Melinda moaned and threw a leg over his thighs. Gently lifting it off, he edged closer to the wall, moving silently to keep from waking her. Melinda did not react. Carefully, gingerly, Gavin climbed over her and off the bed, silently making his way to the window next to the tub. He stopped short when he heard Melinda moan. Her hand was reaching out beside her as if she were feeling for him. He doffed his coat and quickly placed it near the hand. Just as he'd hoped, she touched the decoy, buried her sore nose in its scent, and retreated into dreamland with a little smile.

Snuffing out the candle and fastening his shirt and trousers, he moved back to the window and quietly eased it open. Melinda must have been so certain of her wiles, she could not imagine Gavin wanting to escape, and had failed to have her goons nail her window shut. Or perhaps they had just forgotten. Stepping through the opening one leg at a time and slowly easing himself to the ground, Gavin made his way to a nearby window, which he figured must be Alex's. Peering inside, he could see little in the deep inner gloom. But the window was open!

Looking into the night as his eyes adjusted, Gavin urgently sought to find his Angel. Searching the soft muddy loam in the dim light before dawn, he spied her fresh footprints. Without another thought, he trotted quietly after her.

Chapter Eight

Earlier, at Arlington House, Jack was searching intently for his master, missing his evening treat. He soon picked up the scent of Gavin's blood and tracked it through the wide-open front doors, though forbidden to do so. His plaintive yelps and wet tongue at last recalled Andrew to consciousness.

As he returned fully to his senses, Andrew's mother and sister entered the hall to find him sitting on the floor by the front door, rubbing a knot on his head and taking stock. When Amelia inquired as to his incomprehensible state and made it clear that Gavin and Alexandra had departed, the desperate circumstances dawned on him. The dog was still licking Andrew's face and whining urgently.

Realizing there was no time to waste, Andrew got to his feet and briefly described what he could remember to his mother, while waiting for a footman to respond to his urgent summons. He quickly dispatched the carriage, long standing ready to take Alex home, back to the Earl of Bedford's estate without her, telling his startled driver to inform Daniel Rosenshire that his daughter had been abducted, and to come at once. Mrs. Ravenstock, hastily awakened, rode home in confusion, chagrined that her charge had gone missing but not fully grasping the circumstances.

Perhaps it was time to get a hearing trumpet, she worried.

Daniel Rosenshire was aroused from a quiet evening in his study by a late rap on the door, and learned that his beautiful, precious Alex had been kidnapped.

He did not pause before taking charge. Ordering his fastest horse to be saddled and brought around, he quickly instructed grooms and footmen to ride out to the nearby tenant farms and to awaken other villagers. Every man was to saddle his best horse and meet back at Bedford House within the hour for instructions, preferably bearing arms. Daniel knew how to raise a private militia.

Then he dispatched Andrew's driver to inform the village constable his presence was required at once by the Earl. He gently awakened Elizabeth to give her the bad news, so she could share it with Alex's sisters. Feeling sorry Richard was away, he mounted his tireless and stalwart bay stallion and headed for Arlington House at a gallop.

The Earl of Bedford had never been introduced to the Marquess of Arlington, and this was an awkward way to meet. Daniel's hostile questions began almost as soon as Andrew admitted him. Daniel refused to adjourn to the study and insisted on interrogating Andrew then and there, while a groom held his striking mount just below the grand steps.

Daniel was impatient. "I must devise a plan, and begin a search at once! How could this happen? I entrusted Alex to your care. It is unthinkable that she should go missing, and I shall soon have every able-bodied horseman in Bedford searching for her. You will know my wrath as I grow more concerned for her safety. So I warn you, Lord Blake, do not leave out any detail. Give me everything you know of these most unfortunate events. And tell me, where on earth was her chaperone!"

Andrew, still a little dazed, was holding a poultice to the knot on his head, and still trying to make sense of what he had heard while lying stunned on the parquet floor. He quietly described being summoned by the butler from the dinner table to find Melinda and her large henchmen in his entry hall. He said he knew the Lady Melinda Blackstone of London only as his cousin's former fiancée.

Andrew described being coshed by one of Melinda's brutish helpers when he refused to fetch Gavin from the dinner table. After that, he explained, his awareness was often blunted by his injury. But he could describe Gavin's arrival, his angry words with Melinda, and Alex's dramatic intervention. Daniel then learned that Andrew's cousin Gavin was the target of the attack, and had been kidnapped along with his daughter.

Then, Andrew explained, almost an hour had passed before coming to his senses, to find the pair must have been abducted, probably at a little past nine o'clock. He had immediately sent the carriage to Bedford House to alert Daniel. It was well past eleven now. Any hope of catching up to the perpetrators or finding them in the darkness was slim, but Daniel was becoming more enraged, worried and determined.

Andrew gathered his wits and tried to explain more clearly, "The woman who created all this chaos, Lady Melinda Blackstone, sir. She is a dangerous, vengeful, duplicitous person. When Gavin discovered her true nature, he called off their wedding. This outraged her. She vowed to take her revenge, and now, unfortunately, Lady Alexandra is caught in the middle. That evil woman has absolutely lost her mind!" He controlled himself, and hoping to calm the other man's obvious fury, went on, "I know how you must feel, sir... Please understand, my dear cousin Gavin is a very strong and capable man, and would never allow any harm to come to your daughter." Andrew was tiring under the onslaught of anger and worry and questions. His head was throbbing, the poultice abandoned.

"I feel it only proper, considering these circumstances, that you address me as my lord!" Daniel was becoming peremptory in his frustration. "Whether your cousin is capable of taking care not only of himself but also of Alex in this dire situation is unknown. He may be injured or unconscious. His judgment is questionable if he allied himself with this terrible person Melinda. And my daughter means the world to me, whereas Gavin means little.

I do not know him, nor do I know you. Do you have anything to add to your bizarre story?"

Even under the respected Earl of Bedford's penetrating gaze, Andrew knew little and could add nothing. But Daniel had recalled a certain detail. "Why is it that Alex said she was Gavin's wife? I understood she was *your* dinner guest?" he demanded, perplexed. Andrew had been in and out of consciousness at the time, but he had a vivid recollection of that part of the argument. And Melinda had made her intentions clear as soon as he arrived at the door, to take Gavin away with the help of her goons.

"Yes, my lord, that is correct. But I do believe Alex has feelings for Gavin, whether she admits them or not. I also feel that Gavin has feelings for Alex, but he tries mightily to keep them hidden. It is only because we have such close brotherly affection for each other that I was able to discern them." He paused to gather his thoughts. "It was... so that they might get to know each other better, that I invited Lady Alexandra to dine."

Andrew took a breath and tried to explain more clearly. "After his eyes were opened to Melinda's character, or lack of it, some months back, Gavin shut off his feelings. I fondly hoped that this would change. Now Melinda has come back to do Gavin harm. She does not care about your daughter, my lord. I believe Alex thought she was aiding Gavin when she stepped forward and said they were married. I was so dazed at that point, I surmise the only logical explanation would be to persuade Melinda to drop her threats, her plan of reconciliation, and leave Gavin alone. However, Alex did not know whom she was dealing with, and her involvement apparently did little to change Melinda's plan, except to add abducting the Lady Alexandra along with my cousin. Her revenge appears to be aimed against Gavin for not marrying her, and she was most adamant— and she had a lot of help."

Daniel was thinking over these details. "Now, they met the night of that party Alex last attended in London? As I recall, there was some beastly trouble with Lord Harrison the next day, and it was this Gavin who lent Alex some timely assistance? When she told me of this, I was more concerned with how she had been treated by Harrison, and that she didn't have a chaperone with her." This reminded him to demand again, "Where the hell was her chaperone tonight?" He threw his hands in the air in an angry gesture.

"My lord, if I may interrupt, I really am feeling quite useless, standing here going over this again and again. It does not bring us any nearer to effecting a rescue. I would rather be out searching. Would you care to join me, or shall we go our separate ways?" Andrew was growing frantic to release his mounting frustration with some form of action. He politely added, "Her chaperone tonight was dear old Mrs. Ravenstock, hardly a person who could protect her from abduction. My lord."

"Indeed! Andrew. We shall ride out together, but first I must organize my men for the search. Now. Tell me, is there anywhere that you can think of that this woman would take Alex... and Gavin? She must have had a plan. Where can can she get to from here, traveling with two light coaches, each with only two horses? Could you discern what direction she would take, given her intentions?"

"I shall think about that, my lord."

Daniel waved his hand. "While you think, let us go. We have to gather arms and supplies. My wife will be sick with worry and I must take the time to explain things."

Andrew called for his horse and went to let Amelia know he was leaving, with no idea when he would return. He stopped in his den to take up his favorite hunting rifle and fill his pockets with shells, and put on a warm woolen jacket against the chill of the night. He had a word with his trusted butler about looking out for the family and household staff, instructing him to send out grooms and footmen to ask about sightings of Melinda's carriages, once the new day dawned and villagers were about. He wished he too had a platoon of able-bodied riders, but most of his staff were elderly or otherwise unsuitable. His most reliable footman had taken off with Mrs Ravenstock, the grooms and stablehands were too young, his valets did not ride.

His usual driver was away to visit a sick mother. And he did want some staff at home to look after his family. Besides, he only kept the two carriage horses and his own stallion and Gavin's at the moment. His tenant farmers' houses were on the far side of the village. Not much help He sighed.

Meanwhile, Daniel had mounted and both horse and rider betrayed impatience. The two men were soon cantering toward Bedford House with one thing on their minds, rescuing Alex and Gavin in the most expeditious manner.

Back at Bedford House, Elizabeth, Cassandra and Ashley were all fully dressed, sitting tensely in the drawing room waiting for news. All were too alarmed to carry on a conversation. A pot of tea grew cold beside them. Their faces were pale and drawn in the candlelight.

Cassandra was thinking hard about how Alex could get herself kidnapped. All she could imagine was that Alex would step in to protect her secret love from some threat that lurked at Andrew's home. She knew her sister's daring and courage well.

Breaking the silence, Ashley said, "Mother, I do not understand how Alex could be missing! She would not deliberately put herself in danger."

It was Cassandra who responded. "Ashley, why is it you never listen to what I say? Alex is in love with Gavin. I just know it! When she came home from that trouble with Lord Harrison she was very upset, especially when she spoke of the person who had helped her. That person was Gavin! She was angry because he treated her so gallantly, and then turned stone cold. Then she was quiet at dinner and didn't really want to talk about her ordeal until I brought it up. She must have been trying to protect him. Think about it, Ashley, it is true!"

Elizabeth blinked away a sudden rush of tears. "Girls, now is not the time to bicker over our circumstances. We simply have to wait for your father's return in order to have our questions answered. Trust that the dear man has a solution." She quickly composed herself for the sake of her daughters, telling herself it was important to show them courage and poise in a time of danger. Deep inside, she was sick with worry. She wanted nothing more than to let herself burst out crying.

Just then they heard the front door fly open and Daniel's rapid footsteps in the hall. With Andrew trailing him, the Earl entered the drawing room. With a solemn expression, he tried to find words of comfort and reassurance for the family he loved so dearly. Everyone had questions, but he held up his hand silently to say there were no answers yet. Only Cassandra noticed how distraught Andrew was. As her father and mother left the room, Cassandra respectfully addressed the Marquess.

"Lord Andrew, please, can you tell us more of what is going on?" Realizing he had never met her little sister, she introduced Ashley hastily. It was hard to remember her manners with everyone so anxious and upset.

Discerning the deep worry written on the young woman's pale and lovely face, he strived for a kind tone, suppressing his own concern for his cousin to offer her some comfort. "Lady Cassandra, we know little. My cousin's enemy has taken off somewhere with Gavin and Lady Alexandra as her captives, with the aid of two strong men. Unfortunately, we know little more, as I was knocked out cold before some of the events transpired. I know the name of the perpetrator, a certain Lady Melinda Blackstone, of London. What else could I tell you?"

"Gavin is kidnapped too!" But she was beyond the point where she could be more shocked.

Even as her face betrayed her fright and tension, Andrew was struck again by Cassandra's loveliness. Unshed tears caught the light of the lamp nearby, causing her eyes to glow. Her tresses were unpinned, falling over her shoulders with a most flattering natural beauty. He was ashamed to entertain these thoughts while his dear Gavin was in danger, but was unable to control them.

"Oh, Andrew, please, I know that Alex is a very strong woman, and that for the most part she can take care of herself. But I always feel a need to protect her, as she protects me. We have always shared a deep sisterly affection. So... perhaps I might ride with you and Father? You know I could keep up! But gaining his permission shall be a challenge. Perhaps you could put in a good word for me?" She implored him with her whole heart, yielding to her implicit faith in him.

"Lady Cassandra, how am I supposed to put in any kind of word for you? I do not believe I am in a position to say *anything* to your father. As it is, he holds me responsible for your sister's situation, as she was *my* guest... and who could blame him," Andrew concluded sadly.

"Well, I understand your position, but *you* must understand that I can not just sit here and do nothing! Seeing as how I cannot rely on your intervention, I shall find another way." Turning on her heel, Cassandra climbed the stairs to the second floor, where her father was stuffing blankets into a large saddlebag. She knocked on the door to make her presence known.

"Father, may I enter?" Cassandra asked.

"You may enter, Cassandra. But whatever you must say, do so quickly. I am in a hurry, as you well know. Has anyone seen the constable who was sent for?" Daniel was impatient and preoccupied by the needed preparations.

"No, Father, I have not heard him arrive...." She took a deep breath. "I wish to join you and Andrew in the search. Now, I know your impulse is to say no, but please reconsider! You know I am one of the best equestrians in the county, and sitting here doing nothing is as hard for me as it would be for you." She stood with her fingers tensely knit to hear his reply.

"Thank you for being quick about it. The answer is no, and I shall not change my mind. It is not proper for a young lady to be involved in such matters, especially when there will be a lot of unsupervised young men on this hunt, and I might not be at your disposal should something untoward happen. Your big sister needs my full attention now, and it would not be fair to her if I had to worry about you as well. No discussion! Is that understood?" He fastened up the bag and left the room with it, giving no opportunity for Cassandra to utter a response.

She followed her father's hurrying footsteps down to a pantry. The cook was bustling in her cupboards and Elizabeth was making a bundle of provisions for Daniel, who soon headed for the stable with his burdens.

Once he was out of earshot, Cassandra implored her mother for permission. "This really is not a time for ladylike behavior! I would think that the more people searching, the better," she concluded.

"Cassandra, please. Your father needs to concentrate on Alex, and if you went along you could get in the way. Besides, you're not thinking clearly. It is not as though your sister just wandered off. There are dangerous persons involved, and you could get yourself in trouble instead of helping. That would just make this terrible situation worse!" Imagining countless harms to her darlings, again she fought back hot tears.

Then she studied her daughter's defiant expression. With kindness, she admonished, "Now, dear, please wipe that look off your face. I have seen it before. You must not do anything foolish. Do you not know that I too want to be there right next to your father?" Her patience was running thin in the face of Cassandra's stony countenance. "For God's sake, Cassandra, that is my child out there! Try to understand how important it is for us to stay out of the way." Her mother finally pleaded, "And think about what your father and I have said to you."

"I understand, Mother, but I feel so useless just waiting and waiting here! It is so frustrating at times to be a girl!" Cassandra exploded.

"I know dear, I know." And with a stroke of her child's locks, her mother turned to go check on her youngest, who seemed terrified by these late-night developments. Cassandra, finding her resolve after a moment, called after her, "Mother, I am going back to bed as there is no way for me to help."

Daniel was gathering up his firearms and ammunition from their locked cupboard in his study, after bidding goodnight to his youngest and asking her to go up to bed. A groom led his horse around to the front of the house, and the mounts stood calmly, both now heavily laden. Daniel and Andrew checked over the lashings and were about to mount when Elizabeth caught up with them.

"My love, may God be with you. I pray you will find Alex and bring her home safe and sound. I love you, Daniel. Please be careful." She kissed him long and hard. Elizabeth and Daniel never hid their feelings for one another, and although Andrew was standing right there, Elizabeth embraced her husband with a passion reflecting the deep love she held for him. Their open affection was far outside the norm in most circles of society. Andrew politely looked away.

"We must move along. You will tell the constable everything when he arrives, yes?"

"Yes, Daniel, now go with God."

Cassandra was watching as they disappeared into the night. She was near the stables, finishing tacking up her horse, hastily garbed as a young man. She had borrowed warm, dark garments from a young, lanky stableboy, who was so sweet on her he could be trusted not to give up their secret. Her hair was pinned up beneath a close-fitting cap and she had applied a little dirt to her pretty face. She hoped her disguise would work.

As soon as she felt she could escape notice, she followed after her father and Andrew. Her only plan was to trail them without getting caught. She would find out in the hours to come exactly what her rash impulse might bring.

Elizabeth and Ashley, tiring but too anxious for sleep, stayed in the sitting room close by the low fire, sipping a soothing herbal tea, lost in worrisome thoughts, with the considerate butler looking on. Ashley kept herself busy building a house of cards. The preoccupied looks on their faces spoke volumes but they remained wordless. No one knew what to expect. Would Alex be found harmed or unharmed? More importantly, would she be found at all? It had been an hour since the men's departure.

Daniel's envoys had knocked awake riders from all around little Bedford village. He had organized the volunteers as soon as he returned from Andrew's estate, ordering groups to head east and west and seek news of Melinda's passage, choosing four strong men to join himself and Andrew. He doubted the evil woman would head south toward London, and he intended to head northward himself as he was most familiar with that territory. Most members of this ragtag militia were well-mounted and well-armed. However, he knew they would tire before morning, being hard-working servants, tradesmen and farmers who were used to getting a good night's rest. Also he knew it was unlikely they would find anyone awake at this late hour who could give them information, but he was determined to do all searching that could be done.

All her thoughts focused on Alexandra, Elizabeth suddenly looked up from her tea and said, "Ashley, have you looked in on your sister? I am surprised she is able to find rest. Perhaps she would wish to join us."

"No, Mother." Ashley had been expecting her sister to come back and resume her defiance.

"I think I should go and look in on her. She can be so like her father, too stubborn sometimes for her own good!"

"Wait, Mother, I will come with you," Ashley said, tired of her game, and sleepy from being up so late. Together they walked up the stairs and checked Cassandra's room and bathing chamber, then separated and looked all over the house, dispatching wakeful servants to the butler's apartment, the wine cellars, the maids' rooms. There was no sign of her anywhere.

"Ashley, run out to the stables and check to see if her horse is missing. The searchers would not have taken it, it's too small and fine-boned to bear a man's weight. It should be the only one left. I have a most unsettling feeling that your sister has done something foolish!"

Without a word, Ashley turned and ran. When she returned, Elizabeth could see what she was going to say. "Mother, Cassie's horse is not in the stable."

"It is unfortunate that your sister did not listen to reason when she was told why she could not go. I am afraid that there is nothing we can do. We must wait here for that constable. Cassandra will have to deal with me when she returns. For now we must pray for *her* safety as well as Alexandra's."

Daniel halted the riders at a fork in the lonely country road.

The northbound search party had been riding about half an hour, while Daniel continued to question Andrew every few minutes. "You must try to remember! Is there any place you can think of that may be abandoned or hidden from view, where this Melinda might have taken them?" The men surveyed the moonlit countryside, hoping to be headed in the right direction, hoping for inspiration or divine intervention, losing hope with every mile that passed.

Andrew said, "My lord, I have tried to think of such places, but I have come up with nothing. I have never ridden up this way before. I am keeping an open eye for anything that might serve as a hiding place, searching for articles they might have cast from their carriage... "

Daniel interrupted to demand, "Just what do you suppose this Lady Melinda's *aim* could be in her deceitful endeavor?"

At that, Andrew had a new thought. "Melinda was always most determined to get Gavin to marry her," he mused aloud. "It has always been her foremost objective. Do you think... perhaps Gretna Green could be her destination?"

Daniel took only a moment to ponder that before signalling to the foursome of riders behind him. "We are approaching Shambrook. You two! Take the road to the left; both forks lead north, and we'll go right. Continue northward, and we should meet up near Thrapston in another hour at most. Your route is more direct so you may get there first. Remember to look out for carriage tracks, and observe your surroundings well. In the village, question everyone you come across, even drunkards leaving the taverns. Knock on doors if you see a light on. We will camp just this side of Thrapston until there's enough daylight to see the way ahead."

The Earl turned to the other two riders, both farmers known to have a taste for fast horses. Their steeds were indeed taller than the others, and still looked fresh. "You, Murphy. And Kelly. Head back toward Bedford as fast as your horses will carry you. We've come less than ten miles. You know the directions the two other search parties have taken. Split up to catch them as best you can. Everyone is to meet us by Thrapston before dawn. Tell them to get fresh horses along the way if they need them, and to take the byways rather than main roads." As an afterthought, he added, "Kelly, after that, go to Bedford House and speak to that damned constable. Let him know we think the kidnappers may be heading for Gretna Green. Perhaps he can telegraph ahead."

The four men complied at once, glad to have a direction that was not random.

When Daniel and Andrew neared Thrapston, they espied the encampment set up by their men at the edge of the little village, with a small fire already burning, and horse blankets spread on the damp ground. Unsaddled horses were pegged out nearby, grazing on the new spring grass of the common in fading moonlight. The night was growing colder. No one had anything to report. Two men were soon dozing near the campfire, but Andrew and Daniel were too anxious to settle down.

In the next few hours, the menfolk of Bedford began arriving in ones and twos to join the encampment and rest until dawn. By the time the last star winked out, a company of fourteen strong men had assembled to serve their lords.

Cassandra was not far. It had been a close call when two riders had reversed their direction and suddenly come toward her, but they did not recognize her in her disguise, a roughly dressed lone boy on a nice horse in the midnight, probably journeying home from a rendezvous with a ladyfriend or a late-night carouse in a public house. They cantered on without giving her a thought.

Now she hid herself and her mount behind a hedgerow twenty yards away, careful to stay out of view and make no noise. She grew a little cold after dismounting, but could not start a fire without drawing attention. She huddled on a log where she could just make out her father's tall, dim form in the firelight. Her horse, tethered to her wrist by his reins, remaining saddled in case a quick departure was needed.

The little gelding nuzzled her neck and blew out gently, enjoying a midnight adventure with his mistress.

Chapter Nine

Alex had been running for what seemed like hours when the effects of fatigue took over from her fear of recapture. She slowed her gait along the narrow forest path, probably only a trail used by wildlife, regretting her decision to wear such fashionable, now painful, little shoes. A little way farther along, a modest stone cottage nestled against the wooded hillside revealed itself in dawn's first light. The tiny house was almost consumed by overgrown shrubbery and dense vines, half-hidden in the shade of all the young trees around it. Alex could see no windows except for a very small one in the door. There was no smoke rising from the chimney, and no signs of recent activity in the grassy little dooryard. A woodcutter's little retreat, she surmised, having noted old stumps of many large trees for the last several miles. Finding enough courage to creep closer, she drew her face close to the dirty window and used her thumb to clean a place to peer through. In the dimness within, she could eventually make out a small bed against the far wall, covered by a rough blanket. Close by the door was a little table, two chairs, and what might be a cupboard against a wall. Under the cylindrical tin chimney was a small cast-iron potbellied stove. Only a weak beam of early light struggled through the dirty little window, and she was mostly blocking it. Quietly, aware of being exposed to view as the dawn light increased, she explored around the little dwelling quietly and concluded that it was abandoned, at least for the moment.

Alex's dirty, torn dress was dripping wet from the morning dew on branches that had brushed against her as she ran, and from her own long exertions. She was getting chilly, now that she had stopped moving. Hoping Melinda's men were not drawing close, she forced the door open with a strong pull and entered to the sound of creaking hinges.

She doffed the dress with some difficulty, no maid to assist with the tiny fastenings, and hung it over a rickety chair to dry. More comfortable in her chemise, drawers, corset and petticoat, she ran her fingers through her matted hair. It was warmer inside the house than out, if gloomy with so little light. Alex finally allowed herself to fall into the other chair at the small table and breathe out a deep sigh.

She wondered if Gavin had gotten away, or if he would still be lying with Melinda, and just now waking up. If he had escaped, would he be able to find her? Would he even look for her? What if he headed in some other direction? The way his mood turned hot and cold made Alex wonder if he truly cared.

Her next thought was for her family. What they must think! She knew her father would come for her... but he would not know where to look. He was stubborn, protective. She hoped he would not have a run-in with Melinda and her two hulks. That was trouble no one needed.

Alex decided that even though the bed smelled musty, she would lie down for a while, and give her poor dress some time to dry. She undid her corset and cast it under the bed, a garment her slim, shapely figure did not require, and stepped out of her petticoat, which had become muddy and tattered around the hem. It would have to do for a pillow.

She thought about her long, hard journey. She knew her plight was not over, and she was not accustomed to this constant, draining undercurrent of fear. In the dark woods, every noise she heard had frightened her, and pushed her to run farther, faster. Her father had always taught her to be wary in unfamiliar places, where you never know if someone is secretly watching you. He had also cautioned her never to appear vulnerable, which, she was sure, was just how she did look now.

She could only hope that Gavin would soon find her. She had tried not to leave tracks, but often there was little choice as to where to place her running feet, especially after the moon had set. When the only route through the fields and forests was on soft soil, she had tried to cover her footprints by sweeping a leafy branch behind her. This too, was something her father had taught: keep your head, no matter what the circumstances. Never panic. Her father would not think her very smart for the actions that put her in this predicament! She

knew she would hear about it when she got home...
if she ever got home.

She shook her head to banish useless
worries from her mind. Then she remembered her
mother's frequent admonition: always think
positively. She told herself she would soon find
familiar territory and feel a little safer. The room
was close, airless, too long shut up, but its warmth
was welcome. Her thoughts started to drift and she
let herself fall asleep.

Gavin searched for Alex. He had come
across several spots that looked as though someone
were covering their tracks, but how would a Lady
know to do such a thing? Then he realized that if he
could track her, so could their pursuers, who were
surely on the hunt by now. He could only hope that
he would find Alex first. If Melinda were to capture
him again, Gavin was certain he would be spared.
However, Alex might not be so lucky.

He was tiring from the long run. He had not
slept. He ached from his beating even more now.
The night was dark since moonset. In his fatigue
and pain, he escaped into thoughts of what it would
be like to have a happy life with a woman like Alex.
She was everything he had yearned for. Beautiful,
poised, smart, fine character, a warm personality...
and she had the most radiant smile he had ever seen.
She was a woman any man would be lucky to marry

and keep forever. Even with all this brutality and violence, she somehow always remained... an angel. Her innate radiance, purity and innocence held the greatest appeal of all.

Returning to his senses, he quietly repeated his vow to be done with Melinda before he ever allowed romance into his heart.

Loping on in hope of coming across new signs, Gavin was cold without his jacket, and drenched to the bone with sweat and dew. He had always enjoyed running and his easy gait could efficiently cover plenty of ground, even after a sleepless night. Here, April nights could be bitter with cold and damp. Looking to the east, he realized the first rays of dawn were snuffing out the stars.

Gavin hoped that Alex was doing her best to keep warm and safe. He imagined her hair, fallen over her shoulders. That fashionable blue dress would be clinging to every inch of her body. Her face would be aglow with the dew that made the leaves sparkle in the first rays of dawn's light. He let his thoughts rest for a moment on the wonderful things he could make her feel once he took her in his arms... .

Then he returned to his senses and thought what a sight he was, dressed only in a wet black dress shirt and filthy damp black trousers. A tear in their fine fabric yawned wide across his knee. His soaking, well-tailored garments outlined his every muscle, clinging tightly to his robust, slim, powerful physique. His dark hair was wild, clawed back from his face to keep the dripping strands out of his eyes.

Tiring, and growing colder every minute, Gavin pushed on at a trot. Always he scanned his surroundings carefully, searching for anything familiar or useful, as the once-dense forest thinned around him and the burgeoning dawn at last gave his vision welcome help. It would soon be full daylight.

At last something caught his eye. A tiny scrap of dark blue lace was caught in a sharp thorn in the underbrush. He knew that lace! He put it in his pocket and broke into a faster pace, chill, pains, and fatigue forgotten.

In a little while, behind some stumps, in a thatch of dense shrubbery against a wooded hillside, a sudden glint of light drew his gaze. A ray of the sun, now well risen, had found a reflective surface. It was a window, he was sure of it. Gavin approached the tiny cottage with great caution, seeking the slightest sign of recent occupation, but saw none, except splinters around the latch where the door had been forced. Looking over his shoulder to make sure pursuit had not caught up while he was focused on the dwelling, he stepped on a branch that cracked with a sharp, loud noise. Gavin froze. There was no sign his presence had been detected. He crept silently up to the low door.

Gavin stooped to peer in the window, noting its one clear little circle in the dust. It took his eyes a moment to adjust to the dim gloom within. Then his heart leapt with relief and elation. Quietly, with great care, he stooped and entered the dusty, barren room, not wanting to wake the chemise-clad beauty sleeping so peacefully on a coarse woolen blanket, her shapely head resting on a balled-up beribboned petticoat. It was like finding a waterfall in a desert. Her striking, unspoiled features were more breathtaking than at any time before. Her thick golden tresses curled over her shoulders and across her neck as she reclined in a relaxed and childlike pose. Her superb breasts, freed from her corset, were rising and falling gently with every breath. Her expression radiated serenity and youth. Gavin stared for a moment longer, then realized his manhood was responding to this sight with a fierce and urgent intensity that he was helpless to control. Quietly he ducked outside rather than risk embarrassing himself... or Alex.

In a few minutes, calm and in control, he returned. Alex had not moved. Closing the door quietly and silently walking over to the chair where her dress was draped, Gavin ran his fingers over the silky material. It was dry, if somewhat shabby now. "She must have been here hours," he murmured.

Alex had stirred at a creak of the hinge as he re-entered. She peered through her lashes just enough to see what was happening. Relief overwhelmed her when she saw it was Gavin. She fought down a wild impulse to run to him and throw herself into his arms. She had felt so frightened and alone for so long. Now she would not be alone... but with *him*!

Alex decided not to let Gavin know she was awake. She remained still, and watched him through eyes barely open. His hand was touching her dress. Her body tingled at the idea that he cared. Then she heard his soft remark.

"I have been here for some time, you are correct, though I am not certain exactly how long I was dozing," she responded with a devilish grin, her tone saying "Yes, I made it all this way alone, and I'm proud of myself." Gavin turned, startled. Their eyes met... and no one spoke for a long moment. Gavin returned to his senses and reminded her that she was half naked, certain this would upset and embarrass her.

She surprised him again. "You're correct again, Gavin, I am indeed." Hoping to embarrass him in return, Alex got up from the bed, shook out her petticoat, and walked over, brushing against him as she plucked up her dress. She could sense his discomfort, just the effect she was trying to achieve. Alex *knew* that Gavin felt something for her! She was going to bring those emotions out in the open, one way or another. By giving him a completely different reaction than he was expecting, she hoped she would catch him off guard enough to expose his true feelings. Being half-naked did embarrass her, but she would let that go for now.

Gavin blinked in surprise and disbelief and edged away. Careful to look elsewhere as she slipped petticoat and dress back on, he felt sure there was something different about her.

"Gavin, I'm so glad you're here. I wasn't sure you made it out. I waited for you, but when you took so long I thought I should go before I was discovered. How did you find this place? I thought it was very well hidden."

"I ... almost didn't find it, Alex. Had a ray of sun not lit up that window, I might have missed it." Gavin's tone was matter-of-fact.

Alex looked at Gavin as though he had all the answers. "Well, now that we are here, what is our plan?" She was struggling with little buttons and hooks that were out of reach in places. It was most inconvenient that fine gowns like this were designed for ladies with maids.

"First things first, my lady. I am glad you were able to get some sleep. Now, as this place is so well hidden, I believe it only fair that I get a wink or two myself. I have had no slumber since well before our dinner at Andrew's, so if you have no objection, I'm going to lie on that shabby little cot and rest a while." Gavin stripped off his wet, clinging shirt, and draped it over a chair to dry. Then he walked over to the little bed, sat down, and kicked his muddy boots off. He stretched out on his back and closed his eyes. His feet hung over the end of the bed. Not once did he glance at Alex.

Alex stood for a moment gazing at him with surprise and disbelief, and a little awe. His naked chest was so masculine, so brawny. The fit of those wet trousers was very tight. There was a hole in his sock. The wound on his beautiful, sensuous mouth had begun to heal. She wondered for a moment what else Gavin might have to offer. Then she shook herself back to reality and said, "Wait a minute! That is fine, sir, that you want to get some sleep, but do you not think you could at least let me know what comes next?"

"Alex, please, where are your manners. I was just plummeting into deep repose when you rudely awakened me."

Alex felt a burst of resentment and fear. "I don't care if you were sleeping! I need to know what's going to happen."

"Quite frankly, I'm not sure what the plan is, except to keep moving, as soon as I have enough rest to continue. I am bone-tired. And sore. I suggest, if you hope to keep up with me, you may want to get some more rest yourself." Still without looking at her, Gavin rolled on his side to face the wall so she could not see his devilish grin. He so loved to get her going! Besides, this was his only defense against some deep feelings he could not afford to entertain.

"Fine, Gavin. I will gladly get more sleep. Do you expect me to lie on this filthy floor? You will have to move over and share that bed."

Gavin's eyes flew open and he craned his head around to look over his shoulder. "You have already had your turn on the bed. Now it's my turn. Surely the chair will do just fine. Lean on the table." He settled back down, facing the wall, tucking his feet behind him. His eyes closed once more.

"I do not agree!" Defiant and annoyed, Alex threw herself down behind him on the edge of the mattress. Gavin tried to inch away from her warmth and salty, enticing scent, but his knees were already touching the wall. He thought how impossible it would be to lie close to such a lovely woman and ignore her for long.

But his perfect, breathtaking, pure, innocent Angel was lying so close their bodies were almost touching. He could feel her soft, regular breath on the skin of his shoulders. His thoughts were drawn to the ultimate pleasure he ached to give her. He could never allow himself to touch her that way! He was now awake, all attention riveted by her nearness, urging parts of his body not to respond.

Not once after getting on the bed did Alex open her eyes, but her face bore a triumphant expression. She was not going to sleep in any chair! However, there was not enough room on this narrow little straw mattress for two people. She was on her side behind Gavin with barely an inch separating them, but she could feel herself slowly sliding off the edge no matter how she tried to adjust her balance.

Gavin realized this the same time she did, feeling her breath on his back fade away and the warmth of her lush body near his skin diminish. There was nowhere for her to go but to the dusty floorboards.

The only way for them both to fit on the bed was for Gavin to lie on his side and cradle her in his arms. He turned over in time to stop her fall, wrapped his arms around her, and drew her close, gently shifting her position so she faced the same direction he did.

Alex shivered slightly when Gavin's hand came across her belly to stop her fall, but that was the only place for it to go. The dampness of his trousers seeped through her thin clothing and she could feel the length of him pressed tightly against her legs, buttocks and back. This gave her a warm, pleasant feeling. She sank into his embrace and manly scent, and let herself wonder what it would be like to have this man touch her in a most intimate way. Her very private thoughts soon lulled her to sleep. She was more exhausted than she thought.

Gavin found it difficult to relax with Alex's perky bottom pressed against his nether regions, fearful of betraying his ardor. He liked the flatness of her stomach under his hand. Every inch of her body enticed him. It took all his will to refrain from answering urges to kiss, to caress, to tighten the embrace. Her full, round breasts were a temptation he felt almost helpless to resist. Finally, he closed his eyes to escape an overpowering desire to have her, and willed himself to just fall asleep.

It was late morning when Gavin opened his eyes. Alex was still sleeping, blonde tresses fallen across her face. She must have moved in her sleep, for the hand that was once on her stomach was now gently cupping a perfect breast. Gavin slowly lifted the offending hand just as she awakened.

"Gavin, what in God's name do you think you are doing?" Alex exclaimed as she slapped his offending limb away and jumped off the bed.

"Alex, please don't go daft on me, it's not what you think!"

"Not what I think, ha! Your hand was not on my... my... ah... my breast. I was just dreaming?" Her face was red with anger and embarrassment, and she was too sleep-sodden and startled to speak coherently.

"Alex, don't flatter yourself! I just now woke up, and there it was. Perhaps it was you who moved it," Gavin retorted heatedly. He had just been so comfortable!

"I doubt that," returned Alex icily. "For now, this is not our major concern, but getting out of here is. Let's just drop it. Do not think it will ever happen again!" Not leaving room for debate, Alex turned and slipped on her sodden, ruined shoes. She kicked her discarded corset farther under the bed and walked out the door to catch a breath of air and collect herself. The truth was, she had quite liked his hand on her breast. She was punishing herself, and lashing out at Gavin, in reaction to her disgraceful, uncontrollable, wanton thoughts.

Gavin sat on the bed pulling on his ruined boots while Alex paced outside. He muttered to himself. "Well! The Lady Alexandra Rosenshire thinks I did that on purpose. Maybe if I keep her angry there will be one less thing I have to deal while getting her home where she belongs." His thoughts were interrupted when Alex came back in.

"Tell me please. What is the plan?" She planted her hands on her hips, waiting for his response.

Gavin was buttoning up his shirt. "Straight to the point, aren't we, Alex? To answer your question, the plan is as follows." He had been thinking hard when not distracted by Alex's shapely beauty. "We stay here in the forest until nightfall, waiting for cover of darkness, then we travel until we find another hideout where we might be safe during the day." He gathered his thoughts. He was getting very hungry, and he was still tired. His thirst was growing extreme.

"Shortly I will scout our environs discreetly, in search of sustenance. There may be a well near here, or at least a stream where I might draw water. We must use great care when we move about in the daylight, to limit the risk of discovery."

He concluded, "Also, we must try to determine our whereabouts. We have been travelling mostly westward from wherever it was Melinda took us, which must have been to the north of Bedford and Arlington. The only region I can think of that is this wild and unsettled would be somewhere in the wasteland south of Wollaston."

He continued to ruminate, as much to himself as to Alex. "I worry that Melinda may have the allegiance of local people. Her family came from somewhere around here... they gained their fortune in lumber when first-growth forests spread across the land, but her people have long made their homes in London."

He finally warned, "We must use great caution. There have been few signs of agriculture since we left Arlington House. These parts are most thinly settled, with few good roads and no towns. Do you have any questions or ideas?"

"No, no questions. Your plan seems logical enough," she answered matter-of-factly.

"Fine. This afternoon we eat and sleep, and prepare for another night of travel."

"Eat what? I don't see any food. Did you find some here?"

"I was able to pocket the bread Melinda was so generous to offer me. Here it is." It was a sorry little lump after all night in Gavin's damp trousers. "I hope to hunt us up a woodland creature."

Gavin searched through a little cabinet and under the bed for a vessel that would carry water, a sharp tool, a length of rope, anything that could be of use. The cottage had few hiding places. Then he was pocketing an object, holding another in one hand, opening the door and stooping to go outside.

"Wait!" she called, and followed him out. "You're going to leave me alone? What if Melinda's brutes should find me?"

"I won't be far. Just stay inside. Bringing you with me probably wouldn't work."

"Why is that?"

"I fear you would scare away the animals." Gavin gestured for her to retreat.

"Really!" She turned in a huff, insulted. She sat down at the table and ravenously choked down the bread. She longed for a drink of water. Finding herself with nothing to do, she settled down on the bed to await Gavin's return and was soon dozing.

Gavin came back in a short time clanking a rusty bucket. He had found it behind the cottage and drawn water from a nearby stream. There was a rusty ladle in the cupboard. He took it to the stream to rub it with a little sand and make it usable.

After dipping out water for Alex and drinking deeply himself, he departed again, to hunt silently for almost an hour, circling close to the little hideaway. He froze in place when at last a fat hare hopped across his path. When it paused to graze, Gavin, barely breathing, reached slowly into his pocket for the stone secreted there, and lobbed it hard at the animal's head. Gavin was pleased when the animal fell dead without suffering. He grasped its ears and headed back to Alex.

"I hunt, you prepare," Gavin said as bent to get under the lintel with a smile, thumping the carcass down on the table with pride.

"What did you say to me?" Alex asked, rising and seeing what he carried.

"You heard me, or was there something you didn't understand?"

"No, I understood. But I have never skinned a rabbit, nor cooked one. On that note, I have never consumed one either, our cook does not care to prepare them. She finds them too gamy. I wouldn't know where to begin."

Gavin found her innocence charming. He did not allow himself to dwell on her charm. "Well, you will have to watch me this time, but any other time I catch food, it's up to you to cook. We must both do our share."

Alex answered, "Fair enough, although I don't plan on being out here that long."

She carefully observed as Gavin stepped around to the back of the cottage and beheaded, skinned and gutted the hare with the rusty pocketknife he'd found in the cabinet, sharpened on a stone, then honed against the sole of his boot. Next he stripped the bark and twigs off a long slim green branch, sharpened one end, and carefully threaded the bloody carcass onto it. He used the blade again to slit the thickest places to let heat penetrate.

Alex noticed low gray clouds were rolling in from the west. She hoped they might hide the sight of their cooking smoke.

Then Gavin gathered up a handful of dry leaves, loaded his arms with dry branches, and carried these and the skewered hare inside. Leaning the skewer up against a wall nearby, he knelt and expertly built a small hot fire in the little iron woodstove whose chimney Alex had noticed on arrival, first dusting off the top with his sleeve and removing the covers of two round openings on top. Alex made note of the way he struck a spark with a flint.

Soon the potbellied fire chamber was glowing red with heat. The little chimney drew well and the stove put out little smoke. Gavin finally lay the skewered animal on its top. As its fat began to drip into the flames, a rich aroma filled the cabin. He used the skewer to turn the animal as each surface browned, while adding more sticks to the fire now and then.

As the hare cooked, Alex began to realize how very little she knew about this gentleman, who seemed to be as much at home in the forest as he was at a London soirée. She mused for some time.

Finally she resolved to get to know him a little better. "Gavin, just what is it that you do?"

He looked up at her, not expecting such an inquiry, and replied, "Is that really important right now?"

"No, I'm just curious. Do you have your own estate near Andrew's, or farther away? Or do you live in London?"

"Farther away," he replied, his attention on the hare.

"I see. So you were just visiting Andrew."

"Something like that. Andrew and I are very close. Our fathers were brothers, and we practically grew up together. We are almost the same in age." Gavin allowed himself to relax a bit.

"Were brothers? Does that mean they have passed away?" Alex asked politely.

"Yes, they have. Andrew's father about five years ago, and then my father just before I came to stay at Arlington House a few months back." As Gavin gazed into the flames, a shadow passed across his face.

Alex watched with an ache in her heart. How sad it must be to lose a parent. Then she realized she smelled something new... "Gavin, the hare!"

Gavin quickly removed it from the stove. It had started to burn because it was cooked through. "Enough questions for now? Let's please eat." He was annoyed that he had almost ruined dinner. He dipped water from the bucket to extinguish the flames with a hiss of steam.

Alex smiled, "That didn't look so difficult," attempting to lighten the mood.

"No one said it was hard, Alex, but those who are pampered don't usually have the pleasure of such tasks."

"And you're one to talk about being pampered. Granted you know how to catch and cook a fat hare, but surely you are just as accustomed to being waited on as I am!"

"Right you are. So if you don't mind, please could you cut some meat from the beast, place it on that plate and hand it to me? Thanks." He smiled. Alex struggled with the tiny blade, then handed him the plate. He had found it with a cracked bowl in the cupboard and rinsed them in the stream, carrying them back with the bucket of water. He had thought of everything.

"Fine, is there anything else I can do for you, my lord?" It was not easy to cut through hot muscle and sinew and release meat from bone with this tiny tool and awkward stick. She had never had to think of such a task, much less accomplish it.

"Some water would be welcome. Thanks for asking."

What she had said was meant to be sarcastic. How dare he demand anything from her! "Fine, water it is." Alex rose and fetched a dipper of water, walked over to Gavin and spilled its contents over his head. She couldn't help herself.

"Oh, Gavin, I am so sorry. I must have tripped," she said apologetically.

"Of course. An unfortunate accident, I'm sure." He was not fooled. He pushed wet hair off his high forehead before it dripped into his plate. Alex resolved to hold her tongue lest her temper get the better of her in her strained and uncomfortable mood.

With considerable difficulty, Alex hacked away at the hare until she had something to eat. Her hunger was overcoming her distaste at the unfamiliar aroma. She discovered she was ravenous, and soon found herself twisting loose a fat hind leg and chewing the meat off the bone. She was glad her mother could not see her.

They ate in silence, piling clean bones on the table. Gavin thought longingly of Jack.

When there was no more meat on the scattered bones, Gavin picked up the bucket, motioned Alex to go outside, and dipped up water to pour over her hands, demonstrating how to rub them on the moss to remove the grease. She tore a strip from her petticoat to clean off her face, and then dipped water for him. She ripped off more petticoat so he could wipe his face too.

Walking a short way into the wood, Gavin showed her how to plant a heel in a soft spot away from roots and walk around it to quickly make a hole. They buried bones, skin and entrails in this way. Then they tried to bring the cottage back to its dusty, unused appearance in case their tracks led the pursuit here. The sun was low in the western sky.

Preparations completed, the pair reclined together gingerly to rest and wait for nightfall. The dusty, dark room was very warm now and strongly scented with smoke and hare. Once Gavin started to snore softly, Alex carefully disentangled herself from his relaxed limbs, removed herself to some nearby bushes, squatted for a minute, and silently returned to rest in his somnolent embrace.

The clouds cleared away. When the sky was almost fully dark and the moon had begun its rise, they drank deeply from a last dipper of water, closed the door of the little stone cottage, put the bucket back where it had been found, and resumed their journey.

Chapter Ten

"How could you let this happen! I leave you to guard their rooms and yet our guests just... vanish!"

"With all due respect, Lady Melinda, you were sleeping right next to the lord, the blame hardly lies just on us," Olaf declared, growing tired of Melinda and her antics.

"Well, of course the blame lies with you. I pay you to do as I say! I told you to watch them and you did not. And it took you until well into the morning to discover they were gone!" It was a waste to further the conversation. Melinda's overindulgence had caused her to sleep deep and late. The men had seen no reason to stir before they heard her arising. It was she who had discovered that Gavin was not in her bed, and raised the alarm.

They had been searching all afternoon, and finding no sign of Alex or Gavin. Olaf and Edgar had been listening to Melinda rant and rave hour after hour. If it weren't for the fact that they needed her money desperately, they would have quit her long ago. Melinda promised a high price to whoever found Gavin first. For the girl there would be much less. Once Alex were found, she was to be killed. Melinda had grown tired of these games. Death was the only fitting punishment for a woman who thought she could take Gavin away from her and ruin Melinda's plans.

The three were warmed by the late afternoon sun, pushing their mounts hard, taking a look down every little path. Melinda had assumed the captives would head straight for home, and was amazed that still there was no sign of their trail. No tracks, no scraps of clothing, and, most surprisingly of all, no Alex. Melinda had assumed that any fine and proper lady, finding herself in this vast wild countryside, alone or with a man, would soon be overwhelmed by circumstance and surroundings, and unable to proceed. If Alex were with Gavin, her chances improved. But if she were alone... Melinda held firmly to her certainty that Alex would soon be recaptured. Her escape was unthinkable.

Melinda was not faring well, outdoors, riding bareback, in sunny but chilly weather, with only discouragement to show for her fatigue and discomfort. She did not feel at all well today after her ill-considered bottles of wine. Long pampered and indulged in the refined pursuits of London, she was seldom in the habit of riding a horse, much preferring the comfort of a well-sprung carriage. Riding bareback was an insult to every inch of her body, but she was proud she was able to do it. Her stubborn vindictiveness kept her to her task, and she would not let herself or her henchmen rest, no matter how great her own discomfort.

The sun was sinking and the day was growing ever colder. She halted her mount at the next crossroads and sighed in frustration, anxiously reviewing the situation. Her determination did not flag. In the end she would have her way.

Olaf and Edgar exchanged looks. They believed Melinda to be insane, as well as a nasty witch who had nothing better to do then make others miserable, including them. If not for the gambling debts they must soon make good on, or suffer unthinkable consequences, they would never have put up so long with her peremptory commands and evil ways. Both had bundles and parcels strapped to their backs with the cordage that once restrained wrists and ankles, unable to devise proper saddlebags from the few materials carried in the carriages. Melinda had changed into a thick tweed outfit intended for wear in Scotland, along with several warm woolen wraps and a good hat, but they had brought few clothes along or anything at all appropriate for a camping trip or a long day on horseback.

The horses were tired, and so were the riders. As daylight faded, further searching would be fruitless, so they chose a sheltered spot in the embrace of a hillside near a stream, and set up camp. Olaf gathered branches and built a fire as Edgar tended to the mounts. Knowing well that Melinda would do nothing to assist, Olaf took bread and meat from one of the bundles as Edgar fetched water from a stream in a carriage horse's leaky feedbag, the only vessel they could locate in their hurry to leave the inn. They drank directly from the stream with the horses, but Melinda considered herself too ladylike to consider the idea and tried to cup water up with her hands. They worked quietly and efficiently, but their mistress still found reason for complaint.

"What one does for love! This is pathetic. I have capable people to wait on me at home, I enjoy the most delectable meals, I have one of the most extravagant wardrobes in London, and I sleep in the softest of featherbeds. I go to so much trouble for the sake of this man! Once I make him a total outcast, as he has done to me, this will all be worthwhile." Taking for herself the lion's share of their provisions, she stared into the fire. Melinda was bereft of compassion, incapable of finer feeling.

Edgar and Olaf did not respond to Melinda's tirade, relieved she was not speaking directly to them and accustomed to her attitude. Any response would merely bring them reprimands as if they were incompetent children. They ate their few mouthfuls in silence.

Melinda brooded for another half-hour, gazing into the dwindling flames with an icy stare. She was ill-suited for camping and had never expected to do so. Her careful planning had not worked out as expected. Finally she drew her ebony shawls close around her and closed her eyes, taking the warmest spot by the little fire. Olaf and Edgar waited for her to go to sleep, and then huddled together near the warmth of the embers to let sleep wash away their day's long ride.

Daniel and Andrew had dismounted in the growing darkness and were helping their men make camp. Once the horses had been freed of their tack and taken to the stream to drink, and cheese, bread and winter sausage from Bedford House's abundant stock had been handed all round, the two Lords sat near the campfire to talk and eat.

Daniel shook his head in anger and dismay. They had all saddled up in the first rays of dawn with the confidence of an invading army. He had finally allowed most of the men to return to their farms and shops this evening while their tired mounts could still carry them home. A few stalwarts remained, bachelors without so many obligations at home. This was not a good day.

Finally his thoughts escaped him. "Andrew, how can this be? There are no signs of them, and for that matter, there does not seem to be any sign of anyone! I am discouraged. We have been searching a night and a day, and we have discovered nothing. No one on the farms around seems to know anything, and the villages are so tiny they don't deserve a name. This is such a wasteland, lumbered so long ago, with some sort of soil that does not invite agriculture. These hilly new-growth forests bear no useful products save an occasional charcoal kiln, and paltry ones at that, half of them abandoned! Even the little flocks of sheep are disgraceful. No wonder these lands are practically uninhabited. I never thought this would take so long!"

He did not mention that their provisions were running low, another reason for dismissing his men. He had not found any way to replenish their supplies. The few farmers and shepherds they had encountered had had nothing to spare, at this time of the year, with spring crops not yet in and winter stores depleted. A kind farm wife had shown them a few little puckered cabbages and carrots, almost the only vegetables left in her cellar. Daniel could not bring himself to add to these people's sorry deprivations for his own comfort.

After Daniel's initial burst of energy and organization, his hurried plans were bearing no fruit. He had imagined a quick, early confrontation with the kidnappers and a triumphant return with the evildoers under armed guard by his militia, to be handed over to the constable with due fanfare, and his precious daughter soon home in her family's embrace, safe and undamaged.

How could his dear, exquisite Alex still be missing, and in the clutches of blackguards! Around and around his thoughts might go, but they always circled back to this. Daniel's spirits were sinking with exhaustion and discouragement.

"Perhaps we are going about it the wrong way..." Andrew began. He had been thinking hard as he rode at Daniel's side. "We have been looking for obvious clues such as footprints, carriage tracks... . Your men have explored every path. We have ridden every road or lane a carriage could manage that goes northward from Arlington House, some more than once. Maybe we should start looking for the not-so-obvious?" He was about to continue his thought, but Daniel broke in.

"What are you talking about, young man? We have been most thorough in our search, only to come up empty-handed everywhere we go. We know our horses are faster than their carriages. They did not have many hours to proceed before we set out behind them. Surely we have covered every inch of ground they could have traversed? What could we possibly have missed?"

"Please, my lord, if I may finish. These people who took Gavin and Alex do not want to be found, so they will be covering their tracks. This woman Melinda is not stupid. She is clever and crafty. Considerable planning went into the abduction. She arranged for a second carriage to confine her prey... she hired hulking brutes to effect his capture. She did not instigate this crime on the spur of the moment! Instead of focusing on what we can see, I believe we should focus on her mental state, and try to think as she might." Andrew concluded with Daniel's full attention.

"You may be right," Daniel replied after a minute, considering Andrew's ideas. "Let's go over what we know. You believe they would be heading towards Gretna Green, due north, where this unspeakable Lady Melinda intends to marry your cousin somehow, to take her revenge. Correct?"

"Yes. That's correct. I did hear her say so. And we have explored most thoroughly in that direction. However... I am almost certain they would not make camp out in the open. The lady Melinda thinks highly of herself and is not accustomed to rough living. Those carriage horses can only be pushed so far without rest and water and feed. I saw them when she arrived, and they are not of the best stock. She too must eat and rest each day, as must her men, and her captives too, I hope. So they must have sought shelter somewhere. She must have devised nightly stops in certain out-of-the way places, where there would be water for the horses, a place to sleep, but no close neighbors to take notice. Either we have not gone far enough, or we have missed it... It's possible she would travel only at night. But her main aim must be to put miles behind her as quick as she can, and you know horses can move much faster when they can see their way in daylight, especially on these rough back roads and byways."

Both men had risen to their feet as the discussion grew more intense. Andrew shook his head as the men paced in the firelight. His frustration and fatigue were apparent in every word he spoke. "I cannot believe they would be far ahead of us. It frustrates me so. I know they are out here, so close, yet not within our reach. Damn that woman for finding Gavin and damn her for taking them both!"

Daniel was of the same mind now. "Well, then, Andrew, let us seek out their most likely stopping place with first light. We will be looking for anything suspicious... any place they might secretly come to rest. We know the direction they took, their destination, and we know when they departed, and what they were looking for, and about how long they may have travelled." Stars were sparkling overhead as the men unrolled their blankets. Daniel's steely resolve had not deserted him in his growing despair. "They will surely be back on the road in the morning. Perhaps we can only discover where they have been, rather than where they in fact are... but that would still be progress." Then he noted, "No doubt Elizabeth has informed the village constable, not that he can be of much help."

Another thought was preying on his mind. He threw sticks on the dying fire and turned to Andrew again. "I tell you this! It's up to us to find Alex and Gavin, and to bring Melinda to justice for her crimes. When we find that woman who endangered my daughter, there will be hell to pay! She will get exactly what she has coming." Finally, Daniel rolled up in his blankets and gazed up at the night sky. Andrew reclined close by but did not hear the older man's whispered, heartfelt prayer. "Please God. She is my darling daughter and I love her dearly. Although I have never met Gavin, I wish him no harm. Please keep them safe, and please let us find them soon." Daniel was soon dozing.

Andrew hoped sleep would soon rescue him from his worries, if only for the night. With his dear Gavin in parts unknown, he felt as though he had lost a limb.

Cassandra was observing from a distance, well-hidden in the woodland. She had become an expert at remaining out of sight, though there had been a few more close calls. She felt her disguise was even better now, with her face and hands dirty, her fatigue adding years to her appearance. She hoped she might still discover something that would lead them to her sister. If they missed something, and she found it, there would be no way her father could be angry with her. Perhaps he would even be happy. She did not count on it.

She still had a little bread and cheese in her pockets, carefully husbanding her paltry, stealthily stolen stores. She was always hungry now. She stoically ignored the pangs and told herself that no matter her own discomforts, Alex's were probably much worse. As the men settled down for the night, she crept over to the nearby stream and watered her dear gelding, and knelt down to drink deeply herself. Water helped allay her hunger. The horse was a good companion, always seeming to anticipate her thoughts, always quiet and alert. She gave him a big hug.

Cassandra had chosen this hiding place for its good grazing and nearby water. Now she huddled in her saddle blanket and sat gazing toward her father's distant campfire, trying to think of what it was she should be looking for. There were no tracks, no footprints, no signs. There were just woods and hills and narrow little country lanes crossed by sheep paths leading nowhere. Settlements were tiny and widely scattered She hoped her father and Andrew had a clever plan, but with every passing hour her hopes diminished. When most of the men had been dismissed earlier, she was deeply disappointed. That was not a good sign. After a long night and a long day... so many questions remained.

Cassandra knew that when pushed far enough, her clever sister could be crafty, perhaps even devious. Alex was more than clever— she was strong, able, thoughtful, proud. And she was brave. Cassandra, nevertheless, felt the need to protect her. The intense bond of love with her big sister had been a big part of her as long as she could remember. They fought and argued and competed in all matters, but they also laughed and joked and rough-housed, no matter how much their father admonished them to be more ladylike. They had been each other's dearest companions all their lives.

A tear ran down Cassandra's face in her fear for Alex's safety. The notion of having to live without her sent her heart into an abyss. Finally she curled up on the ground and cried herself to sleep.

Melinda woke up in her usual fit of pique, stiff and sore from trying to sleep through the cold dewy night on hard ground, and from the hours of discomfort on horseback. "Wake up you two, we have to be going! You fools cannot lollygag around all day in hopes that Gavin and Alex will fall from the sky." Olaf, rising, cringed at the sound of Melinda's voice. He watered and bridled the sleepy horses, clumsily pegged out to graze, and held them while waiting for her next demands. Edgar was tying up the awkward bundles and strapping them on his bulky frame. Having prepared only for carriage riding, not only had they no saddles nor saddlebags, the makeshift bridles had been hastily cobbled together from harness parts. Melinda ordered the men to make sure the area was as they found it, for she did not want her movements detected by search parties seeking Alex and Gavin. Edgar scattered the ashes of the fire and scuffed over the charred area with his boots. He hoisted Melinda up and they continued on their way.

In a couple of hours, Melinda's imperious commands rang out again. "We have to stop. I am famished. Bring me food and water, one of you!"

Melinda ordered. Olaf and Edgar looked at each other. They had just started out. There was little food left.

"Did you hear me? I am thirsty!" she repeated, with an even more threatening tone.

"Of course, your highness," Edgar replied softly, not meaning to expose his sarcasm to her venom.

Melinda heard him and replied, "That is correct, you fool, and don't you ever forget it." With that, she kicked her horse into a gallop and started away, so annoyed by the insolence as to forget her thirst. They rolled their eyes and followed.

She would not rest until their captives were found! Melinda was optimistic in the warm morning sunshine. She was insane with jealousy that Alex could turn Gavin's head the way she had. She had noticed the way they looked at each other. Every time a glance full of emotion passed between the two, her stomach knotted and her fury grew fiercer. Her face burned red with jealous, hurt anger every time she thought of the two together. Melinda galloped as if to outrun these thoughts. Olaf and Edgar urged their mounts to catch up. As far as they were concerned, rampant insanity was the only explanation for Melinda's incomprehensible ways.

Sleep was fitful and fleeting as Daniel and Andrew worried through the night. Daniel shook

Andrew's shoulder. "Wake up boy! We must be moving on. It is a good day to travel. I feel very good about today." He was fastening his saddlebags. The other men were breaking camp with quiet efficiency, having arisen at first light to see to the horses and secure the supplies.

"I am awake. It is unlikely that I will get any real sleep until they are found." Andrew gathered his belongings and was soon mounted and ready.

Daniel, setting off, agreed, "I will not feel rested until my daughter is safely home."

Cassandra slowed the gelding to lengthen her distance from Daniel's group as the terrain flattened in a little valley, and the path through the woodland straightened out, without twists and turns to shield her from view should anyone happen to glance back. She thought they might have passed through this same valley the day before. She was feeling a pang of remorse for her mother's anxiety, with two daughters gone from her embrace. However, the risen sun was already lending more warmth than it usually offered, pouring into this valley over the low hills to the East. New grass along the rutted lane was deep green from recent spring rains, and tall wooded hills in the distance created a pleasant contrast against the brilliant blue sky. Without a cloud in sight, Cassandra was gazing cheerfully around the pleasant scenery when her sharp ears picked out the unmistakable sounds of horses and riders not far away. She quickly turned her horse off the path and hid him behind thick shrubbery at the forest's edge, dismounting to increase their concealment. Her father's party was well in front of her, and these noises had come from behind.

In two minutes, riders approached, and she could soon see through the branches that there was a small raven-haired woman followed by two large men, all riding bareback. The first man had oddly-made bundles strung over his massive shoulders. The woman's footwear was not at all appropriate for equitation, nor was her garb, she observed. The men did not look like they were prepared for this either. As they drew closer she noticed their bridles did not look like any she had ever seen before, with blinders just like harness blinders, and buckles where no buckles should be.

She paused for a moment as they passed, debating about quietly circling around through the wooded hills, and revealing herself to her father to describe this strange group on his trail. He would certainly see straight through this disguise! She feared his wrath when he saw she was not still safe at home. Cassandra decided to wait until these riders had gone past, then keep a close eye on them to learn what she could of their intentions.

Chapter Eleven

The first night after Alex and Gavin left the dusty little inn, clouds obscured the skies soon after moonrise, and keeping any sense of direction was impossible with no landmarks in any direction. The terrain was not as hilly, but more densely wooded, with few good paths, and they rarely found any signs of habitation. Confused by meandering game trails, they took wrong turns and sometimes doubled back to recognize a place they had already been. When Gavin got a glimpse of the moon peeking out from behind a cloud, he figured out which direction was south, and tried to keep heading that way, using moss on the trees and a light breeze on his cheek for guidance.

Gavin's well-made boots were holding up, though intended for drawing rooms rather than for exploring a wilderness, but Alex's fancy footwear soon refused to stay on her feet, and had to be buried beside the path. Fortunately the spring weather had softened and warmed the ground. Alex grew accustomed to trotting barefoot among the trees, peering down to avoid sharp things in the dark — stones, broken branches, sometimes thorns. She finally gave up the rest of her petticoat and tied its shreds around her sore feet.

By dawn's welcome rays, they felt they had made but little progress.

Hunting in the early light had only yielded

one little duck, which Gavin had discovered on a clutch of eggs near a limpid little pond tucked between the tops of two hills. He cast his shirt over it like a net, took up the squawking bundle in a leap, and quickly wrung its neck. He considered robbing the nest as well, but decided it would be too difficult to roast eggs on an open fire... and they might already contain downy ducklings. The fowl had been quickly prepared, and even more quickly eaten, stringy and tough more than tasty. Alex was relieved to note he had stolen flint and steel from the little stone cottage. Her dress might be in tatters, but his pockets held treasures worth more than gold.

Their second daytime rest had been in the poor shelter of a charcoal-maker's abandoned hut, with not even a bed, just a straw-filled pallet on the floor, where they again spent the daylight hours huddled together in an embrace that brought up unspeakable thoughts for both of them. They were so exhausted by now that it was easy to fall asleep, even in this intimate contact. Sleep was their only respite from deep fatigue, gnawing hunger, and scandalous, forbidden musings.

Hours after they set off that evening, they chanced across a little hill farm's modest kitchen garden where they hurriedly plucked and ate early spring peas from their pods. Gavin had a little money in his pocket and he paid for the peas by leaving a few shillings in their place, hoping for the farmer's forgiveness. They felt like they had at last encountered civilization, but as there was no sign of horse nor cart in the tiny farmyard, they could not think of any way this poor farmer could assist them. He was probably off in the hilltop meadows helping with the lambing.

It was full night, and she tried to muster the energy to run, but the best Alex could manage, shoeless, hungry, and way beyond tired, was a long walking stride. Gavin let her set the pace. A bright beam of moonlight silhouetted their shadows to dance across the trees as they made their way downhill along wagon tracks that led away from the little hill farm. The woods were growing less dense, the landscape less hilly. They had been speaking very little, but seemed to be in constant communication.

Gavin realized they were nearing Arlington; their environs had finally begun to look more familiar. A certain line of knobby hills rising in the distance, just visible against the starry sky when they attained a densely-wooded hilltop, was well-known to him. They had journeyed hard and dawn was still an hour away. Perhaps they had finally escaped from Melinda.

When they stopped before first light to drink deeply from a little spring burbling out of a rocky place at the side of the path, Gavin started to tell Alex that he estimated they had less than another night's journey before reaching Arlington. Then the thought of separation from her made his knees weak, for, he had resolved sadly, delivering her home meant saying farewell. It was safer that way. If he were no longer around Alex, he could not put her in any more danger. He knew from the way she spoke of Daniel that her father would keep her safe. The Earl of Bedford surely would be all she would need to protect her from harm.

They hurried on through the waning night as quietly as they could, the little track widening to a path and then almost becoming a lane. Finally Gavin felt she should know that their destination was almost within reach. He tried to offer soft, reassuring words, but he felt her withdraw as she listened. The intimate, silent connection that had developed over these long days and nights seemed to snap. He knew Alex had deep feelings for him... she was not very good at hiding her emotions, just at maintaining a proper demeanor. They would have just one more day in hiding, one more day to embrace, one more day. One last day.

The moon had long since set, and the sky in the east was pink now. Alex was almost too tired to take another step and had wearily seated herself on a convenient stump, all her energy gone. Gavin explored the densest part of the nearby wood in the early light, and finally located a mossy glen behind a big oak. He could hear a little brook bubbling nearby. This place would be out of view and out of earshot of this little lane should any travellers happen by, now that they were on a byway that might actually have some wayfarers once in a while.

"Alex, we shall stop here until dark. Then we will be home free." Gavin led her to the spot he had chosen after helping her up from the stump. "I am going off to forage, but I won't be far away."

Alex sat down on the moss, leaning back to rest against the mighty oak and shutting her eyes. She was soon lost in her thoughts. She had been so hoping that with just a bit more time together, Gavin would finally find a way to reveal his feelings, or to allow himself to care for her, or to admit he cared for her. Some *real* sign of affection that was not immediately negated by his next words or actions!

She did not think herself conceited, but she had had several marriage offers from respectable gentlemen of good character and families. Such men had been showing great interest in her ever since her début, and she had turned them down, every one, without a second thought. Those men cared only about money, and themselves. Some were pleasant companions, but not one made her feel special... until she met Gavin. Gavin was different. When Gavin was near, she felt something new, something precious, something deep and nameless, something that she suspected might be love.

Regardless of all the pride and stubborn willfulness that she was well aware they shared, she no longer doubted that he had deep feelings for her... feelings that matched her own. At moments, he seemed affectionate, and yet, at the very next moment, so distant. She could not think of any explanation for his confusing behavior. Whenever Alex attempted to show him her more sensuous self, he invariably turned away. But sometimes she noticed him gazing at her in a most intimate, embarrassing way, as if she had no clothes on, but it never felt lascivious or lustful, it felt like he *knew* her, and appreciated her. She yearned constantly now for any sort of positive response from Gavin. He had opportunities to kiss her, or to comfort her, but he was treating her like an annoying younger sister. Warm and cold. Friendly and distant. She was so tired of being held at arm's length. There had been a few fleeting, rare moments of intimate kinship, as when he had gazed right into her eyes across the table... but he always drew back from them.

And now... now she might never see him again. Gavin had no understanding of her boiling-over feelings. He could not know that she was going to miss him terribly, and that she hoped with all the hope she had that their relationship would change before this long, painful journey ended. After all the fear and turmoil and pain of Melinda's vicious actions, she had been trusting that she and Gavin were at least growing closer, and that he would soon confess his feelings. She had been depending upon the hope that something good would come out of their desperate situation. Not just something good. Something amazing.

Now they were close to home and there was not much time left for a miracle. Their wounds at Melinda's hands were healing. They were almost out of danger. This adventure was ending.

"Alex, are you in there? I have asked you three times already if you are hungry," Gavin said, touching her shoulder gently.

Alex blinked and shook her head. "Of course I'm hungry. I have been starving all night. I was just thinking how good it will feel to be back home with plenty to eat and a soft bed to sleep in."

"Of course, my dear, I did not mean to be rude. I'm sure you are very eager to see your family."

"Absolutely," she said with a tone dripping with sarcasm. She wanted to pick a fight.

"My, aren't we snippy. Perhaps you're just a little tired, or your hunger has really gotten to you?"

"Yes, perhaps it has." Alex realized how childish she sounded.

"Well, Alex, I know you have eaten better then this, but it's all we have until we reach home sometime tonight." Gavin put a big double handful of tiny wild strawberries in front of her. They glistened with moisture from being dipped into the stream. Then he reached into his bulging pockets and pulled out a bounty of hazelnuts. "When you find a good hazelnut tree, you know the nearby squirrels will have stored plenty to share."

Alex laughed, "What a repast! Thank you

for being so clever." She was trying to mask her hopelessness and disappointment. The long-ripened hazelnut kernels were falling out of their loose husks, so consuming them was easy, and they were tasty and filling.

"I am glad to see you laughing! You have such a beautiful smile, and you're much more attractive when you're smiling than you are with that scowl you show me when you get lost in your thoughts."

"I don't know if I should take that as a compliment or not." She paused and said, "I shall take it as a compliment and let you off the hook for now." She smiled seductively and ate the last berries.

Gavin was more than pleased that, at least for now, they were getting along; he truly enjoyed her company. He knew well that it was his own actions that triggered Alex's sarcasm and defensiveness. For this he felt sorry, and he knew that something must be done to remedy it.

The provisions had disappeared quickly, there was no cleaning up to do, and they sat next to each other in shared exhaustion, leaning up against the magnificent oak, gazing in silence at the greenery surrounding them as it started glowing in the morning sun. Soon they would be back in their own beds. Even more appealing than soft, plump featherbeds was the dream of soaking long in very hot baths. Alex's porcelain skin had taken on a natural ruddy glow, even though they had been avoiding the midday light. Gavin thought she looked remarkable. The color added a certain sparkle to her eyes... and he loved her eyes.

Alex sat in silence with a blank look on her face and Gavin thought she seemed sad. He felt the need to go and hold her, but stubbornness held him back. For now he just sat and admired her beauty and innocence. He knew by now that no woman in this world could ever hold a candle to Alex, not now, not ever, as far as he was concerned.

"Gavin," Alex turned to face him, noticing his eyes on her face, "when we get back, will you be staying with Andrew, or will you be heading back home?"

"I'm not sure yet, Alex. Why do you ask?" Gavin replied softly.

Alex wanted to beg him to stay because the thought of his leaving her forever frightened her terribly. "I was just wondering if I shall be likely to run into you or not, that is all."

"Oh, I see. Well, there is no telling what will happen once we reach home. But do not fear, my dear, I am sure we will cross paths again at some point." He then moved away to stretch out on the moss in the deepening shade of a large bough. Slowly he closed his eyes.

His rugged masculinity was so attractive that Alex often got butterflies in her stomach when she looked in his direction. Only when he was pushing her away could she release this tender feeling. She pined so intensely for him to reach out and hold her. She smiled to think of the delicious surge of pleasure that sprang up inside whenever he shot her one of those crooked, devilish smiles. She lounged under the tree gazing at his impeccable form and asked herself over and over why things could not be different. She had finally decided that his new beard, however scruffy it was, made him look more desirable than ever. Perhaps this was why she was fighting back impure and most unladylike thoughts every time she looked at his face lately.

Since leaving childhood, Alex had dreamed about finding the man of her dreams. To love him completely, and receive the same. Life without love was empty, not worth living. Her parents experienced deep love for each other and let it show. Alex had so long been yearning to, one day, find for herself a love just like theirs... And along the way, the ideal had become her expectation, something she felt entitled to. She knew she would not, could not, settle for less. It was much more than a childish desire for romance, it was an emptiness within her that demanded to be filled. And now... had this great love appeared at last, only to vanish?

She closed her eyes and allowed sleep to take her thoughts away.

"Alex, wake up. We have to go. Alex, come on, we're so close to home. Wake up!" Gavin persisted as he knelt next to Alex, shaking her gently.

"For heaven's sake, Gavin! I was up the first time you called me. What in the world is your hurry? It seems like I just closed my eyes." As her eyes adjusted, Alex realized that night was gathering in. She had slept the whole day away. Once again faced with reality, she was reminded that her time with Gavin was coming to an end. Only hours remained to be together now.

"Come on, Alex. I thought you would be excited. Soon you will be with your family again." He regarded the sad look Alex had on her face and hoped she was feeling something of his own desperation and despair.

"I *am* excited Gavin. How could you think I am not?"

"Of course you are. I don't know what came over me. I thought I caught a hint of hesitation. Would that have been my imagination?"

Resolving to play the game he played so well, Alex was not going to tell Gavin what he wanted to hear, so she replied convincingly, "Indeed, it must have been your imagination."

Alex quickly retied the rags around her aching feet, walked down to the little brook to rinse her face and hands, and soon returned, ready to travel.

Together, they began their journey home.

Miles away, two other companions were resting their horses at a crossroads on a remote country road. "Andrew, I wish we could find some evidence telling us that Alex and Gavin are alive, or had come this way, but we have come across nothing."

"You're right, Sir. I'm at a loss. I'm not sure what we should do."

"I believe it's time for me to turn down this road, head for home, and check on my wife. Perhaps she may have some information by now." He paused to consider his choices, not liking any of them. "Do not take this as a sign of defeat, because as long as I live, I shall never give up on my daughter."

Hanging his head in fatigue, Daniel was saddened by the long fruitless search. He had already dismissed his men. He was thinking perhaps the constable knew something of use by now. If the man had the sense to go talk to Andrew's butler, there would be a description of Melinda and her thugs to send out by telegraph... . He did not think this was likely. And she must be lying low, anyway.

Daniel would do whatever he had to do to get his daughter back. He had friends everywhere, friends he could count on. The search was not over. It would not end until Alex was found.

"I agree with you." Andrew's reply had

taken a minute while he thought about his cousin. "It cannot hurt to go and check. We could use fresh horses, and provisions. And... with luck, maybe Gavin and Alex found a way to get back."

"Ah! That, Andrew, would be the answer to my prayers!"

"Your prayers and mine." The men mounted their horses and guided them southward with fresh energy. They would have to make their way through densely wooded, hilly countryside. It would be a long ride, but their destination lifted their heavy hearts.

Cassandra was still keeping track of the mysterious riders, but had circled round to make sure she could still find her father. The two little groups had been on parallel routes all day, travelling at about the same pace, stopping at about the same times, never becoming aware of each other, or of her.

Soon she realized her father had turned for home. She was disappointed he had not found Alex and Gavin yet, and more and more curious as to who these riders were. She had begun to think perhaps one *could* be that evil Melinda, though it could be anybody. If indeed the little woman *were* Melinda, what had she done with Gavin and Alex? Maybe she was searching for them too? That would actually make sense. No, that was impossible.

She let out a big sigh and her horse responded with a long exhalation himself. She could not show her father that she had been tagging along the whole time. When her activities were discovered his wrath would be immense. Let that happen after she made her way home.

Still making their way through the woods, Melinda, Olaf and Edgar had no idea where Alex and Gavin were, and sometimes lost track of their own whereabouts. Now and again they thought they heard other horses or voices ahead, or glimpsed them when the path was straight, and retreated into the brush or slowed their mounts. At one point, two men on horseback had passed going the other way, looking exhausted and hardly giving them a glance.

Melinda was fiercely angered by her captives' escape. It was still hard for her to believe that her carefully-crafted plot had fallen apart so fast. She had been so focused on redoubling her revenge that she'd lost track of her surroundings. She anticipated her erstwhile captives' return home, but did not intend to give up on Gavin. Gradually, a new plan was coming together in her mind. She would give them enough time to think they were safe. She knew clever ways of dropping out of sight. Then, when everyone thought they were entirely out of danger, Melinda would strike. It would be an attack that no one would ever forget! She took a deep breath and felt some energy returning. She looked up and saw a village clinging to the side of a hillside in the distance.

"Olaf and Edgar, I do not want us to be seen. Start looking now, and find us a place to stay the night where no one will notice us. Do you understand this?" Her tone was imperious.

"Yes. Is that all, my lady?" Edgar answered with a look of boredom.

"Yes." Melinda held her nose high into the air as if she were an empress in a palanquin.

Olaf and Edgar exchanged glances. They knew they were just a step away from becoming surly. It was harder and harder to conceal their extreme dislike for Melinda and her ways.

Chapter Twelve

"Oh, look, there it is! I can see Bedford House! We're almost home!" Alex exploded with excitement as the first rays of dawn revealed the vista, familiar at last. She was so glad she was going to be with her family again, but she knew she would be missing Gavin desperately. Having him at her side during this exhausting trek had made all the difference, keeping her moving ahead, keeping her fatigue and despondence at bay through all obstacles and difficulties. She was not sure she could make it through a single day now without seeing his handsome face, without leaning on his brawny strength, without inhaling his manly aroma. His nearness, his presence, was precious, essential.

She told herself over and over: you must take it one day at a time.

"I will escort you home, and see you settled in. But then I must return to Arlington. I do not wish to distress you, but after today, we shall not be able to see each other. It is for the best, so please, no arguments," Gavin replied in low, serious tones.

Alex gathered her strength and composed herself. "Fine, if that is the way things must be, so be it." Alex did her best to find her accustomed poise, and not reveal her deep sadness and despair. Their pace was slow now, each step painful. Her lugubrious mood made her want to move even more slowly.

Gavin had thought an argument was probable at this long-anticipated moment, and felt relief that he did not have to get into one. However, her prompt agreement surprised him enough to leave him feeling a bit unwanted, rejected, and empty.

They had started off just as night had fallen. It was very early morning now. The air was crisp and clean and the sun was beginning a pink and glorious ascent. There was a promise of a splendid and brilliant spring day, but Gavin and Alex were both privately musing that the sun would never truly shine until the moment they found each other again.

"Gavin, will you be staying with Andrew, or will you be leaving?" Alex asked again in a quiet voice.

"I have answered that question, remember? I am not yet sure quite what I will be doing. I suppose I may be here for a little while longer. My plans depend on many factors. Why?"

"Just making conversation, is there anything wrong with that?" she snapped.

"Of course not, my lady, I thought you would be thinking only of home by now," Gavin's reply was equally cold.

They had only to walk one last mile together before reaching the estate, but neither of them could think of anything to say. Their journey would end in silence.

Alex walked up to the front door of Bedford House, there to suddenly pause a moment, realizing how she must look: Her rent and filthy gown, her lack of corset and petticoat, her exhausted and ruddy face, her filthy, matted hair, red scratches and insect bites on her limbs, her toughened, dirty feet shod only in muddy rags! Then she took a deep breath, held her head high, and lifted the ornate brass knocker. When the butler opened the door, he did not immediately recognize her; he had never seen Gavin, with or without a scruffy new beard. He started to close it again thinking the household was beset by vagabonds or beggars. Beggars knew to only approach a back door! Whomever could these dirty people be?

Then Alex greeted him by name, pushed past him, and raced from one room to the next in search of her family. "Hello? Is anyone home? Father? Mother? Cassie?"

Elizabeth and Ashley were in the morning room, arranging fresh blooms from the garden. It was early, but sleep had been elusive for the denizens of Bedford House.

"Ashley dear, hand me that vase, please?"

"Here you..." she did not finish her sentence or pass the vase, but looked at her mother, bewildered.

"Ashley, what is wrong with you?" her mother asked.

"Didn't you just hear that? Someone yelling? It sounded like Alex!"

"What are you going on about?"

"There it is again, Mother! It *is* Alex!"

"I did not hear a thing. Perhaps you are indulging yourself in wishful thinking. I know you miss your sisters and father, but please, to hear you say you hear Alexandra in the house is most upsetting! I miss her so ...." Elizabeth stopped abruptly, turning her head in the direction of the hallway. Now she too discerned a familiar voice calling "Mother, Father... ."

"Ashley— could it be?" Elizabeth said, as she dropped her secateurs with a clatter, gathered her skirts and ran toward the hallway.

Ashley followed closely behind.

They raced around the rooms together but saw nothing. Elizabeth stopped so abruptly, Ashley crashed into her back. "This is strange! I swear I heard her voice!" Then Elizabeth turned around and saw Alex standing halfway up the stairs, near a tall, bearded, disheveled, but most handsome man.

"My Alexandra! My beautiful baby girl, you're here at last!" She observed Alex's lamentable state, but did not care. She ran to embrace her daughter.

"Mother! Oh, Mother!" Alex ran down the stairs and fell into her mother's arms. Together they cried and twirled. Ashley joined them, and in their loving embrace, they were the only ones in the world.

Gavin was now standing at the foot of the stairs, appreciating the joyful reunion. His Angel's exquisite beauty was newly inspiring, as she was so happy and aglow to be home at last. He was aware that her family meant the world to her, as she did to them. He knew she would be well-loved, once in exile from his own protection. Her parents would be there to embrace her and guard her, no matter what might come next. She would be safe here.

"Alexandra, darling, where is your father? Did he come in with you?" her mother asked, with a tearful expression washing over her face, peering toward the entry hall. Perhaps Daniel had taken his horse to the stables? Why would he not leave that to a groom?

"Father? How would I know where father is?" Alex answered, mystified by the question.

"Alexandra, Father went searching for you, of course. He has been gone ever since you were taken," Ashley informed her.

"Well, I did not come across him," Alex responded, dropping her voice into a low tone, concern and worry on her face now.

"Each day, each night, a few men have returned from the search party, but they have had no progress at all to report. They have been running out of likely locations to look for you two and that Lady Melinda, I gather." She had pinned her hopes on

Daniel's triumphant return with Alexandra on his arm. To greet only one of her absent beloveds without the others... she couldn't bear to think about it. Cassandra... there was still no sign of Cassandra. Her heart sank. She pulled herself together.

"I hope he returns soon, then," she continued. "Perhaps we can get word to him." Elizabeth wondered how such a thing might be accomplished. She could send out a groom... might any of the men, returned from the searching, know Daniel's likely whereabouts today?

"Alex, I have a question for you," Ashley said, politely waiting her turn to speak, though she found it tempting to interrupt. "Who is that man?" She was trying not to point at Gavin, knowing that pointing was bad manners, so she nodded in his direction.

"Oh, Gavin, I am so sorry! I forgot you were there! Mother, Ashley, this is Lord Gavin Blake. Turning to her mother, Alex continued, "Lord Blake was kidnapped just as I was. He is Lord Andrew Blake's cousin. Actually, he is the reason I was abducted. But it was not his fault, and anyway, his assistance brought me home... it was a very long journey." Alex motioned for Gavin to draw near. "Gavin, may I present my mother, Lady Elizabeth Rosenshire, and my baby sister, Lady Ashley Rosenshire... Excuse me please, everyone, for not remembering my manners and more promptly performing introductions." She looked over Gavin's ragged beard, torn clothing, filthy boots, and haggard appearance, and wondered what her family might think of this rather unlikely-looking "gentleman." Nothing to be done about it, she decided.

Alex paused and looked at her mother and sister. "Where is Cassandra this fine morning? Out for a ride already? Not out of bed yet?"

"Your sister got it into her head that she was going to help find you, against our firmly expressed wishes. Alexandra... she has been gone ever since your father left, on the night of your... disappearance. I can only hope that she is all right." She was trying to remain composed, but her worry was apparent.

"Well, it was a generous gesture, she must have been most bothered about me to do such a wild thing, but did she not realize that she could put herself in serious danger? I hope nothing has happened to her. It would be entirely my fault if anything did." Alex's expression was pained and deeply concerned.

"No, Alex, it would be my fault. If it were not for me, none of this would have happened," Gavin interjected, uncomfortable and guilty to see the deep sadness written now on Alex's still-angelic, dirty face.

"Please, I want both of you young people to stop blaming yourselves for a situation beyond your control." Elizabeth's was the kind voice of reason.

"Everyone is entitled to a mistake or two in their lives. Unfortunately, it appears that Gavin's mistake came back to haunt him."

"Indeed, Lady Rosenshire. I would have to regretfully agree with you."

Gavin paused, glanced at Alex, and continued to address Elizabeth. "Now, I hate to take my leave, so soon after making your most welcome acquaintance, but I would like to inform my family that I have returned in one piece... however the worse that piece might appear, due to these most unfortunate events." He was well aware of his unpresentable appearance. "I beg you to allow me to excuse myself."

"I understand." She beckoned to the butler, hovering at a discreet distance, and asked him to have a groom saddle a horse to take Gavin to Arlington House. She continued, "You must return for dinner soon, so that we may properly thank you for bringing our daughter safely back to us." She extended her hand to Gavin.

"That would be lovely." He bowed to place a light kiss on the back of her hand. "I thank you, Lady Rosenshire, for your most kind generosity. Perhaps, it would be safer for everyone if I kept my distance for the nonce? Melinda and her brutes are still out there somewhere, and I could not bear to endanger your family again in any way. It is my prayer that Melinda may soon be brought to justice for her crimes."

"Certainly, I understand. You must do what you think best," Elizabeth responded politely. She knew that this was not what Alexandra wanted to hear.

While Gavin and her mother conversed, Alex stood close by, drinking in the nearness of the tall, disheveled man before her with a suppressed sigh. He was such a gentleman, so strong, so brave and honorable. Why could she not find a man to marry such as he? Why couldn't it be he? Or could it be? Her hopes waxed and waned moment by moment, though her feelings did not waver.

Alex offered to walk Gavin around to the stables. Ashley turned to follow them, most curious about this handsome, burly stranger, but her mother grabbed her hand and shook her head. She knew the two needed a few moments alone before parting. Recognizing well the look on her eldest daughter's face, she knew Alexandra had found love at last.

"Well, Gavin, this is goodbye," Alex said, as they rounded a corner of the garden, stopping to face him, but casting her gaze down, hoping he might not notice her fresh tears that sprang to her eyes as these words left her lips. A groom could be glimpsed with a horse over in the stableyard, some distance farther down the walk, eyeing Gavin's height and adjusting the stirrup leathers to make them longer.

Gavin saw Alex was weeping, and it broke his heart.

"Thank you, Gavin. I shall miss you. Thank you... ." She could not choke out any more words, overcome by emotion.

Gavin moved very close to her, and gently placed his hand under her chin, slowly lifting her face until their eyes met. Tears were making tracks down her grimy, lovely face. There were twigs in her tangled golden tresses. He bent and placed a lingering, sensual kiss upon her lips. He gazed into her eyes a long moment before he released her chin.

"Angel, this is goodbye. If it is any consolation... I shall miss you too." Straightening to his full height, he strode rapidly over to the groom, took up the reins, mounted the horse, wheeled toward the drive, and rode away at a rapid trot.

Alex, still as a statue, gazed after him until he was long out of sight. He had called her Angel again, she realized in confusion. She was so tired and drained and upset. Maybe she had not heard him correctly.

"Alexandra, are you all right?" her mother softly asked.

"Yes... I didn't hear you come up behind me." She turned. The concern upon her mother's face melted her heart, and Alex broke down and released a long-restrained flood of tears and anguish. It felt like a dam breaking.

"You love him, don't you?"

"Yes, with all my heart, but I shall never have him," Alex wailed, sobbing in her mother's embrace.

"Darling, I know this is difficult. If I did not have your father's love, I would surely go mad. Now. You must remember one thing for me." Elizabeth tenderly rubbed her daughter's back, then gently grasped Alex's shoulders and held her away so she could look into her eyes. "Can you do that?"

Alex nodded, entirely miserable and still weeping uncontrollably.

"I want you to remember, for *me*, that when two people first fall in love with each other, as I know you and Gavin have, they often do not say what they mean."

Alex gazed into her mother's kind face, puzzled by this idea.

Elizabeth explained, "Gavin wore his love for you openly, as you wore yours for him, because such things cannot be hidden... especially from mothers. And true love always conquers. He will find his way back to you, darling Alexandra. I *know* he will."

"I hope with all my heart that what you say is true!" Alex embraced her mother tightly. They stood on the garden path, rocking back and forth without saying a word, a mother glad to be holding her daughter again, and a young woman pining for her man.

The distance was not great, but Gavin's journey home was taking forever, and was the loneliest he had ever endured. The kiss he had left on Alex's tear-streaked face was etched in his mind, still burning on his lips. Over and over he recalled an image of her woebegone, still-angelic visage. Never had he thought anything could affect him like this. Like her.

"Ahhh, Angel, you tasted so sweet," he said aloud. Then he shook his head as if to shake away his yearnings, and kicked the willing horse into a gallop.

There must be no change of plan, he said to himself, gladdened by his speed. He must never abandon his vow! It was even more important now, with Melinda on the rampage. He must leave his Angel alone, for her own safety! His resolve at last took over from his longing.

He finally cantered up the drive to Arlington House and trotted around the back toward the stables. Dismounting, he tossed the reins to a startled groom deep in flirtation with a chambermaid.

Gavin threw open the nearest door of the mansion, and a very excited and noisy Jack leapt upon him before he could step within.

Aunt Amelia and cousin Catherine, early risers, just sitting down for tea in the morning room, had sent a footman to discover why the normally quiet and morose Jack had been making such a fuss by the garden door. Amelia had been letting him stay inside these last few worrisome days, as he had seemed so distressed by the absence of his master, and she fretted that Jack might run off to join the search, never to be seen again. Amelia and Catherine had both been trying to tempt the pup with treats from the pantry, without sharing their secret worries with each other, but Jack showed little interest in meaty little bites or rich marrow bones. He stayed by the door all day, letting Catherine take him for short walks, no more interested in the many delights of the outdoors than in his food. Every night he curled up against the foot of his master's bed, but no one considered making him return to the stables.

Gavin knelt briefly to caress and speak softly to his loyal dog, surprised that Jack had lost so much weight.

The footman gawked at his reprehensible appearance, speechless, and closed the door behind him.

"Hello, cousin Catherine, Aunt Amelia," Gavin said quietly from the doorway of the morning room.

Startled, they both looked up, recognition taking a moment to dawn on their faces once they could make out the familiar handsome face behind the unfamiliar ratty whiskers. Catherine jumped up and ran to Gavin. "Cousin Gavin! You're back! Are you all right? Why do you look like this? What happened to you?"

"I am fine," he reassured her. "Where is Andrew? Is he well? As I recall, he was groaning on the floor when last I saw him."

His aunt rose from the table, glad that Gavin appeared undamaged, if bedraggled, filthy, and unshaven. His reappearance was a prayer answered. She wanted to show a warm welcome to her long-missing nephew, but her expression betrayed deep concern for her son, merged with surprise, disappointment, and fear, as they had not returned to her together as expected. She did not walk over to him, but stayed by her chair, leaning on it for support, as she finally found the words to explain, "Gavin, Andrew went out looking for you with Alexandra's father, the same evening you were taken." Her face was ashen.

"I had no idea. I brought Alex home before coming here, and her mother did not mention that Andrew had left. Understandably, she was preoccupied with Alex. I did not linger to chat."

"Has Lord Rosenshire returned?" Amelia could not suppress the anxiety overwhelming her.

"No, they were still expecting him, just as you were expecting Andrew. If no one is back by tomorrow, I shall go out to look for them myself."

His plan brought a little hope to Elizabeth's concerned expression. He continued, "Right now, I would like very much to bathe long, and eat heartily, please, and take some welcome rest. Thus I shall make myself more presentable, and worthy of your good company. I shall retire to my rooms now... with Jack, who is going to claw off the last of these poor trousers, apparently." The dog had been forgetting his good manners in his joyous welcome. "I shall look for you both later on today." Gavin smiled at them both, gave Catherine a careful hug trying not to get her dirty, and then turned to seek out his valet, leaving Amelia and Catherine to exchange glances. They could see that Gavin was now as worried as they were about Andrew.

Gavin instructed his most relieved and loyal Stephen to bring up a large selection of everything the pantries might have to offer, then to prepare a hot bath. While waiting for the trays to arrive, he emptied his pockets onto a bureau, stripped off his boots and horrific clothing with relief, and piled all in a heap to be burned. Donning a dressing gown, he ate ravenously, thinking no repast in any fine dining establishment of the City had ever satisfied him more.

Once sated, Gavin dismissed Stephen and sank into his deep, steaming bath. At long last releasing his anxieties and allowing himself to relax, he closed his eyes with relief, and started reviewing these unbelievable circumstances again and again with his tired brain. He had long known of Melinda's evil ways, but had never imagined she would go this far. Now there was the almost certain possibility that she would plot against Alex, perhaps even arrange Alex's murder as threatened, instead of focusing all her wrath on him. Gavin must warn Daniel Rosenshire to watch over his daughter always. Her safety was paramount.

Gavin's head sank beneath the surface of the bath as he scratched at his itchy scalp. The water was already becoming murky, and a few bits of leaf and twig floated up. Emerging to draw a deep breath, he took up a lightly scented bar of Castile soap and scrubbed it vigorously over every inch of his head and body. His feet and hands did not come clean for a long time. He called for the valet to bring more buckets of hot water, and finally stood to have the last one poured over his head. Gradually he was feeling more like himself.

Towelling off with pleasure, donning a new silken robe, he sat at his dressing table and allowed his attentive and relieved valet to shave off his thick new beard, trim his hair and mustache, and attend to his nails. Now that he was clean and fed, his fatigue was becoming overwhelming.

As he cast off the gown and sat naked on his bed, his glance happened to fall upon his bureau. His flagging awareness was drawn to a little pile of random objects. There were a few notes and coins, a flint and steel, one little hazelnut, a fine pocket watch and a rusty little pocket knife... and then he espied a very small scrap of deep blue lace. For a long moment, he closed his eyes, covering his face with both hands. Eventually, he fell back against his pillows, and in seconds he was sleeping soundly, dreaming of an angel. Jack sat close by with his chin on his master's hand.

Waking around three in the afternoon, he saw that Stephen had neatly laid out clean, pressed garments and his newest, well-shined boots. His dreams had all been of Alex. As he dressed, even while savoring the feeling of being clean and shaven again, in clean clothing, and no longer fading from exhaustion, all he could think of was his Angel's beautiful, breathtaking innocence. His love for her consumed him; her safety was of the utmost importance. The two impulses were at war with each other: to gather her close to share his bursting heart, and to keep her at arm's length for her own protection.

He knew he had never before experienced love, and he knew he had found it at last, yet there was still no way to enjoy it. Before Alex, he had not grasped quite what he had been missing. This sensation of emptiness and loss was new and most distressing. A great treasure had been within his grasp, only to be yanked away. He reprimanded himself, trying to gain control of his heartbreak. The only way to express his overwhelming love for his Angel was to protect her, to keep her safe from harm.

Thinking of love only hurt. Thinking of action might help.

At Bedford House, excusing herself politely from Elizabeth and Ashley, Alex stole into the kitchens and asked the cook to produce anything that might be available to eat. Word had spread quickly through the servants' precincts of her safe return, and the cook could not conceal her gladness at seeing her young mistress safe again. Each member of the staff rushed to serve her whenever they could find an excuse.

Alex sat in her filthy tatters and devoured everything that appeared before her, drinking glass after glass of water, tearing off bread from the loaf instead of waiting for it to be sliced, slathering it with fresh creamery butter and sweet quince preserves. She could vaguely recall her last moment of repletion, enjoying that fine chocolate cake at Arlington House, but it seemed like that had been years ago... and it led to thoughts of what had transpired soon thereafter. She could not bear to think of that, and put her attention on the delights before her. Eventually her hunger abated and a feeling of satisfaction grew until, finally, she could eat no more.

It was an equal pleasure to have Sara help her out of her unspeakably foul garments and unwrap her tired, sore feet. The sensation of sinking into a deep, scented bubble bath was so enchanting that it seemed like she had never done such a thing before. She drew the soap over her skin tenderly, observing all the little wounds resulting from her journey. She let Sara lather her hair several times with rich soap, and give it a good last rinse with vinegar so it would return to its usual soft and shining state. She finally lay back and dozed happily in a fresh change of hot water, barely aware of her maid's drawing up a little stool to sit close by, to gently comb out her tangled locks, and carefully attend to her broken nails. Once these ministrations were completed, Sara gently helped her out of the tub, towelled her off, and dusted her all over with lilac-scented talcum powder. Alex was too exhausted to stand unaided by the time a fresh gossamer nightgown was slipped over her head, and she finally let herself fall into the silky sheets and soft pillows with relief and rapture. Alex was deeply asleep in an instant. As she slept, Sara softly rubbed fragrant, healing unguents into her beloved mistress's tired limbs.

Alex awakened in time for tea, feeling renewed and refreshed. Her nagging hunger and constant fatigue and discomfort had ended at last, though, wiggling her toes, she determined that her feet definitely remained sore. One other thing had not changed... she could not stop thinking of Gavin. His handsome face and powerful physique had haunted every dream. She asked herself if she would *ever* stop thinking of him. Alex opened her eyes hoping to erase his image, only to close them again and see him reappear in all his manly power.

She forced herself to keep her eyes open, rose from the bed, and instantly Sara entered and dressed her in a comfortable, casual, soft afternoon frock, somehow forgetting to lace her corset as tightly as was the fashion. She had sought out some especially comfortable stockings and shoes, as well.

When Alex reached the bottom of the stairs looking forward to a big pot of tea, she was astonished and gladdened to see her father standing there with Andrew, with her mother and Ashley close by.

"Father, you're back!" Alex screeched as she ran toward him, giving him the biggest hug she could manage. He crushed her to his chest with what might have been a sob.

"Yes, Alex, I am home! Now step away, please. I would like to take a good look at you and make sure you are all right."

She did as her father asked with a big smile of confidence, twirling around gracefully to face them again.

"Lord Andrew, Gavin is all right too. He brought me home and headed straight for Arlington House early this morning."

"Thank you for letting me know, Lady Alexandra. I am very glad you were not harmed. I must apologize to you for what happened. You were my responsibility, and I failed you," he said most sincerely, pain evident in his voice for her plight.

"Andrew, it was not your fault. I am very much to blame for putting myself in the middle of something I knew nothing about. I thank you both for searching for me. Father, I am most sorry for what I put you and the rest of the family through. I was not hurt, truly. I met with nothing that I could not handle, especially as I had Gavin's able assistance most of the time... ." She wanted to relate some of the adventure, now that the threat of death and disaster did not hang over her head.

Daniel interrupted, "Not now. Your mother has just informed us that your sister disobeyed me. Cassandra has done a very foolish thing." Apparently Andrew and Daniel had not been back for long, Alex realized, suddenly noticing how they were dressed, and that they were dirty, aromatic and unshaven after sleeping rough for three days and four nights.

"Yes, Father. Mother said that Cassandra went off on her own to look for me. I pray that she is all right," Alex replied sheepishly.

"And I pray she is not in danger, as well. However, Andrew has offered to go and look for her. When he retrieves her, she will be in great trouble," Daniel stated, letting fears turn into ire and come into his tone and manner. "I can't keep track of you girls! If you ever put yourself at risk again I swear I will throttle you! The both of you!" He then reached out for Alex and hugged her so tightly she could not take a normal breath. He held her out to take another careful look at her. He noticed a mark on her cheek and was not happy about that. She could not hide all the scratches on her arms, either. It was well she had had enough time to bathe and change her clothes!

Elizabeth was standing quietly in the shadows. "My love," she said gently, "please try to remember that what Cassandra did was out of love for her sister. They have always loved and protected each other."

"Elizabeth, my dear. I will keep that in mind, but what she succeeded in doing was to create more worry for you, and she has put herself in grave danger." Daniel's expression was dark with worry, but his tone was gentle. "I have one daughter back, but another is not yet safe."

Andrew coughed softly to draw Daniel's attention. "My Lord, my Lady, I must be leaving now to seek the Lady Cassandra. Would you please be so kind as to send a messenger to Arlington House to inform my family that I am well?" He moved closer to the door. "And if you do not mind, perhaps I might borrow a fresh mount, so my stallion can at last get some good rest. Our fine horseflesh has carried us far." The men exchanged a brotherly look. By now Daniel and Andrew were comfortable in each other's company, over the recent days discovering many points of agreement, such as the importance of perfect conformation in a thoroughbred.

"Yes, of course, that will not be a problem at all," Daniel responded, nodding to the butler to pass the word.

Elizabeth reached out and touched Andrew's sleeve and looked up into his eyes. "I will ask Cook to send some provisions out to the stable for your journey. By now you must not have much in the way of stores. While you wait for your mount, there will be a flask of hot tea to drink." Andrew gave her a look of gratitude and thanked her. He knew she fiercely wanted her other daughter back.

With a respectful shake of Daniel's hand, and a graceful, polite bow to Elizabeth and then to Alex, Andrew headed for the stables, so anxious to continue the hunt that he could not bear to linger, in spite of his fatigue.

Alex looked lovingly upon her parents, and asked, "I have a question... how is it that you knew what happened to us? Andrew was the only one in the room, he had sent away all of his servants, and he did not look all too coherent at the moment we were forced to depart." Daniel explained that although Andrew appeared helpless and concussed after taking a blow to the head, he was in fact able to hear much of what was said in spite of his daze, and to remember it well enough to promptly raise the alarm when he eventually recovered.

They adjourned to the drawing room, where Ashley had begun her tea without them. Richard had still not returned home and knew nothing of what his family was enduring.

Chapter Thirteen

Andrew was mounted and on his way out of the stableyard, glancing behind his saddle to be sure his saddlebags had been secured, when he almost collided with a mounted young man arriving from the drive, suddenly rounding a corner and about to cross his path.

"What in the hell do you think you're doing? For God's sake, watch where you're going!" he yelled to the boy, too fatigued to find his patience or manners.

"Watch where I am going? I do not think so, Sir, as you are coming out of my stable! I do believe I have the right of way here!" The bedraggled stranger doffed her cap, releasing a cascade of long auburn hair.

"Cassandra? By God! I did not recognize you!"

"Yes, Lord Andrew, it is I. Now I need to know if Alex is back— is that why everyone has returned?" Concern was evident on her dirty but still-lovely face.

"Yes. Alex and Gavin are both restored to us, and, blessedly, little the worse for their journey... they walked a long way after effecting their escape. But I cannot say the same for you!" Dismounting and dropping his reins, Andrew walked over to Cassandra, grasped her around the waist and abruptly hoisted her from her saddle, setting her on the ground in front of himself and grasping her firmly by her shoulders, gazing deeply into her eyes with much more than relief in his own.

"Excuse me? What right have you to touch me as you have, and to tell me I am not all right? Can you not see for yourself that I am fine? Just a little dirty."

"Oh, yes, Cassandra, I can see that you are, indeed, fine in every way." His tone betrayed his deep relief, mixed with a little awe and appreciation. "When your father is through with you, however, you may not feel quite so perfectly fine anymore! I was just starting off to search for you!" Shaking his head, Andrew continued to drink in her visage.

Defiance welled up in Cassie's smoldering green eyes. He released his grip and signalled to the groom, who had emerged from the stables at the sound of an approaching rider. The young man led the horses toward the stable, unable to resist taking a long, unbelieving look at Cassandra's incomprehensible appearance.

Cassandra blushed. She asked herself what Andrew meant by "fine in every way." It sounded much like a compliment, but that could not be; he was interested in Alex, so she must have misinterpreted his words. There was *something* between them, though, it was undeniable.

"Lord Andrew, you will have to excuse me. I do believe my father is going to want to talk to me...

or something. And I must greet Alex and my worried mother." Cassandra brushed past him and started to walk toward the house, but Andrew turned and caught her arm.

"Cassandra, how did you know your father had returned?"

"I may do things that others find inappropriate, but I am not in the least bit stupid about doing them," she replied with a note of pride.

"Quite frankly, my lady, you still have not answered my question."

"I have been riding close behind your search party this whole time, so that if by any chance I might have encountered difficulty, you would have been close enough to hear me and come to my aid."

"Well, that may have been the smartest thing you could have done, but you stupidly put yourself in great danger," Andrew chided.

"Now, sir, it is my turn to ask you a question," she said as she looked him in the eye.

"Anything you want to know, I will tell you."

"Why do you display such great concern about me? Is it not the Lady Alexandra with whom you are so enraptured?"

"You said only one question, yet you have managed to ask two. How sly you are!"

"Are my questions difficult for you to answer?"

"No, not difficult at all. But I might have to reveal my plan to you."

"Now you mystify me. Maybe I do not wish to have your answers after all." Cassandra turned and started to walk briskly toward the house.

Quickly catching up, Andrew stepped in front of Cassandra to explain.

Cassandra took a step back, wondering what sort of game he was playing. She allowed herself to take a long, careful look at him. Andrew was every inch as tall as his cousin, with a strong, lean build and sandy fair hair worn in the current fashion. Normally clean-shaven, he now sported a scraggly blond beard, but he had deep blue eyes and full lips that rested on a square jaw. He was certainly a handsome man, even after several days' hard travel.

"Cassandra, I am not at all interested in Lady Alexandra, I..."

She cut him off. "What do you mean, you are not interested in Alex? Do you mean to tell me you have been *using* her for some silly reason, toying with her emotions? Who do you think you are?"

Before she got too carried away, Andrew interrupted in turn. "Cassandra, please, let me finish. I must do so quickly, before your father learns you are home and I have been detaining you! Your family is most worried over your absence.... Please hear me out. I pretended to be interested in Alex because I knew that my dear Gavin loved her!

Gavin went through a most difficult experience with Melinda, after discovering her perfidy. When he then came to stay with me, he was so distraught that he had sworn off women! But that seemed to change when he encountered Alex at that soirée. I have never seen my cousin respond to anyone as he did to her, even while he thought himself most taken with Melinda, and countless women have been throwing themselves at him for many, many years! After Melinda broke his heart., he built a wall around it, and would not allow himself to be loved, or to give love. But... I know he loves Alex, truly and deeply, and I could easily see her return those sentiments. I thought if I made Gavin jealous, he would let his guard down just enough so perhaps Alex had a chance of breaking through... ." He trailed off and took a deep breath.

Finally he continued, "As you know, my plan turned into a horrible disaster."

"I see... you are saying, your concern was strictly for Gavin?"

"Yes, but I am not yet finished," he replied, starting to appear somewhat nervous.

"What more could you possibly have to say? I thought you covered just about everything," Cassandra said, looking curiously up at him now.

"We did cover most all of it, but for one last thing..." And in an instant, Andrew pulled Cassandra close and kissed her with all the passion in his heart.

After a long moment, Cassandra pulled away and stepped back in shock. "What are you doing?"

"It is you, Cassandra, you are the woman for me. The only one."

"Me?" she blurted. "You could have anyone! There are plenty of ladies prettier and more cultured... Why me?" Her astonishment and shock were apparent. Her delight and joy were not.

"There is no one prettier then you, Cassandra. I love your eyes, your hair, your fire, the way you gallop your horse, the fact that you are so strong-willed and independent. I love everything about you, and would like nothing more than to walk this land with you at my side." He shocked himself with his words. He had not planned to confess his secret, tender and overwhelming feelings, but his worries and fears had been building ever since he had been told of her mysterious departure.

"Oh, Andrew, I feel the same toward you!" Cassie surprised herself with her outburst. "But... I thought you wanted Alex, so I could not permit myself to... ." She was speaking without thinking and trailed off in confusion. She wondered how she could possibly feel that she had always known him, although she had barely met him.

He stepped closer to Cassandra again, and drew her into his arms for a lingering kiss.

"Andrew, I want nothing more than to stay

here with you, but I must go," she said softly when at last he released her. "My family must be most worried, and Father is going to have to deal with me for my adventures, as you are aware. I do not know what to say of this situation... but I do know that I must see you again. Let us pray that it shall be soon."

"I am so relieved and gladdened that you share my affections... and that you have returned safely. We shall soon see each other again, I can promise you that! First, we must get through the upheaval around us, and then we shall proceed. "

"Yes... but... we do face one more problem," she looked at him with worry overtaking her happy expression.

"And what might that be, my sweet?" Andrew was wearing a wide grin. He felt completely witless! This little minx had stolen his heart and soul, and he felt like his boots were not touching the ground.

"My coming-out party will be quite soon, next winter's Season. Until then, I am not to be courted! What shall we do?"

"Ah! Do not worry, I have a perfect plan, darling Cassie. I will explain it to you later, but right now I must take you inside." Taking her hand, Andrew walked Cassandra up the pathway to the garden door.

Before Cassandra entered the house to face her father, Andrew placed a tender kiss on her pliant, willing lips one last time. Then they walked side by side into the drawing room, where the gathered family rose in surprise and amazement to see them so soon. Cassandra's father greeted his prodigal child with relief and a bear hug, and nodded gratefully to Andrew over her head, indicating that at last his new friend could depart for Arlington House.

"Cassandra! Do you have any idea what you put your mother through? What you put *me* through? Let alone yourself! You were in great danger, have we reared you to act so foolishly? And — how is it that Andrew found you so quickly?" Daniel's questions were fired off in rapid succession. He released Cassandra so her hovering mother and sisters could embrace her, but he did not stop berating her, and merely paused to take a breath.

"Andrew did not find me, Father," she replied, when she could turn to face him again. "I followed your search party every step of the way."

"Well, bravo! Perhaps you are smarter than I gave you credit for," he countered, with simmering anger, deep annoyance and great relief in his tone.

His disapproval made her cringe. "That is not fair, father. I went off because I wanted to help find Alex! You know that I cannot sit by any more than you can. I would have gone insane waiting in the house as women are expected to do! I *needed* to help."

"Cassandra, I do not care for your reasons. You were given a direct *order* not to leave the house, which you disregarded without a thought as to what consequences might result, or what worries would beset your mother and sister. Not only did you foolishly put your life in danger, you caused your family enormous anxiety with your headstrong decision! You must be punished for your contrary act of rebellion." Daniel walked back and forth, his anger building and his relief almost forgotten.

"Yes, Father," responded Cassie, hanging her head.

"To begin with, your riding privileges are finished, and you shall refrain from all social activities for at least one month. My decision is final. Do you understand?"

With tears in her eyes, she answered with an almost inaudible "Yes, Father."

"After one month has passed, we shall revisit your punishment. Help your mother and mind your deportment. You may go to your room now. You will join us for dinner."

"Yes, Father."

Cassandra's mother had said not one word. Her face betrayed the emotion welling inside her. Before Cassandra could leave the room, her mother stood up and took her daughter by the shoulders and drew her in for another embrace. Elizabeth was angry indeed, but above all, glad Cassandra returned home unharmed. Alexandra and Ashley were sitting quietly but looked like they wanted to leap from their cushions and envelop Cassandra in their arms. They knew better to interrupt when their father was livid and distressed.

"Go now, dear," Elizabeth instructed, with a look at her other daughters that told them to remain seated.

"Yes, Mother." Cassandra went to do as she was told, but turned and looked back at her mother to say, "I'm very sorry, Mother, for making you worry." Turning to Alex, she said, "I am so very glad you are home and safe." To her little sister, she just said, "I missed you." Quickly she left the drawing room and headed upstairs.

Elizabeth differed from her husband in many ways, and one of them was her sense of the rightness of the punishment just meted out to their middle daughter. She felt her husband had acted as though he were conducting a business deal, instead of looking at Cassandra's motivation, her love and concern for her dear sister. Cassie was wrong to do what she did, but a lighter punishment would have been just as effective. Elizabeth did not say anything for now. She knew how to deal with her husband, and, after a few days, when his feelings had had a chance to settle, she would talk with him.

For now her home was peaceful and quiet. All the Rosenshires were at last safe and sound. Surely Richard was likely to return soon.

Chapter Fourteen

"Alexandra, dearest," Elizabeth said, "you must stop brooding. You are not doing a thing to help yourself. You need to get out, start going to parties again."

Alex sat by the drawing room window. Despite her sadness, she had made the attempt to be presentable today, and was wearing a dark blue blouse. It was a rather plain garment and her hair was loose about her shoulders. Since her return, she did not quite feel like herself. She seldom left the house, and when she did, it was just to take a short walk in the gardens.

"Alex, are you listening to me?" Elizabeth stood looking hard at her daughter. She was aware what a difficult time Alex was having, and it made her heart ache. Alex was usually so strong. She had never known defeat like this. But here she was, sitting by the window as though Gavin would be walking up at any minute. She knew Gavin loved her daughter... and she knew progress would take time, longer than a scant few weeks.

Finally Alex responded: "Yes, Mother, I am listening. You are right. I know I should be going to parties again, Father showed me those invitations, but I do not feel that I could enjoy myself. I miss Gavin more then I thought possible... I had no idea he would affect me in such a way. It hurts... so much." Releasing a sigh, Alex turned back to the window.

"Oh, my sweetheart, it is going to take time for your heart to heal, but you must not let this take over your life. You are stronger than this, Alexandra. I will not have you feeling sorry for yourself any longer. Today is a beautiful day. The grass is green, the sky is blue, and the trails through the woods are beckoning. You have always enjoyed this time of year, just before the heat of summer arrives. You and Cassandra should go riding today." Elizabeth was firm, her tone brooking no argument.

"How on earth are we to go riding? Father said that Cassandra was forbidden to do anything for a month, and she still has almost two weeks to go. Not to mention that Melinda was never found! How safe could it be?"

"Your father has his people watching over Bedford House, and the constable is keeping an eye open for Melinda. Word is out all around the village. If you stay close and ride only on our lands, I feel you would be safe enough. Do not worry about your father! I will take care of him. Now, go and find your sister, and change into your habits."

Alex did as her mother directed, thinking perhaps a fast ride might indeed make the world a bit brighter. She ran upstairs to speak with Cassandra. In a little while, Alex came back down in a floral print habit made up in light pinks and purples. A broad purple ribbon neatly restrained her glorious golden hair. Her gloom appeared to have lifted at last.

Cassandra was already waiting at the foot of the staircase, more than eager to be released from what seemed like endless confinement, tired of playing on the pianoforte and selecting her coming-out wardrobe from among the wares certain purveyors of gowns and shoes and tiaras and gloves had been bringing to the house almost every day. "Well, you could have been a little quicker!" Cassandra said impatiently.

"Yes, I suppose so.... When I was speaking with Mother this morning, something she said gave me pause."

"And what would that be?" Cassandra asked, curious as to what her mother might have said to lift Alexandra's mood. This change was more than welcome.

"She said that I am stronger than I was acting, and she is right! I should not let my sadness get the better of me. Gavin left me. Why should I let him affect me like this? I must appear unmoved and strong in my self-worth, and not indulge in self-pity one minute more."

"That's my girl, now you are talking! Would you please explain to me again how it is that I am permitted to go riding with you?" Cassandra asked, not clear on the terms of her parole.

"I am not sure of that myself. I do know, however, that mother said not to worry about it, and we could take as long as we want, within reason."

Alex continued in the direction of the garden door where they were stopped short by Ashley.

"Just where do you think you two are going?" she questioned, indignant to be left out.

"Out for a ride, what do you care?" Cassandra countered.

"Out for a ride! How is it that you persuaded Father to change his mind?"

"Ashley, you are usually not so rude and inquisitive. Mother told us to go for a ride, and said that she would take care of Father. How she might do so, I do not know," Alex replied.

"Oh, I see, well then, please, be on your way." Ashley waved them off with a sniff and turned away.

"Alex, do you not find Ashley's behavior a little unsettling? That was so unlike her," Cassandra asked once they were out the door.

"Yes, I do. Perhaps she has something on her mind. You know what it's like to be fifteen, too old for childhood and too young for everything else." Shrugging, Alex took Cassandra's arm and headed toward the stables. Their horses had been saddled and bridled and a groom held them to be mounted. Both horses seemed more than ready to finally get some exercise, and were stamping their feet impatiently. Greeting their equine friends with delight, mounting up and trotting away, both young women began to experience a sensation of careless freedom for the first time in a long while.

The day was warm and sunny, with a pleasant, refreshing breeze. The air was clear and clean. Summer would come soon, and the fields and forests were burgeoning with life. Beyond the sound of their horses' hooves on the gravel drive, they could hear running streams, chirping birds, and a swooshing sound the trees made as they danced to the tune of the wind.

The horses needed no encouragement to take up an easy canter, and the young women rode an exhilarating twenty minutes before reining in their mounts. Dismounting near a burbling rivulet, they let their horses browse in the clover on its banks. Taking her boots off, Alex said, "Cass, let us dip our feet in the stream, it will feel wonderful!" Soon both girls ran like children along the banks of the little brook, stopping now and then to wade in the coolness of the clear water.

"Alex! I think I see a person over there." Peering through the trees, they could faintly make out someone on horseback well in the distance. They had been quietly enjoying the brilliant day for some little time.

"I think you are right. But we cannot be certain as to who it might be. Cassandra, we should be careful. Melinda has not been caught. Father has the lands under guard, so it's likely to be someone we know... but we should not take any chances."

Alex's abduction had made her newly cautious, and her memories of Melinda's assault were still fresh. "That person is drawing nearer. We must hide behind the trees until we can see who it is. If it is a stranger, we will mount quickly and ride away. Get your boots on."

Cassandra followed her sister's instructions, and, donning their boots, they waited behind a clump of dense shrubbery, holding the reins of their quiet horses, until the rider drew closer. Soon, they could tell it was a tall, blond man. Alex had hoped to see Gavin astride the horse, which was now more quickly approaching.

Cassandra jumped up and shouted with enthusiasm, "Andrew! Over here!"

Alex was sad and disappointed, her hopes crushed. However, this was not a total loss. Perhaps Andrew would share information as to his cousin's well-being.

"Lady Cassandra, Lady Alexandra! What are you doing out here alone?" Andrew asked as he rode up.

"We thought it was too beautiful a day to waste, and decided to go for a ride. Why do you ask?" Alex questioned.

"I thought that your father would have been more protective of you two, at least until Melinda is caught." Dismounting and standing not far from the girls, Andrew's gaze was on Cassie as he answered Alex. He knew he must stifle his affections until her début, but his feelings were overwhelmed by the sight of her. He so wished to rush to her for another sweet embrace!

Gavin still would not admit his feelings toward Alex. He had told Andrew that it would have been a waste of his time to make sure she got back to safety, if she were not then to remain safe. And so Andrew had promised Gavin that he would determine that Alex was no longer in danger.

Andrew, rightly taking his cousin's words to mean more than such superficial interest, had been quietly patrolling the vast lands around Bedford house each day, seeking a glimpse of the young women, and signs that all was well there. At last, his purpose had been achieved.

"Father is not a fool, Andrew. He has the whole estate well guarded. All the men who joined his search parties have been taking it in turns, day and night, to make certain all is well. The constable comes around as well, and he has alerted everyone in the village. Any stranger coming near will be stopped immediately and questioned. You slipped through the cordon because you are well known by those guards." Cassandra answered him.

"I may have made it through, however, I did not see anyone, nor did anyone let me pass," Andrew replied with a puzzled look.

"Andrew, if the sentries were able to be seen, they would not be able to catch anyone! They would be frightening off the very people they hope to capture," Alex responded.

"Very good. I do not know where my head is today, but it is not resting on my shoulders."

Jokingly, Cassie said: "You are forgiven this time, but next time we will take your head." Playfully, she danced around him with a slender branch as though she were a knight with sword in hand.

Alex and Andrew laughed at Cassie's antics and walked over to the stream as he released his horse to converse with the others. Alex had something on her mind, and her preoccupation was well-reflected on her face.

"Lady Alexandra," Andrew said quietly, "is there something troubling you?"

"No... Why do you ask?" she replied softly, not wanting to draw Cassie's attention, looking down at the stream, and hoping to avoid the question.

"It appears to me that you are not content." Andrew asked, trying to catch her eye.

"Please do not concern yourself. I am just bothered that no one has caught that dreadful Melinda." Then she gazed up at his face. "Your cousin... is he all right?"

"Gavin is just fine, of course. Why do you ask?" He well knew why, but hoped she might be honest about her feelings.

"No reason in particular. It's just that he helped me get home, and I wanted to make sure he was well recovered from our... adventure. Just my curiosity, that is all." Making her way over to a little bed of violets, Alex bent and picked a handful of the tiny blooms. "Cass, I believe I will bring these home to Mother," she called. "Are they not exquisite? What an aroma!" Smiling, she walked along the bank toward Cassandra, picking as many violets as she could carry and genty tucking them into the pockets of her skirts.

Her sister had slowly approached them, hoping to enjoy the sound of Andrew's voice but not wishing to interrupt.

Andrew was soon standing next to Cassandra, drinking in her beauty. The sun's low rays now danced upon her shining hair, casting a delightful red glow. Her eyes in this dappled light were exuberant, a green as deep as the finest emeralds. She was wearing a dark green riding habit with a subtle lighter green for the trim. It did wonders for her, showing off her slender, lithe young figure and her brilliant eyes. Ah! A classic in her own right, he thought to himself. Andrew had been quiet and serious for a time, but was suddenly unable to repress a happy grin. Cassandra asked, "Andrew, are you quite all right? Why are you smiling like that?" Her brows arched with interest and hope.

Shaking his head he said, "Yes, my lady, I am well, I am fine." Still wearing a big smile, he stepped closer to her and placed a light kiss on her forehead.

Alex was looking into the water and daydreaming, and did not catch sight of their dalliance. Then she had a thought that caused her to rise and walk over to Andrew to ask, "Andrew, why are you here today?"

Caught off guard, he stood a moment gathering his thoughts. Not wanting to let on that he was there to assure himself of their safety, especially Cassandra's safety, he finally responded, "I realized soon after I was recovered from the journey that I still had one of your father's horses, kindly lent me for the ride home. And he has my favorite stallion. So I thought I would come by and tell him we would be trading horses shortly. His gelding developed a little lameness, so I have been letting him rest. I know he would have sent a groom over for him, had the horse been needed."

"Why not just send a messenger?" Alex asked reasonably.

"Well, today I happened to have time for a ride, and thought, why not just tell him myself. I became rather fond of the redoubtable Daniel's company when we traveled together, and I would be happy to encounter him again."

"I see. Andrew, it is pleasant to see you, under these so much less distressing circumstances." Alex dropped the subject and started to walk back to the horses, telling Cassandra they should head home now, lest they worry their mother— or their father note their absence. Andrew agreed and felt as though he had been gone long enough from Arlington, as well. He felt he must keep a close watch on Gavin to be sure Melinda should not succeed in abducting him next time. He felt certain she would try again.

"Andrew, thank you for keeping us company today. Please, won't you join us again sometime?" Cassandra asked.

"I would love to. For now, I will leave you both so as not to keep you from your family. I will see you at a later date. Good day." With a polite tip of his hat, Andrew mounted and rode off.

"Cassandra, I find it rather strange that you invited him along on one of our rides. Why, not that long ago, you were upset that he had joined us, and now you're asking him to return. I think you may like him after all," Alex teased.

"You never know, now, do you?" Cassandra replied, giving her sister a wink. Both girls laughed. It would be an unspoken secret between them until the time was right for sharing it aloud.

Alex felt a little twinge of jealousy. Andrew could not hide his interest in Cassie, and love would be so simple for them! They're both attracted to one another and would enjoy a whirlwind courtship. They would simply have to wait until her formal presentation to Society, whereas for Alex, her love was doomed, unless Gavin changed his mind.

The ride homeward seemed much shorter than the ride out earlier that day. The sun was still shining brightly, it was still warm and the sky still blue, but the afternoon was growing late. Not wanting to worry their mother, the two soon dismounted, patting their horses fondly, handed their reins to a stableboy and walked briskly toward the house.

"Alex, I don't think we should mention that we saw Andrew today," Cassandra said.

"Whyever not?" Alex replied.

"Well, we were only supposed to be out for a ride together. I do not want Mother to think we went against her wishes."

"Very well, but I still do not see the issue. We ran into Andrew merely by chance."

"Did we?" Cassandra replied with a hint of intrigue in her voice.

Alex looked up at her sister knowingly. "Cassandra, do tell me what you are talking about."

"I will tell you more... soon. Right now, we must let mother know we are safely home." Taking Alex by the hand, Cassandra opened the garden door.

"Lady Alexandra, Lady Cassandra, do wait a moment, if you please," said Alex's maid, approaching them courteously.

"What is it, Sara?" replied Cassie, feeling a little guilty about her assignation with Andrew, and afraid somehow she was in trouble again.

"Your mother asked me to tell you that your father thinks you were out picking flowers today. So should he happen to inquire what you did, you will know the answer." Sara smiled at the two young women, happy to take part in their little conspiracy. She handed over a little nosegay, freshly picked from the estate's gardens.

"Thank you very much, Sara," Cassandra replied. She smiled to Alex and added, "So that's how Mother took care of that."

"Yes, thank you, Sara. Would you be so kind as to find a way to arrange these woodland violets in a way that will please Father." Digging the tiny purple blossoms out of her pockets, Alex glanced at her sister. "Come, Cass, we must change quickly before anyone else sees us in our boots and habits."

Andrew arrived back at Arlington House in a little while and walked in with a gallant smile on his face. He had found the one for him, and patience would be his virtue. Damn! If only she was of age! But she wasn't, and until she had her grand début he would just have to wait. For now their feelings for one another would have to be their little secret. *How Gavin stays away from Alex I shall never understand*, Andrew ruminated. *Those lovely*

sisters! Shaking his head, he walked toward the study to enjoy a sip of brandy.

"Well, did you enjoy your ride today?" A somewhat shabby figure in black emerged from the darkest corner of the room.

Turning to face the shadow, Andrew answered: "Yes, I did indeed. Is there anything I might help you with?"

Nodding, Gavin asked, "How is she?"

"By 'she,' you are referring to the estimable and courageous Lady Alexandra?"

"You know that I am, must you tease me unmercifully?"

"But of course! What other way is there?"

"Fine, make me wait. But you will please answer me. How is she?"

"She is fine. Perhaps not as cheerful as before all this happened, not quite so light-hearted, but I assure you, the lady is fine."

"Thank you. That is all I needed to know. I will leave you now to savor your brandy." Gavin started to brush past him to the door, but Andrew reached out an arm to stop him.

"Gavin, wait. I so need to know... how do you do it?" Andrew asked him.

"How I do what?"

"How do you keep your feelings for Alex so well buried?"

Gazing at the carpet, Gavin took a slow

breath before replying icily, "I do not know what you are talking about," shook off Andrew's grip on his shoulder, and started to walk out of the room.

The sincere concern in Andrew's voice followed Gavin with his words. "I know you, Gavin, and I know that you have feelings for her, and someday you must give in to those feelings. I just hope that it's not too late by then."

Turning to face his cousin from the doorway, Gavin asked quietly, "Too late for what, Andrew?"

"She cannot remain unmarried forever in this world, and the older she gets, the slimmer her choice of husbands shall be. Maidens of her years can die on the vine and overnight be regarded as spinsters, even if they are beautiful— they are assumed to be damaged goods, unworthy of the finer gentlemen. Rumors build. But she will not remain alone much longer. Soon she shall be married off to someone she does not love, and you will end up alone. Give in, Gavin. Give in while there is still time." Andrew turned back to the crystal decanters. He felt his words would have greater impact if Gavin thought about them for a while.

Gavin considered his cousin's advice as he retired to his rooms, Jack at his heels. He wondered whether Andrew's words would be proven true. Alex was not *old*, not yet, and certainly she possessed enviable good looks, amazing poise, and a sharp mind. She would never have to settle for some man who did not find himself in her thrall. Any man would! However... if she holds a love for me as such as I hold for her... she will never be truly happy with any other man, no matter how much he might adore her. Pacing on the carpet in front of the fireplace, he said aloud, "God help me, I am doing this for her own safety! I must do what I feel right, and though I may have doubts... this is for the best!"

Deciding finally that perhaps a ride would help clear thoughts of his Angel from his worried mind, he headed for the stables. On the way out, Gavin asked a footman to please inform the family that he if he had not returned by dinner, they should commence without him.

Leaving the drive of Arlington House, Gavin soon urged the fine mount to an easy canter, with Jack following along, glad to be out for a good run. Gavin had no idea where he was going, but he knew that leaving this place was fruitless, because no matter where he went, the only thing he would see would be Alex: Alex in the shabby little cottage with barely any clothes on, Alex pressing herself against him on the narrow cot they shared, Alex with her lips of roses, her scent so earthy and intoxicating he could inhale her for the rest of his life. If only it would be so!

These last few weeks, Gavin had stubbornly

refused to let his valet shave him. His hair was always rumpled-looking because he drew his hands through it so often. He had disdained most of his wardrobe and might be seen lurking around the house in a dressing gown, when not secluded in his rooms with Jack, eating very lightly from trays the concerned cook kept sending up. He had had nothing to drink in the way of spirits, and bathed seldom. He had tried to distract himself by reading novels and poems, extracting volumes from the library almost daily, but nothing could take his thoughts away from Alex for long. He was not sleeping well. This morning, Stephen had at last persuaded him to take a bath and don somewhat shabby but most comfortable garments that had been long hidden in the back of a wardrobe. He had allowed his new beard to be trimmed and his nails to be tended. But no matter the valet's ministrations, his mood had not lifted.

The day remained unseasonably warm as the light started to fade. A gentle breeze and the speed of his horse kept him comfortably cool. Kicking his horse to a gallop, Gavin thought he would escape all his frustration the faster his horse ran, knowing Jack would catch up. Then, before he realized the direction he had taken, he was in full view of Bedford House.

"What am I doing here?" he asked himself, halting his horse in surprise. He changed his course to avoid the grand drive, and made his way slowly through an orchard, finally circling his mount around to stand hidden in a copse of slender trees at the edge of the gardens, where he could dismount unseen. Gavin hoped that perhaps he might catch sight of her. One of those curtained upstairs windows must be hers! There was only one with blue hangings, opened now to let in the fine breeze. He knew well that blue was Alex's color. The last of the day's sun shone right on the window.

"This is pathetic," he thought. Shaking his head after a few minutes, Gavin was about to remount when he glimpsed a silhouette in that window. He knew it was Alex even at this considerable distance. Trying to make sure his horse was well hidden, he watched, crouching behind the shrubbery, his heart pounding, weakness rolling over his entire body. Lord! She really had found her way into his heart. His plan was proving to be a lot tougher to execute than he had at first imagined.

For her sake, he must remain strong! He tried to justify watching her as if he were merely assuring himself of her safety. He strongly felt the need to offer her his own protection, even were she to be unaware of it, no matter her father's strength and power. His heart told him that she had been given into his personal care, and would be so forever. She was his Angel, from the first day he saw her, and would be until the end of time. Watching over her was all he wanted to do. Jack arrived at his feet, panting hard, and gave him a delighted bark of reunion.

Alex had bathed again after tea and a rest, and Sara would soon come to dress her for dinner. She stood by her window in her dressing gown, hopelessly dreaming in the purple light of sunset. Perhaps one day she would find some man who would love her, and want her, and say so. As soon as that thought had flickered through her mind, a darker vision appeared, in which she was quite alone, and lonely, and old, her parents passed on, her siblings rearing families of their own. "Oh, please! I pray for God to help me," she said out loud.

Then Alex thought she heard a dog bark, and peered toward the back of the gardens in the gathering gloom. Where the orchard began was where the sound had come from, she thought. Something caught her eye. Yes! There, over in the trees, she had a glimpse of movement of some sort. There was no reason for a dog to be in the gardens.

Gavin saw her peering in his direction after rising to quiet Jack. "Damn if she saw me!" Deciding now would be a good time to leave, he stuck close to the trees and when he thought it safe to mount, he proceeded back toward Arlington at a walk, with Jack trailing behind him.

"It was he, it was Gavin, I know it!" She flew out of her room and down the stairs, nearly toppling her mother, who was headed toward the dining room.

"Alex, my goodness, what has gotten into

you? You are not dressed!" her mother asked.

"I saw him, Mother. He was watching me at the window. I saw him!" she said, nearly out of breath.

"Who, who was watching you? Alex, I do not understand!"

"I am sorry, Mother. I heard a dog, then I could just make out a horse and a man by the trees at the edge of the gardens, and I think when he saw me looking, he got nervous and left. But I know it was Gavin! He does care, I just have to see him... ." Alex was heading for the door as if to run away. She did not even have shoes on her feet.

Taking her daughter's arm, Elizabeth walked Alex toward the stairs and told her firmly, "Dear, I do not think you should get your hopes up. You cannot be certain that it was he, correct? Those trees are a long way off. It could well have been one of the guards."

"I did not see his face— I can't know who it was for certain— but I know Gavin has a dog— I just *know* it was he, Mother!" Alex went on excitedly. Her hopes were renewed, and her heart overflowed. All her heavy cares had lifted.

"Just be careful. That is all I want to say. I do not want you to keep hurting yourself over and over again." Her mother's voice was soft and gentle.

"I will be careful, I assure you, Mother." Alex kissed her mother's cheek and ran upstairs to dress for dinner, calling for Sara.

Chapter Fifteen

More than two weeks passed, but Alex had not seen her mysterious rider again. For the first week she did exactly what her mother had told her not to do— her hopes soared higher and higher as she lingered by one window with a particular view as long as there was enough light to see the distant trees. By the time a second week had ended, those hopes had long come crashing down. Richard stayed for a few days, then returned to the townhouse in London, but she hardly spoke with her brother, or walked in the gardens with Cassie, or amused herself with Ashley's games.

One early afternoon on an overcast Sunday, Alex told her mother she was going for a ride to do a little thinking. Elizabeth, worried over her daughter's delicate emotional state, nodded in acknowledgment and permission.

Meanwhile, at Arlington House, Gavin suddenly announced in a rush, "Andrew! I cannot wait any longer!"

"For God's sake, Gavin, what in the world are you talking about—and why do you sound so daft?" Andrew responded.

"It has been over two weeks since I saw her in the window. That scene appears over and over again in my mind, and I cannot be strong any longer!"

"Gavin... are you saying what I think you're saying?" Andrew asked, cautiously optimistic. He had been approaching despair himself, while trying to devise a way to invite Alex and the entrancing Cassie to Arlington House without the inclusion of a chaperone.

"Yes! Damn it, yes! I need her, and I can't live without her," Gavin answered with great ardor. He was almost shouting.

"Well, quit wasting time, and go get your woman!"

Gavin was through the drawing-room door before Andrew had finished speaking, on his way to claim his angel at last. He did not even think to bring Jack.

Alex quickly donned her purple riding habit, leaving her hair falling about her shoulders. Soon she was urging her gelding into a gallop, as if his speed would lift her despondency. In a little while they arrived at her favorite woodland glade, where she had picked violets with Cassie, and there Alex dismounted. The water in the stream was warmer now, and the trees so green that despite the clouds overhead, the bucolic beauty around her was vibrant and lush. She dismounted and loosed her horse to graze in the clover, then took off her gloves, boots and stockings so she could dip her feet in the refreshing current of the little rivulet and dabble her fingers in its clear waters. Soon she felt a sense of relaxation for the first time in many days. But even the soothing waters and the pleasant little grove with its sprinkling of fragrant violets did not allow her to forget how sad and lonely she always felt, ever since she had found Gavin— only to lose him.

Riding at an easy canter, eschewing the carriage roads and taking a short-cut on rural paths through the deep forests and broad farms that separated the two estates, Gavin knew he was nearing Bedford House when he heard a certain little babbling brook on his left. He slowed his mount as soon as he espied a purple-clad figure sitting on its mossy bank a short way downstream.

"Could it be?" He wondered... he hoped. He turned his horse in that direction and approached at a quiet walk.

Alex's reverie was interrupted when she thought she heard the jingle of a bridle's curb-chain, and at once she stood and hid herself behind a big tree. She cautiously peered in the direction of the noise, hoping to see a sentry, but ever concerned about Melinda's return.

Her stomach leapt, and a rush of intense feelings stopped her breath for a moment. She could recognize that horse and his tall rider anywhere— meanwhile, he knew no woman in any nearby county sported such glorious golden tresses.

"Angel!" Gavin shouted as he drew close enough to be heard.

"Gavin, is it you?" Alex shouted back, thinking she might be lost in a familiar dream.

Vaulting from the saddle before his horse had halted, Gavin ran to Alex, crushed her to his breast, and kissed her lips with overwhelming passion.

At length pulling away, Alex took a step back, her hands on his shoulders, and gazed up into the handsome, adoring face of the man who had appeared before her so many times in her nightly visions. "I must be dreaming... this cannot be real! I have waited so long for you, so long... ." Shocked, her voice trailed off. She was speechless.

"No, you are not dreaming, Angel. I am here with you now, and I want us to be together always. I know it seems sudden, but my Lord!— I cannot live without you! Can you ever forgive me for wasting so much time— apart— when we might have been together?" Gavin asked urgently, appeal and sincerity and hope in his voice, gently drawing her closer.

"Oh, Gavin, I can forgive you as long as we shall never be separated again!" She lifted her face for a long, hot, sultry kiss, tears of joy and ardor streaming down her face.

After quite some time, they drew apart, just arm's length, the better to look into one another's eyes. Alex wiped away her tears.

"Gavin, I must ask. Did you stay away because you were afraid Melinda would come back?"

"Yes. I was afraid for you. It seemed likely for her to seek vengeance against you. I tell you, I had no idea that she was so deranged, so dangerous! I knew she was wicked, but I did not grasp the extremes she might go to— until it was too late, and we were in her clutches. Needless to say, she has not been back, and it's been weeks since that horrible night. I have started thinking, hoping, that perhaps... perhaps we won't hear from her again. There is no way I can be without you one moment longer!" Gavin pulled her close once again.

Alex leaned slightly away and asked softly, "What if she does come back?"

"Then I shall always be at your side to protect you." Gavin dropped to one knee, took her soft hands in his, gazed up into her azure eyes with his deepest feelings brimming in his own dark orbs, and added firmly, "If you will have me."

"Gavin, yes. Yes. Yes! And... I want to be with you... completely." She firmly pulled him to his feet. "I am ready for you. I was ready the night I first met you." Alex was looking directly into his eyes and gently caressing his face, making sure she had memorized every part of its familiar contours. She knew she sounded wanton, immodest, unladylike, but she didn't care. She needed him. Her heart had been bursting with these feelings since that night at the soirée, under the stars. Soon it must explode!

"Are you very, very certain, Angel? I do not want to rush you. I want our first... time... to be special for you, perfect for you." He was whispering in her ear as he gently placed light, feathery kisses on her face and neck, yearning now to tear open all the buttons of her prim purple habit.

"I'm more than certain. Besides, haven't we taken things rather slowly, so far?" Alex's smile was seductive, her expression eager. They were both remembering the long days of their dusty travels, when they had nestled so tightly together, each yearning to *know* more of the other.

"What about your father's guards? It would not do, to be observed."

"We will simply walk over to this dense copse of trees and shrubbery and use it for cover." Without waiting for a response, Alex took Gavin's hand and led him a few yards, ducking under low branches to enter into a secluded spot. "As good as my father's sentries are, they can't be everywhere at once on an estate this large."

Gavin squared his shoulders and took a breath, trying to regain control of himself. He looked deeply into her eyes. "I shall be gentle with you. I want to make sure your pleasure is as great as mine will be."

"Why? Is something going to hurt?" she asked, for the details of lovemaking were all new to

Alex. She only had some vague ideas gleaned from observing animals, and a few rather confusing fragments from her governess when she was about seventeen years old.

"Oh, my Angel, so sweet and innocent. This is your first time. The first time for a woman may be a little uncomfortable, but I promise to do all I can to make sure any pain only lasts for an instant. After that, I will take you to another world where only your pleasure exists." He placed a long, soft, tender kiss on her willing lips.

"Take me, Gavin! Take me to that world," she begged, not trusting her continued ability to stand, breathing in his kiss and sinking to kneel before him on the soft, sun-warmed, mossy ground, in the dappled light of their own private bower, grasping his hands and pulling him down to face her.

Hidden between the densely spaced trees and bushes, lit by a tiny ray of afternoon sunshine, they traveled inch by precious inch to the world of intimate pleasure and delight that only two partners deeply in love may share. Kneeling close, Gavin slowly unbuttoned Alex's purple jacket and slid it gently off her shoulders, making sure as he undressed her to kiss lightly each new area of her skin as it was exposed. He carefully undid the tiny hooks of her pleated bodice and drew it away. Following his lead, Alex unbuttoned and removed Gavin's shirt, to expose his brawny chest, finding the sight of his masculine, well-muscled body once again had made her quiver. His chest was so broad and strong, sparsely covered in fine, dark, downy hair. She lay her cheek against the warm skin of his breast and took in a deep breath, drinking in his manly scent as if it were the nectar of the Gods.

Gavin carefully unbuttoned the skirt of her habit, drew it off with a little help, and spread it on the soft moss. Each of his actions was slow, gentle, adoring. Her blouse followed, then her creamy, starched petticoat, with its drawstring waist, he untied and slipped down and off, as Alex smiled up at him, her eyes on his face, seeing the care and delight and affection written there. Her deeply ruched and ruffled whalebone corset was soon undone, and followed her petticoat onto the pile. She took a deep, happy breath of freedom. Soon the thin blue silken ribbons of her chaste ivory chemise were untied at its deep neckline, and it slipped quickly over her head as Alex lifted her hips a little to help free it. Now she was clad only in her lacy, long, beribboned drawers.

Gavin proceeded to study with great care and attention every little shapely curve of her pink, blonde nakedness, admiring her full, round, youthful breasts, her slender arms, her shapely calves, her flat belly. His hands rested on his knees as he gazed upon her body, head to toe, for a long minute.

"Angel, you are so perfect, so utterly lovely," he breathed, as he leaned down to place a soft kiss on her right breast, just above its rosy center. Gavin's lips and the tip of his tongue lingered upon the right, the left, the right breast, slowly, lightly circling but not touching her nipples, paying them close attention as they signaled her arousal, becoming longer, darker, larger. His weight rested on his hands, one on the moss on each side of her ribs as she reclined on the skirt of her habit. He touched her only with his mouth. Alex reached up and gently stroked his neck, resting a fingertip in the delicious hollow at its base.

Then she blushed. This was all so new to her. Unsure quite what to do next, she inhaled his scent again slowly, taking in a sense of being comfortable, safe, loved, appreciated. She felt... worshipped. She relaxed with a happy sigh, and closed her eyes to experience the touch of his mouth without the distraction of his good looks.

Gavin slowly made his way a little lower, lightly covering each morsel of her torso with kisses as soft as the wings of a butterfly, until at last his mouth rested upon the ribbon-ties of her ruffled silken drawers. Alex remained almost frozen, not out of fear, but so intensely savoring every feathery, delicate, loving touch that she was unwilling to move a muscle, lest she miss one instant of this novel pleasure and intimacy. Experiencing searing heat from his lips was so new, and so intense... the hairs on her arms were standing up, and she was surprised to notice a pleasant, strange, tingling sort of moisture developing in a very private place. Her nipples had surely never felt like this before! Her every sense was on alert, waiting, ready, yearning for more.

Gently, drawing out every action, Gavin pulled loose the ties of her drawers with his beautiful white teeth. At last using his hands again, he gently, slowly, drew down the drawers, and cast them on the little heap of discarded clothing. Now that Alex was entirely naked, Gavin paused again for a long moment, drinking in the slim, lovely, rounded, womanly but youthful form that lay relaxed and still before him. The smile on her angelic face was beatific as she lay breathing deeply. He delicately, slowly, smoothly ran his fingertips up her inner ankles, calves, and thighs, starting from the arches of her feet, using soft, brief strokes, pausing every second, finally halting when he had almost reached the delicate blonde triangle that hid her most inner desires, desires he was about to unleash. Alex's thighs were starting to fall open, though she was not asking them to do so.

"Wait, Gavin," Alex said, opening her eyes, sitting up and reaching to take his hands in her own.

"What is it, Angel? Is there something wrong?" he asked, surprised and concerned, feeling as though he had been awakened from a dream.

"Yes, something is wrong." Alex paused to catch her breath, and shook her head to emerge from her reverie and rapture. Then she continued, "Here I am, entirely naked, and yet you are still half-dressed!" Her tone was lilting, loving, teasing, inviting.

"Well, I can change that." He stood up and doffed his boots and stockings, then began to unbutton his trousers, but Alex stopped him.

"Let me. I want to please you, and make you feel how you have made me feel."

She rose onto her knees and carefully undid each button, finally pulling the trousers down to his ankles so he could step out of them. She cast them on the pile. Noticing the large shape trying to escape his drawers, Alex was a little nervous, feeling unprepared for what a man might look like when fully aroused. A thought of her horse's anatomy passed briefly across her mind.

She took a breath and continued, feeling completely alive, willing and eager. Nothing could stop her now. Reaching back up, she carefully unfastened his linen drawers and let them drop. Gavin's manhood stood up straight and long and proud. Innocently, she guided her hands around it, admiring and exploring for the first time a firm, manly beauty never before encountered.

Standing then, she kissed Gavin on the lips and took two steps back to admire the naked man before her. "Gavin, you are so appealing, so amazing, so very handsome and strong," she whispered, studying the sight before her with overwhelming pleasure. She stepped close to slowly run her fingertips lightly down his face, his neck, his chest, his belly, and at last, the length of his hard, reddened shaft. A sigh of agony escaped from Gavin's lips, his control almost failing him. Pulling Alex close, he gently lowered her to the habit-covered moss and knelt between her legs. She loved the way her body felt something all over whenever his skin was touching hers: naked, warm, perfect, exhilarating, and previously unknown.

Keeping his eyes on hers, Gavin gently placed his right hand on her most intimate place, and observed her lovingly as she gradually abandoned all her poise and self-control, soon writhing off the ground to thrust up her hips and deepen his touch, her moistness rapidly increasing under it. Her eyes had closed and her mouth had opened a little, with small, involuntary moans soon escaping her lips. Alex did not want him to stop, though she thought she might soon die of this exquisite pleasure! Easing his now-wet fingers slowly in and out along the ceiling of her most private cavern, he hoped to bring her closer and closer to her moment of ecstasy. He then explored carefully with his fingertips, seeking her maidenhead, to slowly, gently, gradually stretch its little opening larger and larger, until it had at last relaxed to a welcoming size, more than equalling the girth of his personal magnificence, which was now calling urgently for relief and release.

Ignoring his importunate organ, Gavin leaned forward, resuming his rhythmic stroking with one hand, his other hand close above, finger and thumb gently seeking and finding and caressing another special place. Alex could not stop her hips from moving in time to his efforts. Eventually he took one hard, tall nipple into his mouth, to stroke its length lightly between his tongue and his upper teeth.

At this, Alex begged him, "Stop! Gavin, please! You must take me now! You're driving me insane, I have never felt such... such... such passion!" Drawing his face close to her own with both hands, she bent his tall form to her, and kissed his lips with such ardor and greed, Gavin could not deny her what she demanded. He lifted her hips and guided himself into her, smoothly, firmly, gently. She received him with gladness, and no pain at all.

Alex swooned in ecstasy, her eyelids fluttering.

"Are you all right, Angel?" he whispered to her.

"Oh, yes! Never stop what you are doing, please do not stop!" she whispered back, transported.

Gavin gathered her up into his arms and held her close as he knelt, deeply thrusting inside her. Rocking back and forth, they held each other tightly as they continued their journey into mutual, joyful, expanding pleasure. Alex found herself experiencing wave after wave of indescribable peaks of delight, and wondered if they would ever stop. Gavin at last permitted himself to release his own passion with an irrepressible moan, and almost fainted from the explosive moment, having to catch himself quickly and regain his balance lest he let all his weight collapse forward upon her tender, soft, eager and voluptuous body.

Smoothly, together, they rolled down to lie face to face, never releasing their embrace, limbs tightly entangled. He vowed never to leave her, never! There was no denying their love, there would be no going back. They would forever savor this pleasure they took in each other, now, the now that lasts forever. And always. He covered her face and eyelids and ears and neck with passionate kisses as she tried to catch her breath.

"I love you, Gavin," Alex whispered, after a long spell, as she caressed his hair, his brow, the precious little hollow at the base of his neck, relaxing at last the intense grip of her thighs and sighing deeply.

"I love you too, Angel," Gavin replied, spent, as he gently rested his head against her generous, soft breasts, continuing to hold her very close as she released him.

"Gavin?" Alex questioned. "What will happen next? I mean, where do we go from here?"

"Angel, I intend to wed you, as soon as is proper, and then make it known to all men that you are forever mine. Starting, of course, today, with your father. I will let him know at once that I wish to have your hand in marriage, and I shall ask his blessing. However... until Melinda is in gaol, we must only let our families know. Agreed?"

"Yes, you are right. Gavin, I am so glad that we are finally together. I am yours forever and always. Nothing will come between us now." Alex placed a kiss on top of his precious, beautiful head.

"Alex, every day we must meet here, between luncheon and tea, until we may safely be seen in public. If one of us cannot get away, a message must be sent. In this way we will always be assured of one another's safety. Now, I think, before our families start to be concerned, we must head back." Disentangling gently and standing up, Gavin assisted Alex to her feet and they helped each other to dress, finally turning this way and that, checking each other over for signs of disarray.

"Gavin, before we part, I have a question for you."

"What is that, my love?"

"I would like to know what it is my future husband does for work, if you do in fact have work. Perhaps you just sit in the House of Lords and argue. It is silly, I know, but I need to know everything about you. I did learn that you are a Duke. This whole time, I should have been addressing you as Your Grace!"

"My family has long been involved with the trading of textiles. It is a very old and prestigious company, that long, long ago helped gain us our Duchy. Andrew is active with the business as well. Our reach is long and broad, and should you ever call me Your Grace, it will be urgently required for me to spank that perky bottom of yours!"

"Impressive," she said, as she smiled up at him and took his hand. "I shall endeavor never to be so formal with you."

Embracing again to savor one long, sweet kiss after another, they resolved next to tell her parents about their feelings and intentions, after which Gavin would ride to Arlington House to speak with Andrew.

Returning hand-in-hand to their drowsing horses, Alex put her boots on and they rode together to Bedford House at an easy loping gait, to walk briskly inside as soon as their reins were in the hands of a groom.

The Rosenshires were seated in the drawing room, waiting to be served their afternoon tea. Gavin strode right up to a surprised Daniel, who was leaning on the mantel, and formally requested Alex's hand in marriage, with a little bow to acknowledge Elizabeth and indicate he hoped for her blessing as well.

Elizabeth rose from her chair and embraced her daughter warmly. "Oh Alexandra, I am so happy for you," she said with a big smile and a warm kiss.

Then Elizabeth pulled her close and whispered in her ear, "I knew that stubborn man would come around!" and both women laughed. Elizabeth could easily see how her daughter was bursting with joy, all any mother could hope for.

Daniel, too, was happy with this turn of events, having seen at once that Alex's deep despondence had at last fled, but he remained concerned for his lovely, precious princess. "Yes, indeed, I agree that no one but the most intimate family members should have the glad news until we have more information about Melinda's whereabouts. That evil, vengeful woman needs to be caught! She must have gone into hiding, to strike again when we let down our guard. We must remain vigilant. I am adamant. No further violence may ever happen again to my little girl!" He paused briefly.

"And..." Daniel added, "We do not stand on formality here. If you would be so kind as to permit me, I prefer to address you by your name, rather than by your title, now that we shall soon be of one family."

Gavin appreciated the closeness of the Rosenshire clan, and was delighted to be welcomed into it. He preferred for his title to be forgotten in many informal situations. He responded, "I am most pleased by your acceptance of me as Alex's ever-devoted soon-to-be-husband, and I vow that your beautiful, entrancing daughter shall always enjoy my personal, and most assiduous, protection." He warmly shook hands with Daniel, then with Elizabeth, who drew him into a hug.

Cassie was jumping up and down, her hands over her mouth to stifle squeals of delight. As soon as she could, she embraced her big sister with joy and happiness, and Ashley did the same.

As a bottle of Champagne was brought up from the cellars and shared, Daniel inquired as to Gavin's background, knowing little of the Blake family or the Chatham duchy, having had more pressing concerns during the days he had spent with Andrew.

Gavin described his situation forthrightly, without a hint of hauteur. He had recently come into his father's half of an old, well-established firm known as Blake's Textiles and Clothing, along with a rather considerable sum of very old family money. He had been involved in these affairs since finishing his degree at Oxford, working at his father's side. The other half of the company had gone to Andrew upon his father's demise a few years back. When not visiting Arlington House, as he often did, Gavin made his home with his mother on his vast ducal estate known as Chatham, southwest of London.

The Rosenshires had been impressed with Gavin ever since he had helped Alex return safely from the frightening abduction, and Gavin returned their growing, warm affection. With daylight now fading, he wanted to return to Arlington House before Andrew started to worry about him. Politely declining tea, just arrived, and taking his leave, he made sure to find his Angel alone one more time before mounting up to depart.

"Gavin, you have made me the happiest woman in the world," she said, as she turned her face up for a deep, soulful kiss.

"And I, Alex, am the luckiest man who ever lived. It is most rare for a man to find a true Angel to love, but I found *you*, and I shall never give you up." Holding her tightly, Gavin gave Alex the most sensual, passionate kiss she could endure.

Alex took his overflowing love in, right down to the tips of her toes, and finally released him with reluctance. Gavin left Bedford House feeling more happiness than he had ever imagined to be possible. The delight and passionate intimacy of lying with her still overwhelmed his senses. He felt warmed by Alex's love despite the early evening's growing coolness. His horse sensed his joy, and galloped off with a toss of his head.

The sun had just sunk below the horizon when Gavin arrived at Arlington House.

"Andrew, where are you? I have news you must hear!" Gavin shouted as the butler admitted him, astonished at his sudden change of demeanor.

"Good God, man! This must be good news! Your noise could wake the dead!" Andrew yelled back from his study, relieved at Gavin's obvious change of mood.

"Good news! Yes." Gavin strode into the study. "I have seen Alex, and nothing on this earth will ever separate us again," Gavin said, beaming broadly, his joy apparent in his bearing. "I have spoken with Daniel Rosenshire, and Alexandra and I are now betrothed, with his blessings."

"Well, congratulations, Cousin! Couldn't happen to a better man! What comes next?"

"Well, first, I must ask you not to say a word to anyone. The only people aware of these events are the Rosenshires and yourself. You may tell Amelia and Catherine if you should see them first, of course, but the servants must be instructed to refrain from all gossip," Gavin threw a glance of warning at a nearby footman. "I ask you this because I do not want one word to reach Melinda of our betrothal. She could be most dangerous to Alex, and myself. Until that perfidious wench is caught and safely under lock and key, Alex and I will not be seen together in public."

Gavin went on to tell Andrew how Alex's family had reacted. Observing everyone's happiness with the match, and noting Gavin's boundless joy at last emerging from the long, grim bowels of darkness, Andrew felt a toast would be appropriate, and sent the footman for an old and treasured bottle of his very finest Champagne.

At Bedford House, Alex was celebrating as well. Everyone was happy to see her win the man she had so desired from that first moment in London, even the staff. Her mother wore a satisfied smile, having known it would be only a matter of time before Gavin came around. Cassandra was happy for her sister, but could not help but feel a little sad, for she, too, was in love, yet had to find her patience each day, and wait her turn to experience what her sister was enjoying now.

Alex's father was pleased and delighted and a little relieved that his oldest daughter had found love at last. The passing years with no serious courtship in view had been a concern, if not a worry. Elizabeth had warned him of the hidden feelings between Gavin and Alex, so their betrothal had not come as a surprise. Overlooking the situation with Melinda, for which, he knew, his daughter was partly to blame, he felt that Gavin was an honest, decent, trustworthy and likable man. The love Gavin felt for Alex was now as apparent to Daniel as it had long been to his wife, and he felt certain it was genuine. However, a preoccupation with his daughter's safety had not left him since he had first learned of her abduction, even after her safe return. As long as Melinda remained at large, Daniel would remain on guard, no matter how much he approved Alex's long-awaited match.

As for Ashley, she thought it was wonderful that her recently-gloomy big sister was at last happy, and in love. Someday she, too, would experience this joy and companionship. Her mother and father had promised she would.

"Oh, Mother, I do not think I could ever feel this wonderfully happy again," Alex said, fully enjoying her moment.

"You may not feel *this* happiness, Alexandra darling, but there will be times in your life when you will feel a similar, not very different happiness, that will lighten your heart and give you a feeling so wonderful, tears will form in your eyes," her mother said softly as she held her eldest daughter close.

"Such as what?" Alex asked.

"Such as when you and Gavin have your wedding day, and the first time you hold your own sweet babe. There are many different feelings of happiness, and they make up a long list of times full of wonder."

"Oh Mother, I can hardly wait until Gavin and I shall share a home as husband and wife!"

"I know, dear, but remember, time goes by very fast. You must always savor each moment you have together." She kissed her daughter on the forehead. Walking over to her husband, she placed a kiss on his lips and softly whispered the words "I love you" to the only man she had ever loved.

Chapter Sixteen

This early summer afternoon was ineffably lovely. The lands of Bedford House were aglow with sunshine, every field and garden and woodland bright and cheerful. Alex was just setting off to see Gavin, and having difficulty concealing her eagerness in front of her family.

They had met secretly each day without fail. The excitement of the relationship was so new and enthralling, passionate lovemaking hardly seemed sufficient to express their ardor; they could not experience enough of each other, each overwhelmingly in love, each ever hungry for more and more and still yet more of the beloved.

A broad smile seldom left Alex's face, and her eyes always sparkled with life. The moment she wed Gavin would mark the public proclamation of their love, that it would last forever, that no one could ever come between them. Often, Alex would lie abed at night and dream about walking down the aisle and taking his hand and... she wondered just how long would she have to wait! The day could not arrive soon enough.

By age twenty, most women of her class, by far, had already started their families. Alex knew her Society friends in London had no idea she was spoken for, and she longed to describe to them all how lucky she was, her continuing spinsterhood's still being a topic of gossip. Soon she would have everything a woman could want and more, the man she loved and a family of her own, to say nothing of a duchy. She dreamed of moving into Gavin's homes and how lovely they would be. There would be vast gardens at the Chatham estate, a large townhouse in the City, new trails to explore with her horse. She dreamed of bearing Gavin's first child, and the nursery they would furnish, and the many children that would follow. She let herself drift into a dream as she rode forth to meet her love.

Gavin had already arrived by the stream. He too, was in his own happy world. He knew how very content he was going to be for the rest of his life, now that Alex would always be beside him. He vowed, once wed, his adored Angel would never be farther away than he could reach. Not having ever imagined the possibility of loving any person so much, he yearned to be one with her always. It was a feeling that was so intense and indescribable, only another person in love could understand... and he could imagine few couples except the Rosenshires who would grasp exactly what he was thinking about.

Gavin continued to wait for Alex for what seemed like an eternity... but, these days, every moment away from her was agonizing. At last, she cantered up to their special woodland spot and halted her horse.

"Alex, thank God! I was starting to get impatient," he cried, as he swept her off her mount and into a close embrace.

"Thank you, Gavin." Looking up into his beloved, familiar, masculine features, Alex placed a warm and affectionate kiss on the tip of his square chin. Leaning down, Gavin captured her lips with his own in a rapturous way that caused her knees to weaken.

When he pulled away, Alex asked coyly, "That was nice. Would you mind doing that again?"

"Not, at all, my Angel." Leaning in once more, his kiss was deep and long. He thought her kisses were intoxicating. She thought his kisses were delicious. They were utterly lost in their embrace.

Their passions consumed them in each secret daily rendezvous, but lovemaking was not all they did. They walked and talked and laughed and lay by the bank of the stream, planning their future. Soon they would be able to shout their love to the world, but for now, with Melinda's whereabouts still unknown, this time together would remain their private joy.

The friendly sun was beginning its descent behind the hills as they sat by the brook with their arms around one another, already anticipating their next meeting. The western sky started glowing pink, reflecting their contented, peaceful mood. The days were growing longer.

"Gavin, I wish we never had to say farewell, but I am late for tea," Alex said softly.

"I know. This is always my least favorite part of the day as well. Remember, Angel, soon we will be together forever, and then I shall never be separated from you again."

They shared a tender farewell kiss, then reluctantly rose and mounted their horses. Gavin accompanied Alex most of the way home, and when he felt she would be safe, approaching the big drive of Bedford House, he blew her a kiss and waved his adieu. Daniel had been clear that Gavin must not come to the mansion, hoping to lessen the chances of any rumors reaching Melinda. Gavin turned and glanced back at Alex to see her horse and her lovely form enter the drive, then urged his mount to a gallop.

Alex's horse picked up a stone in his shoe, so Alex dismounted to walk him the rest of the way. Although nothing had changed, the grounds of Bedford House lately seemed to posses a beauty she had never before noticed, so she liked the thought of lengthening her sweet journey. "Ah, to be in love, how very grand!" she laughed to herself.

The horse stopped favoring his leg, but Alex was enjoying the walk so much she did not remount.

Alex soon heard the sounds of an approaching horse. She wondered if Cassie might be setting out for a quick run before dinner. A rider was soon revealed, rounding a bend in the long drive where it looped around some tall trees. She was shocked at the sight. "What are *you* doing here?" she demanded, wide-eyed with surprise to see Lord Harrison approaching.

Halting his horse and dismounting, the man declined to answer, hoping his silence would make her nervous, as it did. Backing away with her horse slowly, Alex was suspicious of his sudden appearance. It felt like an attack. She asked again, "What are you doing on this estate?"

"Lady Alex, tell me, do you like playing the whore for that man? Gavin Blake, is it not?" he questioned with a haughty sneer, walking closer.

Staring back in utter disgust, Alex demanded: "How is it you know of him? And how dare you call me a whore!"

"Very naive, my dear. I have been watching you, so I know that you will perform for me as you did for Blake, and that I will thoroughly enjoy myself. You will be coming with me now. While I would like to say hello to your dear parents, we do not have time for that."

Alex realized that he must have been in hiding close to the streambank where Gavin had been making love to her each afternoon. The guards must have only been told to watch for Melinda, and let Harrison, a well-known neighbor, go by. No one had suspected Harrison to be much of a threat.

Alex shouted, "No! No! I will not go with you! I will not make love to you! Oh, God, the thought of it makes me sick! I despise you! Gavin will not let you get away with this! He will kill you!" While screaming, Alex dropped the reins and tried to run, but she did not get very far. Lord Harrison tackled her and whispered in her ear, "I did not *ask* you to make *love* to me, I *told* you to have *sex* with me."

Harrison knocked Alex unconscious with one swift blow to her temple. Quickly throwing her limp form over the back of his horse and fastening her roughly in place, he mounted and made a hurried departure, reaching for the reins of Alex's mount to buy more time. A smug expression crossed his face, satisfaction that a plan was working perfectly. He was confident that when his partner saw his work, the rest of the plan would fall into place as well.

Daylight grew into darkness, and the warmth of the sunny afternoon yielded to the coolness of night. Bedford House was vibrating with worry, and nothing else. "Wherever could she be, Daniel?" Elizabeth asked again as she paced the floor of the drawing room. She knew something was terribly amiss. No one had had much appetite for the evening meal, as Alex was always home in time to join them.

"I do not know. She has *always* returned well before this hour. It is time to send a rider over to Arlington... perhaps the Blakes know something we do not." Crossing the room past his wife to ring for a servant, he brushed his fingertips gently against her cheek and they exchanged a wordless look. The butler appeared at once. Daniel instructed him to pass the word for a fast horse to be saddled, and to produce a footman, who soon was in the doorway, doffing his cap to Lord Rosenshire.

"Ride at once to Arlington House and speak there with Lord Gavin Blake. Should he not be present, you are to inform Lord Andrew, instead, of our growing concern over Lady Alex's inexplicable absence. She has not come home from her afternoon ride. This is urgent. Do not spare your mount. Lord Gavin must return with you at once."

The footman was soon headed to the Blake estate at a gallop, where he dismounted near the front door, ran up to it and used the knocker with force. Waiting only a moment for a response, he knocked again even harder.

At the peremptory summons, recalling the visit from Melinda, Gavin opened the door warily, to find an unfamiliar and liveried stranger and a very fine but lathered horse, who was blowing hard.

"Is there some way I may assist you, young man? You have come from the Rosenshires?"

"Yes, Your Grace, yes, do you know where the Lady Alexandra may be?"

"And who might be asking?" his growing concern apparent.

"Forgive me. Your Grace, I am Derrick, from Bedford House. My Lord Daniel Rosenshire sent me here to speak to Lord Gavin Blake or Lord Andrew Blake. He is most worried for his daughter Alex, as she has not returned from her afternoon ride."

"What? That is impossible! I escorted her home. We were in sight of Bedford House, just by its drive." Gavin grew pale, and a sudden, sickening feeling overwhelmed him. He had been home for an hour or more.

"So she is not here," Derrick said.

"She is not, but I am returning with you. Something is wrong."

"Yes, Your Grace. Please, sir. Let us leave at once." Derrick turned to take a few steps and remount his horse.

Gavin shouted for Andrew, passed the word, and ran to the stables. He quickly bridled the fastest stallion, too rushed to wait for a saddle. They galloped back to the Rosenshire lands, pushing their mounts hard, Gavin leading Derrick the back way through the woods and fields to shorten the distance.

Back at Bedford House, Daniel had once again sent for help from nearby farms, called in all his sentries, and mustered every servant who could sit a horse. Men were already searching the grounds thoroughly, and finding nothing. Female servants were walking through the gardens and lawns with lanterns.

Daniel was beside himself with worry and Elizabeth was in tears. "Not again. Please God, let her be all right. Let my dear Alexandra be with Gavin." As Elizabeth finished her heartfelt prayer, she opened her eyes to see the butler escort Gavin into her drawing room. Elizabeth at once sank to the floor in a swoon. Daniel ran over to his wife, carefully scooped her up, and gently placed her limp form on the chesterfield by the fire.

"Elizabeth? Elizabeth, are you all right?" He tenderly shook her shoulder and after a long moment, she opened her eyes.

"Are you all right?" he asked again.

"Yes. When I saw Gavin was alone... I realized something horrible has happened again to Alexandra."

"Yes, dear, something is wrong. Just remember that we got her back before and we will do it again." Daniel leaned forward and kissed his wife gently on the forehead. Patting her hand, he stood to look into Gavin's face.

"Gavin. How could you not escort her all the way home? You know that Melinda has not been caught. You both remain in great danger." Daniel's tone was cold and bitter. He was thinking of chaperones again. Too late. Again.

"I rode Alex to within a few feet of your drive, as we had agreed I should not come in. I watched her... she was almost here! This looks bad. I am just as terrified as you are. I cannot understand for the life of me what could have happened to her..." He paused to take a deep breath, compose himself, and continue.

"Daniel. Please make no mistake. I will find her! I promised her that we would never be apart again, and I meant it." Balling his fists as he spoke, Gavin was anxious to get moving.

"Perhaps you did make that promise. However, as I see it, you have already broken it," Daniel snapped.

Gavin said nothing. Perhaps he deserved the blame. He could have seen her to the door, but they had all agreed.... Pity the person who has interfered, he fumed, because that person will not be living very long once found!

The butler spoke quietly to Daniel. "My Lord, the horses are saddled, and a message has been sent to the constable."

"Gavin, let us begin our search." They turned and departed for the stableyard, as Daniel offered a reassuring nod to Elizabeth.

Just as the men were about to mount, Gavin tapped Daniel on the shoulder.

"What is it? We must not waste time!"

"I must ask you— where were all the men who were guarding your estate? How is that no one saw what happened?" Gavin was looking Daniel straight in the eye.

"I cannot say for sure why none of my sentries saw what happened, but you may rest assured that I will take care of them once my daughter is safe at home. However, you are not blameless. You should have been more careful!" Daniel turned away and mounted his horse. His worry and frustration were almost too much to bear, so soon after the first abduction.

"I do blame myself, and I always will," Gavin replied.

Soon the two men were galloping forth.

Chapter Seventeen

"Melinda! Melinda, darling, where are you?" wheedled Harrison from outside the open door, leaning his head just inside while remaining concealed.

"I am right here, my love," Melinda trilled, as she came out to meet him from the back of the remote cabin.

"You are *really* going to like my surprise," he announced with pride.

"It better be what I asked for," she responded impatiently.

"Oh it is, dear. It is!" Harrison, with lifeless Alex draped over his shoulder, stepped inside and pulled the door closed behind him, then unburdened himself and to lay his gift before Melinda.

"Well, well. You are not a total idiot after all!"

Dalton Harrison took offense and his reply was icy. "Do not treat me like a servant. Remember, I am not just another of your goons, who quit because they could not stand sight nor sound of you. Need I remind you of this? I have high standing in Society. You are merely a woman, do not forget that!"

"I may have the body of a woman, but I am smarter and more ruthless than any man. *You* do not forget *that!*" Melinda said, snapping her gaze around to sneer up at him in anger and disdain. It aggravated her whenever he brought up Olaf and Edgar, who had demanded their pay and abandoned her the moment they received it. They had refused to endure more of her arrogance and malice at any price. Because of their untimely departure, she was forced to work with the despicable Dalton Harrison, whom she believed now was no more than a stupid, childish boor.

Dalton turned his attention to Alex.

"Alex, wake up, my precious." He vigorously shook her by the shoulders.

Alex responded to his rough handling and opened her eyes. To her horror, Melinda was standing not two feet away!

"Oh, put your eyes back in your head, young lady. I do not know why you are so surprised! If you remember our last conversation, I am quite sure I mentioned that you had to die."

Alex pulled herself up to a sitting position, closing her eyes against a splitting headache that even the poor light of a kerosene lantern seemed to intensify. She turned her head away from it. Melinda was going on.

"Now, imagine my surprise when I learned that you were not *really* married to Gavin. So many people love to gossip. It was not difficult to discover that you were that beautiful *spinster* everyone has been talking about. I decided to ride out your way. Avoiding those silly guards was not difficult for someone like me. That is where I encountered Dalton here. Can you image my disgust when I realized what it was that he was so preoccupied watching? The thought of it makes me sick! Gavin touching you like that...Ah! Well, the sight— and sounds— only fueled my ambitions. Your escape did spoil my plan last time, but I can assure you that no such thing will happen again. Your timely demise will occur within the hour!" Melinda's prideful countenance was transformed by a delighted smile at this thought.

Alex could listen no more. "Why are you going to such extremes? Gavin did not want to marry you because of your own actions. *You don't even love him!"* Alex shouted. She was so frightened, and her head ached terribly, and she would say anything that might buy time to escape or be rescued. But who would know where to look for her? As she looked around, she knew she was in desperate trouble, and this time... she was alone.

"Alex, you are such a naive child. What on earth does *love* have to do with anything? Love has nothing to do with revenge! I must repay Gavin for embarrassing me, breaking my engagement, ruining my good name. He shall not get away with it! I was born to be a Duchess!"

"You did that to yourself," Alex replied, a little calmer. "Had you not been sleeping with someone other than Gavin, your name might still be worth something. Being the woman you are, your name was destined to be mud!"

"Why, you little witch! I would rather my name be mud and remain alive, than have the reputation of an angel and be six feet underground!"

At this point, Harrison interrupted. "Melinda, remember our deal. Before anything happens to her, I must make Alex mine. What a lovely memory for her to take to her grave. Do you not agree, Alex?"

The thought of his appalling intentions made Alex feel quite ill, and she let him know so. "I would rather die now then have you lay one finger on me!"

Melinda let out a raucous laugh. "Harrison, you do bring out the best in people."

The imperious Dalton Harrison grabbed tiny Melinda by the arms and hissed "Shut up, little woman, I have just about had it with you!"

"Take your hands off me! I would not hesitate to kill you if you gave me an excuse." Melinda's low, threatening tone dripped with venom and hatred. Her cold black eyes were void of all emotion.

Harrison released his grip and turned away so neither woman could see the fear in his face. He was easily frightened and not a proficient fighter. He knew that thinking for himself did not come easily. However— the more he was around Melinda, the more certain he was that he could kill her, if need be. He was coming to believe that soon he *must* kill her, because she could easily kill him without batting an eye, and she well might try it.

"Well isn't that cute, a lovers' spat!" Alex interjected.

"I advise you to keep your remarks to yourself. I will not hesitate to kill you if you continue to irritate me. You should be thanking that tall dolt over there. If it were not for his base desire for your living body, it would already be growing cold." Melinda's warning tone was soft, and promised to make good on her threat.

"I think I would prefer that to anything he has to offer," said Alex as she stared at them.

"Well, we do not always get what we want," Melinda answered, and left.

Lord Harrison walked out after her, so Alex quickly looked around, rubbing the knot on her temple. Her limbs were not bound, but the only way out was the front door, very near which Melinda and her other vile captor were standing and talking. The windows she could see had been well boarded over on the outside. A small tidy kitchen occupied one corner of the room, and in the opposite corner were two little bedrooms, their doors open, beds made up neatly. This was no ordinary rustic cabin, however remote or secret its location. It was clean, with braided rugs on the floor. Crisp, sprigged curtains hung at the windows, and the hearth had been swept. The walls were hung with the mounted heads of dead animals. Alex considered that this might be one of Harrison's father's hunting cabins... unfortunately, he bragged of having ten hunting cabins sprinkled throughout rural England, Scotland and Wales. How long had they traveled to get here? Two hours? Most of the night? All she knew was that no light came through the windows.

Harrison entered and was coming near her. Too close for her liking.

"You really should think about what you are doing," Alex warned him, edging toward the kitchen.

"And why would that be, my lovely?" he asked, reaching for a lock of her golden hair.

Alex recoiled from his touch. "Because no matter what you do to me, Gavin will find you, and he will kill you, whether I am dead or alive."

"Oh, stand still, young lady! You're not going to get away from me. This cabin is not all that big. Oh, and... Melinda is sitting right next to the front door. If you get out that way you are out of the frying pan and into the fire. But you can't! She has locked us in. Isn't that romantic?" He taunted her in an oily tone as he sidled closer and reached to grab her breast.

Alex stepped quickly away, placing the kitchen table between them as she slapped away his hand. "Stop it! I will not let you do this to me. You are deranged! Gavin will kill you!"

"Lady Alexandra. Spare me these threats about Gavin! He does not know where to find you, nor does he know who has taken you. He may think that Melinda has something to do with it but... there is no way would he ever put the two of us together!"

"Don't count on it, you stupid fool. He is a very smart man and my father is just as bright! The first thing they will do is ride over to your father's estate and find out your whereabouts," Alex's tone was defiant and confident, and she hoped to buy time.

"Whyever would they do that?" he asked with surprise.

"My father knows all about the day you attacked me and tried to ruin me, so you are an enemy in his eyes. And as no one knows where Melinda is, he will question your father and every other neighbor first thing, to discover if any strangers have been sighted near Bedford. When he gets to your father's place and finds you absent... this will raise suspicion and spell trouble for you!"

Briefly he considered Alex's words, and then replied: "I think you're rather optimistic on that one, my dear." He lunged and chased her around the table until, losing patience with the game, he dove across and clutched her around her waist.

With all the strength she could muster, she reached out for a rickety chair, raised it high, and let it come crashing down on his head. His body went limp as he slid to the floor. Realizing the noise would be heard by Melinda, Alex quickly grasped the chair again, hoisted it over her head, and waited just behind the door.

The door flew open. Melinda glanced around, and seeing Dalton's crumpled body, shouted, "You idiot! What are you..." But Alex was summoning all her strength and nerve, empowered by her deepest fears of rape and murder. With another loud crash, Melinda fell unconscious. Alex ran from the cabin and saw her horse tied up close by with the others. Moving as fast as she could, she untied the reins, leapt on his back and urged him into the dark forest, asking him to gallop where there was no path, ignoring her reins and stirrups and clutching his mane.

After riding about twenty minutes, trying to keep the moon in view to keep her from turning in blind circles, she pulled her loyal gelding to a stop, beginning to feel more cautious. Crashing through a forest at night as fast as possible is not a quiet process. After listening hard over the horse's loud breathing and not hearing any pursuit, she coaxed her mount forward, praying that something familiar would soon appear. Soon there was a little stream, and the going was more open along its bank. She followed it upstream.

"That whore!" Harrison shouted upon coming to his senses, shaking with rage and anger as he rubbed his aching head. Seeing Alex had escaped, he headed after her, not to be denied. Melinda's limp form was stretched out near the door. He chose not to wake her. Instead he lifted a glowing lantern from its hook and departed.

Grabbing his reins, he took a moment to find the fresh tracks impressed in soft earth and leading straight into the forest. Soon he was on her trail, holding out the lantern whenever it was needed to reveal her path.

Alex was now cantering her horse along the banks of a little river, the woods becoming more open and changing from oaks to evergreens. Her stomach was nothing but nerves. The more she urged her horse to continue, the more she realized how lost she was.

"Please God, let me find my way!" she prayed out loud, in hope of divine intervention.

Easing to a stop, she dismounted, walked him to the water to drink, then knelt and splashed cool water on her face and neck. There was more light as the moon rose higher. Standing, she took a careful look around in the dim moonlight. She made a frightening discovery.

"Oh, no! How could I be so stupid?" she asked herself. "My tracks! Tracks as far as the eye can see. They're going to find me!" In a desperate hurry, she remounted, and rode through the shallows hoping for a place where the river offered a good place to ford. When that plan did not work out, she turned for the shore, rode up the gentle slope of the bank, and turned her horse back into the forest.

Harrison had been following Alex all the while. "That silly little girl," he laughed to himself. He knew that it was her desperation that kept her from thinking clearly, and he was pleased she was making herself so easily followed and found.

He pulled up to the river where Alex had stopped not ten minutes earlier. Climbing down, he examined her tracks closely. "Fresh, good! She should be right ahead of me." Remounting, was unable to find the next trail. Again dismounting for a closer look, he saw the earth was harder here. These were pines and other evergreens, and the thick bed of needles beneath them did not hold impressions. Around them were little clearings of hardened earth and gnarled roots. It was barely possible to find a path through them while dodging their branches. But he knew what direction Alex was taking, so having her tracks was hardly necessary any more. He was so close he would soon hear her. He extinguished his lantern and cast it aside.

Back at the cabin, Melinda was awake, furious, overflowing with rage. "Damn that whore to hell! God help Harrison when I find him!" she screamed, in anger and disappointment and outrage.

She was aghast that he'd had the gall, the effrontery, to leave her on the floor! Not that she would have given a thought to helping him, of course. That man did not know his place. It was entirely his fault that this had happened, for without his lust to deal with, she would have dispatched Alex right away.

Melinda hated Alex with a deep and boiling passion. Alex was kind, cultured, well-bred, beautiful, educated, bright, younger by at least five years, had plenty of money of her own... and could easily win the affections of any man in the whole country. The fact that Gavin had ended up with Alex turned her stomach. Now Melinda intended to take Alex out of the picture for good.

It was time for action. Melinda walked to her bedroom, unlocked her carryall and removed a fine smooth-bore flintlock pistol, with its balls, rod, and other necessities neatly fitted into a cunning little case. She made sure it was clean and ready, returned it to the case, tucked it into the capacious pocket of her dress, and strode outside to her horse.

Alex slowed her pace. She was tired, and hungry, and completely lost, as her horse slowly picked his way through the trees. She listened carefully to the sounds of the forest; the trees whispered, no birds chirped, sometimes animals rustled amid the shrubbery. No noise of an approaching horse or person.

"How will I ever get home?" she asked herself in a whisper. Suddenly, she heard a nearby noise. She had no time to react as Dalton Harrison came charging right at her and knocked her to the ground. She remembered nothing after that.

Harrison tied up the horses. He was tired from transporting Alex all through the night. He did not want to drag Alex all the way back to the cabin until he had rested, and he was not sure of Melinda's welcome there. He would just wait a bit and have a rest right here, and proceed when daylight had returned. He sat down where Alex lay and cradled her head on his lap, running his fingers through her hair in anticipation of her waking. She had to be awake before he would take her. It would be much more gratifying to watch her eyes as he overpowered her, to savor her terror as he thrust himself into her.

Melinda also grew tired, having slept little in recent weeks, especially since arriving at the cabin the day before. She sat against a tree uncomfortably, and wrapped her arms around herself to think. The woods were dense here, and tall trees blocked most of the light of the moon. It would be sunrise soon. Her discomfort only fueled her anger. She must find her prey! For an hour, she practiced loading and priming her firearm though she knew she already could perform all the motions swiftly, accurately, without looking. Then she placed the pistol and the items it would be needing in her most accessible pockets, without the case.

Chapter Eighteen

Asking everyone around Bedford about what they had noticed in the area since tea-time, finally they talked to a farmer who had been tending to a hilltop field toward the end of the day. He thought he might have recognized Dalton Harrison's bay mare, with a rider too distant to identify, leaving the neighborhood of Bedford House in the late afternoon, some sort of strange bundle bouncing behind the saddle. This detail caused the farmer to recollect the sighting, although he had enjoyed a pint or two by the time Gavin found him in a public house.

Daniel and Gavin rode to Harrison's nearby estate at once. Their suspicions of his involvement were confirmed when the Earl could not explain where his heir might be, or why his horse had not returned to the stable. The young man had been riding out often lately to destinations unknown.

Gavin and Daniel spoke at some length with the Earl, who denied his dear son could possibly take any part in a kidnapping. Gavin had to describe to him the day Dalton Harrison had assaulted Alex. "Proof, young man, proof! I need proof of such a wild accusation against my son. Especially as he is not here to defend himself!" the Earl bellowed and blustered, knowing well that his son was foolish, headstrong, and not very bright.

"Proof, I will give you proof!" Gavin responded with heat. "I was there that day. I was the one who tackled your son when he was chasing down Alex at a full gallop! I heard her screams of terror a half-mile away, and I was the one who knocked your son off his horse. Now I see that I should have killed him!" Gavin was bursting with fury, and found he had balled his fists, about to unleash his anger on this angry old man.

Daniel soon demanded that the Earl produce a list of all his properties, then determined which ones Dalton was most familiar with, and which were most likely to be unobserved by neighbors or passers-by. The Earl, grasping his errant son's folly and mischief, eventually drew a map to every property he owned. Finally his patience came to an end. "Get out! I have been cooperative. I have given you locations. I cannot help you any further!" His dismay at his son's behavior was equal to his anger as he stalked from the room.

Finally the men rode out again, some dozen strong, planning a route that would take them to the likeliest hideaways within reach.

"Well, Gavin, it shan't be long before we find that sorry person. I knew in my heart Harrison had something to do with my daughter's disappearance! It is the only explanation as to how anyone got past the guards. For that I blame myself. This damned Harrison was not even a thought at the time I set the sentries, and the men would recognize him as a near neighbor who had been courting Alex." Daniel shook his head out of frustration and guilt.

"I agree, my lord. Harrison has something to do with Alex's disappearance, and God help him when I get my hands on him. He will not live long! I cannot believe that he acted alone. He does not strike me as capable. From what I have heard of the man, he's a coward."

"I have heard the same. And we are armed with enough men and weapons for a war." Daniel 's determination was still growing. "It is not likely to be much of a fight."

Gavin rode onward in silence. His need to hear and sense everything around him was becoming intense. He had failed to keep his Angel safe, and his grief and regret overwhelmed him. He should have been there for her. He should have seen her all the way home. He had been careless, and now Alex was paying the price. For all the days of his life, he would never forget this one, and never again would he allow such a disaster to occur.

They soon visited two of the Earl's nearest hunting cabins, learning nothing, travelling through the darkness with the aid of a few lanterns. Grimly they proceeded to the next.

As dawn broke, Alex opened her eyes slowly, sensing considerable pain in her head and chest and a cramping hunger in her stomach. Slowly she brought herself up to a sitting position and was startled when a big boot pressed on her shoulder to crush her back down.

" Is that really necessary?" she asked, as loud as she could manage.

"Alex, you never cease to amaze me. Here you are, caught again, and you want to question my every action." Pacing back and forth, Harrison tried very hard to look like a domineering bully. "This time, there will be no talking, there will be no pleading, your time is long overdue!"

Seeing a look of horror in her eyes, he pulled a knife from his boot, and growled, "Lie down flat if you know what is good for you!" and, terrified, Alex obeyed. Harrison placed the tip of the blade at the base of her neck, and harshly sliced it down through all the layers of her clothing. Her skirt, jacket and inner garments fell open, excepting only her chemise, which was slit in several places, exposing delicate white skin and revealing the perfect shape of her breasts beneath its thin lawn fabric. Alex had a line of vertical scratches down her body where the chemise was rent. The thin red line was starting to well up with tiny droplets of red blood.

"Oh my God, no!" With fear controlling her every action, Alex fought to regain her modesty, pulling at all the ruffles and pleats and laces, but finding no way to cover herself with her garments destroyed. Harrison was still in control and he still had the knife, and he knelt between her legs now.

He had only to rip open her chemise to expose her full, round breasts. The excitement welling up made him shake with anticipation. Slowly, holding the knife lightly to her neck with his right hand, he slid his left hand into a slit to grasp a tender, firm mound.

Letting out a whimper, tears rolled from Alex's eyes. Then she drew in a slow, deep breath and let out a scream that could be heard for a mile. He quickly removed his hand from her breast, and placed it firmly over her mouth to silence her.

"Try that again and I will use this knife on your pretty throat! Do you understand?" he warned, uncovering her mouth just enough to permit a reply. "I watched your lover do much the same, and *then* your noises were completely different."

"I would rather feel the blade of that knife in my neck than have you touch me one more time," she said, fiercely refusing to let her tears fall.

"It does sting a bit to know that you would rather die than have me touch you. But not enough to make me *not* touch you. If you scream again, I will use my blade on your pretty throat. It matters little now whether you are alive or dead."

Harrison bent over Alex, right hand carefully controlling his knife, left fumbling to unbutton his breeches from the wrong side. He had learned nothing from that earlier encounter. When he saw Alex close her eyes, he assumed that her resistance was over and she had accepted the inevitable, but he was wary and kept the knife on her ivory throat, pressing lightly, enjoying the sight of another little upwelling of blood under its blade.

Alex summoned all her strength and attention, and finally brought up one knee as fast as she could, striking him hard enough in a tender spot to make him fall away and drop the knife. Leaping up and trying to clutch the front of her garments together, she fled to the nearby riverbank in the early light, changing her direction to go back the way she had come, hoping to be seen and rescued somehow. Then she remembered she could have taken her horse. And she realized Melinda might find her first! Too late now. She kept running like the Furies were chasing her, finding good footing on the soft clay riverbanks. She had considerable pain in several places. The petticoat was interfering with running, its drawstring slashed. She let it fall to the ground and ran away from it. Soon most of her tattered garments followed, leaving her in her ruined chemise, drawers, stockings and boots.

Hearing the scream, Melinda arrived where Dalton lay cradling his privates. She could not believe Alex had managed to escape again.

"You fool! How could you let her get away from you?" Standing over Harrison, Melinda felt like kicking him in the same spot. But she needed him to get up and help catch and subdue Alex. She roughly forced him to his feet, as he continued writhing and stooping in pain.

"Melinda, stop! Enough! I am in considerable pain!"

"Through no fault of your own? How might a stupid wench like that manage to outsmart you not once, not twice, but three times!" she shouted at him angrily. She soon mounted her horse and waited impatiently for Harrison to do the same.

"She cannot get far. She is on foot," he managed to say. "This adventure was not supposed to be so taxing."

The search party had finally reached the right cabin, relieved to find signs that someone had been there recently. There was a carryall in each bedroom containing items for one man and one woman, several kerosene lanterns, water, a little food. Signs indicated a hurried departure, and a broken chair in the well-kept place suggested a struggle. Gavin was positive it was Harrison and Melinda. And dawn would soon break.

"Daniel, there is something I have to tell you." Gavin said as he stood in the doorway of the cabin.

"Just tell me, do not play games!"

"Melinda is involved. It is far more dangerous for Alex than we thought, as she has proved she has defenses against Harrison. Melinda is heartless, violent. We must find Alex at once!" They were soon all mounting their horses, a man having discovered the trail of hoofprints entering the wood.

When they heard a scream of terror Gavin and Daniel glanced at each other in despair. Perhaps they were too late. They rode blindly into the forest well ahead of the rest of their men, hoping to find the source of that devastating sound.

Alex, out of breath and tired, a stitch in her side, heard two horses behind her. Their hooves beat like drums on the hard sandy bank. The sounds grew louder as they neared. Her captors taunted her and yelled her name, but still she pressed on as best she could. She did not stop. The light was a little better now that the sun was rising at last.

"Stop! You cannot outrun our horses!" Melinda shouted, enraged. Alex did not stop.

"It will hurt far more if we have to make you stop!" Melinda shouted at her again.

The cramp in Alex's stomach had grown much worse, worse than the sharp stitch in her side. Something told her to stop, a feeling she could not identify. Finally she brought her mad rush to a halt. She panted, leaning against a tree, and waited for her captors to do what they would.

"Daniel, these tracks... ." Gavin had memorized the Earl's map. They were ahead of the men and had paused to let them catch up. "One party must follow the river, the other should head through the woods over there," he advised.

"I agree. I will take half my men into the forest. You and the others follow the river. We will meet up somewhere ahead." The men nodded and separated, divided their riders who had just caught up, and spurred their tired horses forward in the first of the sun's gentle rays.

Melinda dismounted and walked up to Alex. "Ever since I first saw you, you have been nothing but trouble." Melinda walked in a circle around Alex, laughing and leering at her pitiable condition. She continued: "You do not resemble an angel now. That is your little pet name, isn't it? If Gavin could only see you! Do you think you would strike his fancy? I think not! But I could be wrong. So... to ensure that you will not ever strike anyone's fancy again, I am going to kill you, right here and now." Melinda pulled out her loaded pistol, swiftly added primer from her other pocket, cocked it with a click, and pointed it at Alex's forehead from a few yards away with her arm extended straight, taking careful aim. She was a good shot, especially at this short distance.

Alex had nowhere to run or hide, and could think of nothing to say that would prolong her life. She held her chin up proudly and attempted to show confidence, fearlessness and poise.

Harrison at this moment vaulted clumsily from his horse and stepped in front of Melinda. "Wait just a damn minute!" he shouted to her. "We had a deal! In case you have forgotten, I have yet to cash in on my half, I get to stick my shaft in her first, remember?"

"My God! All you do is think with your rod. Put it away and think with your head for a minute. She has escaped you three times, it is not meant to be! Now get out of my way, before I have to shoot you to get at her," Melinda demanded, making it clear that she meant her words.

He was fed up with Melinda and this threat to his life was the last one he was going to take. Early light was glinting on Alex's golden locks. He charged Melinda like a bull in a ring, reaching to wrestle the pistol from her hand. It went off with a loud explosion and a cloud of smoke. Alex closed her eyes in horror.

When she opened them again, she couldn't believe what she saw. Harrison's body was lying motionless atop Melinda. Alex stood frozen a moment. She could not tell whom had been shot. Slowly she edged backwards into the river, hoping this would put enough distance between her and whoever would rise. Suddenly there was movement.

Alex watched as Harrison's body slowly rolled off Melinda and stopped short in an awkward, unmoving pose. It was he who was shot!

Alex shook her head back and forth. She finally turned to run and thought if she could make it to the other side of the river, Melinda would have a harder time catching up.

"Stop right there, *princess*! You're not going anywhere! Turn around!" Melinda shouted as she finished reloading, her movements swift and sure. She let off a careful shot over Alex's head. She wanted to see the damn wench's face when she died. She reloaded swiftly.

Alex froze, startled by the explosion. Turning slowly, she saw Melinda was raising the pistol and aiming straight at her heart.

"Did you really think that I would ever let you get away? You are such a fool! I told you I would have my revenge, and so I shall!" Melinda's evil nature dripped from every syllable. Her voice was louder and more raucous than ever as she recovered her hearing.

Alex threw her head back, squared her shoulders and waded toward Melinda, glad she still had her boots on with these sharp rocks underfoot. She knew this tattered chemise was transparent even when dry and fought against the vulnerability of being almost naked. She could feel the current trying to push her downstream, but she had good footing and persevered.

"You are the most evil person I have ever come across, and if there is only one thing I ever learned, it is that one day you will get exactly what you deserve. You must be a most desperate and lonely soul." Her voice was level and firm.

"And why would you say such a thing, you almost-naked Miss Debutante of the Year? Princess? Angel?" Melinda loved having Alex in her power, and her sneering tone betrayed her satisfaction with the situation.

"Because only a woman who thinks nothing of herself would take another life for the sake of revenge! You must be consumed with jealousy, to hate me as you do. Even so, killing me will not win you Gavin. Nothing will! My death will buy you nothing but more trouble, more pain, ruin, and heartache!" Alex paused and caught her breath, trying to maintain her posture and not grab for the pain in her belly. She was drawing close now, staring down the barrel of the pistol. Melinda stood at the very edge of the stream, trying to avoid getting her dainty boots wet. "*You* must be the foolish one, to ask for all that," Alex concluded quietly.

"Shut up! Shut up! I have heard enough of you! Look at you, you're about to die and still you speak with such superiority! How can you wonder why I hate you so?" Melinda gestured with her weapon in a spasm of intense fury, staring into Alex's angry eyes.

Seizing her opportunity, Alex put her head down and charged full speed into Melinda, ramming her to the ground. They struggled for the pistol. Alex managed to slam Melinda's wrist into a root so hard that her hand went numb and the gun was sent flying to land a few feet away, higher up the sloping bank. Melinda started rising to her knees to go after it. Alex grappled her, and rolled with her into the water.

The river deepened here, and the current was becoming stronger as the sun rose, and both women were soon pulled under by it. When her head finally popped up a few yards downstream, Alex felt a firm hand yanking on her hair, and was quickly pulled under again. Alex twisted around and reached for Melinda's hair, pulling hard to duck her under. They were moving faster downstream now as they struggled. Alex heard a rumble and realized a waterfall would soon seal their fate, throwing them to sharp rocks in the shallows just below as the main current of the river eddied away. Alex tried to break loose from Melinda's grip and swim to shore, but was pulled back by a strength born of blinding rage. Alex's boots searched for the bottom.

"You're not leaving this river alive!" Melinda cried, as she moved her hands to grip Alex's neck. They were both afloat. Melinda had not heard the rapids or the waterfall, deafened by the gunshots and consumed by her fury. Alex butted Melinda's nose hard with her head, freeing herself for a moment. Wiping the blood away, Melinda reached out again to drown Alex. But Alex had been able find her feet, dodge away and fling herself toward the bank. Just far enough. Melinda was swept past by the current.

"AAAaaaaaaAAAAAhhhh!" Melinda's scream was cut short. Then there was only the splashing, roaring sound of the waterfall.

Crawling up and along the riverbank, the dripping, transparent chemise hoisted around her hips to free her knees, Alex forced herself along until she could safely peer over the falls. Then Alex placed her hand over her mouth to stifle a whimper. Hot tears cascaded down her wet face.

The bloodied body of Melinda lay lifeless on the jagged rocks below.

The sun had fully risen.

Exhausted in every sense, with pain in her belly and her head and along the scratches made by Harrison's knife, she slowly followed the riverbank back toward the spot where Melinda had first fired her pistol. Her plan was to mount her horse and ride as far as she could. Surely there must be some way to get home... to get to Gavin.

Alex found her way to the spot, but...how could this be? Harrison's body was missing! He was dead. How could he have moved? Melinda shot him! Alex cautiously moved from tree to tree, looking over her shoulder, reached for her horse, and suddenly Harrison jumped in front of her.

Alex screamed as loud as before, terrified, sure she was seeing a ghost. "No, this cannot be! I watched Melinda shoot you! I heard the gun go off! I saw you dead beside her!" Alex wondered if she could ever escape. She had no energy left, and little hope.

"Yes, you heard a shot. And yes, you saw me lying still. But it was merely a flesh wound, you see," Harrison showed her a small bloody slash through the sleeve of his coat. "I am good at playing possum." His tall figure loomed over her threateningly.

"Please, Lord, you must not do not do this! I am tired, I am sick, and I cannot take any more!" she pleaded, finally reaching her breaking point.

"I have waited too long and have gone through too much. There is one thing that I must do, even if it kills me, and that one thing is bedding an angel! I have to have you. You are a temptation no man could resist!"

Harrison reached for Alex as she filled her lungs to scream, swiftly grabbed her by the hair, forced her head back, and placed his lips over hers, clutching her arm in a painful grip. Her screams were smothered, her strength was drained. With one leg, he roughly kicked Alex's legs out from under her, then lowered her to the ground by her hair. He secured both her slim wrists over her head with one beefy hand and knelt heavily on her spread thighs. He slowly, deliberately brought his hand up her thigh, dragging her chemise and drawers up to expose her naked leg. Alex cried out in anguish. Her hands were useless, her legs were useless, her breasts were exposed... and she was too exhausted and weakened to fight.

"Get off her now!" a deep, commanding voice boomed from nearby.

Turning his head with surprise, Harrison was shocked to see Gavin standing close behind him.

"Oh my Lord! You're here!" Alex whispered, grateful, relieved he had found her in time. One more minute would have been too late.

There was no reply. Gavin's priority was to deal with the bastard who had dared to defile his Angel. She lay motionless, too spent to move. Later she wondered if she had fainted with relief.

"I told you to stay away from Alex, or suffer the consequences! I only warn once!" Lifting the brute by his collar, Gavin punched Harrison in the face with a thunderous blow. Released, he fell over face-first in the dirt. Gavin gripped him by his hair and dragged him into the river as he opened his eyes helplessly, too dazed to offer resistance. Gavin knelt in the shallows, grasped the man's ears, and plunged Harrison's face under the surface, releasing him to draw a breath at the last possible second, then doing it again. Harrison tried to plead for his life, but could not get a word out— whenever he had enough breath to speak, he found himself under water once more. Gavin wanted the bastard to experience the fear he had inspired in his Angel.

Eventually, Gavin held him under... until he no longer struggled. He continued to press his face into the stones of the river bottom until one of the other men arrived and gently pulled Gavin away. Leaving the lifeless body where it floated, Gavin turned to see Alex still lying there. The sight of her brought tears to his eyes. She looked bruised and beaten, tired and damaged and worn. Her clothes were almost gone, her lovely body exposed in the moonlight. He ran to her and gently raised her to her feet. He held her as tightly as he could and tenderly rocked her back and forth. He placed a kiss on every inch of her face and she finally started to respond under this barrage.

"Alex!" She looked up at him vaguely, lost in a dream. She could not respond. "Alex, was Melinda part of this?"

"Yes." She answered softly, looking down.

"Where is she now?" he stroked her face gently.

"Dead. We struggled... she went over the waterfall. Her body lies on the rocks below." She buried her face in his chest and after a little time, she felt at peace. There was enough light to see his heavenly face.

"Were there any others?" Gavin remembered the two hulking henchmen and their brutal treatment.

"No, not this time." Alex was feeling faint. The pain in her belly was returning.

"Alex, I swear to you I will never let this happen again. I am so sorry I let you down," Gavin whispered into her ear. He quickly took off his coat, his only garment that had any dryness and warmth left, and wrapped it around her, then took her back in his arms.

"Oh Gavin, do not blame yourself." She reached up from the deep, warm folds of his coat and placed her hand on his cheek. "This was not your fault. All that matters now is that you're here and those people will never hurt us again." Alex lifted her head and gently guided his lips to hers.

Gavin scooped Alex up in his arms and walked over to his horse, his wet boots making noises, and gently raised her to perch on his saddle sideways. After picking up her horse's reins, he vaulted up behind her, gently turning her to face him, helping her move her leg over, adjusting her torn chemise, making sure she was well enfolded in his coat. Placing her arms around his chest, settling her slim hips securely into his lap, he finally wrapped one brawny arm firmly around her waist and took up the reins of both horses with the other hand. "Your father needs to know that you're still with us. He has been searching for you, too."

She nodded and nestled her head into his shoulder. He led them away from the river and its tragedies, far away, to begin their new life together.

"My sweet Angel, I love you," Gavin told Alex, kissing the top of her head, with words that had never sounded more true.

"And I love you," Alex said. She felt so worn and hurting and empty that she succumbed to sleep, all her weight pressed against him. All threats eliminated, she was confident that Gavin would keep her safe, and soon bring her home.

Chapter Nineteen

Daniel caught up with Gavin soon after they started off, and he dismissed his tired men with thanks. The nightmare was finally over, and the journey back to the estate seemed to pass by quickly. He was most relieved to find Alex alive and apparently undamaged, or at least, that she had not been raped. A very close call indeed.

When the little group arrived back at Bedford House under the mid-afternoon sun, Elizabeth, Cassandra, and Ashley came running out the door before the horses had halted, with most of the servants close behind. As soon as Alex could be gently lowered into Daniel's arms, the women of the family were kissing her and shedding tears of relief and welcome. Daniel carried Alex into the house and gently placed her on the sitting room chesterfield, still enfolded in Gavin's coat. Ashley and Cassandra knelt close by, stroking her limbs.

Gavin recounted briefly to Elizabeth everything important that had occurred. The constable and some of his men soon arrived, and were given a more detailed account. Alex and Gavin related the facts leading to the deaths of Lady Melinda Blackstone and Lord Dalton Harrison in response to the constable's questions. Considering Daniel's highly respected name in the community, and aware that this was the second time Alex had been abducted, the official found no reason to keep them engaged very long. Taking the map Gavin produced from a pocket, he dispatched men to a marked location to retrieve the bodies, and sent another to inform Earl Harrison of his son's demise, then took his leave.

Alex did not say much, merely aware how exhausted and filthy she was, and of the gnawing pain in her midsection. Her only desires were to bathe, and to sleep. She pleadingly, tearfully told her father she did not want Gavin to leave her side even for a moment. Daniel and Gavin exchanged a long look. Daniel nodded slightly, indicating his agreement. Daniel took Gavin by the arm, led him out of earshot, and quietly gave his blessing for the wedding to proceed as soon as Alex regained her health. Without taking this step, he could not permit Gavin to be in his daughter's rooms one minute.

"Alex, are you feeling any better now?" Gavin asked softly. His concern for her health was growing. Normally she would be well recovered by now, but as far as he could see, she seemed worse. Her face was pale and damp, her eyes a little glassy. Her usual spirit was nowhere to be found. Her strength and energy had not rebounded during the journey.

Alex replied, "No, darling, I am not. My stomach feels awful. I am dizzy and the thought of food makes me sick. This has all been too much. I... I have never seen anyone die before." She suddenly began to weep. She had never cried in front of anyone, since childhood.

Elizabeth stepped in and sent Sara, hovering near the door, to prepare a hot bath. She summoned the butler next. "Please send someone for the doctor. I want my daughter to be examined right away." After a little while, she softly asked Cassie and Ashley to go have their tea so Gavin could carry Alex upstairs.

Andrew, summoned by a messenger, arrived to assure himself of his cousin's health and welfare, and was relieved to find him merely dirty and tired and hungry, and undamaged. After Gavin and Daniel described recent events to his satisfaction, Andrew went in search of Cassandra to join her for a friendly cup of tea before returning home.

Everyone in the family was now preoccupied with Alex's fragile state. Elizabeth was most concerned about the stomach pain and Alex's lack of appetite. Daniel thought the shock of observing two violent deaths might have been too much for any fine young woman's delicate constitution to bear.

Once Sara had once again bathed Alex with great care, anointed her wounds, seen to her hair, dressed her a nightgown, and assisted her into her bed, Gavin was permitted to enter her rooms, where he seated himself on a footstool so he could be near enough to hold her hand. He murmured into her ear how much he loved her, and that no other terrors would ever visit her. Alex weakly grasped his hand, and whispered her undying love, a grimace on her face, one hand on her belly. "How very scandalous of you, Your Grace, to be sitting in my bedchamber. I am an unmarried woman." She was barely conscious, but still attempted to lighten his mood. After a little while, she fell into a fitful doze.

Elizabeth quietly sat nearby in an easy chair with her needlework.

"Mother?" said Alex, opening her eyes.

"Yes dear?"

"Where is Richard? I did not see him when everyone came outside." She wondered if he was not concerned for her safety.

"Richard did not come home this morning as expected, and we have been unable to locate him and tell him of the situation. We hope he shall return soon."

Alex murmured into Gavin's ear. She could not tell Gavin enough how much she loved him. She could not stop touching him. She loved the way he smelled, the way he talked, the way he stood and walked. Everything about him she loved, and everything he stood for, she would stand for too. She mused, she had suspected love would be grand, but had never grasped the impact it would have on her life. She sank so deep in her thoughts that she did not hear Sara return to tell her mother that the doctor had been located, and would be along in a little while. Gavin gently nudged her.

"Angel, where have you been?"

"I have been right here, my love," she answered softly.

Gavin tried not to let his concern and worry for her delicate state show on his face. He was frightened by her moist pallor and limp grasp. He did not want to lose her after all they had been through. She was his one, true love.

Alex's mind was wandering a bit.

"Mother, could you ask Sara to burn that chemise? I want no reminders... ."

"Yes dear, I will take care of it. My poor, poor baby. I am so sorry all this has happened to you," her mother said with tears rolling down her face. She walked a few steps to kneel by her daughter's bedside and take up the hand that was not in Gavin's grip.

"Please do not cry, Mother." Alex's voice was faint. "This is not your fault and there is no reason for you to be sorry. I believe that there will always be bad people in this world and you cannot stop them from causing harm to others. They will do what they want... but they pay the price." Alex gazed lovingly at Elizabeth. "No matter how old I get, I will always need you. I love you, Mother."

"I love you, my dearest daughter. Now, please, rest. The doctor should be here any minute." Alex had not been restored by her bath and rest. She was pale and damp. Elizabeth, too, tried not to let her fears and worries show on her face.

"Does your stomach still hurt?" Gavin asked quietly.

"I do not have the aching pain that I had before, but I do still feel very ill." Just being near him and touching him made her feel better.

"Well, not to worry. I am sure the doctor is going to tell you you're fine. Probably just depleted by your ordeal. He'll prescribe rich food, strong wines and lots of rest in the sunshine and fresh air."

The butler knocked on the door, and Elizabeth rose and spoke with him. Gavin turned at the sound of footsteps, and stood to meet the stranger, reluctant to release his Angel's hand.

"Gavin, dear, this is Doctor Albert Roberts, who enjoyed a thriving Harley Street practice before moving to the countryside. Doctor Roberts, this is my daughter Alexandra's betrothed, His Grace Gavin Blake, Duke of Chatham," Elizabeth said.

"It is good to meet you, Your Grace. And a pleasure to encounter you in good health, Lady Rosenshire. However I must request that everyone leave the room, so that I may examine Lady Alexandra." The doctor walked over to the side of Alex's bed and placed his black bag on the little footstool just vacated by Gavin. Elizabeth and Gavin were still hovering, and he turned to them to say, "I understand this young lady has just endured quite an ordeal."

"Yes, that she did... . We will be right outside," Gavin and Elizabeth turned and left the room. Gavin asked, "Lady Elizabeth, where is Daniel?"

"Daniel is outside," Elizabeth answered as they paced side by side in the hallway.

"Outside? Why is he not in here waiting to hear what the doctor has to say?" Gavin asked.

"Let me explain my husband to you: You see... things that concern his family's well-being make Daniel feel very helpless. Feeling helpless is something that my husband does not tolerate well. He feels that he should be in control of every situation. If his daughter should need his help... well... then he can fix most everything. But when it comes to their health, he has no idea what to do for them. So his way of dealing with such things is to be by himself until I ask for his help, and perhaps, guide him a little way down the right path."

"Yes, I understand. People deal with such situations in very different ways."

"Gavin, dear, Alexandra needs to keep you close by. Please know that you are welcome to stay here as long as you like. I will have Richard's valet look for some fresh clothing for you, as you are both about the same size, unless you prefer to send for your man at Arlington House to bring your things. Just let me know what you need. There are vacant rooms near Alexandra's which I have asked the upstairs maid to make ready for you."

"Thank you, Lady Elizabeth, you have been most kind and considerate. And thank you, also, for accepting me into your home and your family, and for allowing me to remain at your daughter's side. I realize I have put you and Daniel in a most awkward position, appearances being as important as they are, and gossip being such a scourge in this society. However, I know my nearness will help Alex. I do not wish to put you to any trouble, but it will be most difficult for me to be away from her for even one moment ever again. I have taken the liberty of sending word with Andrew for my valet to bring me some things and stay here a while to look after me, so your staff will not be inconvenienced. He should arrive within the hour."

They looked at each other with affection and understanding, and then resumed pacing up and down the hall, side by side. Gavin's fatigue was almost overwhelming but his love for his Angel kept him going.

"Cassandra, I do not want to wait any more," Ashley said, extremely anxious to know what was going on with Alex, and finished with her tea by the time Andrew had sweetly taken his leave.

"Neither do I, Ashley. Let's go find out what is happening." Both girls headed for the stairs, but they were stopped by their father.

"No, girls, you must wait a few minutes more," Daniel said as he stood behind them.

"But why? We are so concerned for Alex!" Cassandra asked.

"Gavin and your mother are up there and I do believe they may need a few minutes together." He gave each young woman a light kiss on the forehead and walked away.

"Oh, well! Let us go back to the sitting room, Ashley." Cassandra took her sister by the arm and they walked away scowling in disappointment.

Gavin and Elizabeth paced and paced, waiting for the door to open. They often exchanged worried looks, growing more and more concerned over how much time the doctor was taking.

"Alexandra dear, I am going to gently push on your stomach next, and I want you to tell me if it hurts. Are you prepared?" said Doctor Roberts as he placed his hands on her lower abdomen and slowly pressed down. He had checked her pulse, which was rapid, and observed her pale, damp skin, slowly proceeding with all the steps of a thorough, careful physical examination.

"Does that hurt you in any way?" he asked.

"No. It does not hurt at all." Alex replied.

"I see... ."

"You see what?"

"I must ask you a few questions now, and you must be honest with me, dear."

"Of course."

"When did the pain and nausea start?"

As he listened, the doctor examined her limbs with care, observing cuts and bruises where Melinda had grappled with her. A tender lump on her temple still marked where she had been first knocked unconscious. A bruise remained from Harrison's brutal blow in the forest. There was a very fine red line visible under her thin nightdress, running straight down her body from throat to belly, and another line on her neck from a sharp blade.

"I'm not exactly sure, but... it was some time soon after I was taken, yesterday afternoon or evening. Why?"

"I'm just trying to understand how much time has passed. Now, tell me, what have you had to eat in the last day or so?"

"Well, I ate luncheon yesterday... Father and Gavin gave me cheese and bread on our journey back today, but I ate very little, I have had no appetite."

"And yet you still feel sick?"

"I do."

"This next question is rather personal, but do not get offended as it is my profession to ask such things."

"Well, what is it?" Alex asked, puzzled by the notion of a doctor asking something offensive.

"When did you have your last monthly flow?"

"Oh, well, that is rather personal," she said, a blush overcoming her pallor briefly. "It would have been about three weeks ago... or was it four? I am not certain exactly."

"I see...."

"You see what? Please, tell me your thoughts, you are making me nervous!"

"Sorry to worry you, my dear. I think you will be perfectly fine. You just need to give it some time. Lots of rest, and good food, and proper digestive habits. You have been through a lot physically and mentally. These things take time."

"That is all?" Alex asked him.

"That is all, my dear." He covered her with her sheet and coverlet and propped her up against a pile of pillows. "Now let me go out into the hall and inform your mother and fiancé of the good news." He restored a few items to his black bag, picked it up, and headed for the door.

At the first sound of the door's opening, Gavin and Elizabeth were ready to shower the doctor with questions.

"What is it? What is wrong with her?" Gavin demanded.

"Calm down, young man. She will be just fine. She needs to rest and eat and in time you will be surprised just how well she is!" the doctor told them.

"What is causing the pain in her stomach?" Elizabeth questioned.

"Just nerves. She has endured a grievous shock. Also she has undergone at least two strong blows to the head, which can cause weakness, vertigo, pallor and many other problems, often for several days. This has been a very anxious and strenuous ordeal. She merely needs to take plenty of time to rest and recover."

"Thank you for coming so quickly, Doctor Roberts. We shall give her the best possible care. Please return to check on her when you can." Elizabeth took the doctor's arm to escort him out.

Gavin turned in the other direction, quickly resumed his place at Alex's bedside, and picked up her hand. She stretched toward him, turning her face to his for a deep, lingering kiss. He wrapped his arms around her shoulders and hugged her tightly. The embrace was long, and neither party wanted it to end.

"Excuse us," Daniel said, as the family entered the room.

"Of course." Gavin released his love and leaned back toward the wall at the head of the bed.

One by one her parents and sisters gave her hugs and kisses as she clung to Gavin's hand.

"Alex, we are so glad you are safe and home," Cassandra said.

"Thank you, Cassandra."

"My turn for a hug!" said Ashley, nudging Cassandra out of the way.

"Now that we have all had hugs and kisses, there is another matter we need to discuss," Elizabeth said.

"What are you talking about, dear?" Daniel asked, cocking an eyebrow. As far as he was concerned, the only thing that mattered now, with everyone safely at home, was Alex's return to robust health. The constable had stopped by to say Lord Dalton Harrison's body was being delivered to his father; Lady Melinda Blackstone's remains were apparently destined for an unmarked grave in Potter's Field, unless a notice in the next day's London papers alerted some family member to come forward promptly. What other matter could there be?

"I am talking about the wedding," Elizabeth answered.

"The wedding? Goodness, Elizabeth, don't you think that could wait a few days?" Daniel replied as he sat on the edge of his daughter's bed.

"No, I do not think so. Alexandra has waited long enough for the day to come, and I know she will not want to wait any longer than necessary, dear. We should start the planning right away." Organizing a wedding would be the perfect way to distract Alex from her traumatic experiences, Elizabeth was certain.

"I see. I know I will not be able to talk you into waiting long, but I encourage you to wait a little, just until she feels better. Please don't tax her with anything tonight."

He continued, "Alex, I am glad to hear you are going to be fine. Forgive me for not staying long, but I am tired." Daniel smiled and, placing a loving kiss on her cheek, whispered in her ear, "I am happy for you. I know this is what you want."

"Thank you, Father. This is exactly what I want." Smiling up at her father, Alex bid him a good night.

"Gavin and Alex, it is your wedding, so you must tell me exactly what you have in mind." There was a moment of silence as the two glanced at each other. Then both started to tell Elizabeth their ideas. Every now and again Ashley and Cassandra would offer suggestions and thoughts as well. After a little while, at a signal from their mother, they kissed Alex goodnight and left the room. The butler knocked, and Elizabeth rose and went to the door to speak with him briefly. Turning back, she said to Alex, "We shall resume in the morning. By then, I expect you to have a date chosen. I will call in a seamstress tomorrow to begin the fittings so you may wear my gown. I am delighted that you want to share it with me instead of asking for the latest fashion."

Elizabeth turned to address Gavin. "Your man arrived a little while ago with your valise. I shall ask him to prepare your bath now, as I am sure you are more than ready for it! And Cook has our dinner waiting for us. Please tear yourself way from Alex's side for a short while and join me and Daniel downstairs for a meal once you have had a chance to bathe and change. And you must get some rest." With a light kiss on Alex's forehead and a kind nod to Gavin, she left the room.

"Gavin, now that we have a few minutes to ourselves I would like nothing more than for you to hold me," Alex said.

"Angel, I'm going to hold you for the rest of your life." Gavin stretched out next to her on the coverlet and embraced her, adjusting her pillows for the night.

Her head was against his chest, his head on top of hers. This was a love so real and strong, their bond could never be broken. Alex soon fell into a deep sleep, dreaming of her wedding day, and Gavin gently untangled his limbs and tiptoed from the room, turning down the lamps.

Chapter Twenty

The first beam of sunshine peeked through an opening between the draperies and danced across Alex's face. Slowly she opened her eyes and looked around. Rising to a sitting position, she could tell it was very early, the corners of the room still in dimness. Next she noticed she was alone. The last thing she remembered was Gavin's holding her as they planned their wedding. She wondered when he had left her side. I must have drifted into sleep, and he must have gone home. Soon I shall wake up to him every morning, but for now I must be patient, she reminded herself.

Swinging her feet to the floor, Alex brought herself to a standing position. She realized just how weak she still was when she had to clutch a chair for support, dizzy, and rubbery in the knees. She decided to sit a minute. Waiting for strength and energy, she finally regained her balance and took a few careful steps to ring for Sara. Sara appeared quickly to learn that Alex felt hungry, and had an intense craving for toast and jam, pots and pots of jam! And she wanted to have it downstairs, no tea tray in bed for her this morning! Sara protested that she must stay in bed, but, ever loyal and obedient, helped her into a light summer dressing gown.

Sara worried, "Lady Alexandra. Your mother would have a fit if she knew you were not in bed." She was relieved to see Alex's color so much improved, and asked her to sit a few minutes more so her hair could be brushed, her face and hands washed, and slippers put on her feet. Minimal preparations completed, Sara carefully helped Alex move slowly down the stairs, leaning on the bannister and linking arms, then into the morning room.

Alex was pleased to see a sleepy footman arriving to pull out her chair. "For now, I would really appreciate a pile of toast and jam. Don't be shy with the jam. And tea as soon as possible, please." Just as pleased with Alex's apparent recovery as Sara was, the cook hastened her preparations and poured tea from her own pot so Alex would not have to wait. She also passed word to the servant's hall that young Lady Alexandra had already come downstairs. Gavin's valet had just started sipping his first cup of tea, but banged his cup down and ran up the back stairs to rouse his master.

Alex gazed out the window at the beautiful pink dawn of an early summer morning. It would be a perfect day for a ride, she thought to herself. But perhaps she did not quite have the strength for that yet. Instead she could stroll in the gardens. The weather was becoming warmer, the days longer. Flowers were in full bloom and all the trees were leafy.

"Sara. Do you know when Gavin left me last night?" Alex asked, sipping her tea. Sara was hovering at the doorway while the footman served breakfast.

"Yes, my lady. He left your room around eight o'clock. He is a great catch, Lady Alex. Very thoughtful."

"How do you mean?"

"He did not leave you until he knew you were comfortably sleeping. I thought that was very kind of him. And then he dined with your parents, my lady."

"It was most kind. I just wish he were here now."

"He will be with you soon, I have no doubt." Sara was enjoying the little surprise she knew would soon be coming.

"Good! I cannot wait to see him!" The toast and jam arrived, Alex greeted it ravenously, and Sara went upstairs to lay out Alex's garments for the day and prepare the lady's morning bath.

"Lady Alexandra Rosenshire, for heavens sake! What are you doing out of bed?" her mother scolded as she entered the morning room.

"Good morning to you too, Mother, you have risen early." Alex returned.

"Alex, dear. The doctor said that you needed plenty of rest in order to get well. What is the meaning of this defiance?" her mother questioned her.

"Oh Mother, I did not defy anything. I was

very hungry when I awakened, so I came down to find something to eat. That is all."

"Alexandra, you know Cook would have sent up a tray! You merely had to ring for it. Now do please tell me, just how do you feel this morning?" Elizabeth took her seat next to Alex at the big round breakfast table, and the footman soon reappeared bearing a big pot of fresh tea.

"I feel better! I still feel weak, and my balance is not quite what it should be, but I think it will not be long before I feel like my old self again. My stomach does not hurt any more, and I slept very soundly. My color is better, Sara tells me. Strangely, though, I had a very strong craving for toast and jam this morning, and that is what got me out of bed. I simply was not able to wait for a tray."

"Craving?" Elizabeth looked around to be sure there were no servants near enough to listen, and continued quietly, "Alex dear, when do you next expect your monthly cycle?"

"My next cycle?" Alex asked, puzzled by the question, dropping her voice to match her mother's.

"Please, dear, answer the question."

"My cycle is due next week, I think. Or perhaps this week. I have not been counting. The doctor asked the same question. Could you please explain why you would ask?"

"In my opinion, your symptoms sound much like those of someone who is expecting a baby. It is how I invariably felt, starting with the second month. Cravings and nausea. That was always how I knew I was expecting again."

"A baby? No, that cannot be," Alex said as she choked a little on her tea. The thought was ridiculous! Or... was it?

"Darling, are you sure? For the last few weeks your face has been glowing. You're always happy and smiling. You must remember that I was once your age, too. I love your father as I believe you love Gavin. I know what that love is capable of doing." Elizabeth reached to hold her daughter's hand, trying to be comforting and supportive.

"But wouldn't the doctor have been able to tell, if I were with child?" Alex whispered, certain that such a capable man as Doctor Roberts would know such a thing.

"Doctors cannot always know, this early on. Don't be nervous. Let us just wait and see if your cycle arrives in the next week or two, and then we shall proceed accordingly. I don't think it is necessary to tell anyone of this concern until we know for sure. Your father, I fear, would not take such news well."

"Yes, Mother. Please, say nothing to Gavin just yet! Oh, my God, the scandal!" Alex said very softly. She hadn't even considered the possibility, but it was true. They had made love... without a care in the world, or a thought of possible consequences.

"Not a word, I promise," Elizabeth replied

softly, leaning over and placing a kiss on her daughter's forehead. Elizabeth was worried for more than one reason.

Gavin joined them a moment later. He had taken the time to be shaved and bathed and properly dressed in clean clothes, and though he was not yet feeling rested, he almost felt like a new man. Alex was astonished and delighted to see him. She stood up and gave him a joyful hug. Seeing that she was a little wobbly, he helped her sit back down, and declined to be seated next to her. He explained how glad he was to see her so much recovered, and questioned her closely as to her health. He told Alex he had spent the night down the hall from her in fear for her delicate state, but now he would be returning to Arlington House with his valet, as it was apparent she would soon be well. He promised to return after luncheon, to join her for a walk in the gardens and check on her progress. He thanked Elizabeth for her kindness and hospitality, asked her to share his gratitude with Daniel. Finally he bent down and embraced Alex for a long sweet goodbye kiss, which made her eyes sparkle.

Gavin was soon breakfasting in the bright, comfortable morning room at Arlington House. "Good morning, old chap," came a voice from behind him.

"Andrew, good morning to you too. And

yes, it is a good one," Gavin replied as he kicked out a chair for his cousin.

"I have to say, I am rather surprised to see you back so soon. When your valet went off with your case last night, I thought you would be staying at Bedford House indefinitely."

"I will be returning there after luncheon. She needs more rest than she gets when I am in her presence. This morning her health is greatly improved, so I thought it best to let her return to her usual routine. I will admit that this short time apart from her is torture. Lord! Who would have imagined love could be this powerful?" Gavin wore a huge smile.

"Good God, man! You're almost too happy for me to tolerate! I know that I have never seen you like this in all your life! It's sickening, I tell you."

"Andrew, do not be so serious." He joked, "Someday the love of your life will manifest, and soon you will be as moony and preoccupied as I am."

"Perhaps she already has," Andrew replied nonchalantly.

"Excuse me?" Gavin was shocked. "When did you find the time to fall in love, with all the events that have surrounded our lives these past few months?"

"I was not going to say anything just yet, and I advised her to do the same." Andrew looked down at the table and not at Gavin's face.

"Who could this woman be! Whom did you advise not to say anything?" Gavin was overcome with curiosity now.

"If I am to tell you, you must promise truly not to say a word to anyone, and that would include Alexandra."

"Maybe you had better not tell me, then. I do not want to keep anything from Alex. No secrets! That is the first rule of love," Gavin replied seriously.

"Oh, fine! I will tell you, but you may only tell Alex if you are asked a direct question, and would otherwise be forced to tell her a lie. Deal?" Andrew was eager to share his long-kept secret with his dear cousin.

"All right! Andrew, you have a deal. Now! Who is the girl?"

"It is the Lady Cassandra," Andrew told him with the biggest grin Gavin had ever seen on his cousin's face.

"Cassandra! Alex's *sister*, Cassandra?" Gavin was astonished.

"Yes, that is correct." Andrew hoped his cousin would not put him through the unmerciful teasing he had subjected Gavin to.

"Then that would be the reason you did not want me to tell Alex. But who is to say she does not already know?"

"Perhaps you are right. I really had not thought of that. If Cassandra did say something, it would only be because she trusts her sister just as I trust you."

"I agree completely." Gavin finished his breakfast, rose, and gave his cousin a pat on the shoulder. "I am planning to take some more rest this morning. When I rise, I will have luncheon with you, then head back to Bedford House." Gavin got up from his chair and threw his napkin down. "Andrew, be sure to thank Catherine for taking care of Jack for me. I have had so much going on lately, I haven't been giving him the attention he needs. I know she loves to play with him, but he has quite become her responsibility, which I never intended."

"You poor sap, look what love has done to you," Andrew replied as he rose from the table.

"Don't mock me so soon. You're not far from this state either." Both cousins were laughing as they parted.

After a welcome rest, another bath, a fresh change of clothes, and a hearty luncheon with Andrew, Gavin was eager to mount his horse and gallop all the way back to Alex. By the door, he grabbed some flowers that were nicely arranged in a vase, to take to her.

"Gavin, remember while you're there not to slip and say anything," Andrew reminded him.

"I will not slip. But why all the secrecy?"

"Cassandra is only seventeen, and has not had her début. Until she does, in a few months, I cannot court her properly. People would gossip if I were to call on her now, and that is something I will not put Cassie through... although *that* torture can't be much worse than *this* torture of not seeing each other."

"Why, Andrew, how thoughtful of you. I never knew you cared so much about anyone's reputation, including your own," Gavin said with a teasing grin, mounting up and heading out.

Andrew longed to ride with Gavin to Bedford House, but thought it might seem rather odd or suspicious if both cousins arrived. Besides, this was Gavin's time with Alex, and Andrew did not want to intrude. If he went off and spent time with Cassie in order to give Gavin and Alex time alone, someone would notice. Instead, he would spend another dreadfully long lonely day alone at home. He stood in the doorway and watched his cousin ride away. Soon, he comforted himself, it would be his own moment to ride off and join the woman of his dreams.

"Andrew, what kind of look is that on your face?" Catherine asked as she came across her brother in the hallway, entering Arlington House from a long morning ride.

"What?" Andrew had been lost in thought when she interrupted him.

"The look on your face? It was strange, that is all, sort of... romantic and distant."

"Well, I have no idea what you are talking about, so if you will excuse me, I have a rather busy day to begin. Oh, and before I forget, Gavin said to thank you for taking care of Jack." Andrew brushed past his sister and headed for his study, where work might keep his mind occupied. Somebody had to attend to the family business, and Gavin had not had much time for that lately.

"Fine, Andrew, just fine!" Catherine yelled at her brother's retreating back, annoyed by his abrupt behavior.

Catherine headed for the dining room for her late luncheon. She would not forget her brother's mood. She was very close to Andrew. His mood today upset her and she would not let him forget how he had treated her until he apologized profusely. He seemed to have so little time for her of late.

Andrew had not given much thought to how he treated his little sister. His only thought was of Cassandra. She was considerably younger than he, but love has no age. She was beautiful and smart and had spirit to her, spirit that Andrew usually shied away from, but, in Cassandra, he somehow found beyond charming. Cassandra had him under a spell he could not break, nor did he want to. She enchanted him.

Soon the rest of the family had joined Elizabeth and Alex at breakfast. All were most relieved that this morning she was looking so well. Each one greeted Alex with an embrace, and inquired as to how she had slept, how she was feeling today.

"How do you feel this morning? Better, I hope? You look much recovered."

"Actually, Cassie, I feel quit a bit better, still a little queasy though, a little weak and dizzy. I was hoping that it was something toast and tea would take care of, but that does not seem to be the case. Please, if you would all excuse me, I have to ask Sara to assist me back to my room. I would like to get dressed now." Alex slowly raised herself from her chair and leaned on Sara's proffered arm.

"Please take it slowly, dear. I do not want you to exert yourself so soon. You have been through much distress, and you must try to rest," Elizabeth warned.

"Yes, Mother, I will be cautious. I promise you." Alex headed for the stairs leaning hard on Sara. She had never before paid much attention to the stairway, though she certainly used it often. Standing at its foot, it looked like a mountain to climb, in her unfamiliar weakened state.

The grand stairway of Bedford House was a marvel of beauty, carved of dark cherry, accented by a flowing emerald-green carpet that cascaded down each step, secured by shining brass rods. Green and gold stripes on the pale wallpaper echoed the carpet's tone. Dreaming often of soon having her own homes, Alex was newly appreciative of her mother's talents for decorating. The stairway was straight at the base, then delicately curved as it reached an open, railed gallery at its top. The gallery went left and right to form corridors where large private suites hid behind many doors.

Alex felt her rooms had never been so far away, and slowly began the climb. She was soon feeling far more exhausted than she had expected to, and collapsed on her bed once she finally reached it. She dozed for the rest of the morning, and permitted her luncheon to be served on a tray in her room. After that, she felt ready to bathe and dress.

Downstairs, the butler quietly entered the sitting room to say, "Lady Elizabeth, His Grace the Lord Gavin Blake is here to call upon the Lady Alexandra."

"Wonderful! Alexandra will be so happy." Elizabeth followed the butler to the door, where he relieved Gavin of his colorful bouquet and handed it to a downstairs maid to be arranged and presented to Alex.

"Gavin, it is good to have you return," she said, as she warmly placed a kiss on his cheek and admitted him.

"As it is to see you, my lady," Gavin returned the embrace.

"Alexandra will be so glad to see you. She was up at first light, and, to my dismay, she came down to the morning room to eat her breakfast rather than calling for a tray. I would have preferred she stay in bed, but I was most glad her appetite had returned."

"Please, do tell me more about her condition today." Gavin asked.

"If you would come sit with me, we shall discuss Alexandra's health." Elizabeth took Gavin's arm and steered him into the drawing room. "Alexandra is doing considerably better. She ate well at breakfast, though she is still a bit queasy. She remains rather weak, alas. She required help going up and down the stairs. Some color has started to return to her face, I am glad to say, though she remains pale. She spent the morning resting, and she took her luncheon upstairs. I have a feeling it won't be long before she is back to normal, healthy, ebullient state." Elizabeth patted his hand to reassure him.

"That is most encouraging to hear. I must admit I was more than a little worried, as you well know. She seemed to be in so much pain, and so despondent, so ill, so worn. These are things that I do not want her to experience ever again." Gavin still blamed himself for Alex's disastrous encounters with the late Melinda.

"Gavin, if you would kindly excuse me, I would like to check on her now and tell her that you are here. I will be just a moment." Elizabeth gracefully stood and left the room.

Gavin paced. His anticipation at seeing Alex again overwhelmed him. Time apart from her was agony. Their wedding would have to take place the minute Alex was feeling well! Then Gavin could protect her, and see to her well-being every minute. He would be the one to comfort her when she needed comfort. And hers would be the face he would see every morning upon first opening his eyes. He wanted nothing more than to hold his angel, make love to her, feel her soft skin against his, take in her sweet scent with every breath he drew. He would never forsake her. For the rest of his life he would need nothing more.

Before opening Alex's door, Elizabeth lightly tapped on it and asked, "Alexandra dear, may I come in?"

"Of course," Alex replied.

"Alexandra, Gavin is in the drawing room. He is very anxiously waiting to see you."

"I am almost ready. I cannot wait to see him!" Alex slowly rose from the dressing table, where Sara had carefully worked on her hair and applied a touch of rouge to her face. Clad only in her undergarments, with her corset loosely laced for comfort, she looked critically at the green frock Sara had chosen for today. Then she turned to throw open her wardrobes and look at her other choices.

"Alexandra, why not one of your blue dresses? Blue always brings out your eyes and I do believe it is your best color. Although... I can permit Gavin to join you here for a while, if you prefer not to struggle with the stairs again today."

"Yes, Mother. A blue one. I do want to go downstairs, if you please. Blue is the best choice. What do you think of this one?" Alex drew out a deep blue gown and held it against her body.

"That one is very beautiful, but it might be a little too dark for today, as you are still somewhat pale." Elizabeth was searching through the ranks of hanging garments. "How about this one?" she asked, holding up a simple, elegant, sky-blue silk gown.

"Yes, perfect! Thank you, Mother. Could you please go tell Gavin that I will be just a moment? I don't want him to think that I am never coming down."

"Certainly... I do not think Gavin has the patience to wait much longer! He is a wonderful man, and I know he loves you. That is all I ever want for my children, to be happy with their mates, dearly loved, and treated kindy. Gavin will always treasure you as I do. Cherish every moment, my dear." Elizabeth placed a gentle kiss on her forehead before leaving the room.

Alex whispered, "Thank you Mother, I love you." She found tears in her eyes as she stood while

Sara helped her into the gown and fastened its tiny buttons. The only man she would ever love returned her ardent feelings, and her parents thought fondly of him too.

Elizabeth stifled a little laugh at the sight of Gavin, impatiently pacing the length of the drawing room as though the minutes could never pass swiftly enough.

"Gavin, Alexandra wanted me to tell you that she will be down the moment she is finished dressing, which will be very soon. Why don't you sit down by me? You're going to wear a hole in my favorite carpet with your pacing." Young men had no patience at all, she thought. Her husband had only acquired some patience with his growing maturity over the years, and still it was not his strongest trait.

"Very sorry, Lady Elizabeth. It's just that I have longed for your daughter's company so." He tried to stop pacing, but was too impatient to seat himself.

"Why, you saw her just this morning!" Elizabeth teased. She knew the power of their love. "I would also like to tell you not to be so formal. You must call me Elizabeth now, as we will be family soon enough, and this family does not use titles in addressing one another."

"Very well, if that is your wish... Elizabeth." Gavin smiled, pleased and warmed by the welcome. He was surprised at feeling so close to Rosenshires so soon. They made him feel so welcome. They had forgiven him quickly for bringing Melinda's evils into their home. He let himself relax and sit down near Elizabeth, taking a deep breath and listening for Alex's footsteps.

At last, he heard her approach. It was only a few minutes, but they were hours for him.

"Excuse me, am I interrupting something?" Alex paused in the doorway.

"Angel!" greeted Gavin, leaping up to rush over and enfold her in his arms, lifting her completely off her feet and kissing her passionately.

"I'll just leave you alone," Elizabeth said, as she excused herself quietly. Her departure went unnoticed and unremarked.

"Gavin, I am so glad you're here. When I woke up this morning and you had gone... the loneliest feelings washed over me." Alex kissed him again and again, while trying to speak. She would never be able to kiss him enough! "You left so soon after I saw you at breakfast. It seems an eternity has passed since then."

Gavin gently placed Alex on the chesterfield and seated himself close by. He wrapped his arms around her and pulled her close, inhaling her intoxicating scent, his cheek pressed into her hair. "Your mother tells me you're feeling a little better." Gavin drew away to look into her face. Then he reached for the nearby vase and presented his fragrant, fresh bouquet of blooms.

"These are lovely! Thank you so much. You are so thoughtful." She returned the vase to the end table after inhaling deeply of its verdant aromas. "And, yes, I am feeling much better today, and I dearly hope to be entirely better *very* soon." Alex leaned in close to caress Gavin's ear, studying every detail of his strong chin and straight nose.

"And why is that?" Gavin asked.

"That is because I cannot wait to make love to you!" With smoldering eyes, Alex placed a deep, intense kiss on his full lips. Then her lips traveled across his face to place tiny kisses on every inch of it, with special attention to his eyelids.

"Alex, I think you had better relax for now," Gavin finally said, gently pushing her away.

"What's the matter? Do you not like my kisses?" Her feelings were hurt by his sudden distance.

"It's not that. Of course I love your kisses. Under any other circumstances I would never push you away! But we are in your parent's home, and I fear that if you do not stop what you're doing I will not be able to control my feelings for you." Pulling her close again, Gavin kissed her forehead. "Soon we shall be man and wife, and nothing shall keep us apart for one moment."

"I find it very difficult to control myself where you are concerned."

"But I have been needing to tell you how lovely you look this afternoon, and you have not given me an instant in which to do so. Alex, you look radiant. Your beauty today is intoxicating." Sincerity was written all over his features.

"Thank you, Gavin. I was not sure I made the right choice of attire."

Alex did look more radiant and angelic than ever, perhaps due to her slight pallor and the way it set off her indigo eyes. Sara had pulled Alex's hair away from her face but left its length flowing down her back. The top and sides had been woven into a complicated braided knot at the crown of her head. Her light blue silken gown fell all the way to the floor. It loosely fitted her form with a simple, flowing silhouette. A long line of tiny white pearl buttons fastened by fine hand-embroidered loops began at the notch of the tall collar and continued down well past her slim waist, setting off her curves. Delicate, handmade white lace detailing at the cuffs, collar and hem added to its elegance. Its smooth lines complimented Alex's slim, buxom figure, and at the same time allowed for her comfort, neither too tight nor too full-skirted for ease of movement. Her stylish, white, low-heeled kid boots showed off her tiny feet. She had never looked more attractive to Gavin.

"Well, I think this was the perfect choice. Then again, I do not think anything you could wear would ever detract from your beauty. You would be utterly lovely even in a char's rough overall."

"Why my love, you are so kind." Again they

embraced and kissed as though there were no tomorrow.

Time passed quickly as they delightedly chatted about their future days together, gazing into each other's eyes. Elizabeth discreetly checked on the lovers now and then to make sure Alex was showing no evidence of fatigue or illness. Too soon, time for tea was announced by a gong.

"Cassandra, where is your father? I have not seen him since last night," Gavin asked, noting his absence as the family took their seats around the room and footmen wheeled in domed silver serving platters and steaming tureens.

"At breakfast he mentioned some business with the farmers that he needed to take care of at his office in Bedford Village. He has to pay the men who helped in the hunt, I think. Also, I believe, he is planning to search for my brother."

"I do not understand. Your father does not know where your brother is?"

"Richard and Father, for the most part, get along well. But Richard always feels the need to prove himself by trying to outdo Father in business affairs, even though Father has never placed many demands on him. Sometimes... Richard gets himself into trouble. Since it's been about a week and no one has heard from him, Father feels the need to find him. He made some inquiries at the time Alex was abducted but they proved fruitless. Richard has no idea what happened to her because no one could locate him. Knowing my father as I do, I surmise he is worried about my brother, as is Mother. So today he hoped to find out more, as two families of this county have just returned from Town. He will call on them to learn if they have heard anything."

"I'm sure in time Richard will understand what a wonderful family he has, and how unnecessary it is to put them through such undue worry."

Gavin fell to musing about his own upbringing as the women conversed over tea. His parents were very proper, largely concerned with their role in Society. They believed children should be kept to the nursery or school-room with their attendants most of the time, out of sight and hearing. He had always had very well-trained nursemaids and governesses and tutors to look after his needs, spending at most one hour a day with his parents, after tea, after a stern warning to be on his very best behavior. He had been sent off to a very prestigious boarding school at the age of eight, returning only on holidays, most of which he spent with his cousin rather than with his parents. His mother and father had rarely demonstrated affection to each other or to their only child, though he did not doubt their love and concern for him.

As a result, Gavin had always felt lonely. His mother's mother had lived with them in her later years, and she had been his only reliable source of warmth and affection, aside from Andrew.

He recognized that his parents had shown their love in the only way they could imagine, by making sure he had the very best care, education and opportunities.

Gavin had never heard the words "I love you" from his father. When he was successful at some exploit he might receive a paternal pat on the head. His mother might say "I love you" in an automatic way, as if she knew this was expected of mothers, but she found little time for him. It still amazed Gavin that his grandmother and mother were so different from one another. Once grown, he had a developed a closer relationship with his father by taking on many burdens of the family business, and his mother became easier to get along with then, too.

After his father passed away, his grief at the loss surprised him. He did not expect to feel such emotion for his cold, remote Pater. But for his mother, the loss struck with overwhelming force. Mother secluded herself at the family's Chatham estate and never left it, embracing deep mourning garb and demeanor no matter how many years would pass, firmly defining herself henceforth as a widow. She limited all social contact to close members of her family.

Reflecting on his years as a lonely, isolated child, Gavin was ever more grateful that he had found his love, and the warm family affections that came with her.

"Alex, I want many children," Gavin blurted suddenly, reaching to take Alex's hand now that the last of the cakes and sandwiches and fresh fruits and ices had been cleared away.

"Where did that come from?" Alex asked with delight.

"I was just thinking how lonely it was, growing up the only child, and I want my children to have brothers and sisters who will look out for one another, always be there for each other, especially when it is our time to go. I do not want them to ever feel alone."

"Gavin, you're so sweet! I love you so much, and I want the same."

Gavin enjoyed every moment of his time with the Rosenshire clan. Every time Alex was around her family she was happy, smiling and laughing and talking with delight and energy. Alex had warned him that her family was not perfect— she and her sisters were quite capable of arguing! Gavin had found this hard to believe, so she told him to wait and see.

Elizabeth asked for everyone's attention. "I see everyone has finished tea. Please all stay seated. Let's try to plan this wonderful wedding. It's right around the corner!"

"Ashley, would you please make note of what we decide upon? You have the best handwriting," Alex suggested.

"All right," Ashley replied, bouncing to her

feet importantly. "I shall come right back with pen and paper!"

All were filled with anticipation and eager to bring forth their ideas.

Chapter Twenty-One

As the summer days passed, Alex grew stronger. There were times when she was perfectly fine and others where her stomach would cause her much discomfort. But for the most part her health was improving. She only felt ill first thing in the morning. Today, a week after the abduction, the skies were overcast, yet the weather remained pleasant enough that Alex was eager to get out of the house and go for a walk the minute Gavin arrived for his after-luncheon visit.

Elizabeth waited for Sara to finish fastening Alex's best boots and when Sara stepped out of the room, Elizabeth closed the door behind her.

"Alexandra," asked Elizabeth, "Has your cycle come yet?"

"Actually, no, it has not. Perhaps it is late due to the stress I have been under," Alex replied, somewhat embarrassed to discuss such an intimate topic. She was examining her appearance in the cheval mirror and her eagerness to dash out the door was evident.

"Perhaps you are right. But I do not think you may let this go lightly. It is something to be concerned about, Alexandra. Perhaps you could recall when your last cycle took place? Have you noticed any changes in your breasts? Please attend. If you are with child, we must hurry your wedding along. Your father would not accept any type of scandal that could come from this! He is too proud a man to tolerate any gossip concerning his family. Honestly, for all that has happened, we are very fortunate the county is not a hive of whispers."

"I will not let it go, I promise you. I just want to give it a little more time before I tell Gavin that it is a possibility. I know he would be excited about a baby, but you are right about its causing scandal. If I am with child, we will marry soon. Some people do like to count back from births to weddings! But it just feels so impossible to even think of it." Alex had her hand on the doorknob, impatiently waiting for her mother to finish.

"Why are you in such a rush today?"

"I am rushing because I do not want to waste any time which could be spent with Gavin. I want to make sure I am ready for him the moment he arrives."

"I do not think it's a good idea for you to be moving so quickly, especially when you are just getting better. I am sure that Gavin would not mind waiting just a few moments for the woman he loves," said her mother in a comforting tone.

"I know that Gavin would not mind waiting, but I mind! I have waited long enough and I intend to go for a nice walk and spend some time alone with him," Alex said, fighting an urge to stamp her feet like a child.

"I understand. I still think you should slow down. You may go now. Please, Alexandra, don't exhaust yourself!" With a kiss, Elizabeth let Alex open the door and flee.

Alex hurried down the stairs, ready to greet Gavin. "Ouch!" she said, clapping a hand to her stomach with a grimace as she reached the hall.

Her mother was right behind her, and heard her daughter's sudden gasp of pain. "Alexandra, what is wrong?" Elizabeth said, wrapping her in a supportive hug.

"I...I don't know," said Alex with a trembling voice, pain evident in her face, starting to double over.

"What hurts?" her mother asked.

"I had a sharp pain in my stomach, but I think it is passing," Alex said, standing up straight with an effort as she slowly moved her hand over her belly.

"Alexandra, I think we should call the doctor." Her voice was pitched low, for her daughter's ears only, and Alex also hushed her voice.

"No, Mother. I think you're overreacting. It probably was just a cramp... perhaps my cycle is finally coming today." Alex slowly started to walk down the hall to wait for Gavin's arrival.

"Alexandra, I don't think so. Look at the way you are walking."

"How am I walking?" Alex knew well she was not walking normally.

"You are walking slowly, and you appear to have great discomfort." Growing impatient with her daughter's obliviousness, Elizabeth continued quietly, "I think it only fair to let Gavin know what we think is going on with you and let him have a say in the decision to have the doctor or not. He is soon to be your husband and if you are with child, it is his as well."

"No! I do not want Gavin to know. Not yet, not until I know for sure if there even is a babe. Besides, calling the doctor would only alarm Father, and he must not know about this yet. I know it would disappoint him." They slowly made their way to the chesterfield in the drawing room with Elizabeth wrapping a supportive arm around Alex's waist until she was seated.

Elizabeth was growing more and more concerned. She looked around and seeing no servants within earshot, she continued in a hushed voice. "Alexandra, what more proof do you need? Your cycle is late, you're sick to your stomach in the morning and better in the afternoon, you have had some cramping and feelings of fatigue. You just experienced a sharp pain, and you have no idea what caused it." She took a breath and tried to control her fears. Speaking in a low, imperative voice, she said, "You must listen to me! You must be checked by the doctor."

"Why does Alex need to see the doctor?" Gavin inquired, as he quietly stepped into the room from the garden door, arriving from the stables right on schedule.

"I do not need to see the doctor. My mother is just overreacting," Alex said as she stood up to joyfully hug Gavin in greeting.

"Overreacting to what?" Gavin took Alex's hands and brought them to his lips to delicately kiss, looking into her eyes, deep concern on his face.

Elizabeth stood nearby, waiting for Alex to tell Gavin what had happened.

"I was rushing around very quickly to get ready for you. I did not want to waste any time which could be spent with you. So by the time I was all done and headed down the stairs, I got an unusually sharp pain in my stomach and..." She did not finish before Gavin interrupted.

"What kind of sharp pain? Has the doctor been called?" Gavin said with alarm in his voice.

"No, the doctor was not called. I am fine. It lasted only a minute and completely went away," Alex said as she gave Gavin a big hug and a smile she hoped was reassuring. "Everyone is overreacting."

"Are you sure you do not need to see the doctor?" Gavin asked with worry and love.

"I am sure! I feel fine now, and I would really like to go for a walk."

"Elizabeth, what do you think?" Gavin asked.

Watching her words carefully, she replied: "I think the doctor should be called, however, it is completely up to Alexandra. If she does not want to see the doctor, then we cannot force her to. She is no longer a child." Walking over to her daughter, Elizabeth squeezed Alex's shoulders affectionately and said, "Alex, I love you. Please watch yourself."

"I will, Mother, truly. Do not worry so much. I feel entirely better."

"I will watch her too, Elizabeth." Turning to Alex, he asked, "Maybe a walk isn't such a good idea? It's not a sunny day today."

"Please Gavin, just a short one? I need so desperately to go out of doors."

"Perhaps a short walk through the gardens. We have hours to spend with each other and I do not want you to tire." Smiling at Alex he leaned down and gave her a warm embrace.

"Well, I will leave you two alone. Would you please let me know when you return?" Elizabeth walked toward the door.

"Of course I will, Mother. Please, try not to worry about me."

"That would be impossible, dear. You are one of my children. One day you will see. Once you have children of your own, you will always worry." Elizabeth nodded her farewell and disappeared down the hallway.

"Alex, perhaps you should see your doctor just to put your mother's mind at rest."

"Oh, stop. I am fine, really. Let's go get some fresh air." Taking Gavin by the hand she led him to the garden door.

Gavin and Alex strolled through the manicured paths arm in arm, and finally came to a halt in a beautiful little gazebo surrounded by wildflowers and tall poplars in a remote corner of the grounds.

"It feels so wonderful to be outside again," Alex said as she twirled around in the pleasant warmth of the gray summer day.

"Alex, please. I think you should sit a moment take some rest now." Gavin seated himself on a long, wide, cushioned bench in the pleasant little garden structure, and reached out to take her hand and gently pull her down to sit beside him.

"Oh, all right. But really, I feel just wonderful now. I would like nothing more than for you to make love to me right here, right now." Alex reached around his neck to pull him close and seductively covered his lips and neck with passionate kisses.

Gavin was hesitant, unsure whether making love might put her fragile health at risk. "Alex, are you certain you're ready?" he asked, wanting nothing more than the same.

"Oh, I am more than certain, my love," Alex replied. She took Gavin's hand and placed it in on her breast, looking hungrily into his eyes.

"Alex, I love you very much. If we are to do

this, we shall do it very slowly and gently, and pay attention to your health, understand? You must tell me if you feel faint, or ill, or anything that might resemble pain." He gently caressed her.

"Oh, I understand, but I am ready, so ready, I have missed you so." Alex slowly unbuttoned Gavin's collar and shirt, revealing his broad chest. She gently caressed his skin from belt to neck. Then, leaning forward, she delicately followed the caresses with light kisses, nuzzling greedily, deeply inhaling his masculine scent.

"Alex, I love you more then you will ever know," Gavin said, as he gently helped her to lie back on the wide cushion. "Lie still, darling, I am going to help you relax."

Alex lay quiet, with her hands over her head and her legs stretched out straight, her eyes shut, unable to control a slight shiver of pleasurable anticipation. Gavin unfastened her boots and tenderly slid them off her tiny feet, then slowly undressed her until she was completely naked, piling her garments on a big wicker chair nearby. He gently brought his fingertips to her face and massaged around her eyes, nose and lips with a light, loving touch. She was aglow under his caresses. He paused a moment to remove his own clothing quickly.

His hands slowly caressed her neck, then made their way to her soft, round, handsome breasts. He then placed kisses all over her delicate white skin, leaving nothing untouched by his full, seductive lips. All the while, he carefully studied her face, making sure she was experiencing at least as much pleasure and enjoyment as he was. With his forefinger, he traced a light line down her arm, down the side of her body to her hip and continued to the very tips of her toes. Then he repeated this on her opposite side, going the other direction. He saw the smile on her face and knew what he was doing was working.

"Gavin, you must stop, please, you're torturing me." Alex was starting to squirm.

"Alex, darling, just lie still. I'm not through with you."

"How much longer must I wait?"

"There is no such thing as time for us... just now." Gavin at last brought his lips to hers for a deep, rapturous kiss.

Slowly, gently, he massaged her from crown to toes, caressing and kissing her lovely porcelain skin in many lovely, secret places.

"Now! I cannot wait anymore. Please? Please, just take me! You are making me beg!"

"If that is your wish, but we are going slowly today, remember?" Kneeling before her on the cushion and easily scooping her up into his arms, Gavin very slowly lowered her to enclose his manhood.

Gasping in pleasure, Alex welcomed him within, and soon they found their rhythm, moving in perfect harmony. Gavin was taking his time today, indeed. At long last their bodies erupted with pleasure and they let out moans of satisfaction, holding their arms around each other tightly.

"Alex, how do you feel?"

"I feel absolutely wonderful. How do you feel?" She placed tiny kisses on his cheek.

"I feel like I own all of England! Alex, as long as I have you, I will always feel that way."

They lay on the soft bench comfortably a long time, holding one another, speaking little, until Alex happened to notice how low the sun was getting in the sky. They rose to help each other dress, and soon returned to the house hand in hand.

As they arrived at the garden door, where Gavin started to turn toward the stables, Alex pulled on his hand and asked, "Won't you please stay for tea?"

"Alex, there is nothing more I would like than to stay with you, but I have some business to take care of that can't wait."

"Well, then, here we are again at the part of the day that I most dislike."

"I know, Angel. Remember. Soon we shall never have to part again," Gavin gently placed soft kisses on her face and neck.

"I know, Gavin. It's just that waiting for you to arrive every afternoon makes me so anxious! I have no patience. I want you to be here in the morning when I wake up and gaze into your eyes when I go to bed at night," she said into his shoulder, as they held each other tightly.

"I cannot wait for the day to arrive myself. But for now, until your health is certain, this is how it must be."

"Why can't you stay for tea?" she asked again.

"I'm sorry, Angel. As I said, I have some business to attend to today. I so wish I could stay."

"Well, it had better be important, because I am going to miss you terribly."

"It is. But I promise you that I will be on this doorstep right on time tomorrow. One o'clock, not a minute later."

"I will still miss you."

"And I will miss you!" Gavin gave her a kiss she was sure to remember.

"I love you, Gavin," she told him, looking up into his deep, dark, brilliant eyes.

"And I love you, my Angel."

Finally parting, Gavin glancing often over his shoulder, Alex lifted a finger to her eye and wiped away a single tear.

Opening the door, Elizabeth was curious to see why Alex was so late for tea. She was always worrying about how her daughter was feeling these days.

"Alexandra, why don't you come in? We have started tea without you."

Turning to face her mother Alex replied, "I'll be right in. I just... I don't know. I feel a little weepy." She could not believe what kind of effect Gavin was having on her. She always felt so empty when they had to say farewell.

"Alexandra, darling, what is wrong?" her mother worried at her new sensitivity. Alex was usually so buoyant and cheerful.

"I just hate it when he has to go and I hate waiting until the next time... it is torture for me. I want to be married right away, Mother. Please, I beg you!" she hugged her mother tightly.

"Alex, I think you need to relax! It is not as though he has gone far away. He went home and tomorrow he will be back. In just a few weeks you shall be enjoying your wedding day, and all this will seem unimportant and silly." Patting her daughter on the shoulder and brushing away long strands of blonde hair that had fallen around her face, her mother tried to console her.

Sighing, Alex said, "Perhaps you're right. Maybe I am just tired. I can't believe how emotional I feel right now."

"Don't worry dear, it is natural. Now let's go in and see about getting a hot pot of tea for you. It will restore you."

They entered the house arm in arm.

Chapter Twenty-Two

Gavin cantered through the woods and fields toward Arlington House with a smile on his face.

"Gavin, what are you doing back so early? Is everything quite all right?" Andrew asked as Gavin stepped through the front door, leaving his horse saddled near the steps.

"I have some business to take care of in Bedford, a favor someone asked of me," Gavin explained as he made his way up to his rooms. "Everything is fine."

"That does not explain to me why you are here," Andrew followed his cousin up the stairs.

"I merely need to change my clothes. No worries."

"I see. Now tell me more about this favor." Andrew was puzzled and curious.

"It is no secret. Daniel has asked that I help find his son, Richard." Whipping his shirt off, Gavin snatched a clean black one out of his wardrobe as Stephen arrived from the back stairs, puffing a little in his hurry.

"Why you?"

"It seems that Richard likes to frequent many public houses around Bedford town. I may not enjoy their pleasures much now, but when I was down and out I visited quite a few for many counties around. I know those people, and I know which taverns have the best card games and gambling. Daniel thought perhaps if I inquired I might be able to find out some knowledge that he and his men are not privy to."

Gavin was submitting to his valet's attentions with some impatience.

"From what I have heard about Richard, I thought him to be a fairly sharp young man who indulges in certain business dealings. Perhaps at times these are not quite businesslike." Andrew pondered the situation. "I doubt he is very close to Bedford Village. Were he in the neighborhood he soon would have learned of Lady Alexandra's... er... adventures. Surely that would have chased him home?"

"It seems that Richard has a way of falling off course sometimes, and right now he may need someone to pick him up and set him straight. Daniel has made many inquiries and a few rumors have reached his ears. I will start in Bedford."

"Well, I can understand that." Turning to depart, Andrew paused long enough to ask over his shoulder, "Gavin, did you ever *meet* Richard?"

Gavin responded, "No, I have never met him. But I have a description, and I did see a portrait of him hanging at Bedford House. Granted, it was painted when he was a few years younger, but I think he should look somewhat the same. Sometimes I practically feel like a Rosenshire myself these days, so I know I would recognize his voice, if nothing else."

"I wish you luck on your errand, cousin. Do try and stay out of trouble." Andrew was in the doorway.

"Thank you. I hope not to be long. I need to be back with my angel, taking care of her. And I have had more than my fair share of trouble!" His valet satisfied at last with his appearance, Gavin followed his cousin out the door.

Andrew laughed and shook his head as they walked down the stairs. "I hope you find him, Gavin. It would be a most excellent boon, in the eyes of your new father-in-law."

Back at Bedford House, Alex rose from the settee and yawned. "I think I will head upstairs now, mother."

"Is anything wrong? It's so early yet," Elizabeth looked up with concern. The family had finished the evening meal minutes earlier, and the women sat by a low fire with their needlework, the evening having grown cool. Daniel was reading a newspaper nearby.

"I know it is early, but I feel rather worn out. Perhaps I will read a little in bed before I turn out the lamp." Alex rang for Sara and headed upstairs after embracing her mother and sisters.

"Mother," said Cassandra, "I am worried about Alex. She was quiet tonight at dinner, and she looked very pale."

"I know. I thought she looked pale as well. After she settles herself in bed I will go and check on her. Perhaps it is as she said. She did have an emotional day with Gavin."

"That's right. I was so busy, I forgot she and Gavin actually left the house today!"

"Yes... perhaps it was a little too soon for her to go on an outing."

"Elizabeth, may I see you alone for a moment?" Daniel asked quietly.

"Of course you may."

Once they had moved to the library and closed the doors, Elizabeth asked softly, "Is anything wrong, dear?"

Daniel enveloped Elizabeth in a powerful hug. "Daniel, is everything all right? Your behavior is making me nervous." Elizabeth hugged him back and looked deeply into his eyes.

"Yes, yes, everything is fine. I do not wish to worry you, but, as you know, I have had some difficulty locating Richard. I want to let you know, I have asked Gavin for assistance."

"Gavin? How would he be able to help?"

"Gavin knows people around Bedford, people in the taverns and ale-houses, who may be able to help us find Richard."

"Taverns! Oh, my. That must be the business for which he had to leave early today?" she asked.

"Yes, that is right. We decided not to tell Alex for fear for her health. We did not want to cause her any more distress." Daniel began to pace the room.

"I understand, but why even tell *me* then?"

"I told you because I want to keep no secrets between us, whether it is over something big or something small." Walking over to his wife, Daniel grabbed her around her waist and gave her a romantic kiss.

"And what, may I ask, was that for?" She gazed adoringly at the man she loved.

"That was for being the only woman I have *ever* loved." Looking down at his wife, Daniel realized that at times he still felt like the young man who had fallen head over heels for a beautiful girl.

"Really? Well in that case, I should kiss you back for being the only man *I* have ever loved."

"Don't let anything stop you."

Taking advantage of the opportunity, they engaged in a long, tender kiss. In the privacy of the quiet library, Daniel and Elizabeth then sat side by side and discussed their son frankly. Their one hope was that someday he would put an end to his rebellions and stop causing them worry. Richard was grown. He needed to find someone to love, settle down and get married. If he did not want that for himself, then perhaps he could at least keep focused when doing business. Instead, what money he made, he usually spent on gambling or other escapades with his anonymous friends, whom he never brought home.

Richard had not always been like this. He had, in fact, been in love once with a young woman met on his travels. She was an artist who could paint wonderful landscapes and portraits, and had been working on a painting of a colorful field of wildflowers when he first saw her. Lady Victoria Thorndale and Richard were inseparable for some months. Then she was offered a chance to further her painting skills in Paris. She asked Richard to go with her, but he could not. He had business obligations that kept him in England. She would not give up her opportunity. They parted as friends, but to Richard it was a major heartbreak.

Without Lady Victoria by his side, Richard soon lost his sense of purpose. He started to indulge in frivolities that meant nothing to him. Then he tried to compete with his father as if burying himself in work would make him feel better. The pressure of trying somehow to impress his father was too much to bear at times, and he would end up in a tavern, drinking and gambling. He fell in with bad companions. At times Richard would indulge himself in the charms of women, the kind whose love was for sale.

Half the time Richard was full of love for his family and felt a sense of responsibility to do well and make money. Half the time he was impulsive and lost all his gains. His business brought in good money when he happened to be attending to it. Then it would languish from neglect. He moved back and forth between the two extremes, rudderless.

Gavin arrived at the first tavern around six o'clock. He made a few inquiries and learned that Richard had not been there, so he continued to the next. The search did not go well. No one had heard of Richard. Many people simply would not say anything, yes or no, wary of the handsome, tall, obviously well-bred stranger, and protective of their mates. Gavin patiently continued visiting ale-houses, public houses, taverns and even houses of ill repute, in gradually widening circles from Bedford House. Eventually, Gavin walked into the Royal Hand Tavern. After asking a few people there the same questions he had been asking others for two hours, he ran into someone who knew Richard.

"You have seen Richard Rosenshire of late?" Gavin asked the man, who appeared rather tipsy.

"I have seen the man yer looking for."

"*Where* did you see him?" Gavin asked, hoping he finally had struck gold.

"So yer want more information," said the man, leaning his back against the bar. Slapping his hand down, he said: "Barkeep, another pint, sir!"

"What in the hell is that supposed to mean?" Gavin snapped. Clearly the man was drunk.

"Perhaps you canna' tell by the fine looks o' me, but I do not have a large sum of coin in me pocket. If I tell yer where Richard is, yer will pay me for me troubles." Taking his tankard in hand, the stranger drank it down in one long draught.

"Fine, fine. I will pay. Now tell me, where is Richard Rosenshire?" Gavin was becoming more and more annoyed by this delay.

"Who taught yer how to get information out o' people?" The old man growled. "Show me yer money first."

Gavin took a good grip on the man's collar, hoisted him off the bar and pinned him to the wall so his feet did not quite touch the floor. Holding him there firmly, he said: "Now tell me where Richard is! I'm not in any mood for games and I do not think you shall like what I will do to you if you do not answer quickly. Am I understood?"

Nodding yes, the old man was released and he dropped to the floor.

"Richard is at the StarLite," he said in a hoarse voice as he rubbed his neck.

"Now was that so difficult?" Gavin turned on his heel and headed to the door.

"Hey, wait a minute! What about me money?" the old man shouted.

"Money? That's rich!" Gavin replied over his shoulder, tossing a copper penny at the man's feet.

He soon made his way over to the StarLite, one of the finer establishments in town. It attracted wealthy men because it offered everything and anything: card games, music, dice, liquor, women, more. Though Gavin had never indulged himself with women from these places, their reputation was widespread amongst the local rogues. Entering the StarLite, Gavin noted how charming it was: clean, well-appointed and elegant. He declined to give his hat to an attendant and looked around carefully, noting that the place was not as crowded as the previous taverns and ale-houses, and the few patrons downstairs were not drunk, just enjoying themselves. A piano player was giving most of them a popular tune. Walking over to the bar, he rapped on it once to get the barkeep's attention.

The short, portly man arrived right away. "What can I get for you, my Lord?"

"I need to speak with Richard Rosenshire," Gavin answered.

"Sorry, can you repeat that? It is a little loud in here with the music playing," the man said apologetically.

"I need to find Richard Rosenshire. Has he been here?" Gavin asked again.

"Richard? Yes my Lord, he is here."

"Good! Whereabouts? I did not notice him as I made my way through the room."

"No, I doubt you would have. Right now he is upstairs with Mary," said the man as he pointed to the stairwell in a back corner.

"Mary? How long has he been up there?" Gavin asked..

"With Mary? About two days now."

"Two days!" Gavin blurted, shocked.

"Yes, my Lord."

"Are you sure he is all right up there, man?"

"Oh yes, my Lord. Mary comes down to get him food and drink and take a rest. Besides, this behavior is not unusual for young Richard."

"This behavior, what do you mean?" Gavin asked.

"Richard does this sort of thing often. He may be with Mary now, and has been these last two days, but before Mary he was with Susan quite a while, and before that..."

"Stop! I have heard enough. What room would they be in?"

"And who may I know is asking, my Lord?" asked the barkeeper, suddenly feeling less helpful and forthcoming.

"My name is Gavin. I am soon to become his brother-in-law, and some things have happened at home he must be told about. That's more information than you really needed to have. Now, which room, sir?"

The barkeeper paused, twitching an eyebrow up at Gavin and studying his face. Then he relaxed. "All right, I will take your word for it, but I want no trouble here. I run a clean establishment and I like it that way. They are in the third room to the right, at the top of those stairs. Please do not disturb my other patrons."

"There will be no trouble. Thank you for your cooperation."

" I like Richard and all, but I don't have a wealth of girls here, and they need to be ready for the other men as well."

"Just business, right?" Gavin said, turning toward the stairs.

"Business is right," said the barkeeper, turning to wipe the bar.

Gavin made his way up the varnished stairs and soon found the room he was looking for. He listened at the door before knocking. He did not want to embarrass Richard any more than his father's request demanded. All was quiet, so Gavin proceeded to knock.

"Who is it?" answered a high little voice from the room.

"I need to speak with Richard Rosenshire," Gavin replied.

"For what, please?" came the same voice again.

"My name is Gavin, and I need to speak to Richard about things that concern him at Bedford House."

Some noise came from within the room and then, suddenly, the door flew open. There was Richard, clad only in his long China-silk drawers. "I am Richard, what has happened?" Richard demanded.

"Your father has been looking for you and... ."

"Is that what this is about? You tell my father I do not need his interference in my affairs!" Richard tried to close the door in Gavin's face.

"Wait one minute!" Gavin stopped the door with his hand. "That is not what this is about! Your sister Alexandra has gone through a terrible ordeal, and she is ill."

"What kind of terrible ordeal?" Richard asked coldly, opening the door a bit.

"I do not like your attitude," said Gavin as he stood inches away from Richard, eye to eye. "Your sister was kidnapped again, handled roughly, and escaped rape very narrowly. But that is not all. She had to kill one of her captors, and was exposed to the elements overnight while pursued on foot by armed, mounted assailants. Now she is unwell," Gavin informed Richard in a stern voice.

"Oh, my God! When did all this happen?" Richard now sounded more concerned.

"While you were busy trying to keep all the girls in town happy." Gavin was more than annoyed by Richard's initial reaction, and was not about to treat him kindly.

"What in the hell is that supposed to mean, and who in hell are you?" Richard snarled.

"I'll tell you who I am! I am Gavin Blake. Most address me as Your Grace. I am the man who is going to wed your sister the minute she regains her health! As far as your other question is concerned, your father was looking for you in hopes that you could help in our search for Alexandra, after she was abducted *again*. But he could not find you, because you close yourself in these rooms. The only reason he is looking for you now is so that you will come home to help your sister recover, as she worries over your long absence. And, perhaps, to attend her nuptials."

"Of course I will come home for Alexandra. But do not expect me to stay long!" Richard turned away to find his clothing and gather his belongings.

"I personally do not care how long you stay, as long as Alexandra is soon well. I am disappointed in your lack of concern for your family. Everyone at Bedford House painted such a respectful picture of you, and this is not what it looked like." Gavin stood in the doorway, surveying the tiny, disorderly room where Richard scurried about and a half-naked young woman reclined against the pillows of a wide bed with a glass of amber liquid in one hand

and a small cigar in the other, surveying the activity with a bored expression.

"Really? Well, we all have our unfortunate moments. Mary, it has been a great pleasure." Giving her a wave of his hand, Richard pushed Gavin into the hallway, followed him, and pulled the door shut behind him. Gavin was startled, but managed to keep his composure.

As they made their way downstairs, Gavin spoke seriously. "Richard, we should be on our way quickly. I should like to see Alex one more time tonight before she falls asleep. And one more thing. Do not ever push me again, or it will be a deed you deeply regret."

"You must truly love her. I am pleased that she has finally found someone... and I will endeavor not to push you." He was thinking it might have been better to meet Gavin under other circumstances, and he was truly happy for his sister.

"I love her more than anyone will ever know," Gavin replied.

As they talked while waiting for the ostler to get Richard's horse ready, Gavin learned that the young man was not as cold as he at first appeared, and started to consider him more a person who had momentarily lost his way. Gavin predicted that Richard would find his direction soon, and hoped that Richard and Daniel would settle their differences promptly.

Soon their mounts were cantering off toward Bedford House.

Chapter Twenty-Three

Gavin and Richard were soon delayed when Richard's horse lost a shoe. They were close to a pleasant inn on the Bedford Road, and it was apparent the horse could not continue. They decided to take a room and continue in the morning as soon as a blacksmith could get to work. Gavin was disappointed he would not be returning to Bedford House this evening, but he was relieved that he had completed his errand for Daniel successfully. Not quite trusting Richard yet, he felt it would be wise to stay at his side.

Alex awakened an hour after her family retired, feeling a sudden cold sweat breaking out all over, making her teeth chatter and giving her uncontrollable chills that wracked her body. She pulled the sheet and coverlet over her head to get warm. Suddenly her belly pain intensified and did not retreat. Reaching out for a pillow and hugging it to her midsection tightly, she curled into a ball around it and screamed into the pillow to muffle the sound. Soon she could take no more and screamed out, "Mother! Oh God! Mother, help me!"

Hearing the alarming cries, Elizabeth jumped from her bed, took up her dressing gown and ran to Alex's bedroom with Daniel right behind her, without bothering to put on her slippers. They rushed into Alex's rooms together.

"Alexandra, what is wrong?" she asked, kneeling at the bedside, as Daniel rang for Sara and lit all the lamps.

Alex moaned in pain. "It's my stomach, it hurts so much that I cannot catch my breath!" She had been writhing in agony, unable to find a comfortable position, and had entangled herself in her bedding. Her chills had departed and she was on fire with a fever.

Elizabeth reached to feel her daughter's burning brow. Alex's face was a pale mask of pain, covered in sweat, and her hair was wet. Her pillow was becoming wet as well.

Sara peeped in, still trying to tie her hastily donned apron, and Daniel told her to send a rider for the doctor at once. His urgent tone sent Sara off at a run to wake a footman as fast as she could.

"Daniel! Something is terribly wrong," Elizabeth tried not to panic.

Daniel had been worried about his daughter anyway, and now he was frightened as well. He hated feeling helpless and tried to think of some action he could take. He left the room to get dressed.

Awakened by the commotion, Cassandra and Ashley soon joined their mother in Alex's bedroom. The sight of Elizabeth's look of worry and fear was terrifying.

"Mother, what is wrong with Alex?" asked Cassandra. Ashley was so frightened she was unable to move or speak.

"I do not know. Her stomach pain has returned. She has a high fever. We can only pray that the doctor gets here soon. I need your help right now."

"Anything, Mother!"

"Fetch a basin of cool water, fast as you can. Get some bath sponges as well. She's burning up. At least we can sponge her, to help the fever come down. Ring for the scullery maid on your way, and ask her to keep bringing more basins, as cold as she can manage."

"I will be back in an instant." Cassandra ran from the room.

"Alex, please try and relax your body just a little. Tensing it will only make the pain worse."

"I can't, it hurts too much!" Alex rocked back and forth in a tight ball of pain.

Elizabeth gently untangled her daughter from her damp bedclothes to expose her skin to the cool night air. She lifted the coverlet and sheet and cast them aside.

"Oh my God!" she gasped.

"What is it?" Ashley asked, finding her voice. "May I help, mother?"

"There is blood all over her sheet. Too much. Please bring me more lamps! I must see better to help her." Ashley froze again when she saw the pool of dark blood under her sister.

"Ashley! Now!" Elizabeth reached behind her and shook Ashley roughly by the shoulder. "Fetch two lamps! And ring for your maid to bring me clean rags and towels." Elizabeth's imperative tone broke through. Ashley took a deep breath and ran from the room in tears.

Cassandra encountered Ashley at the top of the stairs. "What! What has happened?" Cassandra asked in a panic.

"Blood! There is blood everywhere." Ashley pulled herself together and ran to her rooms to borrow lamps and ring for her maid.

"Mother, here is cool water, and two bath sponges. The scullery maid is up now and will bring more. What is happening?" Cassandra went to the far side of the bed, climbed up next to her sister, and lovingly took Alex's hand in her own. "Alex, squeeze my hand every time you feel the pain." But Alex went limp, her legs and arms relaxed. Her head lolled back on her pillow.

"Mother!" shrieked Cassie. "Is she dead?"

"Alexandra, can you hear me? It's Mama." Cassie gently pushed hair away from Alex's pale, sweaty face. Elizabeth saw Alex's chest rising and falling with rapid breaths, and said, "She has just fainted from the pain. Maybe that is best, she does not suffer so now."

"Elizabeth, what is going on?" Daniel asked as he returned. He had thrown on his garments without waking his valet and looked rather disheveled, but he preferred not to go about the house in his nightshirt. He had brought Elizabeth's slippers. "Where did all this blood come from?" His face paled and his knees felt weak. Then he saw that Alex was unconscious, and white as her sheets. "My God, what in hell is happening?"

"I don't know yet. Perhaps you should wait outside."

"Yes, dear. The doctor should be here shortly. I will be close by if you need me."

Daniel sank into a chair on the gallery and began to pray. "Please God, let my baby girl be well. She is much needed and wanted here and has too much love left in her to be taken from us so soon. Please God, let her live." Holding his face in his hands, Daniel repeated his prayer again and again.

"Mother, here are the lamps. Towels are on the way." Ashley rushed into the room but tried to speak softly. She placed the lamps on chairs, after setting one on each side of Elizabeth, who still knelt close to the bed. She moved the dressing table lamp in front of the mirror so it would cast more light into the room.

"Good. Now, I will need both you girls to help me. Can you?"

Both girls nodded, frightened for their sister. Ashley saw the scullery maid in the doorway and took the basin from her, asking for another. As soon as she put it down on the bed near Cassie, Ashley's maid arrived with a stack of clean towels and rags. Cassandra reached across Alex for them and set them on the bed near Elizabeth. Ashley asked the maid to wait in the hall.

"Girls, help me get this nightdress off her," instructed Elizabeth firmly, not about to allow Ashley to freeze up again with fear. Together they gently tugged Alex's sweat-soaked gown down around her waist, keeping her covered with the relatively dry top sheet as best they could. Then they pulled the bloody gown and drawers together over her toes and cast the horrific bundle into the corner.

Sara brought in another basin and Ashley set it near the towels. Elizabeth showed Cassie how to sponge Alex's skin and scalp to cool her, then handed the sponge to Cassie. As Cassandra sponged, she tried to keep her gaze on her sister's dear face, and hold back her tears and anguish.

Elizabeth lifted Alex's hips while Ashley spread clean, thick towels underneath, then started sponging blood from Alex's nether regions, wringing the sponge out again and again in the reddening water. Ashley soon took the next basin from Sara in the doorway, who had intercepted the scullery maid at the top of the stairs and sent her back down. Taking the bloody basin from Ashley, Sara left, weeping, to dispose of it.

"Oh dear God!" Elizabeth said out loud. She tried to compose herself and keep her fears from her voice. She needed her girls to be strong, she needed their help. She needed to be strong for all of them.

Ashley had mustered her courage and quietly followed her mother's example. After carefully cleaning blood off Alex's legs, and sponging them again to cool them, she covered them up as best she could. Then she asked her maid to bring clean sheets, and used one to cover Alex, removing the damp one from under it to add to a growing pile of wet, bloody items in the corner. Her maid, waiting anxiously for some way to help, took away the dirty linens and crept back to stand in a dim corner until needed again.

Elizabeth tried to keep Alex's private places hidden as she kept cleaning away the blood, knowing how shy Alex could be about being exposed. Cassie felt her sister's forehead and wondered if the fever was worse or better, then continued sponging. From time to time she caught Ashley's eye to have her replace her basin with a fresh cool one. Ashley brought fresh basins to her mother as well.

"Mother, where is the blood coming from? Tell me, please!" Cassandra could hold back her tears no longer.

"Cassandra, no questions, right now we have to make the bleeding stop."

Ashley had tears streaming down her face too, but tried to stay alert and attend to all the basins.

"I can't tell if the bleeding has lessened because I don't know when or how it started." Elizabeth felt overwhelmed. "I don't know! I just don't know!" She collapsed onto the edge of the bed for a moment, pulled herself together, and resumed her sponging and wringing and rinsing with a determined expression. Her tears kept coming.

Daniel, hearing Elizabeth's muffled sobs, put his head in the door and asked what was happening.

"Oh Father, please tell us the doctor is going to be here soon!" Cassandra begged, sponging Alex's neck and face and shoulders with one hand, and gripping her sister's limp hand with the other.

"It has been a good half hour. Any time. I have a boy waiting at the door for him. What is wrong with her, Elizabeth?" He had stepped up behind his wife and put his hand comfortingly on her shoulder, unable to get closer due to all the chairs and basins and lamps. He blanched when he saw one basin's contents were blood-red.

"I cannot be certain, but I think she is having.. ." Elizabeth could not bear to go on.

"Elizabeth... having what?" Daniel shook her shoulder gently to break the trance.

Elizabeth took a deep breath. "I believe she is having a miscarriage."

Cassandra and Ashley gasped, "A miscarriage?"

"Yes. She and Gavin have been intimate, as they are so soon to wed. When Alex finally came home to us, I assumed that her belly pain was merely from hunger and stress, but as time passed I thought it was possible that she might be with child."

"Why was nothing said to me, Elizabeth? You and I keep no secrets!" Daniel asked, newly upset for at least four reasons.

"She did not want me to say anything until she was certain. She was afraid of your disappointment in her, Daniel. And she did not want to bring scandal upon this family. I had to respect her wishes."

"Perhaps she should have thought of that before she decided to become intimate. However, you all underestimate me! This might have looked bad, but I can handle anything. My family is what is important to me. My children are important to me. You come first, not what other people think. Together, we could have handled this. But now is not the time for this conversation. Alex needs us all to be strong for her!" Daniel looked at his pale, moist, unconscious daughter with immense worry etched on his features. Dealing with his anger and disappointment would wait. He stepped out of the room.

"Does Gavin know?" Cassandra asked her mother quietly.

"No. No, he does not know. I asked her to tell him, but she would not. She said not until she knew for sure." Ashley helped her mother replace the towels under Alex's hips as Elizabeth turned the beautiful, lifeless young woman on her side and sponged off the last traces of blood. Elizabeth finally packed more clean rags tightly between Alex's legs, and waited to find out whether they would soak through. Beyond that she didn't know what to do. She had never suspected anyone could bleed so much. She wondered whether her precious Alexandra would survive.

Elizabeth felt Alex's head for fever. Her skin still burned. "Keep sponging, Cassandra. Not just her face. And change the water often." Sara and the scullery maid had a row of fresh basins lined up on a table in the gallery nearby, each covered with a wet cloth to keep it cool. Sara had stationed herself at the doorway, promptly producing another basin at a look from Ashley or Cassandra.

Elizabeth checked on the bleeding. "It may be slowing... I am not sure. Ashley, more rags please, these are saturated." Ashley was ready.

Elizabeth stood up, rubbing her tired knees, and looked at her daughters. All their faces were pale and wet now. "Girls, listen to me carefully. Not one word of what I have said leaves this chamber, nor is it ever to be mentioned to your sister unless she talks directly about it. Is that understood?"

"Yes, Mother. I understand," said Cassandra.

"As do I," said Ashley.

"Good. Thank you both," Elizabeth said. Kneeling back down by the bed, she wiped away tears that were becoming too insistent to keep under control.

As he reached the bottom of the stairs, Daniel could hear an approaching rider. Running toward the front door, he flung it open to see Doctor Roberts halt and dismount. A stableboy was holding up a lantern to light his way, and taking his reins.

"Thank God you are here! Come, this way!" Daniel motioned for the doctor to follow him and took the stairs two at a time. Servants had lit some lamps in the stairwell, but the rest of the house was in dimness, the sun not yet risen.

"Elizabeth, what is it?" asked the doctor, noting the pale worried faces, the basins, the sponges, the blood, as he hurried to the bedside. Ashley had moved a chair and lamp aside to make room when she had heard the doctor's footsteps approaching at last. She had sent away all the servants except Sara, and they were huddled at the end of the corridor together, waiting to be called back. Cassie continued sponging Alex's arms, shoulders, neck, face. She had draped a wet cloth over Alex's brow.

"Alexandra woke us more than an hour ago with severe pain in her belly and a high fever. Her hair and nightdress were dripping wet. The pain made her scream and roll up into a ball. We discovered very heavy bleeding when we started trying to cool her off. She has been unconscious for quite some time now, and the bleeding has slowed but not stopped. I have packed the area with rags. Her fever remains high, though we have been sponging her with cool water."

"Thank you for the clear description, Lady Elizabeth. I will examine her now, so I ask that everyone else leave the room. Elizabeth, I may need your help." Cassie, Ashley, and Daniel quietly stepped through the door and closed it. Then, once sure he would not be overheard, Doctor Roberts asked, "Lady Elizabeth, what do you think is happening here?"

"I believe she is having a miscarriage."

"Yes, that is my thought as well." Finding a place to set down his black bag in all the clutter, he carefully examined the unconscious young woman as Elizabeth resumed sponging Alex's pale form with a gentle, loving touch. He listened to her heart a long time with an object like an ear trumpet, and spent just as long feeling for pulses in different locations.

"You are doing very well with her care. You must apply pressure where she is bleeding. She could bleed to death. Make sure the rags are packed tightly, and clean, and changed when they become wet. Flannel is best. Do not change or move the one closest to her body in case it is keeping a clot in place. Check them every hour. Do keep sponging her with cool water to help the fever come down. If you are not seeing improvement in an hour, take off the sheet and sponge her all over, and expose her to the air. Open the window, because a cool breeze would help. Or someone could fan her, if there is no breeze."

He washed his hands at Alex's washstand and put his instruments back into his bag. To Elizabeth, the doctor did not appear to be content.

"She is not out of danger yet, is she, doctor?" Elizabeth asked, frightened for her daughter's life.

"No, she is not. I wish I could tell you different. Her heartbeat is rapid. She has lost a lot of blood. She is unconscious. These are not good signs."

"When will we know if she is going to live or die?" Elizabeth was almost too afraid to ask.

"I am not sure. Even if she survives the bleeding, we must worry about infection. It is common with a miscarriage, and fever is a sign of it."

"Please! How long must we wait before we will know?" Elizabeth asked again. She was overwhelmed with worry and helplessness.

Gently taking Elizabeth by the shoulders, the doctor replied, "Lady Elizabeth, I do not know. This is a most delicate situation. We must watch her carefully for signs of any change. We shall get through this one day at a time. I am sorry, but there is nothing I can do."

Elizabeth nodded her head, trying not to cry. "Thank you for coming, doctor. When will you be back?"

"First thing in the morning. Do try and get some sleep, Elizabeth. You look awfully tired, and Alexandra will need your care tomorrow. Someone must stay with her at all times. Perhaps Daniel could sit first? I will make him aware of the situation on my way out." With a nod, the doctor left the room.

"Doctor, let me show you out," said Daniel, waiting by the door with Cassandra and Ashley, who rushed in to their sister and mother as soon as the doctor stepped through it.

"Fine, thank you. We need to talk in any case." Dr. Roberts followed Daniel down the stairs.

"Please tell me everything that is happening with my daughter!"

"Lady Alexandra has suffered a miscarriage. She is in very grave health and must be watched carefully. As I told Lady Elizabeth, someone must be with her at all times. If there is any change in her condition someone should send for me right away. Elizabeth is approaching a state of exhaustion, and I suggested that perhaps you could sit with Alex now so she could get some rest."

"Yes, that is fine... . Doctor, will my daughter live?" Daniel was somber.

"I cannot know yet. I am very sorry, my Lord," he patted Daniel on the shoulder in a gesture of comfort.

"Doctor Roberts, I trust you will tell no one of this matter?"

"My lord. There is no need for you to concern yourself at all. I will be most discreet, indeed." They were standing at the door, speaking in hushed tones. With a firm handshake, the doctor departed.

Daniel sent word that a fast horse was to remain saddled and bridled at all times until further notice, with a footman always at the ready to depart in case the doctor needed summoning.

Elizabeth let Ashley and Cassandra kiss their goodnights to Alex and then sent them to their beds. She did not know how to leave her daughter's side. What if Alexandra wakes up? What if she does not? What if I'm not there and something happens? All of these questions raced through her mind, and when Daniel came in the room and told her to go and get some rest she refused, repeating the questions that plagued her.

"Elizabeth, if I cannot persuade you to leave the room, then you must rest next to Alex. I will stay with you and do whatever needs doing." Daniel spoke to Sara in the doorway, and she went for blankets.

Elizabeth opened a window and drew back the draperies, hoping a cool night breeze might carry away the heat of Alex's fever.

"I must check her now. Please turn your back." Daniel complied. Elizabeth removed and renewed most of the rags, noting some improvement, and glanced at the clock on Alex's mantel. "Daniel, I must tend to her every hour. Do not forget to wake me. Her life may depend on it. And while I rest, you must cool her brow. Like this." Elizabeth took up a sponge, dipped it in the basin, pressed it to Alex's forehead, wrung it out, dipped it again, nodded unspoken instructions to Daniel to do the same. "Sara will bring fresh water. Perhaps you could have Ashley's maid help so Sara may rest as well." She rearranged the chairs and basins so he could sit close to Alex and be comfortable.

"Elizabeth. I will do as you say. Do not worry. Please lie down now, and I will awaken you in one hour."

At last she took a few paces around the foot of the bed and stretched out next to Alex, as Daniel placed a pillow under her head. "Daniel, why is this happening?" Her voice was pleading and weak.

"I do not know. Perhaps we will never know. But I do know we cannot burden ourselves with that question. We must concentrate our energies on making our daughter better, and in order to do so, you must rest. I will remain awake and let you know if anything changes."

Daniel gently covered her with a blanket and tenderly kissed her mouth. "Rest now."

"Thank you Daniel. I love you."

"I love you, too. Now rest." Daniel seated himself and picked up the sponge. A tear ran down his cheek as worry welled deep within him.

"Cassandra, do you think Alex is going to be all right?" Ashley asked, both nestled in Cassandra's bed.

"I do not know, Ashley. I have never been so scared." Cassandra said.

"Me too." They held one another, terrified. They realized now just how much they all meant to each other. But the hour was very late, and they drifted off to sleep.

What morning would bring, no one knew. It would be a long night.

Chapter Twenty-Four

Daniel waited until the first rays of sun beamed into Alex's east window. His wife was kneeling against Alex's bed, asleep. Her lovely head was resting on her folded arms near his frail daughter's face. Daniel shrugged off the blanket wrapped around his shoulders and quietly stepped over to her. When he gently tapped on her shoulder, she jumped to attention in a panic.

"What is it? Is something wrong? Is she getting worse?" Elizabeth's voice was shaky.

"Elizabeth, nothing like that. I think her fever has broken. Her skin is cooler, and dry. I stopped sponging her a little while ago. I woke you so perhaps you could go and freshen up. I know it's time for you to check her, and then maybe you could have something to eat. You must remember to take care of yourself." Daniel's tone betrayed his deep concern.

"I guess that I should keep my strength up for Alex. No telling how long she will need my care. When I checked her bleeding an hour ago, it seemed to have finally stopped. I will just take a quick look now... good. Very good! I will go bathe and change and ring for our breakfast. And I will wake Cassandra to come sit with her so you can join me downstairs."

Tired and worn, Daniel and Elizabeth embraced each other a long moment before she left the room.

Walking down the gallery, Elizabeth began to droop from her deep state of exhaustion. She paused in front of a full-length mirror to gaze in confusion at an unrecognizable woman who had aged ten years overnight. Dark circles surrounded her eyes, and hair that had been neatly braided up at bedtime had fallen loosely about her shoulders. Her nightgown was creased, and blood stained her silk and satin dressing-gown sleeves. She continued to her rooms and rang for her maid. She splashed water on her face and neck and patted herself dry with a monogrammed linen hand towel. Once seated at her dressing table, Elizabeth tried to comb through her mass of tangled hair. Her maid appeared before she got very far, and helped make it tidy again. Word had quickly spread through the servants' quarters of Alex's grave state, so the maid made haste with helping Elizabeth to dress, and tried her best to lift her mood, telling her that Cassandra and Ashley were already up and in the morning room waiting for her, so worried about their sister they had risen before dawn.

Elizabeth soon joined them, and was glad to see that a footman was pouring her a steaming cup of fresh tea before she was seated. She hoped good strong tea would restore her strength.

"Cassandra, I would appreciate it if you would go and watch over your sister for a short while, so your father can change his clothes and get a bite to eat."

"Certainly, Mother, I will go right up. But please, tell us, how is dear Alex this morning?" Cassandra was taking the last bites of her breakfast.

"She has not awakened. Her fever is down and the bleeding has slowed or maybe stopped. How she really is...we will not know until she wakes." She paused and tried to collect her thoughts. "Pray for your sister, my babies. Pray. Please."

The girls had tears in their eyes and they gathered close to their mother to wrap her in a hug as they silently prayed for their sister.

"Amen. Now go, Cassandra, and let your father have some time to prepare for the day. We did not sleep very much last night. I'm sure he will need to rest. If your sister wakes up, or if there is any change at all, you are to come and get me at once. You may give her a glass of water if you are very careful. Do not say a word to her of what happened! I do not want to frighten her. I would like to be the one to tell her. Perhaps I can say it in a gentle way, so that it won't hurt so much."

"Of course, Mother. Ashley, perhaps you would like to keep me company for a while?" Cassandra asked.

"Yes, I would like that very much. Maybe just hearing our voices will make her want to wake up."

"That might work," Cassandra said. "Brilliant idea, Ashley."

"I will come and relieve you when the doctor arrives. Thank you. And thank you for all your good help last night. I am proud of how well you managed in such trying circumstances, and I know it was not easy for you."

"Yes, Mother." Cassandra and Ashley left their mother to sit and sip her tea alone.

"Father, Ashley and I have come to relieve you for a bit," Cassandra said as they made their way over to their sister's bed.

"Yes, that would be good. She has not moved at all, but I would think that your mother would like to be told when she does," Daniel said as he rubbed his tired eyes and rose from the uncomfortable chair at the head of the bed where he had spent the long sleepless night.

"Yes, mother has told us what we are to do, so just go and get some sleep. Ashley and I can handle things from here." Giving her father a kiss on his cheek, Cassandra took her father's chair as Ashley climbed up to sit close to Alex on the bed and take her hand.

Sara had almost finished. She thought to extinguish all the lamps, remove the extra ones, and tidy up the rooms. Alex's bedroom looked almost as it normally did. Sara had taken care to set the fresh pile of flannel rags on a bedside table and cover them discreetly with a pretty lace handkerchief. There was a bin nearby, covered with a cloth, to put used ones in. The other bedside table had a sweet, fragrant little nosegay in a crystal vase. There was a second easy chair where the dressing table used to be, and a few other changes they did not notice at first. The chamber no longer seemed so crowded and frantic and desperately cluttered. A light morning breeze fluttered the draperies.

Gavin and Richard rode up to the stables in the early morning light and handed their reins to a sleepy groom, then turned toward the garden door of the drawing room.

"Richard, perhaps I should not go in just now. Alex has probably not even awakened yet."

"That is silly. From what you have told me, I would bet anything that she would not mind your calling on her so early this morning," Richard assured Gavin, now feeling like they had long been friends.

They entered the drawing room together, trying not to make much noise. At this hour, the servants would be in their hall for breakfast before commencing their duties, and the cook and housekeeper would be busy, but it was too early for any Rosenshires to be stirring. Richard said, "Let's ring for tea and some breakfast. It's too early but we can eat whatever the staff is having. I am ravenous! We never had a bite to eat last night."

"Well, I'm eager to see my angel, but food would not be a bad idea. This way she can sleep a while longer before I wake her up."

They noticed sounds from the breakfast room as they approached.

Both were surprised to see Elizabeth dressed and drinking her tea at this hour. The sun had hardly risen enough to shine weakly through the big windows. "Mother, you're up so early!" Richard greeted her, giving her a hug.

"Richard, Gavin... you're home!" Elizabeth was too tired to stand and hug her errant boy. "I did not expect to see you so soon. Actually I did not think Gavin would be able to find you, seeing how no one else could. But that is unimportant right now.... Welcome home, dear son. I have missed you so." She offered her cheek for his kiss. Her fatigue was evident in her voice and manner.

"What do you mean unimportant? I thought you would have been a little happier to see me!" Richard replied, hurt, too concerned with himself to notice her state.

"Under normal circumstances, I would be," Elizabeth said.

"Normal circumstances? What does that mean?" Richard asked.

Gavin could tell at once that there was something amiss in the household. He looked imploringly into Elizabeth's eyes, trying to determine if Alexandra was in some sort of difficulty.

"Gavin, it is good that you are here. Something has happened that you should be informed about," Elizabeth rose and walked over to him, and gently took his hand in hers. "Please, Richard, would you excuse us? I wish to speak to Gavin alone. I will explain to you later and you will understand." Richard gave her a look of confusion and took himself off to the study. He could get someone to bring his breakfast there.

"Elizabeth, what has happened? What are you talking about?" Gavin suddenly felt anxious and distressed, and overtaken by a nameless fear.

"Last night, after we all went to bed, we woke up to an alarming scream. It was Alex. She was feverish and there was blood and ... we had to have the doctor... and... ." She broke down and began to weep. It was painful to bring back the horrible images of the night before and even more horrible to have to tell her future son-in-law that he had lost a child.

"Blood! Blood? What are you talking about! Elizabeth? Tell me now! What has happened to Alex?" Gavin was trying not to shake Elizabeth by her shoulders. He balled his fists and tried to find his patience. The most agonizing thoughts went racing through his mind. Had Alex been attacked in her bed? That would not cause a fever! He had to hear the whole story. He had to know if Alex was all right, and he needed to hear it from Elizabeth right now.

Just as she was about to tell Gavin everything, Elizabeth heard Cassandra calling.

"Mother! Mother, she is awake! Come quickly!" Cassandra called.

Elizabeth ran for the stairs with Gavin on her heels, soon followed by Richard, who had heard the commotion. Arriving at her daughter's rooms, she asked both men to wait in the hallway.

"Elizabeth, don't do this to me," Gavin begged. "Tell me what has happened. Don't make me wait!"

"Gavin, I do not mean to do this to you but I must tend to Alexandra first. Soon everything will be made clear. Now please be patient while I take a moment with my daughter. Compose yourself for her." Elizabeth turned and quietly entered the room.

"Cassandra, Ashley, please leave me alone with your sister. Wait in the hall. I will be out shortly."

The young women nodded and left the room.

Walking to her daughter's bedside, Elizabeth gently sat beside her on the edge of the bed, and took her hand. White-faced and weak, Alex looked as though the life had been drained from her and it tore at her mother's heart. She gazed into her mother's face looking for a clue.

In a weak voice, Alex asked, "Mother, what is wrong with me?"

"How do you feel now, please tell me first," Elizabeth asked in a soft, soothing voice, fighting back tears. She reached for the carafe Sara had set nearby and poured Alex a drink of water, knowing how dry she would feel from the fever and the bleeding.

Alex took a moment to think, gulped down some water with her mother's hand supporting her head, and fell back on her pillow motionless, pale and drawn, her hair a matted tangle. Then she softly answered in a thin voice, "I feel so weak and tired I can't quite raise my head without your help. I am as sore as if I had fallen off a horse ten times in a day. It is hard for me to speak loudly enough to be heard. And I am very thirsty. What has happened? Why do you look so sad? Please tell me."

"Alexandra. I want you to listen to me carefully. What I'm about to tell you may come as a shock, and I am asking you to remember for me that there is nothing you could have done to prevent it," Elizabeth stroked her daughter's arm.

"Mother, please," Alex whispered, begging her mother to continue, not understanding.

"Alexandra, my darling, you suffered a terrible miscarriage and it almost took you away from us. You are not out of danger yet. The doctor will be along soon to take another look. You will have to stay in bed a while to regain your strength. Recovery will take some time." Then Alex's mouth was open in surprise and shock and her eyes could not get any bigger. Just when Elizabeth was about to ask her if she understood all this, Alex screamed "NO!"

"No! No! This can't be happening." She was whispering, and breathless from the effort. Then her emotions powered her voice and, taking a big breath, she said with a wild look on her face, "I did not think I was with child, yet... I knew I was. How selfish of me to go for that walk! It was such a foolish risk to take! I should have known better. I killed my baby! I killed Gavin's baby!" Tears rolling down her face, she rolled away and curled up in a ball, wrapping her head in her arms.

Everyone in the hall heard Alex's scream and then they heard her words. Gavin faced her door, speechless. Cassandra and Ashley stood with tears in their eyes and Richard did not know what to say. Daniel came running when he heard Alex's scream, too late to hear her words.

"What is happening?" Daniel asked as he reached the group. "Richard! You're back!"

"Alex lost our baby," Gavin said in a fog, unable to move. He was more shocked than he had ever been before and found his thoughts had scattered.

"I know," Daniel said as he walked over to Gavin and placed a hand on his shoulder. Gavin turned to look at Daniel. Daniel lost control suddenly and lashed out. "Gavin, since my daughter has met you she has had nothing but terrible things happen to her. How could you be so careless!" Daniel said with burning anger in his gaze.

"Careless? ... I love her... I care for her deeply. I have never been careless... We never thought anything like this could happen." Gavin thought he and Daniel had grown close, but now there was a great gulf between them.

"Exactly. You did not think, and now my daughter is fighting for her life! If you did love her as you say, you would have waited until after you were wed. Did you not think what people would say about a baby conceived before marriage? It shall be quite a task to keep this matter private."

Gavin struggled to gather his thoughts. Finally, he replied quietly and without heat, "Daniel, I love your daughter. I will not let you question my love for her. I did not force myself on her. We love each other and we expressed that love together. If I had imagined she was with child I would have married her immediately and hushed any speculation of any kind. I am not saying what I did was right, or what we did was right, but I do love Alex with all my heart and soul. Just as she loves me. I know that you blame me, and I blame myself as well, but right now we need to focus on

Alex, on her health and happiness, and not on our anger."

"Focusing on Alex is my first priority, and as far as you are concerned, we will finish this at a later date." Alex's hurt was too much for Daniel to bear.

Gavin looked Daniel in the eye and said, "Fine." Then he turned away and put his hand on the doorknob.

"Gavin, don't blame Alex for this. There was nothing she could have done."

Gavin turned to gaze at Daniel disbelievingly and said softly, "I could never blame her. It's just not in me. I know this was beyond anyone's control, and the last thing anyone could wish for. I resent the fact that you would even think such a thing. I treasure her life more than my own! All I want is for her to get well so I can marry her and be with her every moment of the rest of my life. Of course I am in shock, and I mourn for our child, but Alex is still here, and I need her as much as she needs me."

"Gavin, I did not mean to offend you. Of course you love her," Daniel responded quietly, trying to soften his tone. He knew he was angry and tended to be hot-headed, and he needed someone to blame. His need to protect his daughter was overpowering and his worry was all he could think of.

Richard broke in. "Father, why don't we just wait to hear what mother has to say. Alex does not need to hear people arguing, it will only upset her more."

"The voice of reason coming from my son, who comes and goes as he pleases," Daniel said with a wave of his hand, still spoiling for a fight.

Richard said nothing. He knew his father was concerned about Alex and overcome by his worries.

"Can we all please be quiet? I want to hear what is going on," said Cassandra as she stood with her ear to Alex's door.

Elizabeth gently, lovingly pleaded with her daughter. "Alexandra, stop this! You must not blame yourself. You did not kill your baby! Do you hear me? You did not kill your baby!" Elizabeth cried as she tried to console her daughter. "These things cannot be prevented, no matter what you do or do not do."

No one could reach Alex now with words or with reason. She faced the wall, curled up as small as she could make herself. Hearing nothing, seeing nothing, she rocked back and forth. "I killed my baby. I killed my baby," she murmured again and again.

Elizabeth was so upset she had to leave the room. It was obvious she was not going to get through to Alex. Perhaps someone else could.

"Elizabeth, how is she?" Gavin asked in the doorway as she brushed past him.

"Gavin, she is lost in her own world, feeling sad and guilty." Tears were streaming down her face. "She blames herself. She said she was selfish for taking that walk and now she has shut herself away somewhere... somewhere I cannot reach her. She keeps saying that she killed her baby. She does not hear me!" Elizabeth walked over to Daniel, wrapped her arms around him and let herself weep.

"Elizabeth. She just needs some time," Daniel said consolingly, stroking her hair.

"I'm going in," Gavin said.

No one protested.

"Angel, my love, can you hear me?" Gavin whispered as he sat beside her and gently took her hand, peering into her dear face.

There was no reply. She drew back the hand close to herself and balled her fingers into a tight fist.

"Alex, please don't do this," he reached for her again. Again she pulled away. "Alex I know you can hear me. Please don't shut me out. I know this was unavoidable. You have been through another terrible, terrible ordeal. I feel a loss as great as yours, but I need you. I need you to get through this, and I know you need me." Gavin leaned down to give her a kiss but she jerked away.

"I killed our baby!" she said through gritted teeth.

"No, Alex you did not! Do you hear me?" Gavin said. He lightly grasped her shoulders but was afraid to give her a shake in her fragile condition. His eyes began to fill with tears. He did not know how to make her understand, and he did not know how to help her.

Alex would not answer Gavin, nor look at him. He tried awkwardly to embrace her. She would not acknowledge his presence. He sat in silence stroking her hair for a few minutes, then rose and left the room.

"I don't know what to do," he said as he stood before her family, his cheeks wet with tears. "She won't even look at me."

Elizabeth knew what her daughter's despondency was doing to Gavin. There before her stood a grown man, over six feet tall, masculine in every way. But she saw a lost little boy. She walked over to Gavin and pulled him into her motherly embrace.

"We will all get through this, Gavin. It's going to take a little time, that's all. The doctor will be here soon. Maybe he can help us help her."

Cassandra went into her sister's room to sit with Alex until the doctor arrived. The rest of the family-plus-Gavin went downstairs to wait in the morning room, where the staff had set out a rich array of breakfast dishes on the buffet. Nobody felt like eating. Gavin wanted to sit with Alex but he was afraid his presence was too upsetting for her, and this idea was killing him.

The doctor arrived a short time later, and went up to examine Alex again, sending Cassandra down.

When they heard Doctor Roberts descending the stairs a few minutes later, Ashley excused herself to sit with Alex so she would not be alone. The doctor took a seat at the table in the morning room with everyone else. "I'm sorry Elizabeth, Daniel...but there is nothing I can think of that will make things better. Until Alex realizes that what happened to her was not her fault but an act of God... I doubt anyone will be able to reach her. We will need to watch her closely as her body heals, make sure she has plenty of rest, and do try to get her to eat and drink. Only time will tell us when her emotional state may return to normal."

As Dr. Roberts rose to depart he cautioned, "I will be back tomorrow, and every morning, to ensure that an infection does not set in. It's imperative that you watch for a fever. She must be cared for around the clock. If there is the slightest sign of one, please send for me at once."

Then Gavin asked the doctor a question that was bothering him, and he wondered if it worried the others as well. "Doctor, will she be able to have children?"

"I would like to tell you yes... but at this point, I do not know. Some women recover completely, and some women do not. We must wait and see." Picking up his hat, the doctor bid them all goodbye.

There were sad faces all around the table. "Oh my God! My poor baby!" Elizabeth cried. "Almost every day of her life, that child has dreamed of having a wonderful husband and many babies. If she loses her dreams, she will never again be the wonderful young woman we all love so much." Elizabeth rose and rushed from the room with hot tears blurring her vision.

Cassandra noticed that Gavin had yet to move or say anything. She placed her hand on his arm and gently shook him. "Gavin? Gavin?" she called, but still he did not move. "Gavin, please say something." Richard, Daniel and Cassandra all tried to get some sort of response from Gavin but he sat still as a stone, his expression empty.

Richard took it upon himself to try and jolt his new friend back to reality. "Gavin, if you do not move in the next two minutes, God help me but I am going to hit you," Richard stood up and moved around the table, placing his hands on Gavin's shoulders and giving him a shake.

Cassandra was shocked by her brother's words. "You're not really going to hit him, are you?"

"I will if I have to." Again Richard shook Gavin.

"Perhaps we should try a more peaceful approach," offered Daniel, guessing that Gavin was feeling hurt and responsible for Alex's condition.

"Father, if I seriously thought a more peaceful approach would snap Gavin out of this daze I would do it. But as you can see, he is not responding to our voices or my touch. What else can I do but shock him out of it?" Without waiting for a reply, Richard leaned over and slapped Gavin sharply enough to turn his head.

"What the hell do you think you are doing?" Gavin said, jumping to his feet and placing a palm on his jaw.

"I was bringing you out of that other world you seemed to be stuck in," Richard said, cautiously backing away to a safe distance.

"Good thing. I don't know what happened to me. I remember hearing what the doctor said, and then everything went blank... Where is Elizabeth?" Gavin sat back down.

"She went to check on Alex," Ashley told him, arriving at the table, wondering what was happening. Everyone seemed entirely out of sorts, and her mother had only said that Alex needed rest.

"Alex! What am I going to say to her? How can I tell the woman I love that she may not be able to bear children?" Gavin shook his head in disbelief. Just yesterday he was making love to his Angel. She had seemed perfectly healthy, her normal self... Now she was weak and sick, and in some world far away from him. "How can I help her?" Gavin said as he folded his hands as if he were pleading with the Lord above, looking around at these other worried people.

"Be there for her," Daniel said. "Just be there for her. Give her time to come back, and let her bring up the question." Exchanging a look with Gavin, he left the room.

"Gavin, Ashley and I will be in the sitting room should you need anything," Cassandra said as she took her sister's arm and departed.

"Richard, I think I will go to Alex's room and sit with her for a while. Thank you for your help." Gavin shook Richard's hand with sincere appreciation.

"I will come up and see Alex later. For now I will give you some time."

"Thank you," Gavin said again, and rose to go up the stairs. Still in shock over all that had happened, his main concern was how he would get Alex to realize her miscarriage was unavoidable.

Gavin gently knocked on the door.

"Elizabeth, is it all right to enter?" he asked, slowly opening the door.

"Of course. Perhaps if you talk to her, she will eventually come round." Standing to give Gavin the bedside chair, Elizabeth gave him a pat on the shoulder and looked into his eyes.

"Elizabeth?"

"Yes, Gavin?"

"I'm frightened."

"I know darling. We all are." Quietly she closed the door behind her.

Gavin looked over at his angel, who still was rolled up in a ball on the far side of her bed. A dead, unblinking stare masked her face. Her breathing was barely detectable. Gavin spoke softly as he swiftly removed his boots and jacket and cast them on a chair.

"Angel, please, please, hear me. I love you, damn it, and there is no way in hell you're going to just lie here and die on me. Our baby was taken by God, and there was nothing you could have done. It simply was not our time yet for a child." Straightening the coverlet, he lay down behind her and rubbed her shoulders gently. "Angel, I love you." He leaned over to plant a kiss on her cheek. "Alex, I need you." He drew closer, spooning her, matching her every curve, snaking an arm beneath her so he could gently embrace her. "Alex, please speak to me," Gavin begged. The silence, the motionlessness, was so hard for him. The woman he loved was full of life and love.

The woman he held was empty and sad.

Chapter Twenty-Five

Long summer days and balmy nights crept by slowly as everyone at Bedford House tried to coax Alex to return to them. Tender ministrations and kind words apparently did not penetrate to her mind, so distantly withdrawn. It had been weeks since that awful night, and Alex was barely present.

Elizabeth and Cassandra were sipping tea in the drawing room. "Mother, what are we going to do?" Cassandra asked in sadness and frustration.

"I do not know... I was hoping that in time she would come to her senses, but I am beginning to lose hope."

Fatigue was obvious in their features and manner. Everyone in the household was becoming distant, forlorn and fearful as Alex's condition remained almost unchanged. Until she returned to her usual buoyant spirits, no one would be happy.

Alex was thin, pale and unresponsive. Her bleeding had soon stopped, and she had not developed fever or infection, for which all were thankful, but she shied away from every touch.

Gavin sat with Alex night and day, reluctant to leave her side. He had not been shaved in all this time, and his beard had filled out and then lengthened. His eyes were red and sad and showed his deep fatigue. He seldom let his valet draw a bath or provide a fresh change of clothes, and sleeping in his clothes night after night had not improved his appearance. Stephen had moved to Bedford House with him, but seldom found his services welcome. Gavin had lost so much weight all his garments hung loosely on his tall frame. Gavin slept more on Alex's bed than in his own, taking occasional trays of food at her bedside when Elizabeth insisted, but only while Alex slept. He left her rooms when Sara was tending to her needs, or when her sisters or parents wanted time with her, but seldom went downstairs.

Sara patiently tried to brush Alex's hair every day, and gave her sponge baths, and changed her sheets and nightdress with difficulty. With little cooperation, these tasks were never completed to her satisfaction. Alex did not seem to care whether the draperies were open, whether it was a beautiful day out, whether anyone was sitting with her or speaking to her. She accepted drinks of water and used the chamber pot with Sara's help, never staying out of her cocoon of sheets for long. She rarely spoke except to express her needs to Sara in monosyllables or answer the doctor's questions. The rest of the time she retreated into a hazy doze someplace between waking and sleeping and ignored her surroundings.

After the first week, she sometimes allowed her mother to feed her light, simple meals. She never responded with words or any other acknowledgement to loving family members who came to her bedside day after day and begged her to return to the land of the living, always too lost in her thoughts, her gaze blank when her eyes were open. Daniel could hardly bear to enter her bedchamber any more. Ashley and Cassandra came in faithfully to massage her limbs, kneading her limp body with loving hands for an hour every morning and afternoon as the doctor had requested.

Every time Alex pulled back from Gavin's touch he felt his heart breaking. He tried to hold her as she slept, but there was never the slightest response except to inch away until she was almost falling off the bed. Her rejection was hard on him. He began to doubt their future together. How could he help her get through this, if she did not care if he was there? Day by day, week by week, month by month, it grew harder for him to believe their love would hold them together. Gavin knew that if his angel would not accept him, he would never love again. He understood that without Alex, his life was not worth living.

The days and nights of summer went by with excruciating slowness, the hushed, miserable residents of Bedford House unable to enjoy their usual amusements. Hopes and dreams were forgotten, and sadness remained in their place, everyone preoccupied with Alex and her miserable condition. The summer wedding, once so eagerly anticipated, was never mentioned. Richard lingered at home longer than usual, wondering what to do, then found a way to take a role in Daniel's business affairs. They gradually came to like working together and relied on each other's support through the endless days. Their tentative friendship was fast becoming a solid partnership, and work became their refuge from their despair over Alex.

Finally, Doctor Roberts insisted that she be forced to get up from her bed and take daily walks, lest her limbs become too flaccid or rigid. As soon as the doctor left, Elizabeth and Gavin tried to help Alex rise. She remained curled in a slender ball in spite of their efforts. Every day, Elizabeth and Gavin tried to coax her to walk. Every day, Alex withdrew.

Windy fall weather came early as the days started to grow shorter, and swept the leaves off the trees. One day Elizabeth walked quietly into her daughter's rooms and saw Gavin was asleep. She studied Alex's inert form, hoping and praying for some small indication of improvement. This was so sad. Sleep consumed Alex most of the time. Elizabeth was pleased to let Gavin rest, knowing he badly needed more sleep than he had been getting. She soon slipped away. Her other daughters needed her more than ever now.

Alex heard the door close as Elizabeth departed, and slowly opened her eyes to see Gavin sitting in the big wing chair drawn up against the side of her bed, leaning his head back into its corner. His eyes were closed and his breathing was slow and regular. His hand rested lightly on her own. As she watched him sleep, the love she felt for him was overwhelming. His hair was long and unkempt, his beard shaggy and untrimmed, his ill-fitting clothes looked like he had been wearing them for days, his boots were unpolished, and he looked thin, and pale, and ill. Her heart ached to see him in this state.

"Oh, Gavin, look at what I have done to you," she whispered.

Tears began to roll down her face. She had failed to bring his baby into the world, and now she had destroyed the precious love of her life. This lively, active, strong, athletic, powerful man she had fallen in love with was now just as sad-looking as herself. *How could I do this to him!*

Alex slowly withdrew her hand from his, brought it to her face, and wiped away her tears. Silently, she experimentally moved her legs to the side of the bed and sat up, finding herself weak, dizzy, and drained. She struggled a little with the sleeves, but was able to don the silky dressing gown draped over the foot of her bed. It took a few minutes before she could stand, and then another few minutes before she could let go of the top of Gavin's chair and keep her balance. Her legs felt rubbery. She took a glass of water from the little table by Gavin and drank deeply. Slowly she made her way a few steps over to the window, leaning on furnishings all the way, and, putting her weight on the wall for support, drew back the draperies.

When she saw most of the leaves had turned from greens to reds, browns and yellows, she felt a lump swelling in her throat. The summer wedding she had imagined and dreamed of... gone. Perhaps this was some sort of sign? All her hopes and dreams had vanished on that horrible night. Sadness washed over her as she mourned everything that was supposed to happen, and now would never happen. She could never allow herself that much happiness after what she had done.

Gavin was her whole world, but he deserved someone responsible, someone who could bear his children, someone unselfish... someone who did not ignore her health so she could make love to her man without thinking of anything else! Alex started to feel a little stronger. A deep well of sadness lingered in her heart. "How shall I ever get through this?" she asked herself aloud, tears now cascading down her face.

Gavin had awakened. He observed Alex weeping at the window. He did not want to startle her, especially when he heard her talking to herself. His heart ached at the contempt in her voice, the pain and the guilt. He replied in a soft, tender voice, "You will get through this with me, my angel." He quietly rose from the chair to stand close to her.

Alex turned away. What she wanted was to fall into his loving arms, but she must never allow herself to get close to him again. She did not deserve him now.

"Alex, please do not turn away from me. I have waited for a response from you for three months, and it has been agony. I cannot wait any longer. Do not shut me out," Gavin pleaded.

Alex still did not face him, but hearing his words made it difficult to stand her ground. Her body started to shake with her brutal, warring emotions.

Gavin gently grasped her shoulders and turned her to face him. "You're not going to shut me out again, Alex. I won't let you!" He gazed lovingly into her eyes, desperately wanting to embrace her.

Alex looked up at him, her tears flowing freely. She wanted him to kiss her, but that sort of selfishness had caused all this trouble. She would not let that happen again. Alex looked down at her feet.

"Alex, stop this!" Gavin implored. "You're not being fair. I cannot live without you and I won't! Do you hear what I am saying to you? Alex, you are *my world,* my *life.* No one else could *ever* make me feel what you do. There will *never* be anyone else for me. My heart belongs to you, no matter what the future holds." He shook her gently, unable to control his desperation.

Elizabeth rushed in at the sound of voices in what had been such a quiet, gloomy place. Her heart was gladdened to see Alex out of bed at last, but concerned when she saw the way Gavin was holding her. "Gavin, what are you doing?" she asked.

He dropped his hands to his sides and turned to face Elizabeth. "She refuses to hear me. I do not know what to do anymore. I tell her I will be there for her, I tell her over and over again how much I love her. Still she shuts me out! What have I done to make her like this?" Gavin stormed from the room. Her rejection was tearing him apart. He felt as though he were losing his mind, as she had apparently lost hers.

Alex had slumped against the wall again, shaking with sobs, doing nothing to control her tears.

Elizabeth gently placed her hand on Alex's slim waist and pleaded, "Alexandra, please talk to me."

"I am going to lose him, Mother."

"You don't have to lose him. Just let him help you."

"I can't do that," Alex said, her sobs subsiding. She took a deep breath and sighed sadly.

"Why not? Gavin loves you so much, and he is grieving, too. He has not left your side for a minute. He needs your support as much as you need his." Elizabeth rubbed her daughter's back affectionately, pleased that at last they could talk.

"That day... we went for a walk. I...I wanted to make love to him." Alex wiped her tears, and continued, "He said we should wait, that we had plenty of time for such things, but I was stubborn. I told him everything was fine. I was so selfish! I knew there was a chance that I was with child, but I ignored the discomfort in my belly because I desired Gavin so much.... . Like some common whore, I threw myself at him, I insisted. He was so gentle and loving.... . It was wonderful.... ." Alex was weeping again, and stopped for a moment to wipe away tears and take a deep breath. "I did not listen to you. I did not tell him there was a chance we were having a baby. I did not tell him of my pains. So don't you see, Mother?" Alex asked.

Wiping her own tears away, Elizabeth replied, "See *what*, dear?"

"It is because of my selfishness that our baby is dead."

"No, Alexandra, you are wrong."

"No, I am not! I killed our baby because of my need to be with Gavin!" Alex started sobbing uncontrollably again and covered her face with her hands.

"Alexandra, you did not kill your baby. My God! You have got to stop blaming yourself! Your lovemaking did *not* kill your baby!"

"How can you say that after everything I have told you?"

"Because your father and I made love while I was with child, and you *all* are *here*! It is perfectly safe and normal to do so! All mothers do so! Your baby was just not meant to be born. God took your baby for a reason we shall never know. You had been having pains for days and days. That is not normal, it's a sign of trouble. There is no way you could have prevented what happened! You must accept that this is not your fault in any way. I don't know how such a wild thought got into your head." Elizabeth's tone was firm, but compassionate.

"You're telling me that had I not made love to Gavin, I still would have lost my baby?"

"Yes. That is exactly what I am saying."

"But how can you be so certain? The facts are still the same, Mother. I *did* make love to him and I *did* lose the baby." She turned her face away from Elizabeth.

"Alexandra, stop this! You do not know what caused your miscarriage."

"And you, Mother, do not know that I did *not* cause it." Alex kept staring steadily out the window.

"Alexandra Rosenshire, you cannot blame yourself for something you did not do. There would not be so many unwanted children in this world if making yourself miscarry were so easy! You did nothing wrong. But I will tell you this. If you make that man walk out of your life, you will regret it for the rest of your life! Do not make that mistake."

Elizabeth embraced her daughter and told her she loved her, then left the room. All she could do now was pray that Alex would come to her senses before it was too late to salvage her future with Gavin.

Elizabeth made her way down the staircase just as Gavin was about to start up, having gone to the study to let Daniel and Richard know that Alex had at last risen from her bed. He looked sad and lost and too small for his garments.

"Elizabeth, how is she? Did she talk to you?" Gavin asked, meeting her at the foot of the stairs.

"She did, Gavin."

"She talked to you? That is a wonder! At least she is talking now. What did she say? Why won't she accept my love?" Gavin was anxious for an answer.

"Gavin, Alexandra blames herself because she feels that had you two not made love, your baby would still be in her womb."

"Oh my God!" he said as his face paled.

"What's wrong?" Elizabeth asked. This was not what she was expecting him to say.

"I should have been more firm. I should have said no and meant it! I knew she was not completely well... but she is so beautiful and I love her so much... I could not stop her, or myself."

"No Gavin, I will not let you do that. You are not going to start blaming yourself as Alexandra does. She needs you, and if you're blaming yourself, then neither of you will ever get through this. As I told her, this baby was not meant to be, and this is God's will, not anything you or Alexandra did."

"But had we not made love, perhaps all this would not have happened."

"And who is to say anything would be different if you had not made love that day? She had been having pain for quite some time. That is never a good sign. Why on earth do you think it is as easy as *that* to dislodge an unborn babe?"

Gavin thought for a moment. "You are right, but how do we get Alex to see this? She cannot accept full blame. It takes two to make love. I will share the blame and we will get through this together. She has been through too much! I so wish none of this had happened." Gavin wrapped his arms around Elizabeth and she hugged him back.

"If blame has to be placed, then perhaps it is best shared. I am glad to see you're still determined to be with her." The only person who could help Alex now was Gavin, and Elizabeth was certain of the fact.

"She is the only person I ever will love. I shall never give up on her!" Hurrying up the stairs, Gavin felt a twinge of guilt for making love that day. Not so much the act itself as the timing of it. They would never know if their baby might have survived. Gavin was not about to let his angel slip away. Determined to push his way back into her life, Gavin stormed into her room, ready to do whatever it took to bring her back to him.

Alex had drawn up a light chair to a window overlooking the drive and its surrounding lawns, and now sat lost in her thoughts, gazing at the fall scene. She did not look up to discover who had entered her rooms.

Gavin walked over and knelt at her side, and gently turned her chin so she had to face him and meet his loving gaze. "Angel, I know that you blame yourself because we made love, but you cannot take full blame. I was also there, if you recall, and I certainly did not push you away. If you are going to blame yourself, then you must blame me as well. You have been through a terrible ordeal, much more than you should ever have to experience. But none of it is your fault." He released her chin.

Alex silently shook her head back and forth.

"Please talk to me," Gavin begged.

"You cannot take blame for something I forced you to do." She turned her gaze back to the window.

"Forced me? You did not force me to make love to you! I was more than willing. There is no way to force a man to make love."

"No, you wanted to wait, and I told you I was fine, when in fact I was not. I lied to you, so it was my fault." Alex was struggling to hold back a flood of tears, and her weak, quavering voice was barely audible.

"The fact that you did not tell me that something was bothering you only hurts because I want us to share everything. I want us to be open, and honest, always. But you did not make love without my help! So no matter what you say to me, the fact remains that *we* made love together. Please stop blaming yourself. I could never blame you for this misfortune."

"This was not some mishap. The child that you and I created never got the chance to live."

"But through no fault of yours! This is a sad situation, but you can not stop living because of it. We need each other and I know there will be other children. You need to live for the ones that await us in our future together." Gavin gently took her hands in his own.

"What if there are no children in my future? Would you still want to be with me?" Alex finally turned to look into his dark, handsome, bloodshot eyes.

"Angel, I want to be with you, no matter what. Children or no children. The only future I can believe in has you always at my side. Besides, who said you can't have children?" As far as he knew, no one had mentioned such a possibility to her.

"The last time the doctor was here, I asked him if I damaged myself to the point of not being able to have children. He said he was unsure at this time." The thought of not having babies brought more tears.

"Oh my sweet angel, you did not do this to yourself and there is no other person in this world I could ever be with. When are you going to get that through your beautiful head?" Gavin wrapped his strong arms around her. He held her as her body shook and her tears flowed. He kissed her forehead and drew her tightly to him to feel her heartbeat against his own.

"Gavin, I feel guilty when you touch me... and guilty for wanting to be with you... it is because of my want of you... we lost a part of each other," Alex sobbed.

"Darling! I understand. But can you honestly say you feel so guilty that you would rather live your life alone?"

"I don't know. I do not know what to feel or think."

"Well, I know that I love you, and I will not give up on you. Do you love me?"

"Yes, I do *so* love you," she said with all her heart.

"Then we will start with that."

"I guess... perhaps you could give me a little time to sort out my feelings," Alex pulled away.

"Angel, I only ask you to remember that I love you and you love me. We can build on that." Gavin stood up.

"I know, Gavin. But I want to make sure that when I am with you, I won't always feel this overwhelming guilt and sadness. Just a few days, please?" Alex tried to force a smile onto her face.

"Yes, if that is what you need. I will be at Andrew's. Send someone the moment you have made a decision."

"I will."

"I love you, Angel." Gavin rang for Sara and left the room.

Leaving her side was the hardest thing he had ever had to do. To be back at Arlington House after holding her every night, sitting by her side every day, would be so empty, so lonely. He despaired at the idea of being even more distant from his beloved. But if it meant that Alex would let him back into her life, then he must go.

Gavin spoke with his valet, and to Daniel and Elizabeth, and soon rode away from Bedford House with a heavy heart. He already missed his angel. What on earth was he going to do without her nearness, even if it was only for a few days? He was slumped tiredly in his saddle, head hanging low, knowing his horse could find the familiar paths without help.

Alex watched Gavin leave. His despondent state was obvious. She felt terrible, but unless she could work through her sorrow, she could not bear to be with Gavin. In her heart she knew her love was strong, but she still blamed herself. She was starting to think her mother might be right, though, about how they would never know if making love had caused the miscarriage. A little time to herself might help make things clearer.

Sara entered with an armload of fresh linens, and went off to prepare a hot bath, almost dancing with joy to see her mistress out of bed at last.

Chapter Twenty-Six

For the past few days, Alex had made an effort with her appearance. Sara took extra care with her hair, hoping to lift her spirits. Alex let Sara dress her in her favorite frocks, though they had to be taken in because she had lost so much weight. She soaked in hot, fragrant baths with healing herbal bath salts, and Sara massaged her limbs with lotions and creams, sprayed on light colognes, trimmed and buffed her nails. Alex always felt like a rest after luncheon, as she was not sleeping soundly at night. Her appetite had been improving every day but she usally asked that a tray be sent to her rooms rather than joining the family at mealtimes. She had not ventured often from her chambers since Gavin's departure. She spent most of her time gazing out a window, too distracted for reading or needlework. The weather outside was often gloomy and damp, much like her own mood.

Her sisters visited often, but did not stay long. The date of Cassandra's debut was approaching fast, so she was deeply engaged in a whirl of invitations and preparations, and Ashley was helping her. They felt as if Alex barely noticed their presence, no matter what they said or did for her.

Alex was gazing at her reflection in the cheval mirror, noting she had regained some color in her cheeks and had gained back a pound or two, when Sara tapped lightly on her door and stuck her head in. "Doctor Roberts is here, Lady Alex. May I bring him in?"

"Yes please, Sara, thank you," Alex answered.

"How are you feeling today, Alexandra?" asked Dr. Roberts, as he set down his bag and began his examination.

"I'm feeling better physically... but emotionally, I feel drained," she said.

"Your mother informs me that you blame yourself for the miscarriage. Let me assure you that it was of no fault of yours. It is very nearly impossible to bring on a miscarriage unless there is some underlying problem."

"I often wonder if I might have prevented it."

Doctor Roberts was an elderly man who had looked after the Rosenshires for decades. He tried to find words of comfort and reassurance as he gently completed his examination and started putting items back in his bag.

"Doctor, one question has been weighing heavily on my mind. Last week I asked you if I could still have children, and you told me that you were unsure."

"Yes, I remember, dear."

"Well, now that you have examined me again... can you tell me now?"

"Lady Alexandra, I cannot be sure of anything. It appears that you have healed well, and have no infection, but with internal matters there is no way to know. Wish for the best. Anything is possible." He smiled at her kindly.

"Thank you, doctor. I will see you next week."

"Yes, dear. Try to get some exercise and sunshine, but do not over-exert yourself. You should walk as much as you feel able to, and make sure you eat well."

Alex followed him slowly down the stairs.

"Alexandra, dear, you look more like yourself today," Elizabeth said, meeting her in the doorway of the drawing room where everyone was enjoying their tea. "We are all so glad that you joined us this afternoon."

"Thank you, Mother." Alex chose a plate of sandwiches and little cakes from the footman's proffered tray.

"Alex, tell us what the doctor said," Cassandra asked.

"He said that I look better and that I am healing well." Smiling, Alex sat between her sisters. "He also told me to take walks and eat plenty of food."

"Well then," Ashley said, "will you be sending for Gavin soon?"

"The doctor said *physically* I am doing well."

"What does that mean?" Ashley asked.

"Emotionally, I still have some sorting out to do." A sad, tortured look passed over her face.

"Alex! You know he loves you and you love him. So why won't you let him be with you?" Ashley persisted.

"It's hard to explain, Ashley. Don't pester me."

Cassandra interrupted. "Come on, Alex. A love like that comes once in a lifetime. You did not notice how Gavin stayed at your bedside all summer long? Or how he talked to mother, trying to search out what he might have done wrong, to make you push him away? That man truly loves you. Don't wait too long,"

Cassandra had seen Gavin at Arlington House the day before, and the poor man looked so sad and worn he broke her heart. As far as her family knew, Cassandra had only been out for a ride. Her budding romance with Andrew was still a secret, but with the family's attention so focused on Alex over the summer, she had taken to riding over to see him whenever she thought she could get away with it.

"I know that he loves me, thank you. But you do not understand what I am going through, and I hope you never have to. I would really appreciate all of you giving me time as far as that topic is concerned, and letting me make my own mind up."

"That sounds like a good idea," Daniel said. "Let's let Alex take her time. I am sure she will make the right decision."

"Thank you, Father. And I must ask you not to blame Gavin for everything that has happened to me. This may disappoint you, but I was a very willing partner. Gavin never had to force me to do anything. I deeply love him." Alex wanted her father to understand that she was responsible for her own actions. Cassandra had told her how Daniel had lashed out at Gavin. She wanted her men to be on good terms. They were both so important to her.

"Alex, I was disappointed that you could not wait until you were married to do what you did. The repercussions of your unwise decision could have been disastrous. But somehow your mother always has a way of making me view things from a different angle. All that matters now is that you are getting better. Should you choose to marry Gavin, I will respect your decision." Daniel's voice was stern, but his tone was affectionate.

Elizabeth sat next to her husband, proud of his willingness to be open-minded when it mattered.

"Thank you, Father. I love you." Alex admired her father's strength and compassion.

"Now that you are feeling so much better, would you like to join us for dinner tonight?" Elizabeth asked.

"Yes, mother, I am ready. Where is Richard?" Alex asked.

"Richard went over to check on Gavin and find out how he is doing. He and Gavin became good friends when Gavin brought him home," Cassandra said.

"Oh, well, that's interesting." Alex had not expected this.

"Does that bother you?" Cassandra asked her.

"No. I guess I also want to make sure Gavin is well."

"But you're not ready to see him yet?"

"Not yet. Now can you please stop?"

"Sorry, I did not mean to get on that subject again. I do not want to upset you."

"Thank you, Cassandra. Maybe when things are clearer to me, I will be able to explain them to you." Alex wrapped her arms around her dear sister in a warm hug.

Elizabeth made her way back to her seat next to Daniel. "What shall we do after tea?" The footman was handing round the last of the little cakes.

"I should like to get some fresh air. The doctor told me to take walks every day."

"I think the weather is not appropriate for a walk this afternoon. It's very chilly and damp and windy in the gardens and you must be careful in your fragile state."

"Elizabeth, if she wraps up well a walk might do her good," Daniel chided.

"I guess it won't hurt as long as you you bundle up." Elizabeth gave in.

In a little while everyone was standing and heading off in different directions. Sara helped Alex into her coat and hat, and wrapped a warm woolen shawl around her. Elizabeth said, "Now, don't stay out too long, Alexandra dear. We don't need you to catch a chill on top of everything else."

"Yes mother. Don't worry, I won't be out long. I don't have very much energy, but I do feel that a walk and some fresh air might do me some good." Alex kissed her mother, smiled and walked to the garden door. After a short stroll down a gravel path, she returned to the comfortable chairs set in a protected corner of the brick terrace behind the house that was catching a few late rays of sunshine. Alex seated herself comfortably and looked out over the gardens as they dropped the last of their colorful blooms.

Memories flooded her mind, and everything she had tried so hard to push away came racing into her heart. She remembered the time she caught Gavin looking at her through her bedroom window from behind those trees. Then there were the long rides, and the lovemaking by the little creek. Lord! How she loved that man! But... the pain of losing their babe was still fresh in her heart. How on earth could she so treasure someone she didn't even know? But she *did* love that poor, lost, unborn child. Alex had only been with child a short time, and had stubbornly refused to admit that possibility. But somewhere inside, she did know about it, in spite of all her denials. When she lost it, her heart had crumbled into a million pieces. And Alex would always blame herself.

Was it fair or right to shut Gavin out of her life forever? This was the question she had to ponder. Answering it proved difficult. All she could think about was Gavin, and how sad he had looked that day he left. She respected Gavin more and more for letting her have the time to think.

At Arlington House, Gavin was having a difficult time dealing with the separation. When he first returned, he soaked in a long bath and then spent the rest of the day and the whole night sleeping. When he rose at last, his valet was finally permitted to shave his beard and cut his hair, attend to his nails and provide clean clothing. Once properly dressed, he descended to the dining room and asked the footman to bring him everything there was to eat in the pantry and larders. He ate like a trencherman.

Though considerably more slender, he soon almost resembled the old Gavin.

Once his most urgent needs had been attended to, however, he found he could not read or ride or work or sit still. All he could do was think about her. He was constantly plagued by questions. Is she sleeping now? Is she thinking of me? His mind would not rest and he passed the next nights with only fitful, unrefreshing sleep.

Today Gavin had nothing to do but chase more thoughts of Alex around his head. Gavin's heart leapt when the butler escorted Richard into the study and departed with his coat and hat. He jumped to his feet with a broad, hopeful smile, and asked, "Richard! Do you bring a message from Alex?" Then he could see from Richard's surprised expression that this was not the case, so he swallowed his disappointment, gathered his manners and stepped forward to shake hands. "Richard, good to see you, what brings you by?"

"I came to check in on you and see how you are doing. So how are you doing?"

"How am I doing? That is a good question. I am driving myself mad thinking about Alex. I don't function at all because I'm thinking about Alex. And pretty much around the clock, I am thinking about Alex. It is killing me! How is that for an answer? Do tell me, how is she doing?"

"She is looking better, and I think she is coming to her senses," Richard said. "She has been getting dressed and fixed up every day, which I think is a good sign. She is eating well. She has even ventured downstairs once or twice."

"What does that mean, coming to her senses?"

"Just what I said, she is speaking more rationally and she looks well. I have not heard her say lately that she blames herself for what happened, so perhaps it will not be long before you are back together. You are looking better as well. A good shave and a haircut was all you needed." Both men laughed at the understatement.

"What do you say to a little ride? I gather your cousin is quite a landowner in these parts?"

"He does own a good bit of land, and a ride sounds good." Gavin rang for the butler to bring their coats and hats, and they soon walked through the garden doors nearest the stables toward the rear of the mansion. Gavin waved off the stablehand and soon had saddled and bridled his favorite horse without his help. Jack was looking at him with an imploring expression, whimpering and wagging his tail, so Gavin gave him a pat on the head and said, "Yes, Jack, you can come along."

The day was overcast, chilly, windy, and rain threatened. At least, Gavin thought, he was getting out of the house. They had been enjoying an easy canter for almost half an hour through random, lightly wooded trails and farm fields when Gavin pulled his horse to a stop. They had just gained the top of a small hill. Looking at the wide vista, he gestured to Richard to indicate where the Arlington lands ended. Then a strange look appeared on his face.

"Gavin, is something wrong?" Richard asked, unable to decipher the expression.

Gavin pointed to a spot a little ways off and said: "Right over there on that hillside, I saw a woman being chased by a man, both galloping hard. I'd heard a scream, so I went to have a look, and that is when I realized it was my angel, my beautiful Alexandra, being chased by that cad Harrison. I went after him, tackled him off his horse, and threatened him. Ironic, isn't it?"

"How is that?" Richard asked.

"Last time, I did not get there in time to save her. She had to save herself. Alex was forced to fight Melinda and watch her die when she went over a waterfall. She was tormented and beaten by Harrison, he cut off her garments, and he was about to rape her before I got there to help. I should have been there the whole time she was ill. I should have been there the night it happened. I was not." Looking off into the distance, memories good and bad came racing back.

"Gavin, don't do that to yourself. When I think back, I should have been there for my sister as well. I would not be here today if you had not found me. For that I am grateful. But if you're going to start blaming yourself for everything, then you can blame me too."

"No, that won't be necessary. You know... the one good thing that came out of that day on the hillside is that after I made sure your sister got home safely, I went to a neighbor and purchased a considerable tract of land between Bedford and Arlington. I felt a yen to stay close by, and I was going to set down my roots close to Alex, although at the time I would not have admitted that. I also wanted to stay close to my cousin, as I always find myself spending more time here with him than home at Chatham with Mother." Gavin lowered his head and tried to shake off his sadness.

"It will all come right, Gavin. I really believe that. She loves you truly, I can see it, everyone can."

By the time they neared Arlington House the dinner hour was nearing, so Richard said his farewells to Gavin and headed his horse for home.

Though Andrew, Amelia, Catherine and even Jack were all in the house, Gavin felt lonely again. It was as though his only link to Alex were Richard. In Richard's absence, Gavin was left once more to his maddening thoughts of Alex.

More days passed, much longer than Gavin had expected it would take for Alex to make up her mind. He thought for sure he would have heard something by now, but it had been five long days and nights. He was worried. He wanted to go over and demand an answer. Why was she taking so long? But he could not disrespect her wishes. He would wait for her no matter how long it took.

At Bedford House, Alex was not having an easy time of it either. She wanted to be with Gavin but was unsure about all her lingering guilt. Would it ever go away? Her mother kept telling her that time heals all, and perhaps she was right. But until Alex had some sort of certainty, she would wait. Guilt was such a burden to deal with.

When Richard returned, Alex questioned him eagerly. "Is he well, Richard? Please tell me how he is doing."

"Alex, I will not go into details with you on Gavin's condition, because you are the one who asked for time. However, I will tell you that if you let someone get away from you who loves you as much as he does, you will never experience true love again." Richard walked away. He hoped to make her want to go to Gavin that much sooner.

The doctor returned and pronounced Alex fully recovered. She could return to her normal activities as long as she did not overexert herself. He wanted her to gain back the weight she had lost. She should increase her daily walks to build up her stamina, but not walk so long she became exhausted. She was allowed to resume riding as long as the gait was gentle.

That night was much like so many others. Alex had trouble falling asleep, consumed with thoughts of Gavin. Hours after midnight she at last fell into a doze, and soon was lost in a vivid dream. It was the most heavenly sight she had ever seen and she was lost in it. There was a verdant, tranquil landscape as far as her eye could wander, with green, lush grasses vibrant and alive, and trees swaying gently in a warm, soothing breeze against a blue sky with puffy white clouds. The scene was lit with brilliant sunshine, and the warm rays soothed her skin. Alex felt a sense of great peace and serenity, and overwhelming, encompassing happiness. Then she glanced around and realized she was alone. What good was all this beauty, if there were no one to share it with? If there is no one to talk to, no one to enjoy the experience with, what good is any of it?

Waking in distress, Alex realized that she was about to lose the only thing that mattered to her. Life without Gavin was not worth living! Jumping from her bed, she ran down the dark gallery, feeling her way to her parent's rooms an hour before the servants would light their lamps. Daniel and Elizabeth were sleeping soundly when Alex burst in to awaken them, giving them a fright as they opened their eyes in surprise at the sound of their door banging open.

"Mother, Father, I know what I must do!" she almost shrieked, rushing to embrace her mother.

"Alex, what are you talking about?" Daniel reached to the nightstand and lit a candle.

"I have wasted all this time away from Gavin. I realize that I have no life without him! I blame myself for not being more careful, but to punish myself by staying away from him would kill me!"

Daniel and Elizabeth smiled at each other over her head. Their own dear Alex had returned to them at last! Tears came to her eyes, but Elizabeth could not be happier. She clasped Alex tightly. They rocked back and forth. "Alexandra, you're back! I love you! I knew things would eventually come right!"

"I am glad you are back to normal, but do you not think this could wait until morning?" Daniel asked gruffly, barely awake, but with a twinkle in his eye.

Hearing the commotion, Richard, Cassandra and Ashley awoke and poked their heads out their doors. Following the sounds, they rushed down the hallway to their parents' rooms.

"Mother, what is going on?" Cassandra asked, seeing Alex and her mother rocking each other, and a candle lit, and Daniel looking much happier than he had been of late.

"Cassandra, I feel great! I feel like my old self now! And the most wonderful part is that I want to marry Gavin as soon as possible." Alex embraced each of her sleepy siblings in turn. "Thank you for your patience with me, everyone."

"Well, I guess this won't wait until morning," Daniel sighed, realizing he would get little more sleep tonight.

"Well, I do not think we should wait until morning to tell Gavin. The poor chap has had his head hanging low since last he saw you," Richard said.

"This is so exciting! Alex, I am so glad you are back with us," Ashley said.

"I think we should all go downstairs and celebrate with a bite to eat and a pot of tea," Cassandra suggested.

"That sounds like a good idea," Elizabeth concurred, thinking it was close enough to morning to awaken the staff.

"I think I will pass," Daniel said.

"Oh no, you will not, Daniel. You get out of bed this minute and join our family celebration," Elizabeth ordered. Daniel had learned over the years that often it was smarter to give in to his wife's demands then to argue with her, and threw off his covers. Elizabeth rose and rang for her maid, who would pass the word to the staff.

"Well, I won't be at the table," Richard said. "I am going to ride over to Arlington and bring him back to you, Alex."

"Richard, it is far too early to disturb his household," Elizabeth said. Cassandra and Ashley headed back to their bedchambers for dressing gowns and slippers and a look in the mirror and a quick wash-up before heading downstairs.

"Mother, if I don't go and get Gavin right now, he would most certainly kill me for wasting a single minute! And by the time I reach Arlington, the sun will be coming up." Richard kissed his mother and Alex, rang for a servant to pass word to the stable, and ran to throw on warm clothes.

As the family gathered around the morning room table, they heard him calling out, "I will be back soon!" Then they heard a door slamming behind him.

A sleepy footman was lighting lamps. A downstairs maid was hastily building up a fire in the grate. The cook was bustling around the kitchen to get a fire going under the kettle and mix a batch of scones. The scullery maid was fetching fresh cream from the cellars.

"Father, is everything all right?" Alex asked, noticing her father's silence.

"Yes Alex, everything is just fine. I'm just so bloody tired, and your mother won't let me go back to bed."

Alex laughed and leaned over to give her father a kiss on the cheek. "I love you, Father," she said, as though she were a small child again.

"I know darling, and I love you," her father told her.

They soon were having their tea around the big round table and awaiting the return of Richard and Gavin. The draperies had been thrown open to admit the first rays of dawn.

"I just can't wait to see Gavin's face when you tell him you're ready to wed him at last," Cassandra said.

"Neither can I," Alex replied. Butterflies had been fluttering in her stomach since the minute her brother left the house. She wondered if Gavin would be angry for making him wait so long. Maybe he understands? Maybe everything will be well. She chose to believe the best, and tried to control her excitement and anticipation.

By the time Richard galloped up to Arlington House, the sun had risen. Servants were attending to their early-morning chores, lighting the fires and taking their own tea, but Andrew and Gavin were deeply asleep. Richard's insistent knocking was so loud it woke them.

"Who the hell is knocking at at this hour?" roared Andrew, emerging from his rooms at the top of the stairs, tying the sash of his dressing gown.

Gavin was rushing out of his rooms down the hall in his nightshirt, alarmed for Alex's state.

"For God's sake, Andrew! Your butler is taking his own sweet time getting to the damn door! What if something is wrong with Alex? " Not waiting for an answer, Gavin ran past Andrew and arrived at the door just as the sleepy butler admitted Richard.

His knees weakened. He thought for sure something was terribly wrong to have Richard arrive at this hour.

"Richard, what is wrong with Alex?" Gavin demanded.

"Calm down, Gavin..." He did not get to finish before Gavin clutched him by his lapels roughly and demanded to know why he was there so early.

"What is wrong with Alex?"

"Nothing! Would you calm down so I can talk to you?"

"Well, how can nothing be wrong if you are here in the middle of the night?"

"Let me finish and you will find out," Richard told Gavin. "Calm yourself, old chap, dawn has broken... in more ways than one." Slowly Gavin released his grip and stepped back.

"Sorry. I am calm now. Speak to me!"

"Gavin, Alex wants to see you right away, and she is perfectly well, so this has nothing to do with her health," Richard explained, with a broad grin on his face.

"She is well, and she wants to see me?" Gavin asked in stunned disbelief.

"Yes, Gavin. Alex is back— the woman you love— and she wants to see you right away."

"I can't believe it. I thought this would happen, but not like this. Not at this hour... ."

"Is this a problem, Gavin? Perhaps it would have been best for me to wait for full daylight?"

"No, I would have killed you if you had waited one minute! This is the moment I have been waiting for. For so long I have waited for a knock on the door that would tell me my angel was ready to be loved. I guess now that it is here... I must be in a state of shock... I will go and dress so we can leave right away." Gavin ran up the stairs with more speed then he knew he had in him.

Andrew had heard everything that was said as he slowly descended the stairs. As Gavin brushed past him he said, "Good luck, Gavin. I am most happy for you." Then he asked the butler to find a stablehand to saddle Gavin's stallion as quickly as possible.

"Me too, cousin, me too," Gavin called over his shoulder, taking the stairs two at a time. As Richard and Andrew waited companionably on a bench by the door, Gavin ran to his rooms, threw on his clothes as his sleepy, bewildered valet tried to help, and started back down the stairs, calling out, "Let's go, Richard! I cannot wait to hold my angel in my arms again." In a flash they were galloping back to Bedford House.

Soon he and his angel would be one.

Chapter Twenty-Seven

Richard and Gavin reached Bedford House in the promising light of a brilliant, sparkling fall morning, with the sun gaining warmth as it climbed higher, and not a cloud in the sky. Without waiting for Richard to dismount, Gavin jumped from his saddle as a stableboy hurried up to take his reins, and ran for the house in long, swift strides.

Throwing open the doors without knocking, he ran toward the morning room calling out "Alex! Alex where are you? Alex!"

"Gavin! I'm here, my darling. I'm here!" Alex leapt up from the table and ran toward the sound of his voice. As he appeared in the doorway, she threw herself into his arms.

"I knew we would get through this," Gavin drew her close and graced her lips with a kiss that made the rest of the family blush. With glances around the table, they quietly rose and departed, unnoticed by the happy couple, lost in their own world.

"Gavin, I am so sorry," Alex whispered against his lips.

Gavin said softly, "This was hell. Pure hell! But I do not intend to be parted from you again." He gazed lovingly into her angelic face.

"Gavin... the doctor said again... I may not be able to bear children." Alex's eyes were filling with tears at the thought, but she felt it was important to be clear about this before they went forward. For a long time, Alex would feel twinges of guilt and loss, and at times she would stare into space for a minute, and her eyes would glaze over, on the verge of tears. No one would interrupt her when this happened, recognizing that she needed such moments in order to heal.

"Alex, darling, I love you for you alone. Not for anything you may ever give me."

"Oh, Gavin, I love you so much!" Alex felt relief and love and joy and gladness all mixed together. They stood long in their embrace, vowing never to part. Finally, they released each other, and walked hand in hand into the drawing room to join the waiting family. Everyone had bright smiles on their sleepy faces, sharing in the couple's abundant happiness.

Elizabeth stood and drew them both into her arms. "I am so happy that we are finally going to have that wedding."

"Mother, about the wedding..." Alex began.

The room filled with silence. The joyous mood was broken.

"Oh, it's nothing bad! I just wanted to say that perhaps the wedding should wait until after Cassandra's début. I feel as though I have taken all of your time, and caused you so much worry, for so long, so much worry, so much pain. Someone else in this family should get some attention, too." Everyone let out a silent sigh of relief. There was something unpredictable about Alex now. They had grown accustomed to living their lives focused on her health, her emotional state, her wishes, her needs. Had she come up with a reason to the delay the wedding, they would not have been shocked, just surprised.

Cassandra walked quickly over to Alex and took her hand. "Alex, I am not going to make my début until you are married. I really mean it."

"Please Cassandra, it is only right," Alex asked seriously.

"There is no possibility I will change my mind! How could I enjoy my big Season without your being a married woman? I would be forced to listen to all those dreadful gossips!" Cassandra smiled.

Gavin interrupted them. "Sorry, I do not follow. What is it you would have to listen to?"

"All the older women advising me slyly not to wait too long, warning me I could become a spinster like Alexandra, or asking me when she is going to be married." Cassandra waved her hand, trying to dismiss these notions.

"All right, I think we get the idea," Alex said as they all laughed.

"Well then, that settles it, doesn't it? We have a wedding to plan," Elizabeth added.

Daniel rose from his chair. "Good. I am glad we settled that. Now, I was awakened hours too early, and I know this family does not appreciate my company when I am tired and out of sorts. So if you will excuse me, more sleep is in order!" He walked over to his wife and gently kissed her. Nothing made him happier than to see that smile of hers lighting up a room. He gave Alex a kiss on her forehead and Gavin a pat on the shoulder as he excused himself.

"You know, sleep doesn't sound so bad right about now," Richard commented, finding his mind drifting from fatigue.

Alex said, "Richard, go to bed. There is no reason you have to stay up. Thank you so much for riding out so early."

"Are you sure? You won't be offended?" Richard asked.

Gavin laughed. "No we won't be offended."

So Richard made his way back to bed.

"If there is anyone else in the room who wants to go to bed, don't let us hold you back," Gavin asked, looking around the room at sleepy women still clad in their nightdresses and dressing gowns.

Ashley stood and stretched her limbs. "I think I will take you up on that offer. Good morning, Alex, Gavin. I am so glad that everything has worked out at last." She kissed them and departed.

"Well, I can't go to sleep yet. I am too excited that you two are finally going to wed!' Cassandra was eager to get busy with the preparations.

"Yes, you can, dear," Elizabeth said, looking straight at her.

"No, Mother, really I couldn't," Cassandra replied, puzzled.

"Cassandra darling, Mother knows best, and I can tell you're tired, as am I. You need your beauty sleep before your début. So you and I will go to bed now. Come along."

Finally grasping the hints, Cassandra complied. "Yes, tired, I must be. I presume I will see both of you later on?" she asked Gavin and Alex.

Nodding, Alex answered, "Yes Cassandra, you will see us later."

"Good. Then I wish you both a good morning."

"Good morning, you two." Elizabeth gave both another kiss.

"Good morning, Mother."

"Good morning, Elizabeth."

And then they were alone.

"Now that I have you alone, I want to tell you everything I love about you. I want you next to me, and I want your lips on mine." Gavin swept up Alex, carried her over to the chesterfield and set her down. Gavin brought his lips down in a warm, loving kiss, then settled in close beside her.

"Oh Gavin, I love you so much." Tears

formed again in Alex's eyes. "To think I pushed you away from me!" Her lips wandered from his lips, to his cheek, down to his neck and up to his lips again.

"Angel, I want to be married as soon as possible." Gavin gently ran his fingertips over Alex's shoulders and down her arms. "I do not want to let go of you ever," he whispered in her ear, pulling her to his chest.

"Who says you have to?" she whispered back. So there they lay, one body nestled into the other, whispering their ardor, lost in their feelings. Alex unbuttoned Gavin's shirt so she could place her cheek on his chest and listen to his steady heartbeat. Their love had survived its first challenges, and not succumbed. Eventually they drifted off to asleep in each other's arms and dreamed of their overdue wedding.

Bright noontime sunlight and voices woke them from their blissful sleep. Pulling themselves to a sitting position, they turned to face each other.

"This is what I want every day," Gavin told Alex, gently touching his palm to her cheek.

"And what is that?"

"Waking to the sight of your beautiful face."

"How sweet."

They laughed and kissed until they were interrupted by a certain grumbling sound.

Alex took her hand and placed it on her belly. "Perhaps now would be a good time for something to eat. All I could manage so early this morning was tea."

"I would not mind joining you, darling." Slowly rising to stand, Gavin stretched. Alex savored the sight in front of her. She wondered what she had ever done to deserve such a kind, loving and passionate man. And so attractive, too! The sight of Gavin made her tingle from head to toe.

Gavin noticed the silly grin on her face and leaned over, grasped her hand, kissed it gently and asked sweetly, "What makes you smile?"

"I was just asking myself how I am so lucky to find a man as fine as you." Standing, she exposed his chest again and placed a kiss directly over his heart.

"Alex, if you keep this up, you're going to drive me insane."

"If I keep this up I will drive myself insane!" she laughed.

They adjusted their clothing as best they could and headed for the dining room, from which the voices emanated. The family was just being seated for luncheon.

"Hello, Alex, Gavin," came a familiar voice.

"Andrew, what are you doing here?" Gavin asked, surprised to see his cousin sitting at the table.

"I just couldn't be left out of all the action," Andrew explained.

"I see. So when did you get here?"

"About an hour ago."

"Really?" Alex asked. "Was anyone up yet?"

"We have all been up for some time, Alexandra, dear,"

"Oh, what time is it, Mother?" Alex asked.

"It is twelve-thirty," Cassandra told her.

"Twelve-thirty? I am shocked!" Gavin looked down at his Angel. She was still in her nightdress and dressing gown, having never entertained the first thought of leaving Gavin's side to dress properly.

"Well, I think I should eat, and then perhaps have a bath. A change of clothes sounds good, too," Alex said. "I beg everyone to excuse my inappropriate garb."

They joined everyone at the table, and luncheon arrived. Alex caught Cassandra and Andrew glancing at each other, and was happy that her dear sister would soon be eligible for proper courting by the man she so loved. All the more reason to get the wedding over with!

"When are the nuptials?" Andrew asked.

"We haven't picked a date yet, Andrew. But it will be soon!" Alex answered.

"Not good enough! You need a date, so let's pick one." he demanded in good humor.

"Well, aren't we peremptory today?" Gavin laughed at his cousin.

"Peremptory? Me? No. I just think you two have waited long enough, as have the rest of us."

Planning for the wedding of the year finally began in earnest. Spirits were high at Bedford House and everyone offered thoughts and comments about the date, the location, the hour, the food, the guest list, and the appropriate flowers for this time of year.

Alex and Gavin sat holding hands and exchanging kisses. This was a happy time for them. This was a time worth remembering.

Chapter Twenty-Eight

By a certain day in early October, the final preparations were underway for Alex and Gavin to become one in the eyes of the Lord. The mood around their homes was cheerful and hurried.

Alex had asked Ashley to take charge of the floral arrangements, which delighted Ashley, who had a flair for artistic touches. Now in the scullery, Ashley supervised four downstairs maids and a valet as they artfully arranged a mountainous, colorful assortment of the season's best blooms in highly polished silver and crystal vases. Asters, delphiniums, chrysanthemums, phlox, cosmos and brilliant marigolds would soon wreath the walls and line the tables of the ballroom, with the most perfect blossoms set aside for the ceremony. On another table nearby were dozens and dozens of long-stemmed red and white roses and miles of dark green satin ribbon.

Catherine was almost finished writing out the last of the place-cards. She and her mother had spent the previous morning inspecting all the guest chambers where overnight visitors would stay, servants having opened up and aired out an unused wing at Bedford House for kin of the Rosenshires, and another at Arlington House for Gavin's relatives. Family and friends from far and wide had been arriving since the afternoon before, and today all had been asked to gather at Arlington House for a special luncheon before the ceremony, with Amelia as their hostess. Elizabeth met at length with her housekeeper and the butler to discuss the best way to deploy armies of servants for the grand event, having filled out the ranks of Bedford House staff by borrowing maids, cooks, footmen, grooms and valets from Arlington House as they became available.

The women attended to every detail to make the day perfect, assisted by flower-sellers, tailors, servants and haberdashers. They transformed the grand ballroom of Bedford House into a romantic bower, with flowers and ribbons adorning the walls and tables, and a nosegay on every candelabra. A formal dinner would be served here after the ceremony, and a small orchestra would provide music for dancing. Round tables, each seating eight, would ring the dance floor, and each needed the perfect decorations.

The menfolk had been busy as well. Gavin had arranged for construction to begin on his newly acquired land between Arlington and Bedford, to become the home of Alex's dreams. Every day he rode over to talk to the builders and make sure they were working hard, demanding the foreman hire more masons and carpenters to speed things up. As this dwelling would not be finished for nearly a year, Daniel and Richard chose a large cobblestone cottage located near Old Bedford River, and had it freshened up for Alex and Gavin to honeymoon in, where they could remain in comfort nearby until their new home was completed.

Gavin and Alex also made plans for some travel. First they would spend a few weeks in London for the débutante season, to make sure Cassandra enjoyed a proper send-off. All the relations who were coming to the wedding would also be in town for the Season. The honeymooners would then be spending a month or more at Chatham, so Alex could get to know Gavin's mother and enjoy Gavin's famous ancestral home.

Alexandra was in her rooms, shivering with anticipation. Spread across her bed was her mother's own ivory silk and satin wedding gown and its veil, everything newly tailored to fit her perfectly, aired and refreshed and looking like new, every little seed-pearl securely fastened, every bit of Alençon lace perfectly starched.

The night before, she had been sternly instructed by Cassandra that she was not to see Gavin until she walked down the aisle, but this was proving to be difficult. Just knowing that he was somewhere in the house made her want to go and search for him. For weeks and weeks they had stopped short of total intimacy, as she insisted on waiting for the big day, but they almost always found time to be alone together. She felt this mysterious reluctance was the final vestige of her lingering sense of guilt, but it also added to the excitement of the big day's approach.

"Alex, I'm coming in," Cassandra called out, opening the door and stepping in.

"How does everything look in the ballroom?"

"Everything looks just amazing!"

"So have you seen my future husband around?"

"Actually no, I have not. But don't worry, I am sure he is around here somewhere,"

"You haven't seen him? Isn't that strange?"

"No. No one has seen much of you, either!"

"That's because I'm getting ready," Alex chirped, pacing. She was so excited she had not touched her luncheon, and she wasn't able to sit because she felt the need to be doing something. Now she was making herself nervous over the fact that Cassandra had not seen Gavin.

"Alex, please calm down. Gavin is probably just as excited!"

"Yes, you're probably right. It's just that this is the day I have been waiting for since the first time I saw him. So many things have tried to keep us apart that I wouldn't be surprised if another obstacle were thrown our way." Alex faced her sister, suddenly worried.

Taking Alex's hand, Cassandra led her over to a chaise-longue and sat her down.

"Alex, you and Gavin have had your share of troubles, but that is all over now. Please relax and think positively. In a few very short hours, you're going to be Your Grace."

"You're right. Help me then. Should I wear my hair up or down?" Alex asked as she piled it up on her head and released it.

"I think that with your dress it would look really splendid up, but loosely, and make sure you have some locks falling down on your shoulders and around your face. You will be wearing your veil, most of the time, don't forget. But I am sure Sara will do fine with it. She has a talent for it."

"That's very true." Alex continued facing the mirror, turning her head this way and that as she played with her hair. "And how are you going to wear your hair today, Cassie?"

"I think both Ashley and I will pull the sides up but leave the back to flow long. With our gorgeous gowns, that should look very elegant, as we will have our backs to the congregation during the service." Smiling at her sister, Cassandra joined Alex in front of the mirror and asked: "What do you think?"

They studied each other in the mirror. "I think that will look grand." They exchanged warm glances and then Alex asked: "Could you please let Sara know I am ready for my bath, then she can help me with my hair, and start getting me dressed."

Cassandra gave a deep, well-practiced curtsey and answered, "Today is your special day, I shall do whatever you ask."

"That may be, but you have a special day all your own coming soon." They flashed loving smiles at each other and Cassandra left the room.

Gavin was a bundle of nerves. The Rosenshires had given the Blake family a large suite of rooms remote from Alex's, everyone had moved in this morning, and Andrew was there to keep an eye on him. Leaving his valet to pack up his formal clothing to be carried over to Bedford House, he had neglected to pocket the wedding band! Andrew offered to ride over and get it, but Gavin refused to let him.

"Gavin, I would not mind going back to Arlington to get the ring. As a matter of fact, I would prefer it."

"And why is that?"

"Because if something were to happen to you before the wedding, it would fall upon my shoulders, and that is one weight I wish not to bear."

Gavin was having a difficult time staying away from his bride-to-be.

"Fine, go and get it!" Gavin growled.

"Good God man, loosen up! Today is the day you have been waiting for!"

"I know that. I really think that I would feel so much less nervous if I could just go and see her," Gavin flung himself into a chair.

"Now you know such a thing would be most inappropriate. Today of all days, one abides by tradition! Not to mention that her mother, her sisters, my mother, and my sister are all acting as her bodyguards. There is no way you're going to get by them all."

"That sounds like a challenge," Gavin rose with a sly smile on his face.

"Gavin, what in hell are you thinking now?"

"Perhaps Alex wants to see me as much as I want to see her."

"You're speaking in riddles and I do not like it."

"I think before I marry Alex today, I will find a way to see her. Yes, it shall give me something to do until it is time to dress!" Gavin rose from his chair with a look of determination.

"You shall do no such thing! If you feel the need to keep busy, perhaps it would be best if we both went to fetch the ring."

"What fun would that be? Besides, this is like a game, and I need something to occupy myself for a few hours more. One hour to get myself ready will be more than sufficient."

"I'm not going to have to Mother angry at me because you feel the need to act like a child!" Andrew stood and positioned himself between the door and Gavin.

"That's what love does to you, chap. I can act silly in front of her and she does not care. I can make jokes and pranks and she always laughs. I highly doubt that she would get upset if I popped in for one little kiss."

"It's not Alex I am worried about. It is the traditionalists in this place who scare me. And quite frankly, there are more of them then there are of us!"

"So when did that happen?" Gavin tried to keep from laughing.

"When did what happen?"

"When did you lose your nerve, your sense of adventure, coz?" Gavin backed away from the door.

"Oh, stop! I think you are overreacting. It's not like you haven't seen her for days. You have been spending just as much time here as you have spent at home, possibly more."

"This whole business of being proper— being apart before the wedding! I don't know what the purpose of it is."

"Proper? Well, that is funny."

"What is that supposed to mean?"

"I just meant that you two have already been rather intimate. Perhaps it is a little late for formality now. Her parents have placed few restrictions on her lately."

"That may be true, but I think her family is trying to keep some traditions alive, though we have broken most of them. However, it is not like we did anything wrong. What we have done was done out of love. It's just that, ever since her miscarriage, she has refused to make love. Now my nerves are a little on edge. Andrew! If one of us does not leave soon, then I shall not have a wedding band to give to my beautiful bride."

"Of course— now which one of us was going to get it?"

"I think it would be fine if we both went. That way you know where I am and I will be doing something to keep busy. It will give me a moment to spend with Jack. My poor dog hasn't seen much of me lately, he has been sadly neglected."

"Sounds good to me, let's go!"

"Cassandra, where is your father?" Elizabeth asked, as her daughter came racing down the hall.

"Father has not come home yet. Is there a problem?"

"Are you sure he did not come home? I could have sworn I heard his voice."

"Yes, I am positive. I believe the voice you heard was Andrew's. I ran into him on the stairs."

"The stairs? I thought they were all upstairs getting ready?"

"They were. It seems that Gavin forgot to bring the wedding band when he rode over this morning. Now he is a nervous wreck, so they went to get the ring,"

"Goodness! I hope they are back in time. It would be just awful if something were to go wrong now."

"Oh Mother, stop worrying so much. Arlington House is only thirty minutes or so away, if you take the back way instead of the roads. They will have plenty of time to prepare for tonight."

"Yes, you're right, of course. I know that, but I feel so emotional and I want everything to go according to plan."

"Mother, please let me make a suggestion."

"Go right ahead, dear."

"I know that you like to assist all the servants to do things just the way you like them, but just this once, please could you let them do the job you pay them to do? You need to take a little rest today, or you shall not enjoy yourself this evening as much as you should. They all well know by now exactly what must be done, and how to do it to your satisfaction."

"You're right, dear. Really, you are. It is only that I would feel so badly if anything went wrong."

"Then let Ashley and me and Catherine oversee the staff. Lady Amelia shall be helping too, now that her wedding luncheon has ended, so don't put so much pressure on yourself," Cassandra begged.

"Well, we can try that. I cannot, however, promise that I won't offer my opinions." Elizabeth gave her daughter a smile. She was very proud of Cassandra for taking on much responsibility lately. How very adult her daughter had become!

"I am certain you cannot make that promise, but that's perfectly fine with me. Just try to take a little rest. It will do you a world of good."

"Richard!" Daniel called out. They had been inspecting the cottage and its grounds, to make sure the workers had followed their final instructions, and put every last thing into perfect working condition. They made sure there was hay for the horses, oil for the lamps, plenty of well-seasoned firewood and a load of coal. They had brought two chambermaids to do a final dust-and-polish, air the rooms, place a few vases of flowers, and stock the larder and wine cellar properly. Servants' quarters had been completed over the stables for a valet, a maid, a cook and a stable-boy. Then Daniel realized that for the last thirty minutes while exploring all the rooms and outbuildings, he had been alone.

"Where in God's name did that boy go?" he asked himself. Leaving the front parlor, Daniel went down the hall toward the kitchen. No sign of Richard there. "Richard!" he called out again.

"Father, I'm right here!" replied Richard as he made his way from the scullery in a hurry, looking flustered.

"What in hell were you doing?" Daniel asked him.

"I was helping that new maid you hired. Oh, what's her name again?" Richard said as he scratched his head.

"Her name is Emily, Richard. Now fix your shirt, and stay away from the help, at least until we are finished here."

Blushing slightly, Richard said: "Right. There is not much left to do here, and thank God for that, because mother will have a fit if we are not home soon!"

"Don't I know it!"

Alexandra was in her sitting room, dreaming about her wedding. She told herself that soon enough, her dreams would be coming true! She couldn't wait to see all the people her parents had invited, all the people who used to lecture her on how she should be married by now. She would show them! Some things in life are worth waiting for, and Gavin Blake was one of them. A knock at the door interrupted her musings.

"Come in," she called.

"Alexandra dear, I do not mean to interrupt you. I am sure you have a myriad of things that you must do, but I wanted to speak with you alone." Lady Amelia entered and chose a comfortable chair.

"Lady Amelia! I'm a little surprised to see you," Alex made her way over to her Aunt-to-be to kiss her lightly on the cheek.

"I know, dear. I just wanted to take a moment to welcome you to our family. I'm very glad that Gavin has opened his heart to you. I say this on behalf of Gavin's mother as well. It's a shame that she could not make the trip, but since Gavin father's passing, she seldom leaves Chatham House, and I think she shall always keep to her deep mourning."

"Thank you, Lady Amelia. I'm equally glad that he opened his heart to me. I hope that soon I shall be able to meet Gavin's mother! It's such a shame that she could not share in our joyous occasion. Gavin explained everything to me when he received her letter."

"There is one other matter that I would like to mention. Now that we are going to be family, I hope you will call me Aunt Amelia?"

"Yes, thank you so much," Alex said with a sweet smile, and gently wrapped her new aunt in a hug. Aunt Amelia was a very easy woman to get along with. Alex was already feeling as if they had known each other for years with deep mutual affection.

At Arlington House, the retrieval of the ring was becoming a bigger task than expected.

"Andrew, did you find the damn ring yet?" Gavin asked as they searched his rooms.

"No, I did not. Are you sure you left it on the dresser?"

"That is exactly where I left it!" Gavin shuffled through items on his dresser, in his desk, and in the night-stand, while Andrew searched through the pockets of garments in the wardrobes. "I am not going to disappoint Alex by not having the ring I have been telling her about!" Gavin was growing more irritated by the minute.

"Perhaps there is somewhere else we could look?"

They continued to search Gavin's rooms, but still there was no ring. Jack stayed close on their heels.

"I cannot believe this!" Gavin shouted. "Somebody took that ring!"

"Gavin, you're being ridiculous. Who in the world would come in here and steal your ring? It isn't like I leave the doors open!"

"Andrew, you're not helping! I know where I left it. Perhaps it was not very smart to leave it on my dresser, but I did! I left it on my dresser, and it is not there now!" Gavin was starting to raise his voice.

"Well, you can't hold up the wedding because of it."

"What am I supposed to slide on her finger when it's time to put the ring on? Tell me that!"

"Don't you think you would disappoint Alex more if you did not get married today?" Andrew hoped his cousin would come to his senses.

Running his fingers through his hair, Gavin said: "You're right. It's just that I wanted everything to be perfect, and now it is not. Not to mention that the ring has been in my family for generations, and is far more precious than I can explain."

"We can search for the ring in the future, but your wedding shall not wait. My suggestion to you is that we head back to Bedford House so you shall have time to get ready."

"What other choice do I have?" Gavin sighed, most upset. "I hope she understands. I really wanted that ring for her, Andrew. It's a piece of my mother, and as she could not be here, the ring symbolized her presence and acceptance of Alex."

"I know, Gavin. It may still turn up. You have to think positively!"

Gavin gave Jack a pat on the head for luck. "Think positively. Right!"

Soon they were riding through the woods again. It was a brilliant, sparkling fall day. The sun was shining and it was unseasonably warm. Though the leaves had fallen from the trees, evergreens brightened the forest and a flock of migrating birds sang cheerily.

"Cassandra, have you seen Andrew and Gavin yet?" Ashley asked, as her sister came out of Alex's rooms.

"No, I have not. They had better get here soon. There are only two hours before the wedding!"

"Does Alex know they are not here?"

"No, she does not. I do not think it is worth mentioning, either. We don't need to upset her. There is really no need to worry yet." Cassandra and Ashley retired to their rooms so they could start their own preparations.

Catherine was in the drawing room enjoying a cup of tea before heading upstairs to bathe and dress, when in through the garden door came Andrew and Gavin. Catherine could see at once that they were out of sorts.

"What's wrong with you two?"

"I forgot to bring Alex's ring, so we went to look for it, and it was gone." Gavin said, scowling.

Catherine suddenly had a strange look on her face.

"Catherine, what's wrong?" Andrew asked, suspicious.

"Nothing."

"Catherine, I know you. Now what is wrong with you?"

"Well, I... I... Gavin, I went into your rooms looking for Jack just before I left to come here, and when I saw the ring on your dresser I put it in my pocket to bring, and I meant to tell you, but mother has kept me so busy I forgot. I am so sorry, but here it is!" Catherine reached into her pocket and produced the ring.

She expected Gavin to explode, and hung her head.

"That's great! Now everything will go as planned!" Gavin ran over to Catherine, took the ring, then picked her up and gave her a huge hug.

"You're not angry with me?"

"Oh, I'm angry. However! Today is the happiest day of my life, so you are pardoned," Gavin gave her a big kiss on the cheek.

"Oh, Gavin! You know I hate it when people kiss me," Catherine said, wiping the kiss off her cheek.

"I'm not people, Catherine. I am your cousin. Besides, I see Jack kiss you all the time!" Gavin laughed.

"Jack is cute and cuddly," she responded. "I have to go and get ready now, before mother has a fit."

"I think I shall follow suit and get ready myself." Gavin bowed and left the room.

Andrew was alone in the drawing room when Richard and Daniel came in.

"Hello, Andrew," Richard said.

"Hello! So how has the cottage shaped up?"

Daniel walked over to a settee and sat. "Everything is ready for Alex and Gavin. They're going to love it."

"Good! I am not surprised. I think you have been employing every workman for miles around who was not engaged by Gavin. Now if you will be so kind as to excuse me, I have my own preparations to commence." He politely took his leave, and Daniel and Richard realized they must adjourn to their chambers as well.

"Alexandra, darling, it's me," Elizabeth said as she gently knocked on the door.

"Oh, come in Mother," Alex said as she turned around to greet her. Sara had stepped out to fetch something a minute ago.

"Alex, your hair looks wonderful!" Elizabeth commented.

Alex, clad only in her chemise, corset and dressing gown, answered with tears in her eyes. "Thank you, I can hardly wait. I am so nervous and I'm already shaking. Silly, am I not?"

"No, why is that silly?" Elizabeth took her daughter by the hand and stroked her arm.

"Because this is a man I have come to know inside and out, yet I'm acting like I'm going to experience something that I never have before."

"That's because you are! Marriage will be new, and very different from courting. It's an experience unlike any other. It can be wonderful but it also has its moments. I think it is all completely worth it." Brushing a curl out of her daughter's face, Elizabeth gently caressed Alex's cheek and handed her a tiny, elegant jewel box.

Alex delightedly opened the box to see within an exquisite, delicate, golden filigree-and-sapphire brooch in the shape of an angel.

"Oh Mother, it's so lovely," Alex said, teary-eyed.

"Your father and I had it made especially for you, Alexandra. It is our fondest hope that you have a long, happy and healthy life with Gavin, and we felt that it wouldn't hurt to have an angel watching over you."

"Thank you, Mother. That is a very sweet thought." Alex gave her mother a warm hug.

"The next time I hug you, you will be a married woman." Elizabeth tenderly rubbed her daughter's back.

"Yes, but I shall always be your little girl."

"Yes, you shall."

Sara tapped on the door and entered, and Elizabeth took her leave.

The Bedford House Chapel was located on a remote corner of the estate, far from the mansion, mainly frequented by the villagers and farmers, seldom attended by Rosenshires. It was barely big enough to hold everyone, but it had been the traditional place for Rosenshire nuptials for many generations. Today it was richly decorated, with deep green and ivory-white satin bows and fall flowers on the ends of the pews. A white runner with green borders led to the altar, which had dozens of stems of red and white hothouse roses in tall, shapely golden vases at each end, next to a dozen tall, glowing white and green tapers in golden candlesticks. Strewn around the ornaments were colorful local flowers. Stained glass windows reflected the candlelight in the dusk of the setting sun.

A parade of elegant carriages had been arriving at the door of the chapel for almost an hour, footmen helping down guests promptly as they halted, ushers escorting everyone to their pews, drivers being directed around to a lane where they could wait. The guest list consisted mainly of close friends and family, and a long list of individuals who would feel sorely slighted were they not included, and the pews were packed with elegantly dressed gentry. Elizabeth was excited to show her friends just how lovely her daughter looked and what a dashing young man she would soon wed.

Cassandra, Catherine and Ashley, the excited bridal attendants, were overcome by nervous giggles as they pulled up in a large carriage with Elizabeth and Amelia. Their elegant gowns had been carefully chosen by Alex. They were of shimmering, rich emerald green satin, floor-length, their plunging necklines lined with modest, off-white lace panels. Matching lace set off the waistlines and draped gracefully over their shoulders, and formed little fans on the waist in back. Sara was there to hand them their bouquets of seasonal local flowers tied with green and white satin ribbons. Elizabeth's gown, a deep sapphire blue watered silk, swept to the floor as well. Lace and satin touches adorned its hem and neckline. Amelia's gown was similar, in a rich burgundy tone.

Next to arrive was a black brougham polished to a high luster and drawn by two shining black stallions, the Chatham House family crest picked out on its doors in gold leaf, bearing the groom and his best man. As they stepped out, Andrew thought it best to tease his cousin and tell him it wasn't too late to back out. Gavin gave a laugh. "I would not back out for anything! I have waited far too long to marry my angel." The men all wore black long-skirted cutaway coats with dove-gray waistcoats, boldly striped long cravats, striped shirts with white turn-down collars and cuffs, and striped trousers, completing their formal attire with top hats and gloves. Each sported a fresh rosebud in his buttonhole. Gavin's was the only red one.

The guests were seated and the wedding party had gathered in an anteroom before Alex arrived with Daniel in his shiny new white brougham, a freshly-gilded coat of arms emblazoned on its doors, drawn by two magnificent white thoroughbreds. Seeing Daniel's horses approaching, Elizabeth asked everyone to take their places in the anteroom, and after casting a critical eye over the young women, took Amelia's arm, and escorted her to a side door that would allow them to discreetly take their places in the front pew without attracting attention.

"Has anyone seen Gavin?" Cassandra inquired.

"Yes, I have," offered Andrew. "He just left to take his place by the altar. I think I should take my place as well." Flashing a grand smile, he bowed and departed.

Daniel carefully helped Alex step down. She had fastened the end of her train to her wrist to keep it from the dust. He then stopped, speechless, as he held her hand. "Alex, let me take a good look at you now." Out in the fading daylight, after the dimness within the brougham where he had waited for her to join him, he could now drink in the magnificent appearance of his radiant eldest daughter, dressed just as his wife had been on his own wedding day.

The gown was empire-waisted, sewn of ivory satins and silks with matching lace and seed-pearl panels. It flowed behind her into a graceful, moderately long train. The tight sleeves were of finest Alençon lace with seed-pearl wristlets, and a matching silk and satin headpiece crowned her upswept hair with a cascading lace veil. Alex's hair was loosely and artfully pinned up, with ringlets about her face, neck and shoulders. "So, how do I look?" Alex asked, turning to walk to the chapel on his arm, trying not to crease the train or let it touch the ground.

"You look absolutely stunning, my dear." Daniel was smiling broadly.

Cassandra was standing in the doorway with tears in her eyes. "Oh, Alex. You look absolutely every bit the angel that Gavin calls you. How very exciting that soon you will not be a Rosenshire but a Blake!"

"And what is wrong with being a Rosenshire?" their father asked, as everyone began finding their places close to the chapel entrance. It was time for the ceremony to begin. Daniel covered Alex's face with the veil after giving her an affectionate kiss. Cassandra adjusted Alex's train until it was perfect, took one last critical look, then took her position.

At a signal from an alert usher when Ashley nodded their readiness, a string quartet hidden in the choir loft began to play the processional hymn, and the bridesmaids started down the aisle, with a beaming Ashley leading, then Catherine, followed by Cassandra, keeping careful intervals. No one seemed to notice the wink Andrew flashed Cassandra, nor her sudden blush in response. Once they were stationed in their places, there was a hushed, suspenseful pause, then the musicians struck up a wedding march. The assembled guests rose to their feet and turned to face the rear of the chapel, eager to get a look at the bride.

Finally Alex appeared on Daniel's arm in the doorway, and paused for a moment, waiting for a certain bar of music before taking her first step. She carried a simple bouquet of long-stemmed white roses, gathered with long green and white ribbons. She was stunned to see how the chapel had been transformed into the very essence of purity and radiance, everything she had dreamed it would be! Then she gasped to see Gavin standing at the far end of the aisle, gazing at her. He was so tall, strong and proud in his formal clothes, every bit as handsome as she had ever known him to be, and maybe more.

Gavin's jaw dropped as he took in the sight of his pure, white angel. Never did he imagine that she could look any more beautiful than she always did. And yet... somehow she'd done it again! She was more inutterably angelic than ever.

As Alex and her father slowly made their way down the aisle, hesitating at each step as they had practiced, she was teary with emotion. She smiled through the fine lace at all the familiar faces gazing back at her until Daniel stopped and turned to her. He squeezed her hands, released one, and placed her right hand in Gavin's left, giving them both an approving smile, and seated himself next to Amelia and Elizabeth nearby.

The Right Reverend the Lord Bishop Thorndyke, once a school chum of Daniel's, began intoning the familiar words of the Church of England rite. "Dearly beloved, we are gathered here in the sight of God and in the face of this congregation, to join together this man and this woman in Holy Matrimony... " Alex and Gavin were gazing through the veil into each other's eyes and having trouble following. Finally they heard the words they were waiting for.

"Gavin William Matthew Blake. Dost thou take this woman to be thy wedded wife, to live together according to God's law in the holy estate of Matrimony, to love her, comfort her, honour and keep her, in sickness and in health, and, forsaking all others, keep thee only unto her, so long as ye both shall live?"

Gavin looked into the eyes of his angel with such intensity, it made her quiver. Then he replied firmly, "I do, with all my heart and soul."

"Alexandra Marie Patience Rosenshire. Dost thou take this man to be thy wedded husband, to live together according to God's law in the holy estate of Matrimony, to love him, comfort him, honour and keep him, in sickness and in health, and, forsaking all others, keep thee only unto him, so long as ye both shall live?"

"With all that I am, I do," she replied, her gaze never leaving his.

The bishop blessed the rings. As Gavin gently slid his mother's ring onto Alex's slender finger, he said softly, "With this ring I thee wed; with my body I thee honour; and all my worldly goods with thee I share." Alex did the same. The liturgy continued. Finally the bishop said, "Those whom God hath joined together let no man put asunder....Forasmuch as Gavin William Matthew Blake and Alexandra Marie Patience Rosenshire have consented together in holy wedlock, and have witnessed the same before God and this company, and thereto have given and pledged their troth either to other, and have declared the same by giving and receiving of rings, and by joining of hands; I pronounce that they be man and wife together. In the name of the Father, and of the Son, and of the Holy Ghost. Amen... God the Father, God the Son, God the Holy Ghost, bless, preserve, and keep you; the Lord mercifully with his favour look upon you; and so fill you with all spiritual benediction and grace, that ye may so live together in this life, that in the world to come ye may have life everlasting."

That was the signal Gavin was waiting for. He gently lifted Alex's veil and tucked it over her crown, smoothing it into place, while gazing steadfastly into her blue, blue eyes. He took her in his arms and they kissed with a new sweetness and pleasure, finding their love anew. Holding hands, faces wet with tears, they smiled at each other beatifically. The bishop continued to the end of the liturgy but they did not hear him.

At last, they were presented as the Duke and Duchess of Chatham, and turned to face the congregation. Everyone in the room rose to their feet as the string quartet struck up the recessional. Gavin and Alexandra walked slowly back down the aisle as man and wife, clinging to each other tightly, arms around each other's waists as they accepted blessings from everyone they passed. Cassandra was happy to take Andrew's arm, then Ashley followed with Richard, Daniel and Elizabeth walked together, and Amelia escorted Catherine.

Elizabeth came up to Gavin and Alexandra and hugged them both. Alex showed her the wedding band, which was stunning, of a deep, glowing yellow gold with diamonds embedded all around it, centered on a large, oval-cut diamond.

Gavin and Alex climbed into her father's white brougham, and Andrew shared his black one with Daniel. Once the wedding party had been tucked into their waiting conveyances, ushers began escorting the guests from the chapel, and soon there was a long parade of horse-drawn carriages on the road to Bedford House. Everyone was full of laughter and happiness as they appreciated the joyful occasion. The moonlight night was studded with countless stars.

The candle-lit ballroom exuded a magical aura. Thick ivory damask tablecloths cascaded to the floor, setting off the finest crystal and china. Highly polished sterling flatware reflected the light of the candelabra. White and red roses set off arrangements of local fall blooms, strategically placed to create romance and delight.

As each couple arrived, a footman whisked away their hats and wraps, the butler announced their names, another servant stepped up to offer a tray of crystal champagne flutes, and yet another guided them to the proper table, where most looked over the place-cards to see with whom they were seated.

As a chamber orchestra softly played dinner music, footmen began lifting the silver domes over steaming dishes on the long buffet table and offering delightful morsels to each guest. Elizabeth hovered for a bit until she realized the work was over, everyone on the staff knew exactly what to do, and she could relax and enjoy the feasting and, later, dancing. She started walking among the tables to greet her friends, and finally sat down with Alex, Gavin, Ashley, Cassandra, Richard and Daniel. Andrew and Catherine had been seated with their older sisters, who had come with their husbands, along with Amelia and an ancient uncle.

The meal had been cooked to perfection. A savory soup was followed by fish dressed in a lemon cream, then by a chicken fricassee served with rice. Then came roasts of mutton, suckling pig, and a baron of beef, each accompanied by specialty potatoes or sauced vegetables. Between courses, citrus ices soothed the palate, and fresh, hot dinner rolls with sweet cream butter were tonged carefully from big baskets to go with locally made jams, jellies and sweet pickles. Finally a fancy cake arrived, layered with preserved fruits. Coffee, hot punch, tea and water were plentiful, as were an assortment of fine wines to go with each dish. Eventually big decanters of port were set out on each table along with a few bowls of walnuts and some silver nutcrackers.

"Mother, Father, I can't thank you enough for this day," Alex said.

"Alex, it was well worth the effort, to see how happy you are," Elizabeth said as she gave her daughter a warm smile.

Cassandra and Andrew, seated at adjoining tables, had earlier rearranged their place-cards so they could see each other as they dined. As their attention kept straying away from their own tables, it obvious that something was going on. "Cassandra, you look very radiant today, as do all my daughters. Just think, now we can get ready for your début. Imagine all the suitors you will soon have."

There was no reply. Daniel watched the two a moment longer, uncomfortable with what he was surmising. His thoughts were interrupted when he heard Alex's voice calling her sister's name. "Cassandra? Cassandra, are you not excited about your ball?"

"My ball? Of course I am. Why?" Cassandra brought her attention back to her family.

"Well, father asked you the same question, and you never answered him."

"He did? When?"

"That would be when you were preoccupied with Andrew, dear," her father replied gently.

Blushing, Cassandra responded, "I was not preoccupied with Andrew, Father! I was simply daydreaming about my coming Season, and I must have been lost in my own thoughts."

Seeing her face redden, Daniel decided not to pursue the topic. "Of course, that must be what happened."

Soon couples were rising from the tables to dance, and the orchestra was offering splendid waltzes and quadrilles. Alex and Gavin knew they were expected to take the floor, so they swept around a few times gracefully, remembering to allow Daniel to take a turn with the bride. They were both hoping to make an early exit. As soon as they could do so without giving offense, they graciously bid their guests good night, and Alex went to collect her warm white woolen wrap, after kissing her parents farewell and embracing her siblings affectionately.

Gavin's new black brougham was waiting
for them. His driver had instructions from Daniel as
to where to take them, but the cottage had been
prepared in secrecy and they did not know exactly
where they might be going. Andrew and Daniel had
taken on all the honeymoon arrangements, and
forbidden them to concern themselves. A week
earlier, Sara had packed up several cases and valises
and trunks for Alex and sent them off, and Stephen
had done the same for Gavin.

"Oh, Gavin, this was the most marvelous
day of my life!" Kissing him over and over, Alex
added, "I do not want this night to ever end!"

Gavin looked at his beautiful new wife and
said: "It doesn't have to, my angel of temptation.
Not for a long time." He helped her out of the
carriage, careful of her train, and lifted her into his
arms to carry her through the doorway of the
comfortable, modest cobblestone cottage. She
seemed as light as a feather and he kissed her before
he set her down.

Gavin noticed how neat and clean
everything was. A cheery fire was burning in the
grate, and lamps had been lit. Alex pointed to the
banner that her family had hung over the mantel,
reading "Best Wishes Gavin and Alex Blake, We
Love You!" Sara emerged from the kitchen with
Stephen to wish them well and explain that they had

quarters with the cook and stable-boy over the stables. Sara pointed to bell-pulls by the fireplace that would summon them when they were needed. They bade the newlyweds a warm good night as they departed.

Then, lifting his bride again, Gavin carried her upstairs to consummate their new life. Their bed was covered with rose petals, and the room was dimly lit by several candles. A substantial fire had been built up in a big fireplace to banish the chill of the evening. Their every-day clothing was neatly hanging in wardrobes and folded into bureaus. There was a big bathing room nearby with a stack of fresh, scented towels. A ewer full of hot water stood in a basin on a wash-stand. They barely noticed how every necessity had been thoughtfully provided, but they knew well that at last they were alone together in their own home.

Kissing her face, neck and lips, Gavin gently started to unfasten Alex's gown. She undid his collar, untied his cravat, and ran her fingers down the front of his shirt, making sure not to miss any of the buttons. Tenderly they removed each other's garments one by one and soon engaged in slow, blissful lovemaking to the intoxicating scent of roses. Gently Gavin caressed her naked skin as he ran his hands up and down her back. Alex enjoyed every minute of his touch, savoring the feel of his masculine arms that were so lovingly wrapped around her.

"I promise, my angel. I promise to be gentle

with you," he reassured her.

"I know you will," she whispered back, their embrace never loosening. She had feared that her guilt over losing their child would cause her to hold back from his touch, but much to her delight she felt only comfort, welcome and peace in Gavin's strong arms.

"Oh Gavin!" came a sigh from Alex.

"My Angel! I love you," Gavin sighed back.

Their bodies moved as one until they exploded together in ecstasy. Gavin kissed his beautiful wife and then rested his body close to hers as she lovingly caressed his back and buttocks, delicately brushing off clinging rose petals and inhaling their aroma.

"Gavin Blake, I love you so much!" Alex exclaimed.

"And Alexandra Blake, I love you!" he proclaimed to the angel who was now forever his.

They lay in their bed in front of the crackling fire, holding one another until sleep overwhelmed them. Their dreams had finally come true.

Together, forever and ever.

Chapter Twenty-Nine

"Lady Alex, your Grace, push now, dear, push hard!" ordered the midwife, as Gavin paced feverishly in a corner of their bedchamber.

"All right, I want you to relax for just a moment and catch your breath. Then take in a deep, deep breath, so you can push verrrrry hard when the next urge comes. You can do this, dear." Alex did as she was told, and in a moment pushed with renewed strength. She held the push for ten seconds, took in another deep breath, and pushed hard again. Sweat-soaked and red in the face, she was exhausted, but determined.

Husbands never attended at the birth of their babies, but Gavin had refused to leave the room, and the midwife knew well by now that arguing with him was fruitless. Gavin took a cool, wet cloth and dabbed it on Alex's rosy forehead in an attempt to make her more comfortable. Her laboring had terrified him for the last hour, the pain so intense that she had been calling out in agony.

The midwife spoke sharply to get Alex's attention. "I see the crown when you push! Now, Lady Alex, when I tell you to, you're going to take another deep breath and push very hard. We need to help the head out. Then I will tell you not to push. Even though the urge to push will be there, it is very important that you do not push, is this understood?"

Alex nodded her head, panting from

exertion, so tired she wanted to fall asleep between the overwhelming waves of pain.

"Please, your Grace, support her shoulders so she can sit up. Push now, Alex."

With mighty force and determination, she pushed with all her might.

"Stop! The head is here. Perfect position. Now remember: do not push until I tell you to," The midwife carefully explored around the baby's neck with her fingers, to be sure the cord was in the right place.

"Now you will push again when you feel the need, but only a little push. The babe will slide right out." She readied a flannel receiving blanket as Alex pushed one last time, then leaned back on her pillows, exhausted. An electric instant of anxious silence passed through the room as the midwife glanced down at the upside-down watch pinned to the bodice of her big white apron and grasped the babe's feet to raise it up. Right away came the high, healthy wail of a new baby.

"What is it? What did we have?" Alex begged Gavin, squeezing his hand.

The midwife placed the slippery, bloody, squalling newborn in the warm flannel, and carefully raised the babe atop the sheet tented over Alex's raised knees to display her to her father. Gavin looked down at his radiant wife and said: "It's...It's a girl!" He had tears in his eyes. He added, "And a beautiful baby girl indeed!" Gavin's expression showed awe and wonder as he gazed at his new child, mesmerized at the sight. The infant's cries diminished, and soon she peered around her alertly, balling her tiny fists. Alex beamed with joy through her exhaustion, too elated to feel fatigue now. She looked up at her husband. "We have a girl."

The infant was withdrawn from their gaze. The cord was carefully bound and severed under the little tent of sheets. The midwife finished cleaning, drying and inspecting the baby, weighed her, measured her, and wrapped her loosely in a clean length of flannel. At last, she gently placed the babe in Alex's waiting arms. Before turning her attention to the new mother's needs, she pronounced, "Seven pounds, nineteen inches long, at nine forty-two in the morning. Ten fingers and ten toes. Very healthy-looking. Well done." Then she waited to deliver the afterbirth, which arrived shortly.

"Oh, Gavin, she is so beautiful and so tiny and red and fragile." Alex studied every part of her infant with rapture, unwrapping her for a close inspection.

"Yes. Yes. Yes! What a little princess we have!" Gavin kissed his infant's face and hands and toes again and again. "Such a princess she is! And look at that black hair on our girl! More like me than like you."

"Well, she obviously takes after her father. Dark hair, dark eyes, ruddy complexion... Such a beauty she shall be!" Alex softly nuzzled her newborn's wee button-nose.

Gavin leaned over and kissed his tiny daughter on her forehead.

"Gavin, why don't you take our little babe downstairs now and show her off to the family. They have been waiting how long? What time is it now? More than three hours since you sent for them! Poor things. If anyone would like to come up and see me, I think I would like that." Alex handed the tiny bundle of joy over to the proud new father.

The midwife nodded consent, but made it clear that the baby was to be returned soon, as both mother and daughter needed rest and refreshment. She had been concerned that the baby might have arrived a week or two early, but her weight was good and her breathing was clear. She took the newborn from Gavin and swaddled her tightly before handing her back, only a tiny face with a thick black fringe peering out of the round bundle of warm pink flannel.

"Alex, before I go and show her off... don't you think she should have a name?"

"Oh my dear! How could we have failed to pick a name?" Alex and Gavin had discussed names for boys and girls on countless occasions, without ever alighting upon the one they felt was right. Now they had to arrive at a decision.

"I have it! The most perfect name," announced Gavin, inspired by the tiny beauty resting in his arms as he took her over to the window to catch strong rays of mid-day light.

"What? What is her name?"

"I'm going to give her a name that shall always remind me of her mother, but at the same time be all her own."

"Well, what is it?" Alex asked again.

"Her name shall be Alexandria." He placed a light kiss on a tiny forehead.

"Alexandria? Well— that is certainly beautiful, but don't you think it is too much like mine?"

"Not if we call her Lexie!" Gavin walked to the bedside and bent over to give Alex a loving kiss. "What do you think? Little Lexie."

"I love it! Thank you," Alex said, flattered that her husband thought so much of her that he would want to name his daughter a similar name. "Shall we give her our mothers' names as well? Alexandria Eleanor Elizabeth Blake sounds very pleasant to my ear."

"Good. Now that we have her named, I shall take her downstairs."

Alex called to Gavin as he turned to the door, "Don't keep her from me too long. I will need to nurse her soon." With a smile on her face, Alex sank back into her pillows again and closed her eyes, exhaustion suddenly overtaking her joy.

The midwife bustled around the

bedchamber, washing her hands, adding wood to the fire, and bundling up her scale and other items. She critically inspected the tiny cot and sumptuous layette, and could see that the parents had prepared lavishly for their new arrival. Had there been any little thing amiss about the newborn, she would have stayed a few days, but now there seemed to be no need, and she had other women in the neighborhood who were likely to need her services soon. She blessed the new mother, picked up her bundles and took her leave.

Sara entered just as the midwife departed, having been pleased to see Gavin cooing at a healthy new infant in the hall, and again to appreciate a beatific smile on Alex's tired face. She efficiently set about changing the sheets and putting a fresh, lacy, beribboned nightdress on Alex, topped with a matching bed-jacket, brushing her hair, and preparing her for visitors, while drawing open all the draperies and efficiently setting the room to rights.

"Daniel, someone is coming," Elizabeth said. The whole family had been anxiously gathered in the sitting room since early in the morning, attended by Gavin and Alex's servants, but feeling very little like taking food or tea. They had heard the infant cry, then nothing more but the murmur of voices above. All gasped with happiness at the sight of the tiny bundle in Gavin's arms.

"Lords and Ladies, I am most pleased to introduce my healthy, delightful new daughter.... Lady Alexandria Eleanor Elizabeth Blake! Lexie for short." Gavin handed the baby first to Elizabeth, who was beside herself with emotion at the sight of her first grandchild.

"Would you look at that dark hair!" Daniel exclaimed.

"Oh Daniel, isn't she the most beautiful baby you have ever seen?" Elizabeth asked as tears welled in her eyes.

"Yes, she is, dear, every bit as beautiful as the ones you bore me."

"Mother, let me hold my new niece, please," Cassandra begged with her arms outstretched.

Elizabeth gently handed her over to Cassandra who gave the baby a careful hug and a kiss. Then Cassandra passed the baby to Ashley. Soon the baby had been held by everyone.

"I have strict orders not to be too long. Alex has to feed her," Gavin said with pride, as Andrew gingerly passed the alert infant back to him. No wet-nurses for his family!

"Gavin, I should like to see Alex for a moment, if that is all right?" Elizabeth asked. She wanted to check on her daughter and congratulate her.

"That would be fine. She did tell me that anyone who wanted to see her was more than welcome to do so. I do think, however, you should go up one at a time. I'll wait down here with little Lexie while you all take turns visiting. Please remember not to stay long, she will need rest after her laboring."

"Of course." Elizabeth hurried up the stairs.

Her tapping on the door awakened Alex from a doze. "Come in!" said the new mother, pulling herself to a sitting position as Sara settled more pillows behind her.

"Alexandra, your babe is so beautiful!" Elizabeth beamed as she tearfully hugged her.

"Thank you, Mother. I still can't believe this day has arrived at last."

"I know it! The wait takes forever. How do you feel?"

"I feel surprisingly well. There were hours I did not think I could live through! And I expected there would be more pain afterwards, but I must say I feel nothing more than sore and bruised now. And sort of empty."

"If you are delivered without complications, often there is little pain after... Alex, I am so happy that all your dreams have come true!" Elizabeth hugged her daughter and soon departed.

"Alex, may I come in?" Ashley asked, peering around the door.

"Of course, come, sit right next to me." Alex patted a spot on the bed.

"Well, you look very well, considering, and your baby girl is adorable. Congratulations! I love you, but I won't stay."

"Thank you, Ashley." The sisters gave each other warm hugs, and soon Cassandra took Ashley's place.

"Alex, your baby is most wonderful indeed, but she is not as I had imagined."

"What do you mean?"

"I always thought that when you finally had babies they would all have fair skin and light hair, just like you. She obviously takes after her father."

"To say the least!" replied Alex. "But you know, newborns often lose all their hair, and grow in new hair in an entirely different color. And her true eye color may not be certain for many months. She could well end up with brown eyes like Gavin's, or blue like mine. We just won't know for quite a while."

Alex sighed contentedly and proclaimed, "Today is one of the happiest days of my life."

"It's evident," Cassandra said. "I would love to stay, but I must leave so that Gavin can bring little Lexie in to be fed. Besides, I would like to sneak a moment alone with Andrew when Father comes up to check on you!"

"Cassandra, have you not been waiting with him all this time?" Alex was amused by her sister's ongoing intrigues. She had barely noticed any of the suitors who had flocked around her like a swarm of starlings since her Season, always trying to find a way to be with Andrew.

"Of course I have. But with Father watching over us, we could barely have a conversation. You know he thinks it is too soon for me to limit my prospects, although he very much likes Andrew. How could anybody say it was almost getting too late for you, and now it is a bit too soon for me? When does the exact right moment to settle upon a suitor arrive? It seems like forever since I made my début, and I hope before too much longer, Andrew and I shall announce our engagement."

"I think soon Father will look more kindly upon your romance. You and Andrew don't hide your attraction all that well. I believe Father merely wants you to be courted properly, openly, the way Society expects. Instead of scurrying around in secret like mice chased by a broom, you should ask Andrew to start calling upon you like a gentleman. There is no reason for him not to, now."

"Perhaps. Though we have quite been enjoying our little assignations, especially now that summer weather is here. Well, I will leave you now, so that Father may have a visit." But instead of Daniel, the next person to enter was Gavin, with a fussy little infant chewing on a tiny fist.

"My two favorite people in the world! What happened to Father? I thought he would be coming up?"

"Yes, he was about to. But I think he did not

wish for Cassandra to be left alone with Andrew unless he could supervise. He apparently believes they might make the same mistakes we did! He told me to give you his felicitations, and he will check on you later." Gently he handed Lexie over. "Are you ready? Because I think this one is hungry."

"I am." Alex gently guided her babe's soft cheek toward her swollen breast and the infant at once turned to the nipple and suckled greedily.

"Would you prefer me to leave?" Gavin asked.

"No! Please sit right here with me. I want you near me every minute!"

"Good, because I don't want to be without you, either." Gavin and Alex reclined happily on the bed together as Lexi nursed. Then there was another knock on the door. Gavin rose and answered it.

"Aunt Amelia? Did you come to see my wife and babe?" Gavin asked.

"Actually, no, Gavin, I did not. It's not that I don't want to see Alex, but I wanted to give you three some time alone. I came to tell you that there is a courier at the door, with a letter he says may only be delivered into your hands."

"A letter?" Puzzled, Gavin told Alex that he would return immediately, and hurried downstairs.

The courier explained that the message was important, and said his instructions were to wait to take a reply. Gavin told the courier that he need not tarry, he would find a courier when his reply was ready, and hurried back upstairs with the letter.

Gavin had decided at once that nothing could be more important today than his new family. Tossing the letter on a table without another thought, he reclined again next to his wife. Lexie had started nursing from the other breast, but was looking sleepy now.

"Gavin, shall you not open the letter and see what it says?"

"Not today, my angel. Today is our day, and I do not want to think about anything other then you and little Lexie."

"Gavin, this is one of the happiest days of my life."

"For me as well, my angel. What were the other happy days?"

"One would be the day I met you, and one was our wedding day. Now we can add to the list the birth of our first daughter." Alex rearranged her garments, the infant now sleeping in her arms, and leaned over to kiss her husband's cheek.

"Those were my happiest days, too. Now... about the birth of our *first* daughter. Are you implying that there shall be more? After all the travails you have just endured?"

"Of course that is what I am implying! I think, in the meantime, we are going to have lots of fun practicing!" Laying her head on his chest, and closing her eyes, Alex couldn't have asked for a better outcome to her trials.

Gavin gazed contentedly at his handsome little family, overwhelmed by his love for them. He had never imagined he would end up so lucky.

He woke some hours later and remembered the letter. Gently removing his arm from under his wife and placing a kiss on her forehead, he smiled down at his sleeping baby and rose from the bed. Throwing on his dressing gown, he took up the letter and moved close to the fire for better light. He could see from the seal that it had come from his ancestral estates at Chatham.

Opening it with considerable curiosity, and seeing that it was very brief, he held it out to catch the firelight and read, "Your Grace, your presence is requested immediately..." A gasp escaped his lips.

"What! No!"

Alexandra, groggy with sleep, was watching her husband, awakened by his departure from her bed. "Gavin, what's wrong?" she asked in a hushed tone, not wanting to wake the child at her side.

Gavin rapidly scanned the words of the short letter one more time, unwilling to accept its truth. He took a deep breath, and found an overwhelming sense of sorrow in his breast, swiftly taking over from the elation that had so consumed him with the birth of his daughter. He tried to compose himself before turning to his wife. He shuddered a little as he started to reply, his words caught in his throat, and he found hot tears had sprung to his eyes.

"Gavin, please. What is it?"

"It's... my mother." His voice was barely audible, choked with emotion. "My mother... has passed on."

Alexandra rose from the bed, gently placed the sleeping infant in her cradle, and took her husband in her arms."I'm so sorry, Gavin," she whispered. She could feel his shoulders relax a little in the comfort of her embrace. He put his arms around her and drew her close. Softly she asked, "What else does it say?"

"We must leave for Chatham at once."

CPSIA information can be obtained at www.ICGtesting.com
Printed in the USA
BVOW08s1922200815

414345BV00001B/18/P